cole

EDEN SUMMERS

1

ANISSA

My shrink stares at me over the top of her reading glasses. "I think we need to dive deeper on this. You seem to be fixated on finding a reason for your feelings, and that's okay. My concern, though, is that you're focusing on something that doesn't fit."

"It does fit," I grate through clenched teeth.

She doesn't understand.

I can't blame her. Since our sessions started I've given half-truths and misguided information in a vain attempt to keep the complexity of my time with Cole *conniving* Torian to myself. But it doesn't stop me from needing answers.

"Anissa, I know this is hard, and we're going to work through it together. I just need you to understand that what you feel for this man isn't Stockholm syndrome—"

"That's bullshit."

She clears her throat and straightens in her chair. "Okay. Let me explain again and make things more clear. Stockholm syndrome is a condition where hostages develop a psychological alliance with their captors—"

"Which I did. I also felt sympathy for his cause, and negative feelings toward police and authorities, which is literally the textbook definition, is it not?"

"Somewhat. The problem is, you're leaving out the fact that, even though you were taken against your will, you never truly feared this man."

"Well, maybe when I initially made that admission I was wrong. Maybe deep down I did feel threatened."

She quirks a brow and scribbles on her notepad. "So you believe he was going to kill you if you didn't follow his commands?"

I glare, hating how my insides squeeze in denial.

Cole was never going to kill me. I know that with every breath I take. Yet it doesn't mean I'm willing to give up on this diagnosis.

"You also said Stockholm could occur when the abuser opens up and shows kindness through the trauma. *He* did that. He told me things nobody else knew. And the isolation, too." I push to my feet and pace her light grey rug. "You mentioned Stockholm happens when you're isolated with your abuser. You don't get more isolated than an island in the middle of nowhere."

Now, *that* part I'm still not sure she believes.

I wouldn't be surprised if she thinks I'm making this whole thing up.

"True." She scribbles another note. "However, you would've needed to feel like there was no escape. And from what you've told me, you actually declined the offer to leave. He gave you the option and you decided to stay. Isn't that right?"

Fuck.

"But couldn't that have been a symptom of Stockholm itself?" I ask. "If I was already affected by it, and had these uncharacteristic feelings, of course I was going to stay."

She leans forward in her chair, her pen poised an inch from the notepad teetering on her knee. "Why is this diagnosis so important to you? What will the label achieve?"

I pause, my feet planting an arm's length from the shrink's trusty sofa.

My pulse quickens. My fingers twitch at my sides.

I need the label because it would excuse my feelings. It would explain my obsession and justify why I can't get a bloodthirsty criminal out of my head. Plastering the Stockholm sticker on my chest would help me understand why his world held a semblance of comfort and why my life now feels hollow. It should also dissolve the guilt I feel for my actions. My father would be so ashamed of me.

"Anissa?" She gives a placating smile. "Why do you need this?"

Because it would condone my stupidity. It would absolve me of all these insane thoughts about a man unworthy of my attention.

"It doesn't matter." I grab my purse from the sofa and start for the door. "We're done here."

"Wait. Our session isn't over." She stands, placing her pad and pen on the desk behind her. "We need to work through this."

No, what I need is a diagnosis she won't give.

What I *need* is something to help me understand why I can hate Cole with every breath, yet still tingle with warmth whenever I remember our time together.

Every memory is filtered through a haze of attraction.

Every moment—even those when he drugged, bound, and threatened me—are all relived with a sickening gravitational pull toward admiration. Or worse, lust.

It doesn't make sense.

It's not who I am.

"Thanks for your time." I yank her door open and stalk toward the receptionist, holding out my bank card to pay before continuing my thunderous steps outside into the cool late afternoon air.

I can't keep doing this.

I have to quit thinking of him. Thinking of *us*. Thinking there's some stupid connection between me and a psychotic murderer when those reflections tear my ethics and principles to shreds.

He manipulated me.

Groomed me.

Just like his father did with all those stolen women he turned into sex slaves.

Cole instigated a mind game I couldn't resist. And he won.

End of story.

I continue onto the footpath, thankful for the long walk home because, apart from alcohol, a casual stroll is the one thing capable of stabilizing my pulse.

If only I could find the peace I crave.

Insomnia would be a blessing right now. Instead I pass out nightly, the dreams of Cole luminous and palpable.

"Hey, Fox, wait up."

I freeze at the sound of Anthony Easton's voice behind me, my mindlessness temporarily interrupted. My fellow FBI agent has been the only stability through this entire ordeal. He's the one who convinced me not to go back to work until I'm ready, and I haven't.

He's the lighthouse in the storm. The steady shore.

And despite having limited knowledge of what happened between me and Cole, he's intuitive enough to make sure he bad-mouths that motherfucker constantly, making me despise my inappropriate thoughts like a mentally stable person should.

But Easton also increases my self-loathing. Being around him, with his kindness and generosity, is a constant reminder that I crave the wrong things. He's been my rock, yet I still fixate on poison-filled kisses from a predator.

I turn to find him strolling toward me, his suit crisp, his jawline covered in thick stubble, and those gentle eyes filled with concern.

"What are you still doing here?" I paste on a smile. "I told you I could walk home."

"I know. But after dropping you off, I had nothing better to do, so I thought I'd wait around and give you a ride." His gaze narrows. "You finished early, though. Is everything all right?"

"Everything's fine. Apart from me and my shrink having a difference of opinion." I force out a laugh. "I don't think we'll be seeing each other again."

His expression softens, the kindness transforming to pity. "Is that a good idea? You need someone to talk to. It's been weeks since you last ran into Torian and you're still struggling to cope."

No, not weeks.

He has no clue I had an unscheduled reunion with my satanic libido builder last night. On the side of the road. With a police officer present.

Penny, Decker's sister, had needed help. The recently released sex slave had stolen a hitman's car and wasn't prepared to be targeted for the drive-by shooting that followed.

But that deluge of information is a rabbit hole I refuse to crawl into with Easton.

"It's okay." I continue along the sidewalk, determined to make my way home. "I'll figure it out."

"No, wait." He rushes after me, his strong grip latching onto my wrist. "You're not alone in this. Let me help."

I stare down at the fingers gently embedded in my woolen sweater. I want to feel relief at his touch. Warmth. Affection. I wish something other than the need to compare would overwhelm me whenever he paid me attention, but that's what it always amounts to.

I'm constantly pitting him against Cole and he never wins.

He's not fierce enough. Strong enough. Possessive enough.

"You've already helped a whole heap." I clasp my hand over his and squeeze. "And I'm thankful. But I'm going to be okay. I promise."

He keeps scrutinizing me, his brows furrowing. "He really messed with you, didn't he? Whatever happened between the two of you is far bigger than you've let on." He takes another step, bringing us a foot apart, face-to-face. "I don't know why you're protecting him."

"I'm not." Keeping my lips shut has nothing to do with Cole's safety and everything to do with averting humiliation.

And shame.

I regret everything that happened between me and the manipulative mastermind. If I could, I'd return to the day of Cole's uncle's funeral and catch myself before the temptation to taunt him became too much.

Instead of flaunting my authority, I would've kept to my job, helping my team arrest his father. I shouldn't have become sidetracked by the gorgeous man with the sinister soul.

My stomach flips, protesting the thought.

Goddamnit.

I can never win. It's as if Cole's games never stopped, only became internalized. Now my thoughts wage war against my feelings. My morals battle for supremacy over my yearning.

I'm a fucking nut job in need of sedation—I'm just too stubborn to down the bitter pill.

"Why don't we have dinner tonight?" I stand taller, determined to get a hold of myself. "My treat. We can watch a movie and have a few drinks…"

My insides do that flippy, uncomfortable thing again, warning me against a bad decision. Or maybe hating the possibility of being cut off from a long-standing addiction.

"In your apartment?" he asks. "Again? You don't want to go out and grab a bite from a restaurant this time?"

Like a date? A proper, kiss-you-at-the-end-of-the-night situation?

My brain fumbles for an answer, my hand dropping from his as my internal battle intensifies. I should do this. I *need* to do this.

Stockholm syndrome be damned.

Heated memories forsaken.

Instead, I wince, my fucking weakness claiming victory as I fail to vocalize an affirmation. "Let me think on it." My pulse increases, the pull of want and need dragging me in two different directions.

He's handsome. So goddamn handsome, with his sky-blue eyes and slick blond hair.

But he's not what I hunger for. He's buttered toast pitted against the extravagance of fine dining.

Poisoned fine dining.

"Come on." He jerks his head toward his car and backtracks. "I'll convince you while I give you a ride home. I can be persuasive when I want to be."

2
____

ANISSA

Easton didn't change my mind. He did, however, order the pizza and pick the movie.

He was also the one who made the decision to sit side-by-side on my sofa, putting me on edge with his proximity.

Actually, that could've been my fault.

After genuine conversation and a few laughs at the dinner table, liquid courage had me plopping my ass on the three-seater with him soon following to sit beside me. I'd thought it would be nice to see what happened.

Would he make a move?

Would I like it?

I should've kept with tradition and maintained my distance by claiming the recliner. Now his arm is spread behind my neck, his body so close I can smell his woodsy aftershave, and I can't handle the apprehension that smothers me.

He crosses his legs, his attention remaining on the television. "You're tense."

No shit.

We've worked together for too long, our relationship kept strictly professional since the moment we met, and this, right here, feels like a huge leap into high school awkwardness.

He gently massages his fingers against my shoulder. It heightens my sensitive nerves.

"I, umm... I'm still thinking about my shrink. I should find a new one." I clear my throat, my heart demanding I scoot away but I grin and bear the discomfort. "You're right about needing someone to talk to."

This is Easton.

Straightlaced, by-the-book Anthony Easton.

If he knew half the things I'm guilty of he wouldn't be rubbing me like this. In fact, I'm certain he'd be disgusted. Those kind eyes would turn feral, stripping layer upon layer of my already flimsy pride.

"Want me to ask around and get some recommendations?" He turns to me, his knee brushing my thigh. "I think one of my high-school buddies sees someone on Billow Street."

I clear my throat again, the tickle at the back of my tongue becoming more persistent. "Thanks. But I'd prefer to find someone on my own. I don't want to rush into it."

"Sure. That makes sense."

We fall silent, my attention returning to the television where actors speak words I don't bother listening to as the air turns into pockets of fragile glass around us.

I don't want to budge an inch from fear of destabilizing the atmosphere. I really don't.

Then again, maybe I should.

Maybe I need to beat back this arduous twist of my insides and take a leap of faith.

I should kiss him. Bite the bullet. Dive straight in, getting the experiment over and done with. Because so far, it's working. I haven't thought about Cole in hours. I've been successfully distracted. Until right this second, when his face stares back at me with each blink.

Easton chuckles.

I stiffen. *Can he read my mind?*

I'd almost believe he's capable if his eyes weren't glued to the television. He must be laughing at the movie.

The coaxing massage against my shoulder grows more adamant, awakening tiredness in my weary bones.

I can do this. I *should* do this.

A peck on the lips isn't the end of the world. And my loco, batshit-crazy status gives me a neon-sign excuse if I fail this crash test.

It's a win-win.

So why does kissing someone other than Cole seem like a shitty consolation prize? The bushfire flames of attraction are nowhere in sight. Lust isn't anywhere on my radar.

I clear my throat again, pissed off at the relentless tickle, and turn to face my friend.

He remains lazily focused on the screen, but I know he's aware of my train of thought. His understanding is subtle in the slight lift of his chin, the gentle detour of his hand to the back of my neck.

His fingertips graze my skin, up and down, inspiring goose bumps. It might not be the ungodly heat that engulfed me whenever Cole—

No.

No.

I'm not going there.

This is about Easton. Moving onward and upward. Reclaiming my moral high ground instead of slumming it in the streets.

I suck in a deep breath and regroup, relaxing my muscles one at a time—jaw, shoulders, stomach. I force myself to focus on the handsome man before me with his warm tan and gelled hair.

Finally, my throat tightens with anticipation. My mouth dries. I lick my lips to ease the discomfort and steel myself against what I'm about to instigate.

I'm going to do this. One kiss. One test.

"Are you sure you're okay?" He turns his face to mine, his gaze gentle. "You seem different tonight."

"Yeah…" I nod. "I'm super."

Super?

Fuck me. Who the hell is this ditsy airhead and where did the Bureau bitch rush off to?

I'm not flighty or meek.

I've made fearless criminals cry with subtle threats and intimidation. At least, I used to. Now those moments seem like a lifetime ago.

"Super?" He quirks a brow. "Maybe you should lay off the—"

My cell buzzes from my jeans pocket, the vibration sinking into my pelvis. For a moment, it feels like a sign. I'm just not sure what kind—affirmation or a blinding veto.

The vibration doesn't stop. The *buzz, buzz, buzz* adds to the awkwardness.

He grins. "Are you going to answer that?"

"Should I?" I pause.

He raises a brow and shrugs, the heat returning to his eyes.

It's daunting. The chemistry is all off.

"Just give me a sec." I pull out my phone, suddenly appreciating the disturbance, only to have my pulse stop at the name on the screen.

The Devil.

My heart shoots to my throat, choking me.

All those flames I'd yearned for with Easton—all the thrill and chemistry—engulf me.

"Who is it?" he murmurs.

I reject the call and shove the cell into my pocket. "Nobody."

Nobody I'm going to continue fixating on.

Nobody I can succumb to.

I settle back into the sofa, my pulse taking long moments to find its normal rhythm while I stare blankly at the television.

Did I just conjure a phone call to get out of moving on? Or did Cole perfectly time the interruption at the very moment I was trying to expunge him from my life, like a freaky coincidence?

No, not a coincidence. A succinctly scheduled intrusion.

Has that fucker bugged my apartment?

I shove to my feet, my eagle eyes frantically scanning my furnishings. If there's a camera in here, I'll run him down in my car and reverse a couple of times. I'll shoot and dismember and mutilate.

"What is it?" Easton sits forward. "Who was it?"

"Nothing… Nobody." I rush for the television cabinet and run my fingers over the back of the screen, then the nearby lamp, and the curtains.

My cell vibrates again, the ongoing buzz announcing another call.

I snatch for the device, *The Devil* taunting me again.

"What's going on?" Easton pushes from the sofa, his gentle steps approaching. "It's him, isn't it?"

The wildfire continues to overwhelm me in scorching flames. Head to foot. Organs to nerves.

Even with the threat of Cole yet again breaching my privacy, my body awakens at the mere thought of him being in my home. Touching my things. Paying me attention.

Not Stockholm syndrome, my ass.

If this doesn't scream certifiable, what does?

"Anissa?" Easton stops at my side as the call ends. "Why is he calling you?"

I keep my gaze locked on the cell, asking myself the same question.

I didn't speak much to Cole last night. I couldn't. We weren't alone. There were only a few barbed words to fill the silence before I left Penny in his capable hands. But there'd been unfinished business between us. There has been since Greece—I've just refused to let him close enough to carry on the madness.

One hurdle at a time, please, Satan.

"It's probably nothing." I guide a stray strand of hair behind my ear and nod to myself. "He probably wants to give me an update on what happened last night."

"What do you mean, last night?" Easton's voice thickens with tension. "What happened?"

I sidestep, moving around him to walk to the kitchen. "There was an incident with a mutual contact. I got to the scene before he did."

"You got to the scene?" He enunciates the words slowly. "You saw him? Is that why you're an emotional wreck today?"

"I'm not a wreck." I trudge to the fridge, pull open the door, and grab another beer. "I'm tired. That's all."

"Don't lie to me. You're showing the same crazy upheaval from a few weeks ago. And yet again, he's the cause." He stalks toward me, holding out a hand. "Give me the cell and I'll block his number."

"No." My denial is too fast. Too defensive. I can't help it. "I can handle this on my own."

"Like hell you can. You're not sleeping. Not exercising. Not working. Pretty soon the Bureau is going to write you off completely, then you won't have a job to return to. All for what?" He scans me with pained eyes. "What did he do to you, Nis?"

Oh, God. That nickname is foul on his lips.

An abomination.

Cole was the first person to ever call me Nis, Nissa, and even Nissie. I'd been his little fox, too. Yet the same endearment from a friend sounds sacrilegious.

"You know what he did," I lie. "He humiliated me. He made me his alibi when his father escaped custody."

"The time for bullshitting is over. We both know there's more to it than that. You disappeared for days. You fell off the face of the fucking planet and returned a different person."

I did.

Cole changed me.

"I—"

My cell vibrates again, this time short and sharp with a text.

The Devil: We need to speak. Now.

I grimace, wanting to comply with every breath and loath to do it at the same time.

"I'm turning it off." I press the power button and hold up the device for Easton to see. "I'm ignoring him." I turn away, placing the cell on the counter, my stomach resting against the cool laminate as a jittery discomfort eats away at me.

I want those phone calls. I crave more texts. Everything inside me screams for Cole's attention but I have to deny myself.

I grab my beer, twist off the cap, and down half the contents before gasping for air.

"Why won't you talk to me?" Easton comes up behind me. "What are you afraid of?"

"I'm not afraid." I take another gulp, eager for more liquid to douse Cole's flames while the hair on the back of my neck rises.

"Did he hurt you?"

Yes. "No."

"Did he scare you?"

Yes. "No."

"Are you searching for retribution?"

I sigh, unsure of my answer.

I want so many things from Cole—answers being my most prominent wish. It kills me to have no understanding of how I went from hating a man to willingly sleeping with him within the space of days.

I became lost in a murderer. And it wasn't as if he hid his venom behind that wickedly handsome face of his. He took every opportunity to show me the demon living within. He exposed me to his deepest, darkest depths, and still, I became entranced.

Fucking Stockholm.

"I can help you." Easton closes in behind me, his hands sliding over my shoulders, his fingers massaging softly. "We can take him down together."

I flinch. Tense.

Taking down Cole had been the driving force that pulled me into this mess in the first place. I'd wanted nothing more than to see him behind bars. Now all I can think of is seeing him between silk sheets.

"No." I place my beer on the counter and turn to face him, his large frame looming over me, his hands falling to his sides. "I just want to forget. Okay?" I force a smile, pretending it's all sunshine and optimism in this fucked up head of mine. "I'm going to take this last week off work and really pull myself together. Once I get back into my old routine I'll be fine."

"Is it this place?" He raises a brow, not backing out of my personal space. "Do you feel safe staying here on your own?"

I know where he's going with this, just like I've known what all the lingering stares and constant touches mean. He wants to stay. To spend the night. Again.

"I'm fine. Really." I reclaim my beer and slide out from in front of him, leading the way to the sofa. "And I appreciate everything you're trying to do, but I don't need saving."

I slump back onto my seat, ignoring his approach as he comes to take up the vacant space at my side. I increase the volume on the television, hopefully giving a glaring indication I'm finished with this conversation, and attempt to relax.

One muscle at a time.

One breath.

We don't talk for long moments. I use the lull to think long and hard about my situation.

Cole is my enemy. A manipulative predator who successfully brainwashed me into psychosis.

Easton is my partner. A protective, caring friend, who hasn't grown tired of my constant PMS-on-steroids personality.

He's safe.

He's trustworthy.

He's…not Cole.

And that's a good thing. It *has to be* a good thing.

Any forward momentum with him will drag me further away from where I shouldn't dwell.

I lean over, placing my bottle on the coffee table and settle back into the sofa. When his arm maneuvers from his side to wrap around my shoulders, I fight the need to move away and instead snuggle closer.

I rest my head into him. I breathe in the aftershave that's remarkably different from—

No. I'm not thinking about the devil anymore. Or the way he smelled. Or tasted. I have to cast every disillusioned thought from my brain.

I pull back slightly and turn to my friend, my heart hammering as our gazes collide. It's an all-or-nothing moment. Sink or swim. Fight or flight.

My insides squeeze. My pulse stutters.

I lick my lips and his attention narrows on my mouth.

I'm torn in a million different directions, the static of confusion blaring in my ears.

I shut it all down—the thoughts, the sensations, the warnings—and lean in, placing my lips on his.

3

ANISSA

He sits frozen for a split second, the connection stale and lifeless. I'm about to pull away in rabid humiliation when his mouth slowly moves beneath mine, the kiss tender. He wraps his arm tighter around me but still excessively gentle, as if I'll break.

It's all so slow and calm and…weak.

There's no passion. No possession.

Christ. What am I thinking?

This is a first kiss. It's not meant to be a porn audition. I'd just hoped for more.

I *need* what I previously had.

Ferocity.

Obsession.

I keep our mouths fused as I straddle his waist and cup his cheeks. I've never had a brother, but I'm starting to think this is what it might feel like to make out with one. The more I try to add kindling to the stack, the more my emotions assemble road blocks to all my nerve endings.

There's no fire. No flame. Not even a spark.

I try harder, sliding my tongue between his lips.

Everything is gentle. Soft. Deflated.

Until a knock at the door has his hands snapping to my hips as if in protection.

It's a brief moment of aggressive force, the hold inspiring my heartbeat to rampen.

I pull back, curious, yet thankful for the interruption. Then confusion takes hold.

I don't have any friends. Not apart from the man I'm straddling. And even if I did, I would've trained them well enough to know I'm not the type to want visitors after ten o'clock at night.

"That was…" Easton clears his throat. "Unexpected."

Had I imagined his attraction? Please, for the love of all things holy, don't make his flirtation another part of my vastly increasing mental delusions. "Unexpected?"

The knock sounds again, this time a booming thud.

Not only do I not have any friends who would attempt to beat down my door, I don't have any neighbors who aren't equally as reclusive as I am. And my landlord wouldn't dare to bother me at this hour.

Easton's face turns grim, his eyes narrowing. "It's him, isn't it? He's here."

"No." I should pretend I don't know who he's talking about. That my whole life doesn't currently revolve around one *him*. "He wouldn't be able to get into my building."

He scoffs. "Do you really think—"

The knock sounds again, louder and louder.

"Open the door, Nis, I know you're in there."

Oh, fuckety fuck.

I scramble off Easton's lap. He glides to his feet, far more elegantly than my baby-giraffe fumble.

"Why is he here?" He stretches out a hand to help stabilize me, but I move out of reach, unable to stomach more contact.

"I don't know." I keep my voice low. At least, I try. It's hard to know what's loud with the pulse booming in my ears.

The tingles I'd been hoping for with that kiss flood me. Everywhere. No place more potent than my chest.

My heart.

"I'll handle it." Easton sidesteps me, starting for the door.

"No." I snatch at his wrist, yanking him to a stop. "Hold on a goddamn minute. I'm not a damsel in distress. This is my apartment and my guest… or intruder… or whatever the hell you want to call him." I straighten my shoulders, those tingles turning into tremors at the thought of coming face-to-face with my mysterious syndrome creator. "I can handle Cole." I point a finger at his chest. "You be quiet."

His chin hikes in offense.

"I'm sorry. I didn't mean to snap. I just…" I sigh. I hate this new normal. The confusion and lack of confidence. I want to go back to feeling alive again. And not just in the moments that involve Cole.

The thunderous knock at the door gets louder, probably waking my neighbors.

"I'm *coming*." Fucking hell, that man is an impatient ass. "Stop banging."

I wince at Easton in apology and stalk for the door, yanking it open enough for Cole to see me and nothing else.

I'm poised to yell at him. To rail and curse, but the sight of arrogance personified standing suave and sophisticated in my hall is enough to steal my voice. The dark and devilish hair. The predatory blue eyes. The perfectly chiseled jaw.

"Nice to see you again, little fox."

My blood surges, the anger and animosity colliding. The unwanted attraction, too.

I glare. "What the hell are you doing here?"

His mouth kicks in a cocky grin. It's so subtle. The finest tweak of gorgeous lips.

It's enough to make me gush with intolerable amounts of desire.

Fuck him.

Seriously, fuck him and his hypnotic appeal. I don't know what it is about this man that flicks all my switches, but once I figure it out, I'm shutting down that fuse box.

"I tried calling you. And I know you got at least the first of my texts." He shrugs. "Then I'm assuming you turned your phone off."

I scoot closer, holding the door handle behind me as I lower my voice. "If you've bugged my apartment, I swear to God—"

"I haven't bugged your apartment." He smirks. "Come on, Nis, what do you take me for? Would a man like me really corrupt your privacy like that?"

He corrupts *everything*. Every heartbeat. Every thought.

"You can't do this," I hiss. "You can't just come here and—"

He steps forward, bridging the space between us, making me snap ramrod straight.

I won't backtrack. I can't.

I'm not going to let him win.

"I just want to talk." He stares down at me, those devilish, ocean eyes focused on my mouth.

I swallow, already feeling his lips against mine. The buzz I'd wanted with Easton is right here, without a touch, without movement. The lust is suffocating.

"Let me in." He reaches for the door.

"*No.* You can say whatever you need right here."

His smirk increases, mirth dancing in his eyes as he leans a little closer. "It's not fit for public consumption. We need privacy."

Just the thought of being alone with him, in a confined space, is enough to make my nipples tingle. Harden.

I swallow over the desert taking hold in my throat and stand my ground. "Leave."

Another snicker brushes my ears as he takes one more step, walking into me as he pushes the door wide open.

Shit.

I want to grab him. To stop his momentum.

But touch isn't an option.

If I snatch for him I'm not sure I'll ever let go.

He strides past me as I tense, waiting for the eruption of male testosterone that never eventuates. Easton isn't in sight. He's not in the kitchen or the tiny living area. He's gone. There's only me and Cole, and the realization that my bedroom door is now slightly ajar.

"I'm serious," I warn. "You can't be in here."

What if he mentions Greece? What if he talks about our affair? Or what I did to his father?

My fucking life will never be the same if Easton overhears.

"Having a party?" Cole stops a few feet away, his attention scanning over the mess—the beer bottles, the empty pizza box, the television with its action-packed movie. He turns to face me, one brow raised. "It looks like I interrupted a good time."

"Every day is a party when I don't have to deal with you."

He beams a player smile. White, perfect teeth. Dark, devilish eyes. He knows he's under my skin, and he fucking loves it.

Asshole.

He licks his lower lip and lazily strolls toward me. "Admit you miss me."

My eyes flare. "What's to miss? You're nothing but a pain in my ass."

He chuckles, not stopping his approach, not even once he reaches my hyper-sensitive personal space. I'm forced to retreat. One step. Two. Until my butt hits the door, knocking it shut.

"That's not how I remember our time together." He closes in, caging me with his presence like the most powerful predator.

I'm rendered speechless, my pulse sky-rocketing, my limbs trembling.

How can he control me like this? How can he snatch my common sense and leave me defenseless?

"Something is different about you?" He scrutinizes me. "You're flushed."

"And I bet you think you're responsible."

"No." His gaze hardens. "Your cheeks were already pink when you answered the door. Why?"

I should admit the truth. I need to end this crazy thing we have going on and simply tell him I was with Easton. But the words refuse to make themselves heard over the rush of intoxicating warmth.

"What do you need to tell me?" I swallow, squaring my shoulders. "Hurry up and spit it out so I can go to bed."

That vulturous gaze studies me for long moments before he relaxes into his normal sense of superiority. "You need to lay low for a while. At least a few days. Don't leave your apartment. Don't even cross the street for coffee."

Each demand makes me balk. Not only due to the underlying threat, but because he arrogantly thinks I'll comply.

"I'll have men watching the building," he continues. "However, it's best if—"

"Whoa." I hold up a hand. "For starters, you will *not* have your men watch me. And second, I know how to take care of myself. I'm a goddamn FBI agent, Cole."

"How could I forget?" His expression tightens.

"What's this about?" I hike my chin, matching him stare for stare. "Why do you want me to hide?"

"You don't need the details. Just lay low. It's only for a few days."

"You can't barge in here and demand I put my life on hold for no reason." I scowl. "Who do you think you are?"

I'm gifted with another one of those subtle, taunting snickers. He inches closer, getting in my face, the heat of his breath brushing my lips. "You know exactly who I am."

My pulse detonates. My inhales transform into teeny, tiny gasps.

I want him. *God,* how I want to bite and claw this man out of my system, right on my carpeted floor. Our clothes strewn. Our bodies covered in sweat.

What I wouldn't give to feel his heavy chest pressed down on mine. His lips on my flesh. His cock—

Fuck.

"Why?" I snap, my attention flicking to my bedroom door in guilt before trekking straight back to the wall of dominance before me.

He sighs, his superiority fading under the weight of something heavier. "I need you to trust me."

Trust? Something seriously sinister must be happening if he's asking for such a prize.

"Tell me." My fingers itch to reach out. To physically demand answers and sate my need to touch him.

His jaw ticks, an internal battle coming into view behind those eyes. "Robert might still be alive."

All the air leaves my lungs on a heave.

Robert.

The same Robert who humiliated me. Beat me. Threatened to kill me.

I've worked hard to suppress the memories of that monster. I did everything in my power to pretend those moments didn't exist. Now they all come rushing back in a wealth of icy goose bumps.

"How do you know?" I keep my voice low.

"There was money taken from one of my father's bank accounts. The security image isn't clear, but Decker's sister insists it's him."

I blink and blink, trying to beat back my shock. "Where?"

He winces. It's slight, the minute narrowing of his brows, yet it's enough to make my stomach bottom.

"Where, Cole?"

"Here," he grates. "In Portland."

Frigid fingers of panic grip my throat. "For how long? When did he arrive?"

"I don't know. Could be weeks—"

"And you're only telling me now?" My voice rises. "How could you—"

"I only just received the smallest hint of confirmation." His lips curl in a snarl as he gets in my face. "And you're the first fucking person I've told. I've got a house full of people waiting to find out, and I came here. I came to *you*. I'd never let…" His words trail, and I can't help but bow my head, needing to break the potency of his stare in an attempt to make sense of what's happening.

Robert was meant to be murdered for what he did to me. I heard him beg for his life. The gunshot had blasted my ears.

I'd been the reason for his supposed death.

And if he remains alive, I'd be one of his biggest targets.

"Hey." Cole grips my chin, raising my face until I'm staring back at him. "I'll protect you."

Goddamnit.

The last thing I need right now is protection from an unwanted infatuation.

My lips part as I try to think of something strong and affirming to say. But the squeak of my bedroom door steals the words away.

Cole stiffens, his attention snapping across the room, his fingers tightening on my chin. We both stare at Easton standing in the doorway, his hair mussed, his muscled body on full display as he stands in nothing but his underwear, his shirt hanging loose in his hand.

He's playing the role of awoken lover, and I can't fathom his audacity.

"What the fuck are you doing here?" He scowls at Cole and yanks the shirt over his head.

I'm frozen in a nightmare. Unable to do anything except watch the carnage from behind slowly blinking eyes.

Cole lets out a barely audible growl, his fingers sliding from my chin to leave me hollow. "I could ask you the same thing." His gaze cuts back to mine. "But I won't."

He glares at me. Glares so hard and vicious I'm made to feel worthless under his attention.

He's jealous.

Hurt.

His pain lashes through me like a lethal injection.

"I guess I didn't need to warn you. You've already got all the protection you need." He reaches behind me to pull open the door. "Excuse my interruption. It won't happen again."

No. He can't leave. Not like this.

I want to scream at him to stop. To listen. To understand.

Instead, I let him walk from my apartment, the latch clicking shut seconds later as I remain rooted in place. Stunned.

"What the hell was that all about?" Easton approaches, his sleepy facade disappearing. "What were you two talking about?"

I slow my breathing, taking one long drag of air after another in the hopes more oxygen will decrease my mania.

"Nis? What the—"

"Stop." I warn. "Don't call me that."

"Jesus Christ. I'm sorry, *Anissa.* But you've gotta understand how fucking mind-blown I am at seeing him all over you. I think I deserve some answers."

I puff out a breath. Numb. Cold. Alone.

So goddamn alone.

The wildfire flames have been snuffed. All that's left in Cole's wake are dying embers.

"No." I cross my arms over my chest. "It's time for you to explain why the hell you came out here acting like we'd just slept together."

4

———————

ANISSA

Easton retreats into the room and returns moments later carrying his jeans. "Would you have preferred if I pulled my gun?"

"I would've preferred if you'd let me handle it, like I asked." I grate the words through clenched teeth. "You've only made things worse."

He pulls on his pants, yanking them hard up his thighs. "I was trying—"

"No. Forget it." I raise a hand for him to stop. "I don't want to hear it."

His intent was clear. He deliberately acted like a scorned lover to start some sort of macho pissing contest.

"Please leave." I cross my arms over my chest and stare at the empty beer bottles on the coffee table, unable to keep looking at him.

"Are you serious?" He starts toward me. "What else was I going to do? I could—"

I backtrack, remaining out of reach. "Please just leave."

He plants his feet… sighs… waits.

"Now, Easton. I'm not going to change my mind."

"This is ridiculous." He strides for the kitchen, swiping his keys and wallet from the counter. "I'm sorry, okay? *Christ.* I'm the one who was blindsided. Doesn't that count for something?"

He's not the only one who didn't see this coming. Not only

Cole's appearance, but the resurrection of Robert. The thought of that heinous man still walking the earth has my stomach tied in knots.

"I'll call you tomorrow." Easton starts for the door. "Then we're going to sit down and talk about what the hell is going on."

I don't respond. I wait until he leaves, then make my way to the window to peer at the street below. I remain in place until his sedan pulls from the curb. Then I stand there even longer, hoping Cole's Porsche will follow so he knows I haven't let anyone spend the night in my apartment.

But that black sports car doesn't pass. Nobody does. The city street remains desolate until I drag my weary ass to bed.

The next morning, I didn't hide. I ignored Cole's demands, strapped my gun around my waist in a Velcro holster, pulled on a sweater and active pants, then went for a run.

I jogged block after block, appreciating the thrill of being watched. I knew, no matter how angry the devil was, that he wouldn't stop his men from stalking me.

Protecting me.

And if Robert was around, I wanted to drag him out. Lure him in.

But he didn't show his face. Not during the long morning, or in the afternoon when I made sure I'd ditched my invisible tail with some grade-A driving skills to turn the tables and shadow Cole.

I parked down his street, watching cars pass in and out of his property gates. Last night, he mentioned having a house full of people and that much is evident from the constant back and forth of vehicles. The property is guarded, too. A security team stalks the perimeter. Contractors. I don't recognize the men through my binoculars.

I remain there until night falls, and one by one, a long line of cars leave through the gates. Security in front, then Hunter and Sarah, Benji and Layla, Decker and Keira, and finally Cole, followed by more security.

I follow, trailing in the distance to the Torian family restaurant. I circle the block after all five vehicles head toward the back of the building, and find a parking space within view of the floor-to-ceiling glass out the front.

Staff inside work in a synchronized frenzy, polishing cutlery in an open-plan area previously filled with tables and chairs.

I watch for a long time as guests arrive, the number of people growing by the hour until the entire restaurant is full of mingling criminals drinking alcohol and eating canapés.

Nobody is hiding from Robert. If anything, they're being blatant with their lack of fear.

Especially Cole, who constantly parades the room, suave and sophisticated in his tailored suit, his hair styled, his smile sly yet welcoming. He makes some of the women blush through mere conversation, and I'm sure if I were in there I'd hear their flirtatious giggles.

It seems two can play the jealous game.

Bitterness eats away at me as I sit in silence, nothing but damaging thoughts to keep me company.

Decker, my previous informant turned criminal, talks to an older couple with Cole's sister, Keira, close at his side. Hunter and Sara mingle. Benji and Layla speak with relatives of the Torian empire.

Everyone is in attendance except for Penny and Luca—the other man who was complicit in my abduction to Greece. I can't find them as I skim the crowd slower through my binoculars, concerned for the welfare of the woman once held as a sex slave under the same roof as Robert.

She must be petrified.

I'm seated on the edge of my seat, leaning forward, eager for a better view, when a light rap at my driver's-side window scares the ever-loving crap out of me.

I reach for my gun, yank it from the Velcro as I drop my binoculars to find Easton peering down at me.

"Shit," I mutter under my breath.

He glowers as he rounds the hood to the passenger side, waiting impatiently until I unlock the car.

"Want to know how long I spent driving around trying to find you?" He drops into the seat beside me, slamming the door behind him.

"Not really." I shove my weapon back in place and stare out the window, unable to withstand his visual criticism.

"Don't worry; it didn't take long. This is the first place I looked. And surprise, surprise, you're here."

"Please don't start this again. You've got no idea what's going on."

"Then tell me." He turns to face me. "Fucking clue me in so I understand why you're risking your career and your fucking life by hanging around this asshole."

I clench my teeth, forcing myself not to respond.

"Jesus Christ, Fox." He scoffs. "I don't understand you anymore."

That makes two of us.

I can't figure out where I went wrong. I shouldn't have set my sights on taking Cole down—that much is clear. But when did my need for justice become smothered by my obsession for the man himself?

"I wish I could explain..."

"No, you don't," he grates. "If you wanted me to know, I'd know. But instead, you choose to keep me in the dark and I have no idea why. Especially when I'm one of the only people who has never judged you."

"You're judging me now."

He falls silent, allowing an uncomfortable awkwardness to settle between us.

I wouldn't even have a clue where to start if I did tell him all the wrong turns I've taken to get to this point. I'd have to admit I'm no longer worthy of holding an FBI badge. I'd be forced to confess the feelings I'd had for a manipulative murderer.

The feelings I *still* have.

"Easton..." I sigh, unable to continue. There are no words to explain this mess.

"At least talk to me about that kiss." His gaze bores into the side of my head. "Was it a mistake or did it mean something?"

My stomach flips. Not in a good way.

I don't want to make things worse between us. I can't lose the only person who has been kind enough to see through my flaws and not hold me accountable for my father's mistakes.

"I don't know." It's such a weak, pathetic response. The old me would spit in the face of the woman I've become, but I can't explain something I don't understand.

I can't illustrate how I hoped the kiss would mean something and how, even after the fact, I'm still not sure if it did.

"Did you sleep with him?" He huffs out a derisive breath of a chuckle. "I don't even know why I'm asking. He set you up. He fucking played you. But I can't shake the sex vibes I'm getting between you two."

"He had information on my father." It's not a lie. It's barely a glimpse of the truth, but still, not a lie. Just enough of a fact to hopefully push him away from exposing the worst of my decisions where Cole is concerned.

"What information?"

"It doesn't matter."

"Of course it fucking matters. What did he tell you? And why didn't you fill me in sooner?"

"Because it's nobody's business." Easton knows how I feel about my father's disappearance. It's the easiest escape from this conversation. "The Bureau labeled my father a turncoat. Anyone he worked with has already drawn their own damning conclusions, and I'm not going to waste my energy proving them wrong. I want to move on with my life."

"I'm not asking for them. You used to trust me. What changed?"

I wince, hating how he thinks this is about him. "Nothing changed. I still trust you. You know you're all I've got." I meet his gaze, my wince remaining in apology. "I just didn't want to reopen old wounds."

He reaches out, his palm sliding over my wrist, back and forth. "I'm sorry."

I tense, not appreciating the contact. "Forget it. Can we pretend this conversation never happened?"

"I can…" His hand stops its gentle movement. "But what about the kiss? Do I forget that, too?"

To hell with that kiss.

And to hell with the man who drove me to commit the insanity in the first place.

"Don't worry, Fox." His touch retreats. "I'll put it to the back of my mind. Temporarily. But sometime soon, I'm gonna want to figure out where that affection came from and if there's any hope for a repeat."

I nod, cringing on the inside. I owe him an explanation. Stupidity and shame be damned.

"What are you doing here anyway?" He shifts his attention to the restaurant. "What's with the underworld festivities?"

"I don't know." I follow his line of sight, my gaze immediately seeking Cole only to come up empty. I can't spy him among the crowd. I can no longer see Hunter or Sarah either. In fact, Decker, Benji, and Layla are all gone, too.

I sit taller, scanning the guests once more.

"Is Cole even in there?" Easton asks.

"He was. They all were. I can't find any of them now." I reach for my binoculars.

"Are they up to something?"

"Aren't they always? We both know they live to hatch new schemes. That's not going to change anytime soon." I itch to get out of the car. My skin literally crawls with the inability to find my target. "I'm going to take a closer look."

I unfasten my belt and open my door, only to have Easton grab my wrist again.

"There. Look." He jerks his head at the restaurant. "He just came in from the kitchen."

I narrow my focus. Cole returns to the party. Benji and Layla follow a few minutes behind. Then Hunter.

They all seem different now. Cole is tense, the player smile no longer plastered on his face. Instead, he scowls, his lips pressed tight. And his posture denotes a sharp stick has been shoved up his usually impenetrable ass.

I still can't find Decker.

Something must have happened.

I want to believe the change in Cole has something to do with Robert's capture. But I know him well enough to determine the shift in his demeanor isn't from good news.

He's on edge. His glances pointed.

He's been spooked, which forces me to feel the same.

"It looks like a typical night in their shady lives if you ask me."

Easton speaks softly. "And even if they were up to something you know you're not the person to be handling this. Why don't you let me take over?"

"I'll leave soon."

He laughs. "You're lying to me now?"

"No. I'm tired." Emotionally and physically. Cole has that effect on me. "I'll go home in a few minutes. I promise."

"Is that a hint that you want me to leave?"

I don't answer, letting him form his own conclusion.

"Okay, Fox. I'm outta here. But only if you promise to call me when you get home." He opens his door and waits.

"I'll be fine."

"Just fucking call me, okay? I'm not going to sleep until you do."

He's such a nice guy. A protective, caring, thoughtful man. Why can't my libido be turned on by those attributes instead of predatory darkness?

"Fox?"

"Okay. I'll call." I shoo him away with a wave of my hand. "Get out of here."

He gives me a final look of concern, then closes the door to walk down the street behind me and turn the corner.

For each second of the next twenty minutes, I sit in hope of Cole doing something to give me an excuse to barge into the restaurant. I pray he'll cause a scene or break the law so I have a valid reason to strut my ass in there and face him.

In the same seconds, I fight to drag myself away. To place necessary distance between us so I don't fall deeper into obsession.

I hate what he's done to me.

I absolutely loathe how he took a hammer to my morals and made it impossible to piece them all together again.

I was an honorable FBI agent once. Now, I'm nothing. At least I won't be when everyone finds out how I assisted in criminal activity. No, not just assisted. Participated. *Instigated.*

I start the car and pull from the curb, driving past the restaurant. For a second, I think Cole's gaze meets mine. That there's a tiny spark of recognition in his eyes. But then it's gone, another passing car stealing my attention before I'm forced to focus on the road.

I have to stop doing this. *Why* am I doing this?

Stock-holm syn-drome.

Police sirens wail in the distance as I start toward home. Red and blue lights flash up ahead. I slow behind banked traffic and lower my window, peering outside in a vain attempt to understand what's happening. I can't see anything but cars. There are only frantic shouts for help from unseen people.

I pull over and get out, jogging along the sidewalk. I pass one parked vehicle after another, a crowd building up ahead, as an officer stands on the other side of crime scene tape, staring them down.

"I need you all to take a step back," he growls. "Better yet, go home. Have some respect."

Respect?

The crash comes into sight as I pass the next parked vehicle.

It seems like a truck plowed into a Suburban in the middle of the intersection.

A *familiar* Suburban.

The plates are Luca's.

I run harder, approaching the group of people with their phones at the ready. I shoulder my way to the front, my pulse pausing at the two dead bodies on the road. One up ahead to the left. Another splayed yards away to the right. The crime scene is so fresh the victims haven't had a chance to be covered.

"What the hell happened?" I ask.

The lady nestled against my shoulder casts me a sideways glance. "There was a shooting. This one guy gunned down both men and kidnapped a woman. Even placed her in the trunk of the dead man's car and took off. The only person left behind is the lady currently being interviewed by police."

She points to the Suburban where two officers are nestled close at the open passenger door.

I don't pause for contemplation. I grab the crime scene tape and duck beneath it, running for Luca's car.

"*Hey,*" the policeman yells. "*Stop.*"

"I'm family," I call over my shoulder and keep running, needing to see the survivor, having to confirm who was taken.

Shattered glass blankets the asphalt as I approach Luca's beat up car. The smell of gasoline permeates the air. I close in on the officers at the passenger door and hear the shorter blond guy talking calmly to whoever is caged in front of him.

"I already told you," a woman snaps. "I have no idea what happened."

I know that voice.

It's Hunter's fiancé.

"Sarah?" I skitter to a stop as the policemen turn to face me.

"Ma'am, this is a crime scene." The taller officer stares down his nose at me, his hand moving to his holstered gun. "You need to get back behind the tape."

"I'm her friend."

I'm not even stretching the truth. It's a blatant lie.

The closest I've come to being friendly with Sarah is the silence we shared on opposite ends of a private jet when she escorted me home from Greece.

I lean in, seeing her slumped in the passenger seat, her nose bloodied, one cheek bruised. She straightens at the sight of me, her eyes alighting with strategy as she cradles her ribs.

"Yeah, a friend." She nods. "She's here to take me home."

"She's not taking you anywhere until we're finished talking," the shorter officer warns. "Two people died and another was taken. This is clearly gang-related, yet you're claiming you've got no idea what happened."

"Can't you see she needs medical attention?" My blood boils. "Where are the paramedics?"

"She refused medical help," the taller man snips. "Now, get behind the barrier tape before we're forced to escort you."

Sarah shuffles forward in the seat, wincing as she attempts to climb from the vehicle. "I'm going with her. I've already told you all I know." She jumps to her feet, whimpering on impact. "She can take me to the hospital." Sarah jerks her chin at me. "She's got more authority here than you, anyway."

I cringe, knowing what's coming next as the cops straighten to their full height.

"More authority?" they ask in unison.

"She's a Fed." Sarah hobbles toward me. "She can give me a ride."

"This isn't a Federal case," the shorter officer warns. "You've got no jurisdiction here."

I muster bravado that I seriously lack the energy to maintain. "Not yet it isn't. But one phone call and it could be. So do the right thing and let me take this woman to a hospital. You can ask your questions later."

"I don't even have her name." Short guy frowns. "I need details."

"Jane." Sarah reaches my side and leans into me. "Jane Doe… erty. Jane Doherty."

Goddamnit.

She's not even striving for subtlety.

"I'm going to need to see your badge." The taller man demands of me. "And I'll be noting this in our report."

Fuck.

I do as he asks, snatching my ID from my pocket to flip open my credentials.

I'm going to get in so much shit for this—the involvement in a police matter. Escorting a victim/witness from the scene under false pretenses. And, no doubt, the disappearance of said victim/witness when they later search for her.

Sarah won't go to a hospital. They'll never find her again. Not once Cole gets involved.

"Is there anything else you need from me, Officer?" I keep showing my badge as he takes note of my details.

"No. Get her to the emergency room. We'll check in with her once we're finished here."

"Great." I keep the sarcasm from my tone and start for my car while Sarah hobbles at my side. Once we're out of listening range, the wail of more sirens approaching in the distance, I shoot her a glance. "What the hell happened?"

"Don't know. Can't remember." Her words are sharp. Pointy.

"Right." I stop in the middle of the street, the peanut gallery on the footpath watching our every move. "Maybe I should leave you with the cops then."

She glares, the expression made all the more fierce by the bruising and swelling taking over the bridge of her nose. "I need a goddamn phone. Can I borrow yours?"

"No problem, just as soon as you tell me what happened."

She scoffs, then winces. "You're going to be that bitch? Really?"

"I'm trying to help you. At the expense of my career, I might add, seeing as though you just threw me under the bus."

"Don't pretend you don't have your own agenda." She shuffles ahead, moving away from me.

"An agenda? What agenda could I possibly have right now? I got you out of there and all I want in return is to know if Robert was involved. For my own fucking safety."

She shoots me a skeptical glance, the faintest hint of surprise flashing in her gaze.

"Yes, I know he's still alive." I follow after her. "Cole came to see me last night. I need to know if this was Robert's doing."

"I can't remember." She shrugs. "And I would've kept telling the cops the same thing."

"Okay. Fine." I walk faster, outpacing her. "Find your own way home. God forbid you take my help."

A string of muttered curses brush my ears as I place a few feet of space between us

"It's not like you're more gracious than I am," she snarls. "You were just as thankful for my help when I brought you back from Greece."

I scoff, not stopping my stride until I reach the police tape and duck underneath. "There's a big difference."

"Of course there is," she calls from behind me. "Because I'm in a shitload of pain… and I'm fucking scared. Okay?"

My heart squeezes. Twists.

I keep hold of the tape. Not moving.

I've learned a lot about Sarah through my investigations. About her massive loss. Her orphan status. I don't blame her for falling in with the wrong crowd when she had nobody else in her life. And for her to be scared after everything she's been through would surely mean a woman like me should be petrified.

I wait for her to catch up before I meet her gaze. "Why are you scared?"

Her face hardens. "I don't know, Miss Priss. Maybe because someone plowed their truck into my face, then sprayed bullets like confetti." One hand fidgets at her side. "I really need a phone. Can't you let me make one call?"

"Who was the shooter?"

"Don't know."

Again with the short and sharp response.

She's hiding something.

"It was Robert, wasn't it?" I scope our surroundings, taking in the potential witnesses. "He did this. He tried to kill you."

Any number of nearby people could probably confirm my suspicions. I could simply start asking them. I know what Robert looks like. I'll never forget his features.

"I honestly don't know," she repeats. "I blacked out. I didn't see him. Now can you please give me your goddamn cell?"

"Fine." I reach into my pocket, seeing three missed calls from Easton on the screen before I hand it over. "Make sure you choose your words wisely. That's a work phone."

I continue to my car, giving her privacy as I attempt to figure out how the hell I'm going to explain this to the officers on scene. To Easton. To my boss.

This will act as another nail in my career coffin.

The long list of grievances the Bureau has against me is currently superficial. They align me with the bad name of my father. They despise me for being Cole's alibi when his father escaped custody. But this…

My actions here go against protocol. I'm helping a criminal flee a crime scene.

What the hell am I doing?

I bypass a traffic cop now directing the banked up vehicles away from the area, and slump against the hood of my car, watching Sarah.

She's frantic in her conversation, sheer panic etched across her face.

I want to help her despite our differences, even without the connection to Robert.

It has to be another side effect of Stockholm.

The rev of an engine draws my attention to the back of the

waiting line of cars. The deep vibration transforms into a screech of wheels, then a streak of black as a familiar Porsche accelerates along the parking lane to stop behind me.

Cole climbs out, stalking forward, cell in his hand, scowl set in stone. The closer he gets the deeper his brows pinch, until he's glaring at me.

"Thank Christ." Sarah jogs toward us, her arm tight around her ribs. "I tried calling Hunter but he must be on the phone. And Luca isn't answering. Where is everyone?"

"My house. Or on the way there. What the fuck happened? Where's Penny?"

Penny?

Sarah doesn't speak, but the fear in her eyes says it all as she stares at Cole.

"She's meant to be here?" I ask. "She was in the car with you?"

They ignore me, Cole's face tightening, his shoulders stiff.

"Robert has her?" I push from the car, demanding their attention.

"I was out of it," Sarah pleads with Cole. "I don't know if she ran or if she was taken?"

My stomach free falls.

"She was taken," I confirm. "Witnesses watched a man put a woman in the trunk of a car before he sped off. I need you both to tell me everything you know." I step closer, right up to Cole. "What information do you have on him?"

"The time for shared knowledge is over," he states in a flat tone. Emotionless. Detached. "That was your choice."

"Don't be an asshole. If Penny's in trouble—"

"Penny is none of your concern."

"Cole," I warn. "Listen—"

"No, *you* listen. You made your choice. Now deal with it." He glares at Sarah. "Get in the car."

He stalks to the passenger side of the Porsche, and I follow as he opens the door and helps her inside.

I'm poised to plead my case when he turns on me, his eyes filled with animosity as he says, "Keep your mouth shut. Breathe one word of this and you're going to have a problem on your hands."

"You're threatening me?" My hackles rise, the hair on my neck tingling in response. "What are you going to do, Cole? Kidnap me again?"

He smiles, the curve of lips different than anything I've witnessed from him before. There's no flirtation or superiority. It's pure hostility. One hundred percent venom. "No, Anissa. Our days jetting across the globe are over. You won't be treated that kindly again."

Like so many times before, I'm assaulted with the wrong emotional response.

I should be shocked at the audacity of him calling my abduction a kindness. I should be pissed that I'm being treated like the bad guy. I should even be so entirely fearful for Penny's life that his menace doesn't matter.

Instead, I'm left empty at what he called me—Anissa.

My full name.

Without abbreviation or flirtation.

What the fuck is wrong with me?

5

COLE

I walk past Anissa, skirting the hood of my car to slide into the driver's seat.

I've never had to clutch tighter to my threadbare restraint than I do right now.

Tonight has been a fucking nightmare.

The party at my restaurant was meant to draw Robert from the shadows. I had an extensive team of hired men scattered throughout the neighborhood to catch that fucker. But what I hadn't expected was the revelation that Benji, my own brother-in-law, has been working with him.

It doesn't matter that I know my sister was the driving force behind the betrayal. Benji made the decision to follow Layla's lead. *He* was the one in my inner circle, playing me like a fool. And *he* will be the one who pays the heavy price.

I'd already been on edge, not only due to the threat of Robert, but because Anissa had gone against my directives to stay hidden, choosing instead to flitter around the fucking city all damn morning before outsmarting the men I had following her.

Nobody had been able to find her until she turned up out the front of the restaurant. Right where I didn't want her to be.

I shouldn't give a shit. Not one iota.

After watching Easton walk from her bedroom last night, it

should be easy to forget her. Instead, all I want to do is spend my days destroying his life, and making her watch.

I'll show her how pathetic he is. I'll make him wish he'd never laid eyes on her, let alone his filthy hands.

But seeing her here *now*, after the bullshit of the last twelve hours, only makes my blood boil.

I fight the instinct to gun the engine, escaping in a screech of tires, and pull from the curb slowly, pretending she has no effect on me as she stands on the footpath, her eyes pained.

"Tell me everything," I demand of Sarah. "Don't leave out any details."

"I seriously don't know what to tell you. One minute I was driving; the next, Penny was yelling. I caught sight of the truck plowing toward us for a split second, then I blacked out on impact. I didn't see the driver. And Penny was gone when I gained consciousness."

"What did the police say?"

"They think it's gang-related. The security guard you had tailing us is dead, and I overheard them talking about the murder of an innocent bystander who tried to help Penny. This has to have been Robert."

Fuck.

Luca is going to lose his shit.

And Robert... that fucking prick will make Penny regret her freedom.

"I have no idea what's going on between you two." Sarah fastens her belt. "And I know she's a Fed. But Agent Fox was really only trying to help."

I ignore her, pressing the button on my steering wheel to activate my cell. "Call Hunt."

The car speakers come alive with the ringtone as I inch toward the banked traffic. I blare my horn until the long line parts enough for me to cut through and head in the opposite direction.

"We've got a situation," Hunt growls in greeting. "And I can't find Sarah. She's not answering her fucking phone."

"I'm here," she speaks up, repositioning herself in her seat with a wince. "I'm okay. But Penny's gone."

He releases a long breath. "Thank fuck you're okay. I've been calling—"

"I tried calling you, too. I left a message." She sits taller. "Listen, we were hit by a truck. I got knocked out, but when I came to she was gone."

"Are you okay?" he asks.

"I'm fine. But Penny isn't."

"She's here. Well, she was. Decker just drove her and Luca to the hospital."

"What happened?" I press my foot harder, speeding along the street.

"I've got no idea. I can't figure out the mess. Even the guards at your gate are clueless. All I've got is a damn war zone in your neighbor's house with nobody here to tell the tale."

"And Benji," I snarl the name. "Where is he?"

"He's with me, helping start the clean-up. I told him to call Keira and Layla. They're going to spend the night in a hotel, but they want the kids out of your house asap."

"I'll get them. I'm on my way now. Find out what hotel they're at and text it to me."

"Will do. And Cole…" There's a pause. "Our problem has been taken care of."

Our problem—*Robert*.

Sarah glances at me, her bruised face relaxing.

"Entirely?" I turn the nearest corner, easing my foot off the gas.

"Yeah. Entirely. It's only a matter of getting him off the grid."

I shoot Sarah a grin as she exhales in relief. "Good work."

I disconnect the call, my night finally seeming to change for the better. At least momentarily. I still need to make an example of Benji. There's no way around it.

I've given too many free passes for betrayal lately. I can't do it again.

I'll punish him in a way that ensures everyone knows I'm not to be fucked with. And I'll make sure Layla knows she's to blame.

I pull onto my street, my attention narrowing on Decker's car parked in front of my neighbor's house, Benji's car positioned directly opposite.

I slow, a skitter of foreboding crawling down my neck at the sight of Mavis' house illuminating the early morning darkness. I hope the old girl survived whatever went on in there. Then again, it might be better if she didn't. She'd never feel safe again. Not all alone in that big house.

"What do you think happened?" Sarah asks.

"I don't know. We'll get the details soon enough." I grind my teeth through the mental onslaught of possibilities. That fucker came too close. Way too fucking close. "Once I grab the kids and drop them off to my sisters, I'll call the doc and make sure you're checked over."

"I'm fine. It's a few bruises. That's all."

"You're seeing the doctor. It's not up for discussion." I continue driving to my front gates, opening the thick metal barrier with a click of a remote, and stop beside the waiting guard.

He keeps a hand over his side piece as I lower my window, his gaze stalking our surroundings while he leans down to eye level.

"What happened?" I growl.

"Your guess is as good as mine. We heard an explosion. Our guys on the perimeter thought there were gunshots, too. Silenced, though. But nothing crossed the fence. No bullets. No threat. Nothing."

"You didn't send someone next door to check it out?"

"No, sir. It was our job to maintain the safety of *your* property and the residents inside. My men did their boundary checks every ten to fifteen minutes as scheduled. Then kept a closer eye on your neighbor after the disturbance. But we never left our post."

I don't know whether to be proud or infuriated.

"Make sure nobody disturbs my men." I tilt my chin toward Mavis' house. "I don't want anything coming within a foot of the front yard. No cops. No visitors. Not even a fucking squirrel. You hear me?"

"I hear you." He straightens, retreating from the Porsche. "I'll let you know if we have any issues."

I raise my window and drive through the gates, continuing around the back of the house, passing two more armed guards in the shadows before parking in the garage.

Sarah doesn't say a word. She stares straight ahead even after I kill the engine.

"What's on your mind?" I unfasten my belt and release the steering wheel.

"He took her," she whispers. "Robert took Penny."

"Yeah, he did. But he's dead now."

"And what about her?" She shoots me a glance. "What happened between the time she left me and the moment that rapist died? What did he do to her?"

"Whatever happened couldn't be worse than the life she had in Greece." It's a pathetic comparison. But it's the truth. "She survived living with my father. She can survive this, too."

"I was meant to be looking after her." Her voice wavers. "It was my job to keep her safe."

"It was also the job of the guard you had following you. We should all be thankful your fate, along with Penny's, wasn't the same as his."

She shifts her focus back out the windshield to the darkened garage. "That's not comforting."

"Well, it should be." I shove from the car, waiting as she slowly unfastens her belt, her movements more stiff than earlier. "Stay here. I'll organize the kids."

"No." She opens her door, cautiously climbing out. "I'll get Tobias. You can handle Stella. That little girl is the devil when woken from her beauty sleep."

She isn't wrong. My niece—although, the most beautiful princess I've laid eyes on—can be Satan when the mood strikes. It's an unfortunate trait she gained from her mother.

I lead the way into the house, along the darkened hall, the light from the kitchen the only glow to highlight the closed bedrooms. I pass the nanny's door to gently ease open Stella's, then creep inside, walking from memory because the room is too dark to see shit.

I don't stop until my shins hit the unforgiving hardness of the side of the bed.

Fuck.

I kneel with a snarl, placing my hands on the mattress. "Stella, sweetheart. You need to get up."

There's no response. Not even a shift in the silence around me.

"Stella?" I reach out, swiping my palm over the bed. My fingers glide over vacant sheets. "Sweetheart?"

I can't hear her breathing.

I can't hear a damn thing.

"*Stella?*" I scramble for the door. Flick on the light. Expose a completely empty room.

There's no sign of my niece.

"*Sarah.*" I storm for the hall, into Tobias' doorway, and flick on the light. She stands before another empty bed, the fear in her features mimicking the sensation pummeling my chest.

"Are they having some sort of camp-out in another room?" She rushes toward me. "Could they have heard the explosion and gotten scared? Maybe they're with the nanny."

I send out a silent prayer. I mentally beg the fucking heavens for her to be right as I run down the hall, swinging the nanny's door wide.

"Tanya." I flick on the light and everything drains from me— thought, comprehension, knowledge.

The girl, barely in her mid-twenties, lays strewn on the carpet, face-up, a hypodermic syringe hanging from her arm. Vomit is pooled on the floor near her mouth. Urine permeates the air. And those eyes. Those vacant, unblinking eyes.

"Oh, Christ." Sarah shoves past me and falls to her knees beside the woman to place a gentle hand to her cheek. "She's stone cold."

6

______

COLE

I SEARCH THE HOUSE, SCOURING EVERY ROOM, CALLING TOBIAS AND Stella's names with every breath.

I hope they're in hiding. That they heard someone messing with Tanya and made the smart decision to flee.

"They're not here." Sarah catches up to me in the kitchen, her face pale as she holds up a dirty cloth. "But I found this under Stella's bed."

"What is it?" I approach.

"It's doused in chemicals. My guess is chloroform. Someone took them."

I run a hand down my face, attempting to compartmentalize this goddamn situation. "That means they're not dead. Whoever did this wouldn't go to the effort of sedating them if they were going to kill them."

She cringes. "Maybe. But chloroform isn't a great sign either. It's highly toxic. Inhaling too much could easily kill a child."

The hits keep coming, one after another, the horror compiling.

Anyone accountable won't survive. They won't want to after I start reaping my revenge.

"What do you want me to do?" she asks. "I can go get Layla and Keira if you want. It's better to tell them face-to-face."

"No. I need you to organize a clean-up crew." I hand over my cell. "Don't tell anyone what's happened until I say. Okay?"

"Okay. What are you going to do?"

"I'm going to find those kids."

I stride across the living room and continue through the house to the front door, my ears flooded with the choking beat of rage and fucking fear.

I don't stop until I'm at the front gate, yelling at the guard to let me out.

As soon as I can slip through the opening metal, I stalk for the motherfucker who was meant to be in charge. I grasp his throat in seconds. Slam my fist into his face.

"Where are they?" I pummel him again. "What the fuck happened to them?"

He stumbles as I hold tight to his neck, blood seeping from a cut on his lip.

"What the hell are you talking about?" He claws at my wrist, shoves at my chest. "Get your fucking hands off me."

I cling tighter, his heartbeat frantic under my fingertips. "Someone has been in my house. The nanny is dead. The kids are missing."

He quits fighting. His face falls. "Nobody has come through these gates except you. I vow it on my life. I've been here the whole time."

"Then whoever is responsible didn't use the fucking gates." I release my hold, shoving him backward. "Call your team and have them properly check the perimeter. Until the culprit is found, this is on your shoulders."

I turn on my heels to run some more, this time to Mavis' house. I slam my fist against the front door. Again and again. Over and over. The outlet doesn't lessen the effects of overwhelming adrenaline.

I'm suffocating here. Drowning in my own mistakes.

"I'm coming," Hunt yells from inside. "Hold on."

I keep knocking until the door flings open.

"What the fuck?" Hunter's hard scowl stares back at me. "Are you trying to wake the whole goddamn neighborhood?"

"Have you seen the kids?" I shove past him, the acrid scent of bleach burning my nostrils.

"No. Why?"

I make for one of the curved staircases bordering both walls in the entry and jump the steps three at a time.

I switch on every light.

Open every door.

Search every fucking room.

When the entire floor turns up empty, I hustle back downstairs finding Hunter still waiting for me in the entry, eyeing me with trepidation.

"It's bad, isn't it?" he asks.

"Yeah." I stop before him, not wanting to break the news when I'm sure this has to be a fucking nightmare I'll soon wake from.

"Tell me and I'll sort it out."

This isn't something he can fix for me. Not this time. No matter how much I'd give to have this all be over.

"It's Stella and Tobias." I lower my voice, unsure of Benji's location. "They're gone. There's no sign of them."

He frowns. "Did the nanny take them somewhere?"

"She's stone-cold, wide-eyed on the bedroom floor, a needle still in her arm."

"Holy shit." He stands motionless. "What about Sarah? Where is she?"

"She's beat up and needs to see a doctor. But right now she's busy making arrangements to get rid of the body."

"Fucking hell." He rakes his hands through his hair. "Tell me what you need me to do. Where do we start? What did the guards say?"

"The guards don't know a damn thing. And neither do I. If Robert is dead, where does it leave the damn kids?"

"He had a man working with him. Young guy. California ID His dead ass is still upstairs. If we follow the trail, he might lead us to someone else."

Footsteps approach from along the hall, and I turn my gaze to find Benji walking toward us with a bloody rag in his hands.

"What's going on?" He glances between us. "Did something else happen?"

I don't have to tell him a damn thing. After his betrayal, I'm not obligated to breathe a fucking word. But this is his daughter. His little girl.

"It's okay." Hunt clears his throat. "Whatever happened, we'll ahh… we'll sort it out. We always do."

"Sort *what* out?" Benji asks. "What's the problem?"

I stare at him. The traitor. The snitch.

Earlier, I wanted him dead.

Now, I'm loath to inflict this punishment on him. The news of Stella's disappearance will be a far more painful torture than anything I could inflict.

"Benji—" I clench my fists, struggling to straddle the line between brother-in-law and betrayee.

"What?" He frowns. "What is it? What's wrong?"

"It's Stella." I shake my head, attempting to dislodge the overwhelming horror. The things that could be happening to her… the things that might happen in the future… "She's missing."

He jerks back. "What do you mean?"

"She's gone. She's not in the house. There was—"

He storms forward, walking around me, heading for the front door.

"Where are you going?" Hunter grabs his arm, pulling him to a stop.

"To Torian's house to show him Stella's fine." He yanks his arm free. "She'd be sleeping in a different room. She bed-hops all the time."

"She's not there." I remain in place as Hunt moves to the door, blocking the exit. "Sarah and I checked. The guards are searching the yard."

Benji's frown deepens. "She's there." He shakes his head, denying the dire possibilities. "Where would she go?"

I hold his stare, my jaw tight, my focus lethal. The beats of silence are painfully informative.

He shakes his head harder as Hunter's expression contorts in discomfort.

"No." Benji backtracks, moving closer to the door. "She'd be asleep somewhere. Hiding. It's probably a big joke to her."

"It's no joke. She was taken."

"No." The rampant back and forth of his head is aggressive. "*No.*" He turns, storming for the door.

Hunter blocks his escape. The two grapple.

"Benji, you're not leaving." I keep my voice level. "We don't have time to waste. Tobias is gone, too. The nanny is dead."

A sound escapes him. A guttural cry more animalistic than human.

He quits fighting and stumbles backward, his face draining of color. "No."

"I believe the kids are still alive. There's evidence they were sedated. But who knows how long that will last."

His chest rises and falls in rapid succession. "Why?" he pleads. "Why would anyone…"

"You tell me." I fight a glare as he hunches over, retching. *He* was the one speaking to a sex trafficker behind my back. *He* was the man who betrayed me to a man capable of something as vile as this. "You need to share every single thing you told Robert. And you need to do it now. Because if I don't find those kids, living with the loss of your daughter is going to be the least of your problems."

7

———

ANISSA

I remain at the scene, Cole's lingering fury and rejection making it near impossible to leave. If I go home, I'll only work myself into a mental frenzy, questioning my thoughts, my past, my future.

I'll eat my weight in feelings and this body has seen one too many tubs of ice cream lately to justify the additional calories.

So I stay, steering clear of the cops, taking discreet photos from behind their plastic tape barrier, speaking to witnesses who continue to hang around despite the early morning hour.

"Did you see what happened?" I smile at the young blonde cradling a cell in her hands. She looks on edge. Fidgety. Maybe agitated, as her suspicious eyes meet mine.

"It's okay. I'm FBI." I flash her my badge. "You can talk to me. Did you see what happened?"

"I saw the whole thing. And I tried explaining what happened to one of the officers, but he told me to stay here and wait. I even recorded the whole thing on my phone." She sighs, her shoulders slumping. "I'm just so tired. I've got three jobs and I need to be up in a few hours to start my next shift."

"I understand." I step closer. "Why don't you give me a look? I can take your statement."

"Thank you." She focuses on her cell, pressing buttons until a video starts to play. "This is what happened."

The recording is jolted, as if she were running along the sidewalk toward Luca's Suburban which has already been hit in the middle of the intersection. Horns blare. Onlookers speak in the distance. Then there's the unmistakable *pop, pop, pop* of gunfire.

People scream.

The vision lowers, the cracked cement footpath the only sight as a female swears.

"I was hiding," she explains. "Once I heard the gunshots, I dove behind a car parked on the side of the street. I didn't know what else to do."

I nod, my attention glued to the screen.

The camera is raised over the hood of a red truck. Luca's car comes back into focus. I hold my breath as Robert stalks into view, his stride long, his confidence remarkable. He shoots toward something off-screen, making onlookers scream.

"That's when he shot the man in the car behind the Suburban," the woman says. "Shot him dead. Just like that." She clicks her fingers. "I've never seen anything like it in my life."

"I'm sorry you had to witness this." I remain transfixed on the replay as Robert approaches the passenger side of Luca's car, gun raised. He yanks open the door, drags Penny out, and shoves her down the road.

An innocent bystander steps forward, calling for him to stop. But there's no stopping. Robert barely pauses as he raises his weapon and guns the man down.

"It was horrific," the woman whispers. "None of us knew what to do."

"Us?" I don't raise my gaze from her phone.

"There was a group. About five of us. We were all in hiding, not sure if we should risk our lives to help. I feel so guilty."

"There's nothing you could've done."

Robert drags Penny toward a silver sedan parked behind the Suburban and shoves her in the trunk. Then, as easily as if he's heading out for a leisurely Sunday drive, he climbs into the car and leaves the scene. No screech of tires. No frantic escape.

He abducted her effortlessly. Not one hint of doubt.

"As soon as he was gone, we all rushed to help those people.

But the man from the sedan was already dead, and the other…" She drags in a ragged breath. "He was so scared."

"It's going to take you some time to come to terms with what you witnessed." I give her a sad smile and fight against the need to get more involved in Cole's drama.

He wouldn't want this recording shared.

And Penny doesn't deserve to be a news headline or a viral sensation.

"But this footage is great." I keep smiling, attempting to exude warmth. "Do you know if anyone else recorded what happened?"

"Not that I know of. I think once the gunshots started, most people were too busy hiding. After the police arrived, everyone crowded me to get a second look."

I nod and pull out my own device, deleting the notices of Easton's missed messages and calls. "I'm going to need you to Bluetooth it to me. Can you do that?"

"Yeah, sure."

I talk her through the transfer and wait patiently for the file to arrive, double-checking it as my stomach churns with foreboding.

I shouldn't be getting involved.

I *shouldn't*. But goddamn it, I can't help myself.

"I'm sorry. I don't think I got your name, ma'am." I inch closer.

"Izzy," she offers. "Isabel Masen."

"Thanks, Isabel." I lower my voice. "Before I let you go, I want to make sure you know the legal risks associated with holding onto recordings of a crime such as this." I'm bullshitting, talking completely out of my ass. All for what? Cole *fucking* Torian. "If someone else gets hold of this—if your phone is stolen or hacked—you could be in a lot of trouble."

"Are you for real?" Her lips part in shock. "I thought I was helping."

"You were. It's the aftermath that gets tricky. You don't want to be responsible for leaking information on an investigation as important as this."

Why am I helping Cole? *Why, Anissa? Why?*

"Can I delete the video?" she begs. "I don't want to be a part of this. I just want to go home."

"Of course you can. I have the footage now. If you delete your copy you won't have to worry about anyone else getting hold of it. And I have your name for future reference. But I'd like to take your cell number, too."

"Okay." She nods and recites the digits as she taps buttons on her screen. "It's gone. Deleted. Do I need to go to the police station to make a statement?"

My stomach dips, the hollow organ seeming to fall to my feet. "No, you're free to go home."

She releases a relieved breath. "Thank you so much."

Sickening guilt works its way through me in an increasing tide. I force myself to breathe normally. I'm going to get fired. Not only that, I could end up behind bars.

The woman pockets her cell, gives me a tired farewell smile, then leaves.

I'm so screwed.

Tampering with witnesses. Destroying evidence. Involving myself in a case that isn't even remotely in my jurisdiction while I'm on leave.

I'm in over my head, trying to convince myself I can't walk away because of my fear for Penny's safety when my reasons for being here are far deeper than that.

I'm protecting Cole. Again.

Risking my career for a criminal.

I stare at my phone, the morning hours growing colder, my breath fogging in the frigid air. I should call Easton. After listening to him spit a quick verbal barrage about Cole's reputation, I could be back on the straight and narrow… but I don't call.

I send him a quick message instead—*I'm climbing into bed. Sorry I didn't text sooner. Night.* Then I get in my car.

I should go home. For the sake of my job and my mental health, I should head directly for my apartment building. But I don't do that either.

I drive to Cole's restaurant. Bright lights continue to illuminate the room as I slowly inch my vehicle forward, yet all the guests are gone. There's only a cluster of waitresses rearranging tables and a lone man with a mop pushing through the kitchen doors.

I park at the curb, the engine still running as self-hatred eats me from the inside out. I need to know if Penny has been found. If she's okay. If she's even still alive. I wonder about Sarah, too. Did she see a doctor? Is she recovering?

And Robert. What about him?

The reasons to call Cole mount on my shoulders.

No, they're excuses. Placations.

Sarah isn't my friend.

Penny is just another victim.

Robert is one of many threats I've earned in my career.

I just want to talk to Cole. For no other reason than to hear his voice.

I cringe through self-loathing as I pull out my cell. I sigh as I dial his number. Then I hold my breath and listen to the phone ring.

He doesn't answer.

After two quick trills his voicemail cuts in, announcing loud and clear he rejected my call.

He's rejecting *me* when only weeks ago he was in front of my building with flowers, demanding my attention.

I throw the phone to the passenger seat and grip the steering wheel.

"This isn't healthy." I exhale long and loud. "It's not normal." I suck a deep breath in. "Go home, Nissa."

I don't know what's worse—talking to myself or using the nickname Cole gave me. But this time, I listen.

I pull into the empty street, cranking the music loud to drown my thoughts, and find my way home on autopilot. I don't pause a second in contemplation once I set foot inside my apartment. I head straight for my medicine cabinet to snatch at the sleeping pills, downing two with a vodka chaser.

The liquid burns. Just like my shame.

I don't trust myself to fall asleep unaided. If left to my own devices, I'll toss and turn, my subconscious feeding me unwanted thoughts of dark eyes and a darker soul.

I don't change. Or shower. I fall face-first into bed and stay there, unmoving, until darkness takes me away.

When I wake, the sun is already creeping through my curtains. It's still early, and the heady lethargy from the pills makes it difficult to get my ass vertical.

I shower. Eat. Tug on my light grey pantsuit and then stare at my phone, willing it to ring. I flick from news station to news station, listening to vague information about the alleged gang-related violence from last night. The footage shown includes a snapshot of Robert and Penny, but neither of their faces are visible.

If authorities had detailed descriptions they would've been shared.

The witness I spoke to might be right. I could have the only video of the crime.

I dial Cole's number, pretending I have an obligation to let him know, when the necessity for contact is far more complicated than that. But the call rings out.

He's cut me off. After claiming he wanted me. When I was meant to be *everything* to him. He severed ties without a backward glance.

I've tried everything apart from exorcism to rid myself of feelings for him, and he flicks off the hinderance like a damn light switch.

Asshole.

Well, good for him. But it's not going to stop me from getting answers on Penny.

I snatch my purse, keys and cell from the counter, ignoring the unanswered messages from Easton, and down my half-filled mug of coffee in one chug before leaving the apartment.

Within a short drive I'm at his front gates with a guard approaching my window.

"Who are you?" He glowers at me with unabashed superiority as I lower the glass.

"A friend of Cole's. I need to speak to him."

He sidles up beside my door and rests a forearm against the roof of my car, making his jacket gape to expose the holstered gun beneath. It's deliberate intimidation. I wouldn't expect anything less from one of Cole's men. "No visitors today. You'll have to come back some other time."

I smile, sweet and pure. "I don't need to see him. I just need to speak to him. Tell him Anissa is here and that I'm not going anywhere until we talk."

"He's not going to give a shit who you are, sweetheart. He's given strict orders not to be disturbed."

My lips tighten, venom entering the upswept curve. "Call him." I pull out my badge, enjoying the tiny flare of surprise in his eyes. "You don't want to be responsible for me returning with a warrant and a full team of agents when all I want to do is chat."

It's a bluff, but given Cole's reputation, even the slightest hint of a warrant should put this guy on edge.

He glares, stepping back to right his jacket with a hard yank of the lapels. "Fine. I'll call him. But it won't mean shit. He'll still say no. They're dealing with a family emergency and want privacy."

"I know all about the emergency. Just make the damn call."

He retreats, unclasping a cell hooked to his belt. He turns away, murmuring words I can't decipher in front of a house that looms tall and menacing in the distance.

I've never been inside the perimeter. Not even a foot. But I've heard stories. I've been told about the wealth on display. The secrets hidden.

There's a whir of metallic sound, then the gates open to expose the path to damnation.

My pulse kicks like an unruly mule.

The guard returns. "Park at the front of the house and ring the bell. Someone will meet you."

Wait. What?

I'm not going in there.

That's not what I want.

"I only need to speak to him." I meet the guy's eyes. "Not enter the property."

"I called," he growls. "I got you an audience. Now hurry up and drive inside, or get the hell out of here."

No. I shake my head. I can already hear the snarled anger from my boss, Taggert, as he lambastes me on why I would even approach the property, let alone slip through the gates.

I've crossed so many lines. All of them dark and dangerous, the distinction between right and wrong clearly defined.

"I swear to God," the guard mutters, "once I close those gates I won't be opening them again. Either get in, or leave."

It's not that easy.

I have legitimate reasons for being here. Penny was abducted. Robert was responsible. Men died. Yet again, there's violence on Portland streets.

I need to be updated on what's happening.

But none of those things will appease my boss when I'm meant to be keeping my distance from Cole.

"*Now,*" the guard snarls.

Goddamnit.

I press my foot on the accelerator, entering uncharted territory.

The landscape before me is pristine. The grass, lush and green. The hedges, trimmed.

The whir of the closing gates brings an icy chill to my arms. The quiet calm of early morning that follows puts me on edge. Every sound is amplified. The crunch of gravel beneath the tires. The sweep of breeze through the trees.

I approach the towering two-story mansion with its perfect white curtains in every window, not a cobweb or tarnish in sight across the entire veneer. I park in front, my discomfort multiplying, the tension inside me wringing tight.

But I need answers.

About Penny. About Robert.

And most of all, about Cole.

I don't let doubt take a stronghold. I turn off the car, get out and stride for the front door, ringing the bell twice in quick succession.

For a while, I don't think he'll answer. I wouldn't be surprised if he let me through the gates just to lock me in his yard until I had to climb my way free.

I press the bell again, this time holding my finger in place.

Trudging footsteps approach from inside, the thuds ricocheting through my chest. I hold my breath as the door is yanked open. But the man who stands before me with a monstrous scowl isn't Cole.

"How the fuck did you get in here?" Hunter barks.

"Cole is expecting me."

He stiffens. Straightens. "Since when?"

"Since now. Are you going to let me in?"

His eyes narrow to lethal slits. "Do you have a warrant?"

I sigh, losing all strength in my posture.

I'm tired. Of the fighting. Of the battle. I haven't felt alive in weeks. There's only the memories of the vicious verbal conflicts with Cole to invigorate me. "I just want to speak to him. I'm not here for drama."

"Let her in." Cole's far-off voice comes from inside the house, his authority brushing over me like a favored blanket. His adamance squeezes my belly.

Hunter doesn't budge. He remains imperial in his defiance.

"You heard him." I step forward, testing the boundaries, strengthening my resolve. "Move out of my way."

He snarls, the dog-like threat entirely fitting for such a pit bull as I squeeze past him, my nose immediately assaulted with the scent of bleach.

The chemical hangs heavily in the air, smothering each breath I take.

"What happened here?" The possibilities fill me with dread. Yet there's a curious niggle of hope, too. A sickening sense of pride at the possibility of Cole having killed Robert.

"Hunter?" I swing back to face him. "What happened?"

"Keep pushing me and you'll experience a reenactment." His poisonous smile is slow to form. The bags under his eyes negate the taunt. He's just as exhausted as I am. "He's in his room." The words grate over thinly veiled hostility. "I suggest you watch your snappy mouth. I don't have the energy to dispose of another body."

Another?

"Robert's dead?" I ask.

He ignores me, marching ahead, passing a staircase that he hikes a thumb toward. "Torian is up there."

The thud of his footsteps continues down the hall, the silence closing in once he turns out of view.

The house becomes eerily quiet. Empty.

I glance around my surroundings—the high ceiling, the artistic photography lining the walls, the light, clean crispness of it all. It's spectacular. I wouldn't expect anything less from Cole.

But it's cold. And not only due to the breeze sweeping my skin from another part of the house.

This place is hollow. Without heart.

I walk to the stairs, the light murmurings of haunted conversation brushing my ears as I climb the first step. The whispers of secrets and scandals are hidden in the unheard words. I grab the banister for grounding. For courage.

I can already sense him. Can instinctively feel Cole's presence wrapping around me. Coiling tight.

My pulse increases as I reach the landing and turn the corner, finding more steps leading to a captivating portrait of a middle-aged woman.

His mother?

Their compelling eyes are the same. The warm skin. The dark hair.

"Cole?" I call his name at the top step, feeling like an interloper.

A shuffle emanates down the short hall to my right. No verbal response. No civil welcome. Just the intimidation of his existence.

I approach the sound, my steps leading me toward the daylight sweeping in through an open doorway. I keep my head high, my shoulders straight, my breathing level, even though all three fight against me.

"Cole?"

Again, no response.

I reach the threshold and pause, my attention skimming over the intimidating king-size bed with its shiny black covers and shifting to the man standing at the open window, his back to me, his attention focused outside.

Air congeals in my lungs, the splinters of unwanted yearning punishing me from the inside out.

He's still in the same suit as last night, the material remaining pristine, his posture oozing power.

"Good morning." I attempt to add authority to my tone. Fortitude. My ears hear it for the weak greeting it is.

He remains immobile. Statuesque.

"Cole?"

He shudders out a breath, the sound foreign for a man with such tenacity. He turns to me, slow, controlled, those dark eyes meeting mine, the indecipherable emotion in them twisting my stomach.

He's almost unrecognizable with the defeat in his features.

A Jekyll to his usual Hyde.

"What happened?" I force myself to remain in place. "Is Robert dead? Have you found Penny?"

He scoffs, his frame jerking slightly before the silence returns. There's nothing but a slight whistle from the breeze.

My unease grows. Bubbling. Spitting. "Answer me. I deserve to know."

The demand is the only leverage I have. I can't throw my badge at him—not when he has enough dirt on me to send me to prison.

"You deserve it?" His voice is a low growl of barely contained anger. "You don't deserve *shit* from me."

The spike of aggression squeezes my ribs.

He's been hostile toward me before. Too many times to count. There's been intimidation and unrest. But this is different. There's no energetic anger in his eyes. No mindless rage.

This is clinical hatred.

I open my mouth to say something... anything... Problem is, I'm isolated from reason. I can't think when he looks at me like that. When *he* looks like that.

His hair is tousled, as if he's raked his hands through it a million times. The bags under his eyes are heavy with fatigue. And those lips, the ones that previously brought me pleasure, are one straight line of disdain.

"Two days ago you knock at my door, demanding to facilitate my safety. Now, I'm what? Your enemy?" I move forward, slow and cautious. "I haven't done anything wrong. I came here because I want information on a man who attacked me. A man who has become a nightmare in my life because of you."

His nostrils flare. His jaw clenches.

The energy of passionate anger builds between us. I'm a slave to the flames. It's always been this way. We burn from the heat of animosity. It fuels us.

"We're not enemies." It's imperative I remind him. If he turns on me, my life is as good as over. But that's not what pains me. It's not what scares me the most.

The reality of how close we are to severing ties, after I've fought so long to do exactly that, is confounding. Soul shaking. I don't want this.

"I think our past proves I'm worthy of inside information." I clear my throat. "I tried—"

"Is that what you really think?" He scoffs. "That you deserve anything from me after you fucked another man?"

I jerk back in shock. In gratification.

This hostility can't all be driven by jealousy. Surely not.

But the thrill of this poisoned treat is something I wish I could sink my teeth into. To taste every morsel of his envy. To gorge on the way he covets me.

"Easton is none of your—"

"He's dead," Cole snaps.

For a moment, I'm not sure who he's talking about—Robert or Anthony. Both possibilities leave me shocked.

"There's no longer a threat toward you." His face turns into an expressionless mask. "And now that you've got the information you came for, leave."

I blink through the mass of unfurling questions. I should do exactly as he's asked. Leave. Never look back. But I can't move. There's no will to walk away—only the determination to stay.

"If he's dead, then what's wrong?" I take another step and another, the exotic scent of his lingering aftershave invading the acrid bleach. "What else happened?"

His face hardens. His upper lip curls. "Get the fuck out." He turns his back to me, returning his attention out the window.

Rejection slaps me cold. I've kissed this man with all the passion I contain. I've taken him inside my body and exhilarated in the resulting pleasure. I've craved him.

Hungered for him.

Pined.

I was stupid to think I could turn those memories to ash. I was even more ignorant to assume I could simply switch off what I once felt. There's no easy withdrawal from this.

He's an addiction like no other, requiring more than a twelve-step program and a lifetime of rehab.

"Please talk to me," I whisper. "What else happened?"

He launches a fist at the wall. The crack of impact startles me. He swings around to storm my way.

There's no time to think. To retreat. He gets in my face, attempting to intimidate, but all I feel is passion. Fire. Flames.

"We're not doing this again." He leans close, eye to eye. Feral. "That was your choice."

His breath brushes my lips, the exquisite tease a shot of ecstasy to my throbbing veins.

"Leave." He holds his voice in check, his gaze steady. Unshakable.

The demand skitters over my flesh. Into my bones.

I breathe deeper. Heavier.

I should do as he says. Common sense squeaks in the back of my mind telling me to listen.

But I don't. I steady my shoulders. Hitch my chin.

His lips curl in a snarl, part rage, part hunger. I can feel him. The vibration. The power.

My palms sweat with the need to reach out. To touch.

He doesn't scare me. Never has. What I fear is this ending. What frightens me the most is being forced to walk away from here and never feel alive again.

I've not been adored like I have been with this man. Even through the lies and deception, my recollections of him always come back to the emotions he inspires. The unwitting sense of belonging. The strange click of a puzzle piece finally fitting in place.

He inches closer, so close I can feel the warmth of his lips, the heat in his eyes.

I could kiss him. I'd barely need to move. All it would take is a slight lean. A mere hitch of my chin. And I want to. *God*, how I want to feel his scorching mouth unravelling me one thread at a time. To taste his aggression. To drown in his possession.

I turn my head instead, denying us both.

His chuckle is a whisper over my cheek. A subtle dose of spite.

I stand rigid, close to breaking point, my insides screaming at me to take, take, take.

He gets closer, his nose nudging my jaw, awakening a flood of tingling goose bumps. The slight connection holds the force of an explosion. It's blinding. Shattering.

Air thickens in my lungs as he nuzzles higher, his mouth moving to my ear.

I stop breathing, waiting for erotic words to soothe my yearning. Waiting for him to say something that will signal my surrender. And it's right there. My submission is his for the taking.

"My little fox," he murmurs, deep and low.

I whimper.

"After everything we've been through, there's only one thing I want to say to you." His admission trickles down my neck, awakening every nerve ending. "Get the fuck out of my house," he growls, "And never come back."

I pull away, embarrassment rendering me speechless.

He truly wants me to leave.

Right… Okay… Fine…

I step back, raising my hands in surrender. "I'm leaving."

"*Now*," he sneers.

"Jesus Christ." I'm already retreating, goddamnit. I'm just too gobsmacked at how the tables have turned to move faster than a snail's pace.

I used to be in his shoes. *I* was the one who despised *him*. At least, that was the role I played.

I backtrack farther, slowly, prepared to pause as soon as he asks me to stop.

But he doesn't.

I reach the threshold without a word. Then I turn and trek to the staircase, then to the lower level.

The silence thickens.

There's so much dense, suffocating silence beneath the pummeling drum of my heart as I drag hospital-grade bleach into my lungs.

Where did Cole kill Robert?

In the kitchen? The hall?

Curiosity takes over my self-pity, and instead of slinking my ass to the front of the house, I stride in the opposite direction, along a vacant hall until I enter an open living area.

Glass doors run along one side of the room, giving sight to the manicured yard and Hunter who stands on the grass, his back to me as he talks on his cell.

"Hello?" a grated female voice asks from somewhere unknown. There's a groan, a shift of movement, then Sarah pokes her head up from a sofa, her frown instantaneously spreading across her bruised face. Her features are more swollen than they were last night, her fierce beauty almost unrecognizable.

"Are you meant to be in here?" She holds my gaze, the questioning expression slowly transforming into a wince before she slumps back out of view. "Don't answer that. I don't give a shit."

"I'm glad you're here." I shoot a cursory glance at Hunter, making sure he hasn't caught sight of me, then continue into the room. "I've been worried about you."

"Sure you have."

I pass a recliner and an elegant glass coffee table to sit on the far armrest of the sofa opposite hers.

It's hard not to stare when her blue eyes are startlingly bright against the backdrop of skin mottled in purples and browns.

"I was concerned." I hold her gaze as she repositions her hands under her head. "Did you see a doctor?"

"I didn't need to. I only had a minor fight with an airbag."

That crash packed far more than an airbag's punch. So much more that I feel sorry for her inability to face it. Nobody should ever have to act this tough after what she endured.

"I don't need your pity," she mutters. "You don't know me."

"You're right. I don't." I break our gaze to search the room, looking for clues to explain the necessity for an oil spill of bleach. But even in here, where the smell is far more potent, I don't see any hint of murder or bloodshed. There's only an abundance of gleaming stainless steel in the kitchen, and immaculate white tiles on the floor. "Can I ask about Penny? Have you found her? Is she okay?"

"She's free from Robert, if that's what you want to know."

Relief eases through my tired muscles. "Unharmed?"

She shrugs. "Not so much. But nothing major either."

I nod, genuinely thankful and also hopeful at the prospect of milking this conversation for all it's worth. "And what about Robert? What happened to him?"

Her lips stretch into a wide grin. "Do you really think I'm going to answer that? Come on, Special Agent. Surely you don't think that low of me."

"I don't think low of you at all. I know you're a strong woman. A smart one, too. I would've thought—"

The slide of a glass door cuts off my words. The accompanying slam makes me flinch.

"What the fuck are you doing in here?" Hunter approaches like a wall of muscle and testosterone that clearly needs to be put on a leash. "Does Cole know where you are?"

I slowly rise from the armrest. "Does it matter? You've got nothing to hide, right?"

He clenches his fists, his teeth gnashing. "Get the fuck out."

"Calm down." Sarah pushes to a seated position. "We were only chatting."

"Like hell. This bitch likes to play the field. First, she's the enemy, then she's an ally. And now what? You're trying to straddle both?" He quirks a condemning brow. "Fuck that. You can move your smug ass out of here or I'll do it for you."

"I'm smug?" I slap a hand to my chest. "Let's get one thing clear: I never willingly crossed sides. That option was forced on me when I was fucking drugged and flown out of the country. I didn't ask to be a part of this."

"Like hell you didn't. You turned Decker into a snitch—"

"Decker was always a snitch," I correct. "I just gave him a megaphone to spill the secrets he'd discovered. That's why you hate me, right? Because I easily turned someone you thought you could trust? Because I outplayed you?"

His eyes flare. His fingers flex then clench tighter. "Keep talking, pig. Keep pushing. See where it gets you."

"Don't threaten me. You might hide behind a macho name and a despicable reputation, but I can pull a trigger just as easily as you can. The only difference is that I rid the earth of people like you, not inspire more."

"Stop it." Sarah raises her voice. "Both of you. You're as bad as each other."

"I'm nothing like him." I hold Hunter's glare, not intimidated by his animosity. Yes, he's a murderer, but he's not indiscriminate. He doesn't kill for fun. He won't touch me.

"Maybe I've been looking at this the wrong way," he drawls. "I think I'm finally coming to understand your obsession with this family, and it has nothing to do with justice."

I cross my arms over my chest. "Please enlighten me."

"You want to be one of us." He grins, his deceivingly handsome face turning sick and twisted. "But you're too much of a chicken shit to take the leap."

"Enough," Cole demands.

My focus snaps across the room as he stalks toward us, his suit jacket discarded, his hair even more disheveled.

"Sarah, are you capable of leaving the room?" His attention doesn't stray from mine, the potency sending a shiver through me. "Apparently, Ms. Fox and I need to have another discussion on why our time together is over."

8

____

ANISSA

Sarah rises from the sofa, the hint of a grimace squinting her eyes as she finds her feet and heads toward Hunter. "Come on." She grabs the crook of his arm, tugging him into submission.

I watch them leave, my gaze remaining on the hall once Cole and I are alone.

"Why are you still here?" he asks without animosity.

I deny the real reasons. Even to myself. I can't face the shallow truth when everything else should be far more important than my cravings. "I was checking on Sarah."

"You were snooping. You couldn't help yourself. You're back to scavenging for dirt on me."

I snap my gaze to his. "I don't have to scavenge. You sprinkle evidence of your crimes everywhere you go."

He huffs out a half-hearted laugh, but humor evades his features. "Why are you still here, Anissa?"

Because I can't stay away.

Because I need to understand you. And I need you to understand me.

I cross my arms over my chest. "I want to know what's going on. What happened to Robert? What's the story with the bleach? Why are you so..." I look him up and down, cringing at the potent failure ebbing from him. "...different?"

"Gaining any sort of leverage against me won't help take me

down. Not unless you're willing to go to hell right along with me. I was smart enough to keep receipts of your crimes in Greece."

Rage chokes me. Shoves the air from my lungs. "You bastard." I glower, hating even more how the smallest spark of appreciation flickers in his tired eyes. "I'm not attempting to take you anywhere. I just want answers. I want to know if I'm safe. I want specifics on Robert."

"You're safe. I've always made sure of that."

His conviction deflates me. Slightly.

"What?" He quirks a brow. "Did you expect me to forget what happened between us? Did you think I'd feed you to the wolves after I vowed to give you everything?"

I don't respond. The reminder of his softly spoken promises in heated moments renders me speechless.

"I can give you all the answers you want, Nis. Every single one. But the information will drag you back into my world. You won't be strong enough to resist."

"I can resist you just fine." *Liar.*

"I'm not talking about resisting *me.*" He clenches his jaw, as if hating the strength of my rejection. "You'll want to get involved because you're always inclined to help. Even at your own detriment."

I scrutinize him, sensing another trap. "You're baiting me."

"You're the one who wants answers." His lips curve in subdued satisfaction. "If that's changed, you know where the door is."

Self-preservation is a niggling presence on my shoulder, whispering for me to take the opportunity to run. Flee. Never look back.

"Go." He jerks his head toward the front of the house. "Get out of here."

I should.

God, how I know I should. Yet my feet won't move. My legs won't function.

"Tell me," I demand. "I won't get dragged in."

"Have it your way." He steps forward, bridging necessary distance between us.

I tense, my shoulders straight, limbs taut.

He continues into my personal space, predatory in his approach. I hum, my body vibrating like a tuning fork.

"What are you doing?" I raise a hand in warning.

"You expect me to divulge incriminating information without determining if you're wearing a wire?"

Shit.

I should've guessed.

We're back to playing games. The power struggle has returned. The tit for tat.

I clench my teeth, biting back a snappy retort, and force myself to focus. To *win*. He's disheveled for a reason, and I'm not leaving here until I find out why.

"You're not going to argue?" he taunts, the words not packing quite as much punch when his expression remains defeated. "I thought you'd voice a loud protest at the prospect of my hands all over you."

"I know how paranoid you are. You want me to prove I'm not here officially? Then fine." I yank off my jacket, throw it to the recliner, then raise my arms at my sides. "Have at it."

Victory dances in those dark blue eyes. Subtle but strong. "You surprise me, little fox."

"I doubt that's true."

He steps closer, one leg between mine, our thighs grazing, his feet brushing my shoes. "I'm going to touch you now."

I roll my eyes, determined to ignore the rampant beat of my pulse as I focus on keeping my breathing steady.

His palms slide over my hips, making me flinch at the strength in his possession. I'm thrust into the past. Back to a time when I willingly surrendered. When I took him into my body and prayed the bliss would never end.

He ascends, feeling my waist, the outside curve of my throbbing breasts, my arms.

I tingle. Inside and out. Nerves and skin and bone.

With a touch, he undoes me. Enslaves me. The look of ownership he gives only increases my struggle.

"Are you done?" I clear my throat. "I'm not wearing a wire."

He leans in, his mouth to my ear. "Not even close." He sweeps his hands back along the path he's laid, then lower, over my ass, along my thighs.

I hold my breath as he kneels before me, the sight of submission clenching my stomach.

It's just another game. Another tactic to place me in a false sense of security, made even worse when he glances up at me with hunger.

I look away. "How long is this going to take?"

His palms slide down the outside of my leg, around my ankles, to my inner calves. I close my eyes. Swallow. Breathe. I hate that my body wants him. That *I* want him.

He creeps higher, over my knee, along the inside of my thigh.

Each inch of skin blazes. Yearns.

He approaches my crotch and I have to hold my breath to suppress a moan. But he stops an inch from my pussy, his palms splayed on my upper thighs, his thumbs close to my heat.

He doesn't speak. Doesn't move.

For long moments, there's nothing but silence until I'm forced to open my eyes and look down at him. My regret is immediate. Overwhelming. The subdued lust staring back at me makes me want to beg for him to continue.

"After what I've previously done to your body, I never would've imagined you'd hate my touch." His hands fall away. "What changed in our weeks apart?"

I lick the dryness from my lips. "You know what changed."

"I explained myself."

I step back. "You made excuses."

"Bullshit." He lashes out, grasping the back of my legs to keep me in place. "I told you why my father's death had to happen the way it did."

"After promising me there would be no more games. But that's all there is with you. You're still playing me."

His lip curls, his eyes hardening. The punishing grip on my legs vanishes and he pushes to his feet to tower before me. "Give me your cell, then take a seat at the dinner table."

What?

He's not going to deny it?

"Don't make me wait, Anissa." He holds out a hand.

There he goes again with my name. No sentiment. No tease. I've hit a nerve.

"I guess I was right." I pull out my cell and slap it into his hand.

He stalks away, taking my device to the kitchen counter, the power down sound trilling through the room as he yanks open a drawer and pulls out a tiny metal object.

"What are you doing?" I follow after him.

"Taking out the chip." He places the tiny point of metal into the top of my phone, slides out the chip holder and taps it onto the counter. "There. Now I'm satisfied."

At least that makes one of us.

"Take a seat." He indicates the table to his left with an arrogant wave of his arm. "Let's get this over and done with."

"Yes, let's." I lead the way, taking the middle seat while he takes the head. "I'm waiting with bated breath to find out what shit storm you've gotten yourself into this time. Don't keep me in suspense."

He smirks, settling into the old Cole, the one with oozing superiority. "After that pat-down I would've described it as panted breath, but it's your story to tell."

I don't bite. Nope. Not this time.

I'm above this. I have to be.

He sighs into the growing silence. "Fine, Anissa. Let's talk." He leans back in the wooden chair, crossing his arms over his chest. "Robert is dead."

"Please tell me I didn't endure being frisked for a crumb of information you've already given me."

"What I didn't tell you," he grates, "is that before he was taken care of, he'd made plans to have Stella and Tobias abducted."

My world shifts.

It's an unfathomable flip from uncontrolled emotion and anticipation to pure dread. "He planned?"

Now Cole's appearance makes sense. His deathly complexion. The hair-trigger anger.

I sit forward, resting my elbows on the table. "Am I correct in assuming he made an attempt last night?"

His brow furrows, the expression a mix of cringe and devastation.

"Cole?" My heart thunders.

"He didn't merely attempt. He succeeded."

I'm lost for words, caught in a waking nightmare.

"They're gone." He holds my gaze, his brittle voice betraying his pain.

"Where? Has there been a ransom demand?"

"I haven't heard a word. I don't know where they are. Decker is currently attempting to hack one of my neighbor's security tapes for clues, but…" He shrugs. "He's been at it for hours."

"Where were they? Where did this happen?" I fire the questions at him. "What are the authorities doing?"

"It happened here." He glances over his shoulder toward the far hall. "They were abducted from under my roof."

"Please tell me that bleach didn't dispose of critical evidence." I push to my feet. "And where are the cops? They should still be here. They should be setting up phone tracking and scouring the property. They can't—"

"The police won't be involved."

My stomach free falls. My heart follows.

I shake my head, not believing what I'm hearing. "Cole, you need to call the police. You can't seriously think—"

"Don't start," he warns. "The authorities don't mean shit in my world. You already know that."

"But—"

"*Don't.*" He shoves from his chair, the wood clattering on the tile behind him as he jams his hands into his hair. "Even if I wanted to, I fucking couldn't. Robert was killed next door, along with an accomplice Penny slaughtered. And the kids' goddamn nanny was murdered in my own damn house."

I ache for him. For all of them.

He seethes out a long breath, his hand lowering to his side, his stature strengthening before my eyes. "The nanny had a used needle in her arm. The last thing I can handle right now is a drug investigation that will distract my attention from where it needs to be."

I keep shaking my head, struggling to understand how he's

coping. How his *sister* must be handling this. "Tell me what else you're doing to get them back. What plans do you have in place? What resources?"

He gives me nothing aside from that fixed stare.

"Cole?" I grab the back of my chair and shove it under the table. "Answer me."

"I thought you could resist." His tone is thick with derision. "Isn't that what you said?"

"Do you want me to admit you were right? Is that what you're waiting for?" I clench my fingers around the top of the chair. "Okay. You were right. I can't walk away. Not from this. Not when those kids are gone and you're refusing help from the authorities."

"Not refusing." He bends over, splaying his hands on the table, attempting to stare me down. "It's not an option."

"Either way, you've limited your resources. So tell me how I can help."

He keeps glaring, his jaw ticking, his knuckles white against the wood. I can't tell if he wants me involved or not. My read on him is hindered by his exhaustion.

"I don't know." He straightens. "I've got no fucking idea."

He turns away and paces to the far end of the table. "We spent the early hours going door to door, waking every neighbor to obtain any security footage they had. Every car that passed along this street was identified and their details forwarded to a contact for investigation."

"A contact?"

"Yes, a fucking contact." He pauses. "It may not be legal, but it ensures I get the information instead of the cops withholding it from me."

"What else?" I start toward him. "What's in motion right now?"

"Apart from me wasting time explaining myself to you, nothing. I have no leads. The man responsible is dead. And there's been no ransom call. I've contacted every one of my father's associates. Hunt's been to all the usual haunts, throwing his weight around, but nobody has heard a damn thing about those kids. There's not one fucking trace."

"And the others? What are they doing?" He has an entire team of people working for him—not just Hunter and Decker.

"The *others* are slightly unreliable at the moment." He grits the admission through a tensed jaw. "I can only count on myself."

"Why?"

"Sarah and Luca are injured. Decker was shot in the leg, but he's doing his best. And Benji is..." He huffs an unforgiving snicker. "He's—"

"I get it. You don't have to explain. He must be beside himself."

"Yeah. Something like that."

I swallow over the dryness in my throat. "Your sister—"

"I don't want to speak about my sister right now. I have to stay focused."

I get that, too. An abduction has to be one of the most traumatic circumstances a parent could endure, let alone knowing the perpetrator was a sex trafficker. "Let me help." I eat up the remaining space between us, stopping in front of him, my fingers itching to soothe the furrow of his brow.

"How?"

The word washes over me.

How.

Yes, exactly how can I help him without committing a crime? How can the benefits of my badge work toward securing those children without making this an official case?

"See?" He raises demeaning brows. "You should've walked away when I told you to."

"No. I can help. I could use the Bureau's resources... I could—"

Fuck.

The burden of loyalty drowns me. The loyalty toward Cole, *not* the FBI.

He scrutinizes me. "Last I heard you weren't back at work."

"I'm not, but..." I pause, attempting to figure out a plan. I could ask Easton. He'd obtain information for me. I'm just not sure if he'd do it without the full story.

"But you'd rely on your boyfriend to get whatever you need. Is that it?" He reads me, plucking my thoughts like painful feathers.

"He's not my boyfriend. But yes, Easton is reliable."

Cole creeps closer, his upper lip twitching as he invades my personal space. "I'll pass."

"You'll pass?" Is he serious? "Two children have been abducted after their nanny was murdered, but you'll pass?"

"I'll pass," he repeats in a sneer, then walks by me, heading toward the kitchen.

"Hold up a minute." I grab his sleeve. "Are you joking?"

He stops. "Do I look like I'm bursting with humor right now?"

No, he looks like a man filled with uncontrollable fear, rage, and jealousy, all of them clouding his judgment.

"I know you can be heartless, Cole. But I assumed that was toward other criminals. Not innocent children."

He yanks his arm away. "I guess you don't know me as well as you thought."

It's true. If he can turn down my offer without a second thought, then yes.

"You're right," I admit. "You've just established I don't know the first damn thing about you."

"You've also earned yourself a one-way ticket out of here." He yanks open the fridge. "Don't let the front door hit you when you leave."

"You're kicking me out?"

"You bet I am. I don't need your narrow-minded ignorance. I've got enough shit to deal with."

9

COLE

She waits a second, my misplaced anger seeming to render her speechless.

This isn't her fault.

None of this has anything to do with her. It's all me. All my failure.

"*Fine.*" She stalks to the counter, snatches up her cell and the discarded SIM, then walks out.

I don't move. Apart from the grinding ache of my tensed jaw, I don't fucking budge until she slams the front door in farewell.

"*Fuck.*"

That woman destroys me. Slays me. Without pause.

And now she's gone.

"It doesn't sound like things ended well." Sarah walks in from the far hall, Hunt following her.

I close my eyes, my hands finding their way back to my hair, my fingers ripping at the strands.

"It's good she's gone," he grunts out. "The stupid bitch shouldn't have come here in the first place."

"Don't start," Sarah warns. "The last thing we need is you running your mouth."

No, the last thing I needed was to push Anissa away. Why couldn't I stop myself?

"What do we do now?" Hunt asks. "I've called everyone I know."

I don't have to look at him to understand what he isn't saying. He made those calls and came up empty-handed. Every stone has been turned.

"Someone is lying." I drop my hands to the kitchen counter. "It's not possible that a plan this big has gone unnoticed."

"I'll pay everyone a personal visit." Hunt pulls his car keys from his pocket. "I'll throw my weight around and see what I can uncover."

"No." Sarah shakes her head. "All you're doing is wasting time. We need Anissa's help."

"Like hell we do." Hunter starts for the front of the house. "She's a fucking viper."

"You're wrong about her." Sarah focuses on me, the bruising under her eyes almost black. "Your sisters continue to blow up my cell, asking for updates. They're petrified, and we're stuck here doing nothing. And things will only get worse once Penny finds out, which you're going to have to deal with any minute now."

"I told Decker to leave her in the dark." I push from the counter. "We've got time."

"Wrong again." She flashes her phone screen at me, showing a string of text messages I can't read from this distance. "Luca has walked out of the hospital. They're all on their way here. And as soon as Penny takes one look at us she's going to know something has happened. If our expressions don't trigger her suspicion, the smell of bleach will."

Fuck.

Fuck.

"We need Anissa," she repeats. "And believe me, I don't like admitting it either, but what other option do we have apart from sitting on our asses waiting for a ransom call? Or worse."

"Don't go there," I warn.

Nobody can fucking go there.

It's bad enough that I lose focus on finding those kids every few minutes and fall into a sinkhole of possible scenarios where their battered bodies turn up in a ditch.

"Cole, we've spoken to everyone we know." Her eyes plead

with me. "Benji has been to every transport hub. And your contacts haven't come back to us with even the slightest update."

"They will. We just need to wait."

And wait and fucking wait.

God, I hate this.

I've never hated anything more.

I wish I could throw money at the problem. I'd bleed through my finances to get Tobias and Stella back. If only there was a fucking ransom.

"Anissa has to be able to help." Sarah sighs. "She'd have to have experience in this type of thing. And you've worked with her before, right? She plays both sides."

"Nobody plays both sides." Hunter stalks for the sofa and flops into the far seat. "She's either a turncoat or waiting for an opportunity to take us down."

"She's no threat." I'm not defending her. It's merely the truth.

If Anissa wanted to put me behind bars, she would've attempted it by now. The only risk with her is if she opens her mouth to her piece-of-shit boyfriend.

"Then you have to go after her," Sarah begs. "Think of your niece."

"I can't *stop* thinking of my goddamn niece," I snap.

"Babe, you don't understand how this works." Hunter pats the sofa cushion beside him, wordlessly instructing Sarah to sit. "If Cole's seen aligning with a Fed—"

"Don't even attempt to feed me that bullshit." She cuts him off with a vicious wave of her hand. "Cole has cops in his pocket. He's got other Feds, too. What's the difference?"

"The difference is that she isn't dirty." I scrub a hand over the back of my neck, trying to ease the building tension. "She still believes the legal way is the right way."

"What about Greece?"

"Greece was different." Greece feels like a lifetime ago with the contrast of how things now are between Anissa and I. "She had very few choices while in the islands. And no communication with the outside world. I know her well enough to understand she won't break the law willingly."

Sarah crosses her arms over her chest and straightens to her full height. "Then make her do it unwillingly."

Hunt scoffs.

I don't bother reacting.

Sarah is the most pro-choice woman there is. She wouldn't force an innocent to carry her groceries, let alone be involved in this.

"You know what I mean." She glowers. "Let me convince her."

"It's not about convincing her." I walk around the kitchen counter toward them. "She wants to help—"

"Then why the hell did you let her leave? Go after her."

I didn't *let* her. I *pushed* her. I forced her out of this goddamn house because I can't look at her and not see Easton's hands all over her body. But it's more than that, too. So much fucking more.

I send a warning look to Hunter, wordlessly telling him to pull his woman into line.

He ignores me, sitting forward to rest his elbows on his knees before hanging his head. "We may have limited options, but she's not one of them."

No, we never had any to begin with.

None.

"Please, Cole." Sarah gentles her voice as she pads toward me. "Help me understand why Anissa isn't an option."

"Because she's on leave from the Bureau. There's no way she could gain information for us without causing suspicion."

"But her knowledge alone… Her experience…"

She's right. So goddamn right.

"It all means nothing when she's not one of us," Hunt mutters. "We could never trust her."

Sarah continues to stare at me, her gaze digging under my skin. "You trust her. And you know she can help. So what's really holding you back from running after her?"

Frustration.

Pride.

A whole fucking heap of jealousy.

"She doesn't want to be one of us."

"None of us did," she counters. "Not to begin with. But

whatever reason brought us all here also convinced us to stay. So convince her, Cole. Do whatever it takes to bring her to our side."

"*No*. It's a bad idea." Hunt pushes to his feet. "At any given moment she could turn on a dime and make this case official. Then we'd have cops breathing down our necks, digging into shit that will cause a whole lot of complications. I disposed of three fucking bodies this morning, Sarah. Do you want me to go to prison?"

She shakes her head, still staring, still visually decimating me. "If something goes wrong, Torian will buy off the necessary people. He always does."

"That takes time." He reaches her side, pleading his case with a punishing glower in my direction. "Don't listen to her. You've already got men on your lower levels wondering what the hell you're doing being seen with the Fed. Their trust is slipping. Especially when you've made no effort to hide the association. You've got dealers looking over their shoulders—"

"I've got dealers questioning me?" I ask, incredulous. "And this is the first time you've decided to mention it?"

"Excuse me for thinking you didn't need the added drama. I took care of it. I've made it known you were inflicting a little manipulative revenge after she arrested your father. But all my hard work will mean nothing if you keep being seen with her."

The sharp bite of protection sinks its teeth into me.

He's been badmouthing her. Tarnishing her name.

"All your hard work?" I keep my anger disguised, letting the bubble of rage thicken inside me. "Let me make one thing clear— when it comes to Anissa, keep your fucking mouth shut. Don't justify my behavior to anyone. If people question me, *I* will deal with their mutiny. *I'll* be the one to reiterate that my decisions are not up for discussion. And any further doubts will be seen as disobedience and handled accordingly."

His nostrils flare. His eyes narrow.

"Do you hear me?" I snarl.

"Yes, I fucking hear you."

I edge closer, so far in his face I could headbutt some sense into him. "You don't get to speak shit about her. You don't get to decide if she's helpful or not. If she's trustworthy or not. I don't even want to hear you mutter her name in an unwelcoming tone." I grin, the curve of lips threatening. "As far as I'm concerned, you're not entitled to a fucking opinion. What I do with her is none of your business."

He sneers, his gaze silently roaring with animosity.

"Same goes for you." I step back, giving Sarah a direct look of warning before starting for the front door. "Nobody gets to dictate what happens with Anissa."

Nobody but me.

10

ANISSA

I slam Cole's front door behind me and march to my car.

Every step ratchets my emotions up another notch. Anger, fear, and helplessness vibrate inside me. I'm thrumming with energy and exhausted at the same time. Itching to fight but also begging to surrender.

I reach the driver's door, pull it wide, and slump into the seat. But I can't leave.

I *can't.*

I slam my palms against the steering wheel and blink away the traitorous burn in my eyes. I'm not sad. The tear-filled heat is driven by hysteria. Mental pandemonium.

Cole *fucking* Torian is such a stubborn, thoughtless prick. His inability to see past his own pride and allow me to help is not only careless, it's dangerous.

Those kids…

That little girl…

I don't even want to imagine what she's going through or who she's with.

"Goddamn you, Cole." I pummel the steering wheel again.

I should report this regardless of his protests. I should take this into my own hands despite the threat of arrest for residual crimes. I need to put the lives of those children first, even though the thought of betraying Cole makes my throat dry.

All I want to do is help. I could make things easier, not only for those kids, but for *him*. For the man I should be happily distancing myself from.

Yet I still can't start the car.

My body refuses to vacate the premises.

"Come on, Anissa. Move." I force my hand to the ignition as a dark shadow drifts over my window.

My pulse quickens. I tilt my head to face the large frame of my tormentor looming over me from outside the vehicle. He opens my door, one hand remaining on the handle, the other moving to the roof, caging me in.

"What are you still doing here?" His voice is neutral. No accusation. No apology.

I keep clinging to the steering wheel and shift my focus through the windshield to avoid those conquering eyes.

"I shouldn't have told you." The indifference in his tone is far different than how he spoke to me inside. The aggression is gone. Maybe even the animosity, too. "You've got a soft heart. I knew you'd feel obligated to help."

I'm not soft. I'm determined. Righteous.

Those kids need me.

Cole needs me.

"I'll get them back, Nis. I'll stop at nothing."

I can't stand him talking to me like this. I hated his vehemence, yet his kindness is far more lethal to my sanity.

"Or is that the problem?" he asks. "Are you worried about the blood I'll shed?"

"No." The answer comes immediately. Truthfully.

I meet his gaze, letting him know I wouldn't deny him anything in his search for Tobias and Stella. He can maim and mutilate those involved. Murder and massacre.

I guess that's part of the problem. My ethics are scrambled.

They have been since Greece.

That's the real reason I couldn't return to work. Not because I need more time to get my head around what happened. But because I haven't been able to ditch the mentality of a lifelong criminal. I've struggled to convince myself that incarceration is the right punishment for those involved in sex-trafficking and people-smuggling. The animalistic, eye-for-an-eye way of life has grown on me like a fungus and I can't ditch it, no matter what I try.

"The only thing that matters is Stella and Tobias." I swallow over the bitter taste of surrender. "Please let me help."

He releases a tired breath and takes a step back, pivoting away from me. He's quiet for a moment, glancing across the neatly manicured lawn as if searching for guidance.

The new facets I'm seeing in him today have each become more soul-shaking than the next. First fear, then vulnerability and defeat.

Now it's heartache, his harrowing expression making me fragile.

I never knew he had this depth. I'd always hoped, even daydreamed, but never truly believed.

It takes all my restraint not to go to him. To touch. To soothe.

"Your offer is appreciated," he murmurs. "But you have to realize it's unacceptable when on your terms. You'll want to involve the authorities and that isn't an option."

"Then we do it your way." I release the steering wheel, turning my entire body to face him. "Whatever you want, Cole, I'll do it. Just let me be a part of this."

"At the cost of your career?"

I open my mouth to protest, but he's right. The looming threat is real. "I'll be careful… discreet… I can keep a low profile."

"We don't work nine to five. And this isn't a desk job. It's all in or nothing." He swivels back to me, eyes narrowing. "That means being available twenty-four-seven. Everyone else is living under this roof, and I'd expect you to do the same."

My gut flops. Drops. Rolls.

I ignore it and shrug. "Whatever it takes."

There are numerous beats of silence, the gentle quiet thickening around me.

"You'll move in here?" He raises a brow. "Into my house?"

Having him repeat the insanity doesn't help. My stomach does the same acrobatics. Tumbling. Turning.

It's always been a vicious game of push and pull with him. One hand delights in shoving him away while the other itches to drag him forward.

Right now, it's the itch.

I'm sure there's a multitude of psychological reasons for my behavior. But most of all, it's just him.

Just Cole.

Plain and simple.

"Into your house, but *not* into your bed."

"Of course not." The words are snipped. "I wouldn't want to step on your boyfriend's toes."

I have zero intent of informing him of the inaccuracy of his assumption. Absolutely zero.

"*He* can't know anything about this," he continues. "Not a damn thing, Nissa."

I roll my eyes and slide out of the car, having to concentrate on my movements so I don't brush into him as I close the door. "I won't say a word."

"And Easton won't notice when you don't go home?"

"He won't be a problem."

He huffs. "I shouldn't be surprised you've got him bluffed."

I try to ignore the sidestep into a conversation neither of us want to have, but the diversion reminds me of Cole's perfect timing the other night. "Did you lie when you said you didn't bug my apartment?"

"Me? No." He feigns offense. "I'd never stoop that low."

I don't let anger take hold, because that's what he wants. He's baiting me. Taunting. "Have you forgotten I've watched you stoop far lower?"

He stares at me for several heartbeats. His controlled, superior expression doesn't loosen until he sighs, his shoulders relaxing with the movement. "Believe me, little fox, my imagination has punished me enough with thoughts of you and him. Bugging your apartment is a level of hell I never want to reach."

He walks away, his long stride flawless while I'm left cemented in place.

His admission is more bait. This time the delicious kind.

He wants me to believe he's yearning for me. I won't fall for that again.

I lock the car and follow after him to the front of the house where he holds the front door open.

"You're going to need to be patient." His voice is low as I step inside. "My people won't appreciate you being here. It's best to keep your mouth shut as much as possible. Relay any thoughts to me privately."

"I'll be fine."

"You'll be fine?" He closes the door, then turns to face me. "You can handle Hunter's animosity multiplied?"

"Do you even remember what you've put me through?" The question is more of an accusation. He's acting as if he doesn't recollect our past. "Do you even vaguely recall the actions that led to Greece and how you got me there? Of course I can handle your men."

"I remember everything," he states simply, the potency of those three words blissful in their purity, before he distances himself, leading me down the hall to stop at the staircase. "You need to go upstairs for a while. Stay in my room until I come get you."

"Why?"

He keeps his back to me. "Penny will be here soon and she's not aware of what's happened. I hope you understand the need for privacy when I break the news."

More kindness toward others? Really?

This man continues to surprise me.

"It shouldn't take long." He keeps walking, not giving me a backward glance.

I can't help but watch him place distance between us. I wait until he enters the living area and moves out of view before I start on the stairs.

I breathe a little easier at the top step, the light breeze sweeping away the acrid scent of bleach.

I ignore the stare of the woman in the looming picture and make my way to Cole's bedroom, stopping at the threshold once more to take in the sight.

His power oozes from within the large space. It's in the menacing bed with its inky black coverings and shiny red pillowcases. In the dark, polished dresser that lacks any adornment. In the suit jacket neatly placed across the armchair in the corner.

His aura has seeped into the furniture. Into the walls and curtains.

The crunch of gravel draws me across the room to the open window. Decker's car slowly makes its way up the drive with Penny behind the wheel and Luca riding shotgun. I withdraw, hiding from view as she parks beside my car, and they all climb out, Decker joining them from the back seat.

They walk quietly to the front door, Decker limping a few steps behind. Once inside, the subtle murmurings of conversation sweep my ears. I can't make out the words. I don't try.

I ignore my need to snoop and give them privacy. A howl of pain rends the air.

Penny knows.

Her suffering finds a home inside my chest. I hurt for her. For those kids. For a family who once seemed deserving of punishment, but this is far too much.

I kick off my shoes and creep down the hall, stopping at the staircase to sit on the top step. I stare at the blank wall in front of me, picturing the confronting scene below like a voyeur on the outer edges of this incredibly emotional moment.

My ass is numb by the time another crunch of gravel travels from the window. Additional people enter the house. The hum of conversation grows, the words still out of reach, but the tones of Cole's sisters' voices are distinguishable.

There are tears. Sobs. Wracking, hiccupping cries.

All of it sinks into me, the torment softening me to a family I've spent so long hardened against.

I use my phone to work on a list of names as they suffer. I jot down the contact details of my informants and the vague recollections of local people who have had links to previous abductions. There aren't many. But it's a start.

By the time I hear footsteps approaching from the hall below, I'm starved for communication.

The crying has petered out to long silences between occasional blown noses.

Cole finally sates my starvation as he comes into view at the lower landing, his look of exhaustion aging his face ten years.

"Are you okay?" I'm the first to break the silence as he remains distanced from me, simply staring with hollow eyes.

"Yeah." One word. A lie.

He's far from okay. I don't even know why I asked, I just… talking is a far better option than fixating on his torment.

He approaches, the slow steps bringing him within touching distance. I stand and move out of the way as he continues past me, down the hall and into his room.

I follow, pulled toward him by an invisible thread to find him discarding his shirt at the foot of the bed. I watch in silence from the door as he lays the material atop the mattress, then starts to unbuckle his belt. I swallow, not looking away as he discards his pants, exposing tanned, muscled legs and black boxer briefs.

The sight drags me into the past. It also seems as if I never left. As if our time apart has merely been a blink of contemplation instead of weeks spent agonizingly alone.

"I need to freshen up." He walks for the closed door a foot next to where I stand. "I won't be long. Once I'm done, I'll escort you to your apartment to get whatever you need."

I nod, ignoring his perfectly muscular chest as he continues out of view, closing the door behind him.

I lean against the threshold as I hear the faucet turn on. There's a slush of water. The sound of him brushing his teeth.

I've listened to all of this before, the menial tasks unlocking warm memories of our time in Greece.

I'd been consumed by him back then. Emboldened. He'd awakened my every nerve. Inspired passion beyond my comprehension.

Everything had felt… right.

The differences in our lives hadn't mattered. The lies and manipulation were forgotten because being with him became a calling.

He felt like my goddamn messiah.

In reality, he was nothing but a magician creating emotional illusions. And shamefully, those tricks would still work on me now.

I already want to go back. To relive the nightmares and injuries just for a taste of passion.

Stockholm.

Goddamn fucking Stockholm.

I don't move when the water shuts off. I remain cocked against the doorframe, staring across his room as he enters, now fully dressed in another pristine suit, his pure perfection sucking up the oxygen and replacing it with smothering humidity.

I push from the frame and glance into what I thought was the bathroom door, finding a huge wardrobe filled with hanging suits, shirts and ties. Shoes are neatly placed in tidy chutes. Jeans are piled on a shelf. The area is bigger than my living room, with an open side door to a tiled area, revealing a seductive two-person shower.

"Do you feel better now?" I return my gaze to him before heated memories burn me.

"I needed to wake myself up. Maybe it would've worked better if you'd joined me in the shower."

I scoff. "I didn't ask to give you ideas."

"Then why did you?" He straightens his lapels, all suave and sophisticated. "Are you starting to care about me again, little fox?"

Despite the taunting question, it's becoming more blatantly obvious I didn't discard any heartfelt feelings toward him in the first place. They're all still here, tinkering inside my chest.

"Don't worry. I won't tell your boyfriend." He winks at me. "This can be our little secret."

I wish I knew the best way to shut down his comments about Easton without exposing the truth. But it's best to keep a slight barrier between us. If I'm not careful, he'll figure out I'm not just here for those kids.

This isn't work to me.

I'm here for him.

"Can you please stop mentioning Easton?" I ask. "Don't talk about him."

"Why?" He flicks out his collar to then smooth it down. "To appease your guilt? To ease your betrayal? Or is it so you can have a break from reality and return to the fantasy life of being with me?"

Yes.

Yes.

Yes.

Each question packs a sickening blow, cutting me at the knees.

"How about this?" He bridges the space between us, his

aftershave acting like a drug to my senses. "Admit how you feel about me and I'll forget that piece of shit even exists."

He doesn't reach for me. There are no touching hands or grabby fingers. But I sense them.

Everywhere.

"You're mine, Nissa." There's adamance in his voice. Conviction. "You know this. You *feel* it. Yet you punish me for things I've already explained. You hold me accountable for transgressions that were necessary to ensure our future. And you blame me because it's the only excuse you have to keep me at bay."

His minty breath brushes my lips, sinking into my tongue.

He's right. So right.

And still, I deny him with the shake of my head.

"You'll quit fighting soon enough," he growls. "And when I finally reclaim that sweet pussy of yours it will be worth the wait. But until then, I plan on reminding you of your cheating ways as many times as I goddamn like."

I lower my gaze and bite my lip, holding in a pathetic whimper.

I'm overheating. Sweating.

"You can come downstairs now." He retreats as if immune to the screaming chemistry between us. "Be prepared for a fight and keep your mouth shut."

I blink at the sudden whiplash of topic. "Okay."

He leads the way from the room and I follow a step behind, trailing him down the hall to the staircase.

I'm chilled by the time we reach the lower level. Cole's bedroom is like a sanctuary in comparison to the upcoming firing squad of murmured voices.

He pauses near the opening of the living room, waiting for me to reach his side before we enter the open area together. A united front.

Both of us strip the conversation from the room without a word.

"What is *she* doing here?" Decker pushes from the sofa, his glare more accusatory than his hate-filled tone.

Everyone stares at me. Keira, Penny, and Layla with tear-stained eyes. Hunter, Decker, and Benji with animosity. Luca and Sarah with pity.

"Anissa will be helping us." Cole places a hand at the low of my back, igniting whispers and muttered dissent.

"Help with what?" Keira asks. "What can she do that you haven't already done?"

"Nothing," Hunter answers. "She'll do more harm than good."

"No." I shake my head, directing my answer to Benji and Layla. "I would never risk your daughter's life. I promise I won't interfere."

"Then why be here at all?" Decker growls.

"Yeah, why?" Hunt continues to glare. "You're nothing more than a distraction."

I press my lips tight, keeping my mouth shut because that's what Cole wants.

Whispers of discord arise between them. Layla murmurs to her husband. Penny does the same with Luca. Sarah mouths a harsh warning to Hunter.

"Are you all finished?" Cole adds pressure to my back, encouraging me toward the wolves. "She's here because she has experience on this when we have none."

"She's got no fucking experience when it comes to our people," Decker counters. "The goalposts are different."

"It doesn't matter." Cole drops his hand and moves to the kitchen to open the fridge. "She's here now and she's staying. If any of you have issues, keep them to yourself. I don't have the energy to waste."

Everyone continues to look at me. Hunter and Decker's glares intensify, along with Sarah and Luca's pity.

"How can you help find my baby?" Layla raises from the sofa, slow and fragile. She maneuvers around the coffee table to approach me, her husband soon following. "Are there ways you can search for people on the Bureau's computers? Some sort of facial recognition on public camera or something?"

I glance at Cole, who walks back toward me, a bottle of water in each hand. "She can't help like that, Lay." He reaches my side and hands me a bottle. "Nothing she does can be traced back to the Feds. She's risking her career by being here."

"Then send her home," Hunter mutters.

"What *can* you do?" Benji asks. "I don't understand."

I crack the lid on the water and take a quick sip, needing the liquid to soothe my drying throat. "I've worked on hostage cases before. I know how to negotiate a ransom."

"But there hasn't been a request." Layla's eyes implore me. "There has to be something you can do when we haven't heard from whoever took them."

Her anguish bleeds into me.

I don't know what to say. I open my mouth, not even able to form a response.

"There will be a ransom." Cole's hand returns to my back. The subtle unity drags the air from my lungs in a gentle heave. "We have to be patient."

I remain silent, wishing I could reiterate his words of encouragement, but I can't. I won't lie to Layla. Not about her daughter. Not when a sinking part of me is wondering if that little girl is already dead.

"Whoever has them probably didn't anticipate we'd kill Robert." Cole's palm continues to do circle work against the back of my suit jacket. He's providing *me* with comfort. An interloper. An unwanted intruder. "They might be scrambling to find a place to hide."

"And you know Stella," Sarah adds from the sofa. "That feisty little thing would be giving them their money's worth. I'm sure someone will reach out any minute now."

I nod, making myself believe.

I ignore all the statistics on hostage situations that have been drilled into my brain and nod and nod and nod. This isn't a normal abduction. This isn't a criminal against a naive civilian. The rules here are different. The playing field is entirely new.

"A two-person abduction is a major operation." I meet Layla's watery eyes. "Whoever is responsible would want to set themselves up in a stable environment. Especially if they're on their own. They'd want to keep the kids calm."

"Tobias and Stella are probably still passed out," Hunter growls. "Does she even know they were hit with chloroform?"

No, I didn't.

I glance at Cole, witnessing the tick of his jaw before he turns to meet my gaze. "We still have a lot to discuss." His palm stops the circular assault. "I'll fill you in on the way to your apartment."

"You're leaving?" Layla's voice is laced with accusation. "Please, Cole, stay here. What happens if someone calls? What will you do if—"

"We won't be long." His hand sweeps over my wrist, the touch light. "And I need the fresh air. The bleach is giving me a migraine."

He leads me toward the far side of the room, the prying eyes remaining heavy at the back of my neck even once we're striding down an unfamiliar hall.

I can't get rid of the ache Layla's suffering has awakened inside me. The agony chips at my soul. Little by little.

I sniff to beat back the tingle in my nose.

Usually I can detach from a case.

This one seems far too personal. An attack on me and mine, not Cole and his family.

He stops before a door and releases my wrist. "Pull yourself together."

I cringe, hating his ability to see through me. "I'm…" I shake my head, not sure how to finish my response.

Am I sorry? Embarrassed? Weak?

Ding, ding, ding.

All of the above.

I lower my head and suck in a deep breath. Regrouping.

He leans closer. "Fucking pull yourself together, Nis." It's a warning. A vicious growl. "*Now.*"

I don't understand his venom, but I focus on doing what he says. I try to wring myself of emotion. To siphon the weakness.

"Don't fucking break on me." He grips my chin, raising my face so we're eye to eye.

The desperation that stares back at me strips the air from my lungs. That's when I understand he's not demanding—he's begging. Pleading.

"The last thing I can handle is your suffering," he rasps. "Don't do this to me now."

My heart squeezes. Chokes.

I lick my lips to ease the blooming tingle and straighten my shoulders.

I have to be strong for him.

I *will be* strong for him.

"It was a momentary lapse," I whisper. "It won't happen again."

The sorrow staring back at me speaks of disbelief. Of a yearning that could outstrip my own.

"Good." He releases me, but not before his gaze drops to my mouth, lashing my lips with a visual sweep of unadulterated affection.

I want the kiss he promises. I'd almost kill for it.

"Let's go." He reaches behind his back, sweeping open the door to a garage. "We'll take the Porsche."

11

———

COLE

I FILL HER IN ON EVERYTHING I KNOW AS I DRIVE TOWARD HER apartment. I tell her about the rag that smelled of chemicals. Of the nanny and her staged overdose, along with the gouge marks in my grass at the side of my property, the divots having come from a fucking ladder still laying in my neighbor's yard.

"What's your assessment of the situation so far?" I stop at a set of traffic lights and glance at her, despising the way her hands are coiled in her lap like she's a meek princess.

She's upset and I fucking hate it.

"I don't know. It's too early to tell."

That's bullshit. She's brilliant. She's logical. She would already have an idea of what could be happening to Stella and Tobias, along with the statistics on successful retrievals.

"Don't fuck with me, Nis." I keep my tone amicable. "You think it's a bad sign they haven't called."

Her silence is loud.

"Tell me." I lower my window, needing fresh air. Needing *anything* to clear my head of the static.

"It's too early to say."

The traffic light flashes green and I turn onto her street. "Do you think I can't handle the answer?"

I pull into a parking space across the road from her building's front door and cut the engine. When I glance at her again, she's still staring out the front of the car.

"Speculation is a minefield. It's better if we focus on facts." She unclasps her belt and opens her door. "Give me ten minutes. I won't take long."

"You're not going alone."

She pauses in her escape, her ass half off the leather seat when she huffs out a defeated breath.

I'm still the enemy to her. Or that's what she wants to believe.

"It's bad enough you brought me here in a shiny dick extension when I shouldn't be seen with you." Her eyes plead for understanding. "You're not escorting me into the building."

She shoves from the car and closes the door.

I do the same. "I won't risk you going in alone."

"I can protect myself," she hisses over the roof of the Porsche. "At least for five damn minutes."

She jogs around the hood and across the street, easing into a long stride along the footpath while I follow at a slower pace.

The distance doesn't feel right. She's too exposed to any asshole with a trigger finger. But I grind my teeth through the paranoia and keep an eye on our surroundings.

I scan the pedestrians along the sidewalk, considering each of them a potential threat to the woman I crave. I even scrutinize the buildings, checking windows for a sniper attack.

Robert has already proven I underestimated what he was capable of. Now I'm left to contemplate what else he could've arranged before his death.

"Anissa," a male shouts nearby.

I fucking know that voice. *Easton*.

The piece of shit approaches from the front of her building with a face full of concern, all anxious and uptight.

At least the fucker is wearing clothes.

She stops before him, ramrod stiff. She doesn't glance over her shoulder at me. She doesn't have to. Easton does it for her.

"What are you doing?" he asks, his voice low. "Why is *he* here?"

I can barely hear him, the low volume spurring me to move faster. Or maybe that's the desire to stake ownership.

She murmurs something quick in reply. A fast snap of frantic words.

"You need to move in with me for a few days." He grabs her arms. "I'll take care of you until you're back on your feet."

Like hell he will. Over my goddamn dead body.

"There's nothing to worry about." She shakes him off. "Trust me. I just have to…"

Her response trails as I reach her side, her pained exhale brushing my ears.

"Easton," I sneer in greeting. "Can I help you?"

He keeps staring at her. "Listen to me—this isn't right. Whatever you're doing is going to get you in trouble."

"I appreciate your support." She gives a fragile smile. "But I'm in control. You don't have to keep checking on me."

"You don't need to come around at all," I growl. "It's best if you leave her alone."

His eyes narrow but he still doesn't acknowledge my existence.

"Anissa…" He moves forward, triggering my rage as he reaches for her again.

"Hands off, asshole." I lunge, grabbing his arm.

He yanks away. "Calm yourself, Torian, before I have you arrested."

The threat is real.

Normally, I wouldn't give a shit. A set of handcuffs and a few hours behind bars while my lawyers ensured any charges were dropped would be worthwhile to draw my gun on this pretty boy and let him know exactly who's in charge. But not today. Not when I could get word on Stella and Tobias at any second.

"It's cute that you think you have any power over me." I smirk. "Naive, but cute. Are there any other delusions we can clear up while I'm here?"

Anissa glares at me.

"Stay away from her." Easton puffs out his chest and gets in my face.

"I did." I keep smirking. "She came to me. It was my gate she was banging on this morning."

"Jesus Christ," Anissa hisses. "You two need to quit it. For starters, I was only at your gate because of the shooting last night.

And *you*." She turns her ire to Easton. "Don't babysit me. I'm on leave from work, and what I do in that time is my business."

"You're obsessing over a criminal you haven't been able to put behind bars," he growls. "Let me look after you for a while."

I snicker. This asshole is talking about taking me down like I'm not even here. Like he has a fucking hope in hell.

"I'm looking after her now." I slide an arm around her waist, pulling her into my side. "Don't worry. I'll keep her safe."

She stiffens. Every inch. Every muscle.

"Anissa, this is crazy." Easton's face pinches. "You need to think about what you're doing. Not just with your job, but with me. I thought—"

"You thought wrong." I tighten my hold around her, my jealousy sparking to flame. This asshole has been trying to steal her out from underneath me from the moment we met. But he had his chance. He had all the time they've worked together. Fucking years. He only wants her now because she's mine. "My time with her has proven more productive."

"You've got to be kidding me." She shoves away. "You two can finish this dick-measuring contest without me. I'm not participating."

She turns on her heel and storms for her building, leaving me to seethe at Easton as he watches her walk away.

"You need to leave her alone." He doesn't meet my gaze. "Otherwise, I'll make sure you spend the rest of your life behind bars."

"Is that right?" I huff out a chuckle. "Here I was thinking you should be the one to back off before you go missing."

His attention cuts to me, his fury nothing in comparison to mine. This man has no passion. No backbone. "Are you threatening an FBI agent, Mr. Torian?"

"It sure sounds like it, doesn't it? And if you don't listen, I'll make sure those fragile parents of yours go missing, too."

His eyes flare, the surprise instantaneous before his jaw clenches. "You're blackmailing her as well, aren't you?" He shakes his head, his laugh patronizing. "The righteous Cole Torian is now manipulating classy women for sport. Why is that? Have all your criminal hags grown tired of your games?"

He hits a mark, a fucking brutal target beneath my ribs. Not about the hags, because fuck him, I don't slum when it comes to women. But being unable to get Anissa to engage with me without an underlying threat is a sore spot.

"Manipulation is an art." I keep my voice in check. My smile tight. "What pisses you off more? My ability to easily shape her decisions or the fact you can't?"

His teeth grind. Nostrils flare. "You know what?" He pokes a finger toward my chest. "Fuck you." He steps back. Once. Twice. "She might have fallen victim to your games, but I won't. I'll figure out what's going on, Torian. If I were you, I'd keep my nose squeaky clean."

If I were you, I'd shut my fucking mouth before a gun barrel fills the open space.

I continue smirking as he gives me a wide berth, stalking around me toward the street to climb into a tin-bucket sedan.

He's not what Nissa wants.

He might be the safe option, the *easy* out, but there's no life in that perfectly crafted box.

She needs intensity and adrenaline.

She needs *me*.

I wait until he pulls from the curb and drives away before I start after her, stopping at the security panel to unlock the ground-level doors. I glance around for an approaching resident, find nobody nearby, then pull out my wallet and press the coin pocket against the security pad.

She needs a new building manager. The current father of four took too easily to a three-figure bribe when I demanded an access fob.

The fucker didn't even hesitate when I offered an increased price to obtain a key to her fifth-floor apartment. The only thing keeping him in his job is the fear I witnessed when I assured him he would live to regret betraying her to anyone else.

After a quick elevator ride, I'm standing at her apartment waiting for her anger to greet me after I knock.

She doesn't disappoint, flinging the door wide, her cheeks pink with rage.

"Finished the pissing contest already?" She doesn't wait for a reply before walking off, the door beginning to close in her wake.

I shove my foot inside the threshold and follow her, past the shoebox living area with its tiny kitchen to her darkened bedroom with the closed curtains and messy bed, the sheets twisted, the duvet half on the floor.

Blinding jealousy kicks back in as I picture her disheveling the covers with another man. A split second—that's all it takes for my blood to turn hot and my chest to constrict.

I've got more important things to think about, but her betrayal commands my attention.

"You can't blame me for being territorial." I indicate her bed with a fling of my hand. "Unlike you, I'm not unaffected by our past."

She scoffs, bending over an open suitcase on the floor. She doesn't even meet my gaze before stalking to the closet, her metal coat hangers twanging as she rips out a jacket and several shirts.

"And downstairs wasn't my fault," I add. "He deliberately taunted me with his *move-into-my-place* bullshit."

"No he didn't." She thunders back to the suitcase, dumping the clothes inside. "He's trying to protect me. He thinks you're extorting me."

"He's trying to throw your fucking relationship in my face."

She pauses, hunched toward the ground as she lets out a long breath. She wants to rail on me. To fight.

I want it, too.

Instead, she moves to her bedside table, snapping open drawers to riffle through underwear.

"Admit I'm right." I close in behind her. "He may have you, but he's so fucking insecure he has to shove your affair down my throat."

She straightens. Turns. Glares. "Get out of my way."

"I will once you admit I'm right. Then tell me it doesn't piss you off that he's so fucking weak."

Her face is etched in darkness, but the shadows don't hide her spite.

"I don't know how you can stomach having him in your bed," I sneer. "Let alone your body."

"*Stop.*" She raises a clenched fist that chokes her silken underwear. "You know nothing about me and Easton. All you're doing is proving your jealousy."

"Of course I'm jealous. You're mine. You're meant to be with me."

Her eyes flare in rage. "Don't—"

"Here you go with your feminist bullshit." I cut her off. "You want to call me out on not owning you when you know you've fucking owned me for a lot longer."

I grab her fist, lowering it so I can move closer. "You were my possession in Greece." I hold her noxious gaze. "And I was yours. The only difference is my feelings never changed. I still want you."

Her brows pinch. "No, you want me to lose my job—you made that clear downstairs. You want me scrambling to keep my life together. You want to turn my world upside down, and you have. I still can't pull myself together after what you put me through."

"You forgave me my sins," I reach for her chin, needing to touch her.

She pulls back. "In the heat of the moment, maybe, but not now. You *kidnapped* me, Cole. You *drugged* me. Nobody can simply forgive those things."

"You already did. We both know it's true."

"You're wrong." She walks around me and throws her underwear into the suitcase. "It was Stockholm syndrome."

"Like hell it was. Your fucking shrink has denied that bullshit prognosis repeatedly."

Her eyes snap wide.

"You still have feelings for me, little fox, despite your best efforts to deny them."

"You bribed my psychologist?" Her mouth gapes.

Even in the darkness, I notice her paling skin. She's horrified. But I did what I had to do to get the necessary information. "You'd turned your back on me. I'd been concerned, not to mention agitated. When you refused my calls, I'd been left with no choice."

"I'll have her license revoked." She pants. "I'll..." She stands speechless for long moments, her lips working over silent words before she flees the room.

"The shrink isn't to blame." I follow. "I always get what I want."

"Why am I doing this?" She reaches the far end of her sofa and turns to me. "Why do I keep seeking you out?" She closes her eyes and shakes her head. "The best option was to shut you out of my life."

Her struggle is bittersweet.

The fact I'm still in her head when she's spoken for, and after this time apart, is a soothing balm to my pride.

"I can't do this with you again." Her eyes open, the tired depths blinking back at me. "I'd been ready to move on."

"We never stopped." I continue toward her, despising how she retreats. I don't quit my approach until she's backed against the far wall, her breathing labored, her hands splayed against the plaster. "You might have been with him, but I bet you thought of me."

"Don't." She winces. "My life is here. In the FBI. Doing the *right* thing. I only came to you this morning because—"

"You came because the so-called right thing feels wrong. You hate it there. You can't stand being without me." My pulse chants an erratic beat as I will the declaration to be true.

She loathes being without me. I know she does.

Her wince increases, the furrow of her brow deep. "It's because of Stockho—"

"Bullshit." I step into her, my thighs jolting hers, pressing her harder into the wall. "I bet you can't look me in the eye and honestly tell me you believe your feelings are a mental issue."

She turns her cheek, proving my point by glancing away.

I'm so fucking tired. My limbs are drained of strength. But I could stay here forever. I could live in this embodiment of fatigue if it meant I wouldn't be without her.

I breathe her in. The lavender from her perfume dances through my senses, muddling my control.

"It isn't Stockholm, little fox." I lean in, pressing my lips to her neck, the heat of connection scorching.

She shudders. Whimpers.

The sweetest fucking mewl hums in her throat, turning my dick to stone.

"This thing between us is far more powerful than that." I speak against her skin, tasting her salty flesh.

"I don't care how powerful it is," she whispers. "I don't want it."

"At one point, neither did I. But I'm done fighting. This is going to happen."

"Easton—"

"*Fuck* Easton," I snap. "He was a mistake."

"You're wrong. About everything. I was moving on." She shakes her head softly, her jaw brushing my cheek. "And I will again, once those kids are found."

"No you won't. Not with Easton anyway."

She turns her face into me, her gaze questioning, her lips so fucking close. "How can you be sure?"

"Because I'll kill that man before I let him lay another hand on you."

She's not repulsed by my threat. There's no fear or panic or gasp. Only stillness.

"You know I'm not joking, Nis. I'll make sure he permanently keeps his distance."

"You're insane."

I smirk, pressing my chest to hers, her deliciously soft breasts making my dick jolt beyond salvation. Sex is the last thing I should be thinking about. But going through the start of this nightmare alone has only cemented how much I need her.

Every part of her.

"I'm also determined." I sense the heat of her mouth against mine. The delicate sweep of her breath. "I can—and will— slaughter every man who attempts to replace me. For the rest of your life if I have to."

She groans. Softens.

I'd fucking bleed for her. *Die* for her. If only I could have her.

She closes her eyes.

She's succumbing to me.

It's the most immense victory, spurring blood to pump faster through my veins.

I'm about to bridge the distance and claim the prize of her lips when her arms reach between us, her hands splaying on my chest to push me back.

"I'm not like you, Cole. And I don't want to be." Her eyes open and someone different stares back at me. Someone restrained and in control.

Fuck.

"I want to help those kids," she repeats. "But not like this. Either agree to be professional or I'll have to find another way."

12

COLE

I REMAIN CLOSE TO HER FOR LONG MOMENTS, MY FINGERS WRAPPED around the wrists still shoving against my chest. But she doesn't falter.

If anything, her eyes turned colder.

I'm losing her. All over again.

Without agreeing to her terms of professionalism, I back away, retreating to her room to grab her suitcase. Then I silently walk to the apartment door and wait for her to follow.

We don't speak on the way to the car. She glowers the entire time, climbing into the Porsche to cross her arms over her chest.

"Do you want me to get you something to eat before we return?" I keep my attention on the road, my hands on the wheel. I deny myself the visual and physical connection I crave and stare at the traffic straight ahead.

"No." Her answer is short. Sharp.

"Are you sulking?"

"I'm not goddamn sulking," she mutters. "I'm thinking. I'm trying to do what I'm here for."

"You need to eat. The extra weight looks good on you."

"Oh, wow." Her tone turns incredulous. "You're really going to go there? You must have a huge set of balls to comment on my body."

I hold in a grin. Her anger is like a fucking balm to all my concerns. It's as if I find peace in her volatility.

"Why wouldn't I?" I shoot her a look, my brow raised. "Your body is one of my most favorite things in the world."

She sighs. "You agreed to be professional."

No, she assumed my silence was confirmation.

"How 'bout—" My suggestion is cut off by the vibration of my cell, the ringing connecting with the car Bluetooth to trill through the speakers.

'Unknown number' illuminates across the dashboard screen.

Anissa repositions in her seat, leaning forward. On alert. "Are you going to answer? It could be…"

I connect the call and pray this is the communication we've been waiting for. "Cole Torian."

"Ah, Mr. Torian, I'm glad I reached you."

Apprehension tightens my throat at the unfamiliar accented voice of an older man.

"Who is this?" I drive on autopilot and glance at Anissa as she pulls out her phone and taps buttons to start a recording.

"Excuse me for contacting you out of the blue. My name is Emmanuel Costa. I'm a friend of your father's, although I admit it's been quite some time since we've been in touch."

Foreboding prickles the back of my neck. Any friend of my father's is no friend of mine, but this man's tone holds the quiet calm of a genuine welcome.

"I tried calling him directly," he adds, "but there was no answer. I'm not even sure I have the correct number anymore."

"My father has been hard to contact lately. Is there something I can do for you?"

There's a pause, the quiet deafening.

"No, son, I think it may be the other way around. I'm under the impression I might be able to do something for you."

Anissa's gaze bores into the side of my face as I pull over on the quiet residential street.

"I'm told I may be obtaining something of yours in the near future," he continues.

Darkness edges into the corners of my vision, the build of fury almost blinding. "You're *obtaining* something of mine? I suggest you choose your words wisely before you continue."

"Oh, no, please forgive me." His accent thickens. Italian? "I'm not addressing this correctly. It's not me who arranged these... how should I put this... assets? It's one of my men, who seems to have misjudged a situation and put himself into trouble. Again, I tried to call your father, but when there was no answer, I didn't know who else to reach out to apart from you."

"Cut the shit, Emmanuel. Do you have the kids or not?"

There's another pause, this one siphoning the air from my lungs.

"I don't, no. It's my employee. But I've since instructed him to come directly to me. I assure you they should be arriving safe and sound within the hour. There's no need to worry."

I don't know what to make of this. Is it an olive branch or a Trojan horse?

"Where are you?"

"I've just flown into Sacramento to meet him. He has driven through the night with your two little ones asleep on the back seat. Not a hair on their heads has been touched."

I scoff.

Not a hair has been touched, yet they were sedated. With fucking chloroform. And taken across state lines.

"What do you want?" I cling to the steering wheel, my knuckles white with the tight grip. "Money? Drugs?"

"Son, I don't want anything." He chuckles, the jovial sound a contrast to the sinister darkness surrounding the situation. "Especially not these children when I already have four of my own. I'm merely trying to right a wrong."

I frown. "Are you suggesting I come to Sacramento, and what? Just pick them up?"

"Precisely."

This doesn't add up. Nobody obtains power over me and gives it back willingly. There has to be a catch. A trap.

Anissa's hand slides over my thigh, her face demanding my attention.

She nods at me in encouragement, her eyes filled with

confident hope. But she doesn't understand the smoke and mirrors of my world. She's still naive to the complexities.

"Okay." I hold her gaze, needing the strength that comes with her determination. "I'll be there as soon as I can."

"Perfect. I'll text you the address once arrangements have been made."

Anissa smiles, the curve of lips subtle.

This isn't right. The simplicity. The ease. Someone doesn't go to the effort of stealing children from a notorious criminal to then give them back, even if acting under orders from a man who's now dead.

"I want proof of life." My request sounds like a plea. A pathetic show of weakness.

"That won't be a problem. I'll arrange for an image to be sent to you. Safe travels, Mr. Torian, and I'll see you soon."

"Wait," the demand leaves my mouth before I can think things through. But I refuse to spend the next God-knows-how-many hours anticipating an ambush. I need answers. At least a hint as to this man's comprehension of the situation. "I appreciate you not asking a price for the safe return of those kids, but you need to be aware I will require one of my own for the attack against my family. Nobody steals from me and gets away with it."

Anissa's hand tightens on my thigh, the grip a subtle warning.

"I understand." Emmanuel's voice holds regret. "I will make sure my employee is here to explain his decisions once you arrive."

The call disconnects. Anissa's hold gentles. My thoughts explode.

I rerun the entire conversation in my mind. The nuances of tone. The choice of words. I analyse everything, hoping to find a clue to an underlying agenda, and come up with nothing.

"This is good news." Anissa's fingers slide away, the threat of disconnect snapping me back to the present.

"Don't." I grab her hand, refusing to break the contact. She's the only thing grounding me.

She winces, the slight tug of retreat spiking my instability.

"Allow me this one thing, Nis," I growl. "Just this."

Just one hold. One brief grasp of a lifeline to help me concentrate on extraction instead of bloodthirsty revenge.

Her throat works over a heavy swallow. Her lips part.

But she doesn't deny me.

She lets me entwine our fingers as she turns to face the road ahead of us, resting back into the seat.

"What do you want me to do?" she asks. "What travel arrangements need to be—"

"I'll take the jet."

"You don't seem relieved. Do you think this is a setup?"

"Maybe." I clasp the steering wheel and pull back into traffic.

"Why wouldn't he threaten you to begin with?"

"He might be naive enough to think I'll arrive in Sacramento unprepared. Or that I won't dig into his life before arriving." I press buttons on the steering wheel to connect a call to Decker. What I don't do is let go of her hand.

I guide her palm to the gearstick, placing mine on top of it as I ask Deck to make travel arrangements and start digging up dirt on Emmanuel Costa.

"You aren't going to tell him to keep quiet?" she asks after I end the call.

"I don't need to. He knows we'll be home soon, and he'll keep his mouth shut until then." I sense her continued desire to pull her hand away. But she doesn't do it. She humors me with the connection while also refusing to look at me.

"How can you be sure?"

I guess I can't. At one time, I would've sworn my life on the loyalty of my people. Now I don't have that faith.

I think that's why I crave her so much. I can trust her. Rely on her. I've got too much leverage over Anissa for her to betray me. "Decker won't want to upset my sisters without more information."

She nods, falling uncomfortably quiet.

I turn onto my street, then into my drive, and up to the guarded gate before she slinks her hand out from beneath mine.

"What happens now?" She glances across my gardens as we make our way to the back of the house. "Do you want me to come with you to Sacramento?"

Not only do I want it, I expect it. *Demand* it.

"I was under the impression you planned on seeing this

through." I pull into the garage and cut the engine. "Are you looking for a way out?"

"No, of course I'm not. I just wasn't sure if you'd want me to assist from here or..." She shrugs. "I'll admit, I didn't anticipate having to get on another jet with you."

I unfasten my belt and push open my door. "Are you worried?" I shove from the Porsche and wait for her to follow, but she doesn't.

After a few moments, I lean back into the car to see her still seated in place.

"Please tell me this isn't another game." Her eyes implore me. "Promise me, Cole. Vow it. Because if this is a trick, I'll..."

I want to catch her fragile threat and throw it back at her.

What would she do?

How would she get back at me?

It's the flimsy shield she holds up against me that stops me from retaliating. She's close to breaking point, and I'm the one who carved the initial fractures.

"I give you my word, little fox." I clutch the top of the doorframe, hating the slight wince crossing her features.

"I want to believe you." She unclasps her belt. "But once bitten and all that."

"Trust me, I feel the same when it comes to you walking out on me." It's a low blow that I punctuate with the close of my door.

Our games might be her trigger but we both participated in those. She attempted to trick me just as much as I did with her.

"Don't hold your breath for an apology." She climbs from the car. "I don't regret the way things ended."

I huff out a laugh and start for the door leading inside. "That's the thing, Nis; nothing ended. It never will."

I don't look back as I enter the house. I force Anissa from my mind with each step toward the chatter in the living room and find everyone still sitting on the sofas, awaiting our return.

The only person who doesn't sit at attention at the sight of me is Decker who keeps his attention on the laptop resting on his thighs, his fingers dancing over the keys.

"Who's Emmanuel Costa?" Keira pushes to her feet. "Does he have anything to do with the abduction?"

I don't acknowledge her, don't even flinch as I approach my other sister, crouching before Layla to meet her watery gaze.

For a second, she takes me in, her eyes searching mine with apprehension. "It's bad, isn't it?" She sucks in a breath. "He's the one who took her, didn't he?"

"I don't know." I clasp her hands as she draws in one weary inhale after another. "I don't think so."

"What is it then? What happened? Who is he?"

"Why are we looking into him?" Benji adds from beside her.

"He called to tell me he knows where the kids are. That they're okay and we can go get them."

Her face alights with hope. Misguided, punishing hope.

"Lay." I squeeze her fingers. "Before you start thanking your lucky stars, I'm not sure how good this news is."

Anissa walks into the room as Layla's hope turns to confusion. "Why?"

"Because it's too easy." I don't want to worry her, yet false expectations are dangerous. "This doesn't feel right. This guy led me to believe this will be an easy resolution. Without a ransom or threats. And maybe that might be the case. But…" I shrug. "You know that's not how these things work."

Her lower lip trembles, the unshed tears building in her eyes.

"Why does his name sound familiar?" Benji asks. "Who is he?"

"A heavyweight in the fashion industry by the looks of it." Decker keeps tapping at his keyboard. "Does the brand Alleya mean anything to you guys?"

"Jesus Christ," Anissa murmurs from the far corner of the room.

"I had one of their handbags a few years ago." Keira pushes to her feet. "Dad gave it to me for my birthday."

"That's the other thing." I cringe. "He's friends with Luther. Or was at one point."

"Tell me what this means." Layla clings tight to my hands. "Why is he involved in any of this?"

"That's what I want to know, too. Robert had to have some sort of familiarity with this guy of Emmanuel's to reach out to him for help. Which means it's likely they know about our father's unsavory business ventures."

Keira shakes her head. "But why would a successful businessman risk any sort of association with our father if he knew?"

"Some of the most high-profile people in the world have maintained relationships with suspected pedophiles well after rumors turned into a conviction," Anissa murmurs. "It's either about power or perverted proclivities."

"Show me a photo," Penny demands. "Let me see who this man is."

I release Layla's hands and raise to my full height to take a look at Decker.

He taps a few more times on his keypad, scrolls, then turns the screen to face us. "I'm not sure how recent this image is. It's on his company website."

The smiling face jogs through my childhood memories. He holds a friendly expression full of laugh lines and kind eyes, his Lego-man hair more grey than black as he sits behind an expensive wooden desk in a tailored suit.

"I've seen him before." Keira points at the laptop. "Back when Mom was alive."

I ignore the thought of my mother, determined not to fall into that well of suffering, and nod. "I remember him, too."

There are no specific instances of familiarity. No recollection of good or bad. But I know him.

"Penny?" I switch my focus to her. "How about you? Have you seen him before?"

Did she see him in Greece while my father held her prisoner?

She shakes her head and lowers her gaze. "No. Not at all."

At least that's a start. Emmanuel may not have any connection to the sex trade at all.

"Please, Cole." Layla inches to the edge of the sofa and reclaims my hand. "We need to get the kids back straight away. Where do we have to go? Where are they?"

"Sacramento," I announce the location quickly, ripping off the Band-Aid.

Someone gasps. Either Sarah or Keira. I don't know. But the sound is far better than the crumpling of Layla's face.

"Sacramento?" she whispers. "Some monster has driven my baby all the way to Sacramento?"

"Yes. But I'm told they're unharmed." The weak platitude leaves a bitter aftertaste on my tongue.

"Emmanuel agreed to send a photo as proof of life," Anissa adds. "That's a good sign."

I nod, thankful for the reminder.

"When?" Hunt leans forward, resting his elbows on his knees. "If he's as innocent as he says, then we should be able to track information from the digital footprint." He looks at Decker for confirmation. "Right?"

"Right." Decker turns the laptop back to face him. "If he's got nothing to hide, then he shouldn't go to the effort of scrubbing the information from the image. And then we can get an exact timestamp of when it was taken along with a GPS location. It's not a lot to go on, but it's better than nothing."

It still feels like nothing to me.

An address won't tell us what kind of man he is.

A timestamp won't prove whether he's abused the children or not.

"What do you think?" Layla turns her attention to Anissa, still standing across the room, doing her best not to intrude. "Did you hear the conversation? What do you think of this man?"

Nissa looks at me, her lips parted as if waiting for permission.

"It's okay." I nod. "Tell her what you think."

She walks closer, swallowing before perching herself on the armrest of Layla's sofa to give her a sad smile. "Yes, I heard the conversation, and I think Cole is right. Even though Emmanuel sounds like a positive influence on the situation, we still haven't received the proof. He hasn't sent the photo yet, and we don't even have his cell number because the connection was private. It's too early to tell what we're up against."

Her agreement stirs something inside me. Not pride. But similar.

It's not often this independent woman agrees with me. It's even less common to have her attempting to soothe one of my family members.

"Do you think they're still alive?" Penny asks her.

"Yes. Although this guy was remorseful for what has happened, he also had an air of confidence. There were no pauses for contemplation or stutters where he may have been lying. He either believes what he's saying or he's done this too many times to feel fear." She meets my gaze. "My guess is the former. Especially with him being the man behind a brand as big as Alleya. I just wouldn't be betting anyone's life on a seamless outcome."

"I'd say the odds are pretty good." Decker turns his laptop to face the room again, displaying a Wikipedia page. "This guy is seriously wealthy. I'm talking balls-deep, filthy-rich territory. Anything he could possibly get out of us would be pocket change to him. Which means this could be exactly what he told you—just an easy handover."

I'm still not convinced. Men who know my father don't do business above board.

"It's possible. I'm just not sure if it's probable." Anissa pushes from the armrest. "We can be hopeful, though, as long as we remain cautious."

The room falls quiet. The mental musings of everyone are loud through the silence while Benji stares at me, questioning. Begging. Fucking pleading for more information.

All I see when I look at him now is a traitor.

A conniving, backstabbing, heartbroken traitor.

He's lucky he's still breathing.

"So, what's the plan?" Hunter stalks for the kitchen. "How many of us are going to Sacramento?"

Layla glances at me in panic. "I want to be there."

"I'm coming, too." Keira's hands drop to her sides.

They both stare at me in anticipation, waiting for me to deny them. "You can both come. But you'll do as I say the entire time. I don't want you anywhere near this guy. You'll have to be satisfied with being in the same city, not the same location."

They nod.

"We're all going," Hunter states from the kitchen, his face in my fridge. "If this is a trap, every one of us needs to have your back."

"I have to be there, too." Penny's eyes plead with me. "I want to be close for Tobias."

"I agree." Luca slides deeper into his seat, his expression lax with exhaustion as he leans against the headrest. "There's no way any of us are staying behind."

That's where he's wrong. Everyone else can tag along, but not him. "You're staying."

He straightens. "Me? Why?"

"From what I'm told, you've got a fucking bleed on the brain. You're not getting in a jet."

"Like hell I'm not."

Penny glances from me to Luca and back again, her mouth opening in panic. "Then we'll drive. It can't be that far. By the time everyone gets to the airport, we could already be well on our way." She pushes to her feet. "We can meet you there."

"It's a fucking long drive. And Luca's in no shape to do it." Hunt snaps the fridge door shut and returns to the group. "From the look of him, he needs about a month's worth of rest and a saline drip. Driving nine hours is the last thing he should be doing."

"I can handle it." Luca scowls. "I've had more sleep in the last twenty-four than any of you."

"Nine hours?" Layla's panic increases. "Won't we already be on our way home with Stella by then?"

Benji grabs her hand and she falls silent with the touch.

"Yes." I keep my tone confident despite the lack of emotion to back it up. "It's a waste of time to drive."

"It's a waste of time sitting here with my thumb up my ass while you guys go without me." Luca pins me with a stare. "I'm driving. You can take Pen in the jet. And if everything is squared away before I arrive, I'll just turn around and come back. As soon as I know the kids are safe, I can find a hotel and rest."

"I'm not letting you drive on your own." Penny pushes to her feet. "I'll help. We can take shifts."

"Says the woman who not only doesn't have a license, but is legally dead as far as the cops are concerned." Luca winces as he moves to stand beside her. "It's not a good idea."

"Do you even have a car?" Decker asks.

"Shit." Luca meets my gaze, his lips kicking in a faint smile. "Can we take the Porsche?"

"Don't push your luck." I jerk my head toward the garage. "Use the Escalade."

He nods and leads Penny to the far hall. "I'll go home first and pack supplies. Keep us posted on any developments."

"Now what?" Keira asks. "What do we do?"

"Get ready to fly," is the only response I have. This is new territory. The fragility of having children targeted doesn't sit well with me. The constant nausea is growing old.

"What do you mean?" Layla stands, Benji following close behind. "What do we need to pack? What should I take?"

I don't know. I have no fucking clue what my sister should bring.

"Pack some things for Stella," Anissa answers for me. "A change of clothes. A hairbrush. Maybe even her pillow or a plush toy so she has something familiar to cuddle on the flight home."

God, she's a fucking angel. A spiteful warrior of an angel, but heaven-sent nonetheless.

"Maybe even some comfort food," she adds. "Bring her favorite packet of crisps or candy. It's usually the little things that help life return to normal."

Layla glances at me for confirmation.

"You need to hurry." I jerk my chin at her. "The jet won't take long to get on the flight schedule. I don't want to be here any longer than necessary."

"What about us?" Hunter grates. "What are we packing for?"

I pause a second, not wanting my sisters to be privy to my thoughts. But it's another Band-Aid that needs to be ripped off. If they're tagging along, I can't hide them behind a shield of pretense forever. I don't have the disposable energy.

I start for the hall leading to my bedroom. "We plan for war and pack accordingly."

13

COLE

It takes two hours to get in the air.

Benji and Layla are seated at the front of the cabin facing Decker and Keira across the small serving table. Hunter and Sarah are in the plush leather seats behind them, while Nissa and I sit toward the back of the jet, side by side along the right wall.

The aircraft has barely leveled out after takeoff when my cell vibrates with a text image from a private number.

I cradle the device in my hand for long moments, staring at Tobias and Stella asleep in what looks to be the back seat of an old sedan.

They seem peaceful. Unharmed. Their faces are free from bruises or scratches. But the fact they've slept through their abduction in the middle of the day speaks highly of the amount of sedatives coursing through their systems.

The children are fine. We have moved them into our home and placed them together in a spare room. They're still resting peacefully. I will contact you again once they wake. Emmanuel.

The message aligns with the old man's MO—kind, placating. Yet no phone number is given. My hands are tied in a one-sided conversation.

More than an hour later, I stare out the window across the cabin of the jet, still seeing nothing but those sleeping faces.

The carelessness toward their lives consumes me.

The danger.

I'm livid at the neglect.

"We'll get them home safely." Nissa fidgets in her chair, playing with the recline. "The continued communication is a good start."

"You don't believe that." I keep my voice low, not wanting anyone to overhear. "You haven't relaxed in the slightest since I received that text."

I didn't show the photo to anyone else. I kept it between us, not wanting to add fuel to the hysteria, and I'll continue to do so for as long as I can.

"That's nothing new. I haven't relaxed since you banged down my apartment door two days ago."

It's another lie. The image put her on edge, and I've been talking myself out of questioning her about it, not wanting to face whatever hint she's picked up on that I missed. But I can't ignore it any longer.

"Tell me what you see." I retrieve my cell from my suit jacket and bring the image back on screen. "What have I missed?"

"Nothing." She doesn't look at the device.

"Nothing?" I hold it higher, breaching her line of sight. "You see nothing?"

She cringes, her brows pulling tight. "Put it away."

"Why? I thought you were meant to be helping."

"I am." She shoots me a glance. "Keeping a level head is imperative. We need to remain positive."

I lean onto our joined armrest and she stiffens. "I'm not positive in the slightest. And it doesn't take a genius to figure you aren't either. I know you, little fox, and there's something in this picture you're not telling me."

Her eyes turn sad as she releases a long breath.

"*Tell me,*" I demand, drawing the attention of Hunter, who glances over the back of his chair toward us.

She waits as he scowls at her, not saying a word until I shoot him a warning glare to mind his own business.

"Come on, Nis." I attempt a softer approach. "What is it? What do you see?"

"I see what Emmanuel wants me to see." Her voice is low, barely audible over the hum of the aircraft. "I see two children peacefully sleeping in the back of an old car. Both, presumably, in the clothes they wore to bed. Both snuggled close in a show of shared affection."

I keep eyeing her, waiting for more. "And?"

"I also see what the picture lacked." She doesn't elaborate—just fucking leaves me hanging.

"It's dangerous to withhold information from me right now." Especially when I trust her judgment and the only thing she's giving me to go on is raised apprehension. "Tell me before I lose my temper."

She glares. "Don't threaten me. I've heard so many from you that they're no longer effective."

"Then maybe I need to graduate to action instead of words."

She holds my stare, one brow raised in a complete lack of fear. She won't bow down to my aggression. Not this time.

Fuck.

"*Please*," I grind between clenched teeth. "Just fucking tell me."

Her expression changes with each of my labored heartbeats. Her eyes lose their hardness. Her mouth gentles. By the time she gives a hard swallow what beams back at me is sickening pity.

Shit.

She didn't withhold information to be a bitch. She was attempting to protect me.

"I see a photo that could've been easily staged." She holds my gaze, barely blinking. "I see subtle smudges of dirt on their pajamas and what looks to be blood on Tobias's toes."

I drag my cell closer, narrowing my attention on what she's pointed out. The blindingly obvious now stares back at me.

"I noticed how both their heads are bowed, supposedly in sleep," she continues. "However, it could be an attempt to hide sightless eyes and gaping mouths. What I see, Cole, is a photo that lacks proof of life. And because it was taken while they were still in that car, even if he didn't delete the image data, the GPS co-ordinates won't lead us to where they are now. Only where they were."

The icy chill of death sinks into me, coating my skin in thickening grime. They can't be dead. If I've contributed to the murder of my niece and half-brother, I'll—

"My observations mean nothing, Cole." Anissa places her hand on my wrist, the warmth breathing the slightest sense of life back into me. "Emmanuel had no obligation to send you anything at all. But he did. That alone is enough to leave me hopeful."

"He could be trying to give me a false sense of security."

She cringes "Yes."

"They could already be dead."

Her brows deepen, her gentle fingers sliding back and forth along my skin. "No more than we thought they could've been before. That photo changed nothing. We're no better or worse than we were. We're just the same." She's silent a moment. A bump of turbulence shuffles us closer together. She opens her mouth to speak again, then stops.

"What?" I frown. "What were you going to say?"

Her hand retreats as she sits taller. "With one phone call, this could all be over. Let me get in contact with the Sacramento—"

"No." I know exactly where this is going—straight into unwanted territory. "Don't bring it up again."

"Please, Cole. If you let me reach out to the local authorities, they could handle this. They're far more equipped—"

"Of course they are. Not only to retrieve the children but to dig deep on why the fuck this happened in the first place." I lock my cell and shove it back into my pocket. "Tell me, Nis, do you have an appropriate story to tell about why Robert would've arranged this? Because I'm sure the asshole who drove those kids away from my house wouldn't take the full blame."

She presses her mouth together in indignation.

"The fun will begin once they tie Robert to my father. Then discover my old man is missing." I don't withhold the antagonism from my voice. "What happens when they dig deep enough to figure out he's dead? Do you have an appropriate story for why you pulled the trigger and didn't report the death?"

She sits back in her seat, turning her focus to the opposite wall of the cabin to cross her arms over her chest.

"It's not such a great idea anymore, is it?" I taunt. "That easy call isn't so easy after all."

Her jaw ticks.

"Believe me, Nissa, if I could get those kids out of there without having to wait, I'd fucking do it. But I'm not risking the freedom of everyone on this jet."

I can't.

It might not be the best call, but it's one I can live with.

Everyone here should be behind bars. Nobody would be spared. Then who would look after Stella and Tobias? They'd be no better than they are now.

She doesn't answer me.

Not while I stare at her, and not after I settle back into my seat and wait out the remaining minutes until we start our descent.

I don't hear anything else from Emmanuel by the time we land. There's no destination point. No cell number. I'm unable to contact him, and he sure as shit doesn't seem in a hurry to contact me again.

"Pretend everything is fine." Anissa tugs on a baseball cap she took from my house as we disembark onto the tarmac of the private airport. "Don't let anyone know you're worried."

I scoff. Not because she's wrong, but because she's homed in on my increased anxiety.

"Easier said than done when we've got nowhere to go. I can't even call this asshole."

"You'll figure something out." She walks ahead, her head hung low as she follows behind the airport staffer who carries the only duffle that doesn't contain anything illegal, along with wheeling Anissa's suitcase.

The pilots will take care of the weapons, either bypassing security or waiting until they can pay someone for the privilege.

It isn't until we're out the other side of the airport, our belongings piled onto a trolley at my side, waiting for our rental cars to pull up, that I notice I have an audience.

Everyone watches me—Hunt, Deck, Sarah, and Benji, waiting for instruction, while my sisters blink at me with silent questions. Anissa stands alone a few feet behind us, remaining an outsider as she keeps her head hung, attempting to shield her face from any cameras.

"We're going to find a hotel." I deliberately keep my attention from Keira and Layla. "We'll freshen up and get something to eat. I want to get a lay of the land first. Sacramento isn't what I'd call an even playing field, and we need to make sure we know what we're up against."

"I don't want to freshen up." Layla glances between me and Benji, as if waiting for support. "I want to see my daughter."

"I agree," Keira adds. "We could spend days trying to get familiar with this city. It's a waste of time."

"I said, we're going to a hotel. Regardless of your protests, I've already told you you're not coming to pick them up, so you'll need somewhere to wait."

There's a beat of tense silence before Anissa steps forward. "I'll book the rooms. Do you have any preferences?"

"I'll do it." Sarah backs away from the huddle, grabbing her cell from her jeans pocket. "I already know the drill."

"I know I didn't protest back home about coming with you to pick them up," Layla starts. "But I want to be there. I'm her mother. I should be the first to comfort her."

Anissa shakes her head. "It's best not to—"

"Stay out of this," Layla snaps, jabbing her finger in Anissa's direction. "I've been patient and haven't questioned your sudden involvement. But don't mistake my silence for friendship. Don't even mistake it for civility. You don't belong here."

I narrow my eyes on my sister. "She's helping us."

"Exactly." Layla returns the accusing stare. "She's a *Fed*, yet she's helping us. How can you trust her?"

Anissa looks at me in confusion. Then dawning shock.

She's finally realizing I kept her secret.

I made no effort to clear up the assumption that I killed my father instead of her. And I've also ensured the news would never be exposed by Penny and Luca, as long as the two of them want to remain breathing.

"Send her home, Cole." Hunter follows after Sarah. "She brings nothing to the team."

A crowd of subtle nodding heads bob before me—Decker, Keira, Benji, and Layla all in agreement.

They don't see what I see.

They don't understand the asset. The impeccable resource.

She's much more than that, too, but they're definitely not going to appreciate the chemistry or history that cements Anissa as part of this team.

I'm about to open my mouth and put them in their places when Anissa squares her shoulders, a mask of no-shits-given settling into place.

"You don't want to send me home." Her voice is authoritative. It's the determined confidence I appreciate more than gold. "From what I can tell, I'm the only one here who has slept in the past twenty-four hours. I'm also the only one who isn't emotionally involved. And this isn't my first rodeo."

Her tone is almost a taunt of superiority. A casual *fuck you* to her haters. "You *need* me. Not just for clarity, but for common sense. You have no contacts here. You've got no connections. I can make things happen if your wrong-side-of-the-tracks agenda doesn't pan out."

She fascinates me with her confident tirade. I'm fucking drained beyond belief, but I'm impressed.

"Anyone require me to reiterate what Anissa put so eloquently?" I glare at everyone in turn. "I'm going to lose my temper real fast if we have to continue going over the reasons for her involvement."

They remain quiet, their protests contained to returned glares.

"I just don't understand why we're waiting," Layla breaks the silence. "Why can't we get them now?"

"Because we're not ready." Anissa steps closer to the road as three Escalades pull up in front of us. "Cole needs to strategize. Contingencies have to be made. So we'll go to a hotel and make a plan. As soon as we're ready, we can move."

I walk for the man getting out of the first car, exchange the necessary pleasantries, and catch the key fob he throws at me.

"Nissa, you're with me." I make eye contact with Decker over the hood. "You, Keira, Benji, and Layla are in the next car. Followed by Sarah and Hunt, who will take the luggage."

I don't wait for another protest as I climb into the Escalade and start the engine. Anissa joins me in seconds, clasping her belt and letting out a sigh.

"You did well." I don't look at her. I place my hands on the steering wheel, denying myself the pleasure of reaching out. "They might not like you, but they respect you."

She huffs out a laugh. "Hunter doesn't respect me. Neither does Decker."

"You have a past with Decker." One I don't care to remember. "And Hunter is beyond loyal to him. They'll never be kind but they're not threatening to kill you."

"At least not to my face."

I grin and start the engine. "True."

"Lucky me."

There's a tap on her window. Sarah's face comes into view. "We're staying at the Saffron Towers in the city." She speaks through the glass. "I booked two rooms to give us a little breathing space. See you there."

She walks away and Anissa lets out another sigh.

"The space is a good idea," I offer, hoping to address whatever added to her discomfort. "It also shows that you've got Sarah on your side."

"She's not on my side. She's just…" She shakes her head.

"What?"

She looks at me, her confidence gradually returning. "Smart. She knows I'm an asset."

"Yeah, well, she's not the only one." I jerk my chin toward the navigation system. "Do me a favor and figure out where we're going."

She does as instructed, leaning forward to tap at the small screen until an automated voice directs me to take the first left up ahead.

"What are we going to do once we get to the hotel?" She settles back into her seat.

"We're going to share the photo of the kids to buy us some time, and if Emmanuel hasn't reached out after that, then we pray."

14

ANISSA

COLE MENTIONS HIS NAME TO THE VALET AND WE'RE IMMEDIATELY treated like royalty. Our escort beams a bright smile as he leads us into the hotel foyer while our travel companions are lost somewhere in traffic.

"I'll show you to your room, Mr. Torian. Would you like any bags brought up?"

"No." Cole strides ahead of me, not showing any of the concern I have for the bags of illegal weapons soon to arrive.

I didn't realize the extent of the arsenal we brought along with us until Cole enlightened me on the drive here. Guns, sniper rifles, and ammo are encased in those bags, escorted by Hunter and Sarah. And my FBI allocated weapon is right there with them.

What if they're pulled over? Their car searched?

I'm not sure how these people live with the threat of prison on a daily basis. I've already accumulated enough paranoid arrhythmia to set me on a collision course for heart failure. But Cole lives with this daily. The adrenaline. The naive thrill.

We're led into the elevator. Our escort even handles the button to our floor and we ascend in silence. It isn't until the red neon floor indicator dings our arrival on the penthouse floor that all my accumulated arrhythmia becomes a threatening panic attack.

"The penthouse?" I follow the men into the wide hall, the

glistening lights above kissing their features in a gentle way fluorescents never could.

"That's right." The escort stops, turns, and glances between Cole and I. "Isn't this what was requested?"

"Yes." Cole continues forward without pause. "Make sure our companions get a spare key to our room."

"No problem, sir." The young man nods and jogs ahead, beating Cole to the door to open it with an elegant sweep of his arm. "I hope your stay is enjoyable."

I pass both men as Cole arranges a tip. I peek my head into the room along the hall, finding an immaculate bedroom, the massive bed crisp, the furnishings well above my pay grade, and the view… Even from the hall it's nothing but open skyline.

"Come on." Cole walks by me into the open living area.

"The penthouse?" I follow. "We're not staying the night, are we? Why would you need the penthouse?"

I reach the end of the hall, the breath leaving my lungs at the pristine elegance. There are two corner sofas in the middle of the room, facing floor-to-ceiling glass doors leading onto a balcony with more expensive furniture.

There are flower-filled vases, as well as artwork, and a massive television.

The kitchen has appliances I've never even seen before, the sparkling stainless steel gleaming in the sunlight.

"Kick off your shoes and rest for a while." Cole continues to the doorway across the opposite side of the room. "The others will be here soon."

The temptation of taking off these two-inch heels and sinking my toes into the thick carpet is too strong. I slide my shoes against the side of the sofa and groan with the freedom as Cole disappears into unexplored territory.

I don't follow this time. I'm sure the main bedroom is in there and it's not a place I want to be alone with him.

Not when my sympathy for this crime-hardened man is growing.

I need to reassess the walls I've placed between us and make them stronger. Thicker. I have to Great Wall of China this shit and ensure no unwanted emotions breach the perimeter.

I faintly hear the grate of a zipper, which electrocutes my pulse due to the accompanying heated thoughts.

The unmistakable sound of fluid hitting fluid thankfully sucks all the eroticism from my mind.

There's a flush of the toilet, the rush of water from the faucet, then silence.

The quiet stretches long enough to make me curious to investigate, the space between the sofa and the bedroom bridged in creeping footsteps.

I reach the threshold and suck in another breath at the view. This time, the awe is male-inspired. Cole is laid out on the bed, his shoes and suit still on, his hands behind his head.

He's at home amongst the luxury. A perfectly fit piece.

I can't help admiring the sight. The calm amid the storm. The oozing sexuality which needs to be smothered by professionalism.

He lowers his chin to meet my gaze, his eyes tired, yet so fucking captivating. "You seem nervous, little fox." His tone is smooth, calm, with that infinite cockiness threaded beneath. "Why? Do you fear a carnal repeat of Greece?"

I don't want to humor him, but the innuendo needs to be smacked from his consciousness. "Not at all."

He raises a brow and sits, sliding his feet to the floor. I prepare for him to continue the taunts. Instead, his shoulders slump as his hands fall to the bed coverings. He stares at the carpet, his exhaustion creeping into my chest.

I ache to help him. To make this easier.

No. I need to build walls.

Many, many walls.

"That's probably for the best." He pushes to his feet. "As much as I want to fuck you, I don't think I could bring my A-game right now."

My abdomen squeezes.

Goddamn wrings tight.

It's pathetic.

"A-game?" I drawl as he starts toward me. "I think I've only ever experienced the lackluster version."

A grin is slow to spread his lips. "Is that so?"

Shit. I shouldn't have bitten back.

I swallow, hating myself a little more with each of his predatory steps.

"Don't taunt me, Nis." He stops beside me, his shoulder brushing mine. "I might just be willing to muster enough energy to prove you wrong."

My pulse flutters. A million tiny butterfly wings rapidly bat beneath my ribs.

"You should order room service," he instructs. "When the others arrive, I'm going to need something to keep their mouths occupied."

He continues into the living room as if he didn't just treat me like the hired help.

I don't follow. I remain rooted in place, taking necessary calming breaths.

The others will be here soon.

I don't need to worry about a lengthy isolation with him. With my feelings. With my desires. But the risks claw at me nonetheless.

Seeing him like this is a double-edged sword. The drained, vulnerable Cole is just as alluring as the man who threatens me into a frenzy of lust and carnality.

This man, with his palpable weariness, makes me ache for him because not once has he shown weakness despite his belly being exposed.

He remains a force to be reckoned with. A lethal, conniving soul. And I hate how drawn I am to those parts of him. I'm smothered with attraction even though the facets of his world I despise the most are painted before me in broad strokes.

These feelings aren't normal.

I'm not normal.

"Food, Nissa," he barks behind me, lighting the fuse to my agitation.

I swing around, hands clenched, cheeks flaming. "Who the hell died and made me your bitch?" I raise my voice. "I'm a fucking FBI agent, asshole, not the catering staff."

He smirks as he sits on the sofa, then lays down, mimicking his relaxed position from the bed, only this time his arm moves to cover his eyes. I can still see those lips though, and that conniving son of a bitch maintains the slightest grin.

"You're *a* bitch. *The* bitch. *My* bitch." He crosses his feet at the ankles. "But I wasn't treating you like a servant. I thought you might be hungry, so I disguised my demand for you to eat in a request to order food for everyone. Excuse me for caring."

Well, great. Now I feel like trash.

It doesn't matter that his execution was utter idiocy—his motives were thoughtful.

Through this whole ordeal, he's still taken time to remember *my* needs and *my* sustenance while I stand here struggling to remind myself of the bigger picture through the haze of lust.

"Fine," I mumble. "I'll order the damn food." I glance around the huge space, searching for a phone or menu.

"Kitchen," he drawls, not even raising his arm to look at me.

Damn mind reader.

I pad toward the sparkling stainless steel and round the marble counter, finding the phone beside the fridge and the menu in a drawer. I'm finger sliding through the list of mouthwatering food items when a knock sounds at the door.

"Come in," Cole yells.

The blood drains from my face. I reach for a gun that isn't there. "Are you serious?" I hiss. "That could be anyone."

We're in a foreign city, with foreign threats. This isn't well-known Portland territory.

"Untwist your panties. It's Hunt and the others. They messaged while I was in the bedroom."

The door opens and the familiar mumble of deep voices down the hall has me relaxing my tense muscles.

"You still couldn't have known," I say in defense. "Anyone could walk through that door. So don't do something this reckless again. Not when my safety is in jeopardy."

Hunter and Sarah wheel my suitcase in as I finish my tirade, followed by Decker, Keira, Layla, then Benji, who carries one of the duffels.

"What's going on?" Hunt asks.

Cole shoves to his feet in my periphery, his air of increasing authority building as he approaches. "Bear with me a moment," he growls when he passes them. "Anissa and I need to get one thing straight."

He storms forward, making every inch of me stiffen at his ferocity while our audience watches. Those hard eyes slay me, almost buckle me. He stops in my personal space.

"They followed us to the fucking hotel," he snarls. "They messaged me to say they were here." He leans closer, forcing me to backtrack into the counter.

I should be hating his dominance, despising the demeaning way he talks to me in front of everyone. Instead, my lips tingle, my nipples ache.

I *have to* hate this.

Oh, God, how I have to hate this.

"They even had a fucking key," he enunciates slowly. "Not now, or ever, will I take uneducated guesses. I protect what's mine. I'm not careless with—" He stops, his gaze boring into me, his mouth hinging open a crack.

I hold my breath, struggling to understand what I've done to end the tirade, but then his shoulders lose their stiffness and his face washes clean of the confident aggression.

Have his words come back to bite him? Does he think he's been careless with those children? Does he hold himself responsible?

Yes. I can see it in the slight pinch to his brows. In the uncomfortable scrunch of his nose.

My stomach twists with more unwanted sympathy as eerie silence suffocates the air.

He can't show weakness now. Not in front of his sister, who is resting her daughter's life on his shoulders. Or his men, who need to follow his example.

They're all depending on him to lead them out of this. He has to remain strong.

"I get it. You're the fearless Cole Torian," I seethe back in his face, hoping to resuscitate his conviction. "How could I forget the way you've built an empire on bloodshed and brutality?"

I'm attempting to remind him. Inspire him.

But his stiffness doesn't return. He's still lost in guilt, his gaze unfocused on my cheek.

"Next time, fill me in on what's happening." I inch closer, smothering his personal space, the hair on my arms prickling from the attention of our captivated audience. "I'm not one of your minions who will blindly follow where you lead."

I begin to turn, hoping to end the awkwardness by ordering food, but he grabs the crook of my arm, forcing me back in place, demanding my gaze to his with nothing more than a heated stare.

I shiver. Shudder. Everything inside me quakes under his attention, and I'm sure he feels it.

"Mark my words, little fox." His lips are cruel as his grip tightens. "You *will* follow me blindly. One way or another."

I know I will.

I already do.

He releases my arm and stalks away, shoving past Hunter and Benji to escape into the bedroom, slamming the door behind him.

I don't move. Don't weaken.

I stare at the far wall as Decker mutters something under his breath and limps his way to the sofa. The others begin to follow, allowing me a few moments to close my eyes and slump against the counter to gain composure.

I'm not sure how much longer I can do this.

I'm straddling too many emotions, each one spreading me in a different direction. The calm self-assurance that has accompanied me my entire career is no longer here to depend on. I've got nothing but instability.

"Are you okay?"

Keira's voice snaps me out of my mental shelter.

I straighten and busy myself by reaching for the room service menu. "I'm fine."

"My brother can be pig-headed sometimes."

I huff out a laugh. "Sometimes?" I shoot her a two-second glance. It's a mistake.

Her eyes are kind. Bloodshot and puffy, but gloriously, sympathetically kind.

"There's something between you two, isn't there?" she asks. "Something that makes more sense than the convoluted excuses he's given me about you working together for mutual gain. He doesn't usually lie to me. But I have a feeling he is when it comes to you because he's too tight-lipped."

"I guess it's nice to know something can shut him up."

She gives a sad smile, not buying my attempt at humor. "You know, in my entire life, I've never seen a woman stand up to him like you just did."

I zero in on the menu. The clear-cut words and the crisp white paper. I focus on everything except her admission that's likely to weaken me further. "That's a real shame. Maybe if more women didn't bow down to his smarmy arrogance he wouldn't be such a raging asshole."

"Not only that," she continues, "but I've never seen him walk away from a heated exchange as if he'd lost the fight. And then to hide in his room? That's quite a feat."

My throat tightens. "What can I say? Cole and I have a special sort of toxic relationship only the best of enemies can have."

"Enemies?" I hear the smile in her voice. "Is that really what you are?"

No. "Yes." My response is rapid, and regretted just as quickly. I bit out the lie with too much guilt.

She gives a breathy chuckle, raising the hairs on the back of my neck. I can feel her gaze on me. The narrowing eyes. The scrutiny.

"I know I wanted you to leave earlier, but…" She shrugs in my periphery. "I think that might have been a mistake. Having you here means a lot. We could use someone like you around more often—"

"No." I turn to face her. "Don't even waste your breath. This is a one-time thing. I'm morally obligated to help with those kids. But that's it. Afterwards, I'm done." I snatch the menu from the counter and walk forward to hand it over. "You should order some food. Everyone needs to keep their energy up."

I maneuver around her and take a hard right down the hall, moving away from the quiet conversation to escape into the far bedroom, then farther into the adjoining bathroom.

I wash my face in the basin, over and over again, wishing I could scrub free from reality. But as soon as I turn off the faucet, I hear Cole's voice—the unmistakable growl that collars and enslaves me.

I dry myself with a hand towel and return to the bedroom to sit on the edge of the king-size mattress, listening to him speak. There's no longer any weakness in his tone as he informs them of the photo he received. He's so fucking strong and sure of himself, his authority a commanding force.

He continues talking as someone sobs. He outlines possible strategies for the pick-up of the children. He mentions the names of those who will accompany him, and I'm disappointed to hear I'm not one of them.

Questions are thrown at him. Suggestions are offered. More sobs filter down the hall.

I bow my head, a slave to my unwavering admiration of a criminal, and pull out my cell as a distraction technique.

I do an internet search on Emmanuel Costa, determined to lose myself in the long list of results.

I skim through details of his fashion empire, find out he's a majority shareholder in innumerable well-known companies. He has no fixed address, but owns a rolodex worth of properties around the country and the globe.

Born from poor parents. Father to four children—three boys and a girl. All offspring follow in their papa's footsteps.

I don't find any ties to Sacramento. No real estate ownership or businesses. But all it would take is one text to Easton. One quick question to get him to do a search on the Bureau's database.

I'm tempted.

I clear the browser and open my messages, clicking on his name. I stare for long moments, battling indecision.

Is it worth the risk?

"What are you doing?" Cole asks from the doorway.

"Jesus Christ." The cell fumbles from my hand, falling to the floor. "Did you deliberately sneak up on me?"

"I called your name. Twice." He stalks forward and scoops up my phone, his face hardening as he stares at the screen. "Miss him already? You couldn't even last a few hours?"

I push to my feet and attempt to snatch the device back, only to have it held out of reach. "That's real mature." I try again. "Give it back."

"What did you plan on sending to him?"

"That's none of your business."

He glares. "Like hell it isn't. If you jeopardize Tobias and

Stella's safety, I'll ensure you regret it. Or maybe you've already contacted him. Did you send him a message and delete it?

"No." I hold my head high. "I haven't contacted him."

"But you want to." He scrolls through my screen, probably checking past messages that would clearly outline our platonic relationship. "You would've if I hadn't interrupted."

I don't respond. There's no point. He's in a mood I don't want to trifle with.

"What is it about him?" he murmurs. "What could you possibly find attractive in such a pathetic man? I thought you were smarter than that."

I keep my lips shut, not indulging his jealousy spiral.

"Maybe I should keep this." He holds up the phone, taunting me. "Just in case you're tempted to get in contact with him again."

"Just in case I'm tempted?" I raise a brow. "Or just to appease your jealousy?" He needs to get this out of his system. I may have used my partner as a shield, but we can no longer afford the distraction. "Keep the phone if you think it's the only way you can get between me and Easton."

"Oh, I could do a lot of things aside from taking away your phone, Nis. Trust me."

I start toward the hall. "I don't doubt it. But right here, right now, it's your frantic attempt to stop me talking to someone who threatens you." I pause in the doorway and glance at him over my shoulder.

"Do *not* contact him again while you're with me," he warns.

"And if I do?" It's such a stupid question. Taunting. Provoking. I can't help it.

"If you do?" He swings around, storms toward me, not stopping until I'm backed into the wooden threshold. He pins me with his body—no hands, just hips. And eyes. God, those captivating eyes.

He breathes heavily, the rise and fall of his chest brushing against mine.

There are no more taunts left in me. Only heat. Desire.

I ache to drop this charade. I burn with the need to kiss him.

I sink my teeth into my bottom lip to soothe the tingle, only increasing my suffering when his gaze lowers to my mouth.

Memories from Greece haunt me. The flashbacks of pleasure and passion weaken my knees.

"You might be with him, but you still need me." He pockets my cell. "You fucking want me, Nissa."

I close my eyes, hoping he'll bridge the connection and praying he won't. My desire is potent enough to push the air from my lungs, leaving me starved for oxygen.

"You're with him." He leans closer. "But I'm the one who makes you burn."

It's true. Not the being with Easton part, but the burning. The flames lick higher with every passing second. Scorching. Scarring.

My hands find his pecs. I don't know how. I didn't put them there. I couldn't have. Some unknown force has my limbs working without my direction, tangling my fingers in the silken material of his shirt.

"Say it," he growls. "Fucking tell me you want me."

I shake my head.

I won't.

I refuse.

"Have it your way."

His heat vanishes, my arms falling back to my side as he retreats.

I swallow, desperate for the heat to return. The energy. The life. But he doesn't slow his pace.

"Cole." I push from the threshold and grab his arm.

He turns willingly, his menacing frame seeming so much bigger when I'm practically begging for his attention. He glares down at me, nostrils flaring.

I don't fight it any more. I go to him, surrendering, raising onto the tips of my toes to plaster my mouth against his.

I expect a refusal. At least a fight. Instead, his hands claim me. Tight in my hair. Harsh against my hip.

He walks into me, leading me backward, slamming my ass into the wall as his mouth devours mine.

I can't breathe. Can't think.

There's only sensation. Mindless, consuming sensation that starts in my toes and ends at my lips.

The feelings I held for him in Greece come flooding back. Not just the passion, but the connection. The emotion. The unbearable devotion.

My heart yearns for more as he grabs my waist and lifts me, forcing my legs to circle his hips as he grinds me into the wall. The friction is heaven and hell. Relief and increased torture.

One of his hands lowers and he fumbles with something. His belt? His zipper?

I'm about to pull away, panicked at the possibility of him attempting to remove clothes, when he deepens the kiss, making me clutch at his shoulders for support.

I gasp against his mouth. Mewl into the connection.

I claw at his suit. Scratch and tug.

The trap of mindlessness has reeled me in, closing me into its cocoon. I don't care. Not anymore. I just want this. *Only* this.

Someone clears their throat nearby and I gasp, suddenly pushing instead of pulling, shoving instead of yanking.

"I should've brought a hose." Hunter glares at me. "I didn't expect to find you two at it like dogs."

Cole retreats slowly, waiting for me to find my feet. "What do you want?"

"Room service is here. But it looks as though you're already enjoying an unhealthy snack." Hunter continues to visually berate me for long seconds while the scent of deep-fried food fills the space in my lungs where intoxicating aftershave once lived.

"Keep your mouth shut," Cole warns. "We'll be there in a minute."

Hunter scoffs yet follows the command, marching down the hall.

As soon as his back is turned, I quit fighting the need to heave in deep breaths, my cheeks flaming red-hot.

I don't know whether to feel ashamed or relieved over finally giving in.

"You should eat." Cole turns away from me, lowering his attention to my cell now cradled in his hand, his fingers tapping the screen.

"What are you doing?" I step closer, attempting to see, but he hands over the phone, giving me a clear view of the new message he sent to Easton.

A fucking video.

"What have you done?" I snatch the device and play the recording, feeling all the euphoric goodness slide from my soul one slow inch at a time.

"I'm claiming what's mine." He walks away as I watch myself on the screen, my lips plastered to Cole's, my hands clutching his shoulders.

He recorded us.

He fucking recorded us and sent it to Easton.

"You son of a bitch." I storm after him. My chest tightens with the betrayal. My heart beats in a rigorous frenzy at the thought of the repercussions. "Why the hell would you do that?"

"I already told you." He keeps walking, his stride confident, his shoulders strong and sure. "Now he knows the truth."

"The truth?" I scream. "No, this doesn't show the truth. It doesn't tell him how much of a fucking thoughtless, psychopathic idiot you are."

I throw my cell at him, my rage increasing when he easily leans out of the projectile's path. The phone ricochets off the wall, clapping to the tile floor.

"You're a fucking asshole," I choke out.

He inclines his head. "Yes. But you already knew that before you threw yourself at me."

I gape, stuck for words, filled with shame.

He continues into the living room, the attention of everyone falling on us as I follow close behind.

I want to strangle him. To fucking slaughter.

But he isn't wrong.

I threw myself at him. *I* latched on to his shoulders like a monkey starved of affection.

"You're a sick son of a bitch." My words are barely audible. "You deliberately—"

"Stop it." Layla raises her voice. "Both of you, just *stop*." Tears streak her cheeks as she glances between us, wide-eyed. "Stella is missing and you two are wasting time arguing. Where is my daughter, Cole? Why can't you put as much energy into finding her as you do fighting this woman?"

Benji wraps a hand around her waist. "It's okay. He's—"

"*No*, it's *not* okay." She steps out of reach. "None of this is okay. Not that those innocent children are missing. Or that we're in this godforsaken city waiting to hear from a man we know nothing about. And it sure as hell isn't okay that we've got a Fed here watching our every move. I don't even know what I can and can't say, because I'm waiting for her to arrest me."

"She's not going to arrest you." Cole strolls for the mass of food on the coffee table and picks up a chip from a pile of nachos. "Sit down. Eat. Try to relax."

"Don't dictate to me. Don't for one second think I don't hold you accountable. *You* made us attend that function at the restaurant. *You* gave Robert the opportunity to attack." She jabs a finger in his direction as everyone remains quiet. "*You* promised all of us we would be safe."

He eats the chip, dusts his hands, and takes her vehemence without a flinch.

I just wish I couldn't sense his underlying torment.

"Are you finished?" His face remains impassive, his tone perfectly balanced.

"You know what? Anissa's right." She flicks a glance my way before returning her attention to him. "You're a fucking ass—"

"Yes, I'm a fucking asshole. I'm fucking responsible. The fate of those kids rests on my fucking shoulders." There's no waver in his voice, only an increase in volume that vibrates into my chest. "I fucking know all that, Layla. But have you ever wondered if this would've happened if you hadn't sold me out to Robert?"

"She did what?" Keira gasps.

I have no idea what he's talking about. And the only response comes from a subtle vibration of a silenced cell.

"I'll let your sister fill you in." Cole starts toward me, reaching into his pants pocket to pull out his phone. "Emmanuel," he says in greeting. "Where the fuck are you?"

15

————

COLE

I SHUT MYSELF INTO THE MAIN BATHROOM, CLENCHING THE CELL IN MY fist.

"I'm in Sacramento, son. Have you arrived yet?"

"I arrived a fucking hour ago. I've been waiting for your call. I don't have your damn number."

"Ahh, yes. I forgot my details are blocked. Sorry. Technology isn't my friend."

Bullshit. Fucking bullshit.

"Where are you? Where are the kids?" I pace, not appreciating his chilled tone. He's too relaxed to be concerned for their safety. He's too fucking smug.

I don't trust this piece of shit. Not in the slightest.

"They are here with me. Safe and well. To tell you the truth, my wife has become quite smitten. It's been a long time since young ones were under our roof. She's enjoying this immensely."

"Where are they?" I repeat.

"As I said, they are safe. But still very tired. It's best if they remain with us for the night. That way, I get to indulge my wife's maternal instincts. She was a nurse, you see, and she's making sure they're under constant observation due to the sedatives. You should enjoy your time in Sacramento while you wait."

And there it is—the thinly disguised threat.

The extended hostage situation.

The thickening of his plan.

I pace faster. Harder. I gnash my teeth and pray I have the patience to kill this motherfucker slowly. "As you can imagine," I grate, "my family are beside themselves with worry."

"I understand." His accent thickens "But there is no need. My wife assures me the children are perfectly healthy. They have been laughing and playing. Their smiles are bright when they're with us. We may not be blood, but my friendship with your father ensures we are family."

I press my closed fist against my forehead, pushing harder and harder. "Emmanuel, I insist—"

"Insisting will not help me against my wife's wrath if I return these precious gifts from God too soon." He chuckles. "Trust me, they are in good hands. They are happy. Tomorrow morning we will meet, and they will tell you all about the lovely time they had. Until then, enjoy yourself, Mr. Torian."

"No. This isn't—"

The call disconnects. The hold on my anger goes with it.

I roar, slamming my fist into the tiled wall.

He's starting a fucking war. In unfamiliar territory. I have no leverage here. No assets.

"Cole?" Anissa's voice carries from outside the bathroom. "What is it? What happened?"

I close my eyes and pinch the bridge of my nose. I need to think. I need to figure out how the fuck to get a hold of this asshole.

My cell vibrates. A text message illuminates the screen. A cell number.

What the hell is Emmanuel playing at?

I click the details as the door opens, and connect a call.

Nissa stares at me, one gentle brow raised in question while I plaster the phone to my ear and listen to the monotonous ring.

"Mr. Torian," the fucker answers. "Did you forget something?"

Jesus *fucking* Christ. He's entirely cavalier.

"Listen to me, you son of a bitch." I have to expel all my breath and drag it back in to stop myself from detonating. "I want those kids returned to me. *Now*. Not tomorrow. Not after your wife plays Mary fucking Poppins. *Now*. Tell me where they are."

There's a pause. A frantic beat of silence before his kind tone rockets my rage. "Mr. Torian, your lack of patience is quite disconcerting after I've gone out of my way to help you. But I understand your anxiety. I will send you some more pictures of them to ease your concerns."

Fuck him.

Fuck this pathetic game.

"I don't care about pictures or your fucking wife. If you don't tell me where you are, I'll—"

"You'll what?" Steel enters his tone. "Please, do not mistake my kindness for weakness, child. I do not take well to threats."

There's a pause. One that I can't fill.

I have no power. No fucking move to make.

"I am a man of my word," he continues. "You will see these children tomorrow. But not a moment before. Now please do not call again unless it is urgent. It is not healthy for me to become agitated by such unnecessary concerns."

The line disconnects.

My vision darkens. I raise my arm to throw the phone.

"Cole, don't." Nissa runs at me, grabbing my hand to pry the cell from my fingers. "You need it."

What I need are answers. What I need are those fucking kids.

My breathing quickens. Mindlessness takes over. I can't think clearly through the rapid-fire thoughts screaming in my ears.

My fingers itch to squeeze around that bastard's throat. My arms throb with the need to hear bones crack. I want blood.

"What happened?" Anissa pockets the cell and stares at me in concern.

No, it's pity.

"Nothing." I walk around her and stalk from the bathroom. Every goddamn step toward the living room is a struggle while she remains hot on my heels. What's worse is Layla's face when I enter the room.

She rushes for me. "What did he say? Where do we go to get them?"

I ignore her, meeting Sarah and Keira's gaze over her shoulder. "All the women, out."

"What?" Layla stops before me and grabs my upper arms. "No. I'm not going anywhere."

I sidestep and pin Sarah with a scowl. "Where's the other room you booked?"

"The next level down…" Her voice is hesitant.

"Then get going. Hunt can update you later."

"No." Layla follows after me, still clinging to my arms. "You need to tell me what's going on. Are they okay? Oh, God, did he hurt them?"

"They're both fine." I refuse to meet her gaze. The guilt is suffocating. "Now go."

"*No*," she screams in my face, slapping a hand across my cheek.

I take the impact without a flinch. I prefer the sting to the ache in my chest.

"Fuck." Benji runs for her as she continues her assault.

Sarah and Keira, too.

They grab her arms as she thrashes and kicks, cursing my name and vowing to never forgive me.

I don't back down. Don't even falter. I lock all the punishing shit inside. Keep it buried deep as I clench every muscle in my body.

"Make sure she's sedated until morning," I direct to Hunter, who remains unmoved on the sofa, throwing a French fry in his mouth as if the suffering of my family is just another fucking Friday on his work calendar.

I wish I was as immune as him. As capable of shutting off emotion.

"No." Layla bucks in Benji's hold. "You can't do this."

"Go." I jerk my chin at Hunter, then turn my attention to Decker, then Benji. "Make sure they're all calm before coming back. The last thing I need is a scene."

They nod, Hunter and Decker stalking toward my sisters like enforcers, wordlessly demanding obedience.

I don't hear a protest from Keira. I feel it instead. Her judgmental gaze bores into the side of my head, slicing deep as she's ushered toward the hall in my periphery.

Layla doesn't need to tell me she will never forgive me for this. I knew she wouldn't as soon as I found Stella's empty bed. This situation has fractured our foundations. Permanently. There's no recovering from the damage that's already been done.

"I hate you, Cole," Layla screams down the hall. "Let me see my daughter."

The door clicks shut moments later. The muffled sounds of my sister's wails haunt me until she leaves the penthouse floor.

I close my eyes against the deafening silence. I breathe deep of the stillness that feels sinister instead of welcoming.

The gentle pad of footsteps approaches. I stiffen farther at the potential of another bitch slap.

"What about me?" Anissa asks softly. "Do you want me to leave?"

I scoff.

I don't get her. I fucking don't.

She wants me, then she doesn't.

She needs me, then shoves me away.

One minute, she hates me. The next, she's all over me just like on our last night in Greece.

I can't figure her out. I doubt I ever will. I think that's half of the appeal.

"Do whatever you like." I open my eyes and scan the room until I find liquor bottles perched on a golden cart near the television. Then it's full steam ahead until the scotch is in my hand, a glass in my fist, and the burning liquid is flowing down my throat.

"Is that a good idea?" She comes up beside me, wreaking havoc with my nerve endings.

"Don't mother me." I pour another finger and throw it back.

"You're exhausted. You're panicked." She reaches for my arm and grips my suit. "Alcohol isn't the answer."

"Then what is?" I snap. "What the fuck is the answer, Nis? Because I'm clueless here."

She takes my fury with the raise of her chin. So confident. So composed.

She's a force I want to lose myself in.

Drown in.

"What happened?" Her hand falls to her side. "What did he say?"

I huff a sarcastic laugh. "That him and his wife are having such a lovely time with my niece and brother that they're going to keep them a little while longer." I fling my arms wide in frustration. "Ain't that fucking nice."

"What do you mean? Is he refusing to release them? Did he threaten you?"

"He's not doing shit. Not threatening, but certainly not playing by the fucking rules. He's messing with me. Pushing. Just wait until I get the chance to push back."

There's a buzz of a cell. *My* cell. Coming from her pants pocket.

She pulls out the device, then meets my gaze. "Can I?"

"By all means." I reach out, unlocking the screen with my fingerprint. She can't fuck up this situation any more than I already have.

I refill my glass as she focuses on the screen.

"I don't understand his strategy." She raises the cell to me, showing a picture of Stella and Tobias in a fancy kitchen, the counter smothered in flour, their hands and faces marred with white smudges as a grey-haired woman grins behind them.

The kids wear new clothes. Fresh. Brand name. Expensive.

But it's their faces that speak the truth.

Even though they smile, there's no joy in their eyes. They know they're being held prisoner. They understand the seriousness of the situation and are playing along.

I look away, my throat tightening. My eyes burn.

I'm going to cause unfathomable bloodshed. I'm going to maim and torture and slaughter. I'll kill every son of a bitch Emmanuel knows.

I slam my glass down on the cart and grab the scotch, drinking heavily from the bottle in the hopes it will dilute the venom in my veins.

"Please stop," Anissa begs. "Please, Cole. I need you to help me with this. I need you to make me understand."

I guzzle the burning liquid until it runs down my chin, the alcohol dripping onto my shirt. My shoes. The carpet.

"Cole." My name is a warning this time. "You're better than this."

I almost choke over her lie and lower the bottle to turn to her. "Am I? Am I fucking better, Nis?"

She snaps rigid at my harsh tone.

Fuck.

I throw the scotch. It smashes against the far wall. Glass scatters, the destruction giving me no satisfaction. "Layla's right. *I* did this. *I'm* responsible."

I stalk toward Anissa, getting in her face. There's no point putting off the inevitable. She needs to commit to hating me. I want her to despise me as much as I despise myself. To loathe me. To fucking run.

"I'm the reason they were taken. I'm the one who has to live with the guilt of the nightmares they'll endure until the day they die." I let out a bark of laughter. "And that's if they live at all. Who knows what this sick fuck is capable of?"

She reaches for me. "It's not your fault."

"Fuck off." I back away. "You know it is. It's just more ammunition for you to pile against me."

"No. You're not responsible, Cole. You didn't do this. You would never willingly place those kids in danger."

"But I did." I swing around to the alcohol cart and reach for the gin.

"No more alcohol." She grabs my wrist, holding tight. "Put it down."

"I'm not done."

"Yes, you are." She shoves me sideways, catching me off guard, and places herself between me and the liquor. "You've had enough."

"And you've got a death wish." I bridge the space between us, the heat returning to her eyes as she raises her chin. "Move."

"No." She shuffles her feet apart, taking a fighting stance. "Get a glass of water instead."

"I don't want water." I step toward her.

"Back off." She raises her hands and aims them at my chest.

I snatch her wrist, but she does the same, snapping her palm around my forearm, then lunging in a flurry of movement. She twists my arm behind my back and shoves me face-first into the wall.

My cheek slams hard into the plaster, the pain holding no comparison to the agonizing punch to my pride.

All I can do is laugh.

I laugh because a woman has dared to manhandle me this way.

I laugh because the one person I want by my side is the same person who can easily defeat me.

But most of all, I laugh because despite it all, I wouldn't want anyone else here to witness me at my lowest. Nobody but her. A fucking Fed.

"You need to calm down." Her voice is soothing near my ear as she gentles her grip, no longer threatening to tear muscle.

She's all warmth and stability. Perfection and excellence. Even now, when I'm drowning in defeat, I want her. *Need* her.

I crave the goodness to wash all the suffering away.

"No more drinking," she continues. "No more games. You have to sit down and tell me what happened on that phone call. And while we're working on a plan, we're also going to figure out when you can get some sleep. Your mind has to rest."

My mind and my soul.

I'm so sick of this life. Of the betrayal. The sabotage. I'm ready to burn the world to the ground, along with everyone in it.

Except her.

I'd keep Anissa around, if only to listen to her tell me how much of an asshole I am.

"Are you listening?" Her voice is low. Too fucking gentle and caring for the hard-ass bitch I know.

"Yeah." I shove backward, catching her unaware, and duck to spin out of the twist to my arm. Then I'm all over her, foot to foot, my hand claiming her throat.

She gasps, her eyes widening, her fingers moving to my threatening hold.

I've done this before, felt her delicate neck in my grip. In Greece. In passion. This moment isn't overly different. Her eyes blaze with heat. Her lips part in shock, but also in that sweet, submissive seduction.

Her lack of fight is all I need to tell me she wants this as much as I do.

She craves my control. The mastery—even though it's now clear I'm a master of nothing and no one.

She aches for me to fuck her. Practically screams it through the silence.

My dick throbs, already agonizingly hard.

It wouldn't take much. A yank of a zipper. A tear of her underwear. I'd sink deep before she could form a protest. But we both know she wouldn't anyway.

Those eyes don't lie. Maybe to others. Never to me.

This woman is mine. She has been from the moment I laid eyes on her. And I'd thought I'd been enough. I'd mistakenly thought my concept of right and wrong was better than hers.

Now, my well-defined superiority is crashing around me.

"It's normal to be emotional," she whispers. "But you have to move past it. Push it aside. We need to think strategically. And I can't do that until you tell me what happened."

She's still thinking of those kids. With my hand around her throat and my restraint threadbare, she remains focused on the children I put at risk.

"Stop torturing yourself." Her fingers slide from my hand, her palms moving to cup my face. "Jesus, Cole, I can't stand to see you this way."

This way. This weak.

I walk into her, leading her backward to the elegant dining table, not stopping until her butt bumps into the wood.

"Tell me what you see." I snarl an inch from her lips, inhaling her heat. "Tell me all the shitty things you feel when you look at me."

She sighs, her shoulders slumping. "It's not like that. We just…" She shakes her head despite the restriction of my hand. "We're enemies." The frantic lick of her lips tells a different story.

Her body and mind don't match up. Her morals may dictate that we're adversaries, yet the way she physically responds to me is entirely different. Always has been.

I keep my attention on her mouth. "We didn't leave Greece as enemies."

"Like hell we didn't. We arrived as enemies and left the same way." Color floods her cheeks. "The middle may have contained some shady decisions and a wealth of regret, but that's to be expected through all the adrenaline."

"Shady decisions and regret?" I meet her gaze, stroking my index finger along the sensitive column of her neck. "Is that all you remember about us fucking?"

She breaks eye contact.

"Tell me." I tighten my grip. "I want to know exactly what you think when you recall me being inside you."

She shudders and the fragile tremble rocks right through me.

"We were made to fuck." I lean closer, brushing my stubbled cheek over her perfectly smooth one, my lips near her ear. "Admit no other man has moved you like I have."

"You're looking for a distraction, Cole. That's all this is. You need an outlet." She pulls back an inch and meets my gaze. "You don't want to think about what's really happening."

No, I need her.

I've never been more reliant on someone in my entire life.

This is about us. About forming an unbreakable alliance that will help bring my family back together. It's about the future and a shaky past. It's about strength and power and pride.

I brush my lips over her cheek. "I'll tell you all about that phone call once you admit you want to be with me."

She straightens, her chin jutting higher.

"Tell me I haunt your dreams." Like she haunts mine. "Tell me how no other man compares." Like no woman ever could. "Tell me how you want to commit to me even though our lives are worlds apart."

She stiffens and I pull back to see her glaring in fury.

It's not the reaction I expected. But I've never been able to predict this woman perfectly every time. It's one of her many highlights.

"What exactly did my shrink tell you?" She grates through clenched teeth. "How much do you know?"

I smirk, rerunning those questions in my mind to hear her truth.

I haunt her dreams.

No other man compares.

She wants to commit to me.

That shrink had given me very little information. There wasn't much other than a contempt-filled explanation that Nissa continued to beg for a Stockholm diagnosis to excuse her lingering feelings for me.

"Your secrets are safe, little fox." I part her thighs with a shove of my knee and sink between her legs. "I'm not the bastard you think I am."

"Yes, you are." It's a weak protest. Feeble at best.

I reach between us with my free hand, finding the waistband of her pants to release the button with a flick of my fingers.

"Cole," she pleads. "Don't."

This time there's strength in her voice. Panic. She nudges forward, probably attempting to free herself, but all it does is bring her closer. Hip to hip. Chest to chest.

Her pulse beats harder beneath my fingers. Her breathing increases. And those breasts. *Fuck.* With each pant they brush against me, turning my already hard dick to stone.

"You want me," I whisper.

"That doesn't make it right." She swallows, her throat working overtime beneath my palm. "None of this is right."

"We've discussed right and wrong in the past." I hold her gaze. "And I've convinced you your perception was misguided before. This is just another example."

She blinks back at me, shaking her head. "I can't want this. You just sent a goddamn video of us to my partner."

"But you *do* want it." I lower her zipper, the slow grate of friction loud between us.

She mewls. Whimpers.

I slide my hand beneath the elastic of her panties, expecting her to protest as I delve deeper, but there's nothing.

No demand.

No threat.

Only the frantic grip of her fingers clinging to the arm at her throat as if she's battling the desire to beg for more.

She's done fighting me and the realization is invigorating. Soul cleansing.

I glide my hand lower, past her mound, to her opening and

groan at the slickness awaiting me. She's wet as fuck, her greedy pussy clenching as my fingers part her folds.

"Oh, God." The words are a barely audible prayer as she closes her eyes and clings tighter to my wrist. "We can't do this."

"Yes, we can." I tease her entrance, stroking back and forth.

She shakes her head. "We shouldn't."

"This is fate." I inch my fingers inside her, slowly delving as deep as the restriction of her pants will allow.

"I've tried so hard not to want this," she whispers. "It's not right, Cole."

"It's right for us." I stroke her, making her hips roll. "Perfection isn't meant to be easy."

"Perfection?" She grinds her hips, her nails digging deep into my wrist. "How can you think that?"

"Because it's what you are. It's what *we* are."

She pants. Clings. Shudders.

I press my thumb to her clit and the resulting gasp is heaven to my ears. I'd give anything to fuck her right now. To have my cock inspire those gasps. But I don't deserve it. Not yet.

"Cole," she whispers. "I don't want to do this."

My chest squeezes with the kick to my ego. Deep down I know she's only protesting to save face once all this is said and done. It's a defense mechanism. A shield.

She needs to think this is my fault. My doing. That she had no choice.

I won't allow it.

"Then push me away, Nissa." I place my nose an inch from hers, staring her down. "Stop grinding against my fingers and walk."

Her teeth sink into her lower lip. Her brows furrow. Her eyes plead.

"Or simply enjoy what's meant to be." I inch closer, hovering my lips a breath from hers. "Take what I willingly give."

Her gasps increase. The buck of her hips, too. She grinds against my fingers, driving me to madness with her desire, when a heavy knock sounds at the door.

Fuck.

"Oh, shit." She scrambles like a feral cat.

"Stop," I growl. "We're not done."

"No." She tries to pry my fingers from her neck. "There's someone at the door."

"They can wait. We're not finished here until you come."

She shakes her head rapidly. "I can't."

"You fucking can. And you will." I back her harder against the table, clench my grip tighter around her throat, and work those digits in her pussy like we're seconds from death. "You're going to fucking come, Nis. No woman of mine is left wanting."

I plaster my lips to hers, tasting her, devouring her. She moans, melting her tongue against mine.

The knock sounds again, but we don't stop. I deepen the kiss. Press harder against her clit. Her pussy drenches my palm while her core clamps tighter around me as Hunter yells for me to, "Open the fucking door."

"Come," I demand in her mouth. "Fucking come, little fox, or I'll let them in here and they can watch."

"I can't." She shakes her head.

"You know I'm not bluffing."

Of course I am.

I would never allow another man to see her like this.

Her pleasure is mine. I own these gasps.

But my men have a key. If they grow concerned about my lack of response, they'll quit waiting for permission to enter and simply storm in.

"Fucking come." I reclaim her mouth, squeeze her neck, making her struggle for air.

She trembles. Scratches.

The knocking continues. My cell vibrates in my pocket.

This time, Decker yells, "What the hell is going on, Cole?"

Nissa's trembling intensifies. She shudders. Claws at my wrists.

"Cole," she pleads. "Please, Cole."

"Tell me what you need."

She responds by releasing my arms to circle her hands around my neck, dragging me closer. She hypnotizes me with her frantic kiss. Tortures me with her demand for nearness.

Then soothes me with the release.

She comes undone in my hands, whispering my name, holding me so fucking tight I never want her to let go.

She's the most beautiful thing I've ever seen. Ever felt. Always wanted.

I love her.

That's all there is now—my obsessive worship and the inability to walk away.

Her arms fall from around my neck, her shoulders relaxing. Her eyes slowly blink open, her breathing remaining a frantic mess.

I release her throat and hope to escape to the kitchen before her remorse hits. But I'm not fast enough. My fingers are sliding from her pussy as regret stares back at me.

"Don't look at me like that." I pull a handkerchief from my pocket and wipe my hand. "The time for second-guessing is over. We're done fighting this. You hear me?"

16

ANISSA

I'm still in a mindless trance of reflection and self-loathing, leaned against the dining room table, when Cole opens the penthouse door.

It isn't until Hunter stalks into the living room, his gaze narrowing on me in a new level of heightened spite, that I realize how I must look.

Disheveled. In a post-orgasm haze.

Shit.

I shove to my feet, my head high as I walk toward him and the banked up wall of men behind him to maneuver through the crowd and into the hall. I scoop my discarded cell from the tile floor, thankful I didn't break it in my fit of rage, and shut myself into the main bathroom to stare at my blissed-out reflection in the mirror.

My cheeks are pink, my lips bright red. And the marks on my neck from Cole's restricting grip stand out like a brutal reminder of my flaws.

I touch the flaming skin, still feeling him there, his hand around my throat, the threatening yet erotic grip inundating me with adrenaline.

There's something sick about how much I enjoyed the menace of that hold. Something twisted and unhinged about the undeniable thrill. It's made all the worse when the man inspiring the nirvana is entirely capable of strangulation.

I don't doubt he could kill me.

Maybe that's the appeal. The danger. The thin line between life and death.

Not only do I see flashbacks of what just happened, I feel them. Cole's touch remains tangible, raising goose bumps, stealing breath.

I use the facilities, my cheeks flaming hotter at the slickness drenched between my thighs. I need a change of underwear.

I need a goddamn lobotomy.

Even with the self-loathing and shame, there's still a tingle of exhilaration emanating through my chest. It's a silent demand for more. A hunger that can't be sated by a lone orgasm or stifled by remorse.

How can that even happen after everything Cole's done? Why do I still feel this way when moments earlier he'd humiliated me and risked my career by sending Easton that video?

I should hate Cole.

I *need* to hate him. Yet, I fucking don't. There's only an agonizing ache where anger should be as I unlock my cell and stare at the blank home screen.

The radio silence from Easton says it all. I can't even imagine what he's thinking right now. I don't want to.

I navigate to my text messages, then Easton's folder. I prepare to watch the video again but pause at the tiny red icon beside the message.

Error. Message not sent. Turn on cell data.

I stare in amazement.

The message didn't go through. Cole turned off my data?

He took the video. Prepared a message. But deliberately made sure it wouldn't send.

Why? To trigger my fear? To assert his authority?

Regardless of the reasons, I'm thankful. Almost overwhelmed with relief at Cole's exposed decency.

I delete the evidence capable of ruining my life and ignore the shake of my hands as I turn the data back on.

Notifications of missed calls blink onto the screen. A text from Easton, too.

I'm worried about you. We need to talk. Please call me.

My heart pangs. I can clearly visualize his concern. His face would be somber. His eyes gentle. But I don't crave his sweetness. Not his affection or his attention.

All for one reason—he's not Cole.

Sorry about earlier. I text back. *I'm working on something important. I promise I'll fill you in once this is over. I'm fine. Trust me.*

My moral compass is so far out of whack I don't even feel guilty with the lie that's barely veiled by the truth as I place my cell back in my pocket.

I lean against the basin and stare at myself in the mirror, finger-combing my hair until the freshly fucked look leaves my features. It isn't until I'm completely devoid of adrenaline, lust, and anticipation that I cautiously leave the bathroom, remaining out of sight in the hall to listen to the conversation in the living room.

Cole speaks with authority as he asks for an update on his sister's well-being.

There's a murmur of reply about crying and sedatives. It isn't until Cole cuts back into the conversation, relaying information pertaining to his latest phone conversation with Emmanuel, that I enter the opening of the hall, not caring that I'm in view of Hunter's evil stare.

"He's refusing to let us see them until tomorrow." Cole removes his suit jacket and drapes it over the armrest of a sofa. "He's holding them hostage yet somehow thinks he can downplay the act of war behind false promises and insane excuses."

"What excuses?" Decker asks. "What reason could he possibly have for keeping them from us?"

"Some bullshit about his wife being smitten with the kids and wanting to spend more time with them."

"They could already be dead." Hunter begins to pace beside the wall of glass leading to the balcony, his face stone cold. "He's buying time."

"Jesus." Benji leans forward in his seat at the dining table, elbows on the wood, hands raked into his hair.

He's seated in the same place I'd been earlier, with Cole's hand in my underwear. Panting. Gasping. Now the position is filled with such sickening mourning I can barely stand my own degradation.

"They're not dead. I have a photo." Cole reaches into his pants pocket, coming up empty. "My cell…" His attention raises, his eyes finding mine. "You have my phone."

I nod, approaching him to hold out the device.

He's in business mode now. Stern. Sterile.

There's none of the dominant heat in his expression from before, and there shouldn't be. I shouldn't even be looking for it. I don't know why my head is still back there. Lathered in seduction.

I'm broken.

He takes the cell, navigates to his gallery, then shows the screen to Benji. "They at least made it to Emmanuel like he promised."

I start toward Benji as he pushes from the table, his steps frantic as he snatches the device to stare at it cradled in his hands.

"She looks scared." He shoots a glance at Cole. "She's fucking petrified."

I pause a few feet away, not wanting to encroach on the private moment, while also itching to catch sight of the evidence. "Can I see?"

Benji continues to focus on the image, his eyes hollow, his suffering soul deep.

"Please?" I hold out a hand. "Just a quick look."

Hunter huffs at my request. Decker scoffs. But Benji reluctantly hands the device over and returns his attention to Cole. "What do we do?"

The men continue their conversation as I scrutinize the digital image.

The setting would seem wholesome to the ignorant eye. Even loving. Two young children with a doting elderly woman. Benji is right, though. Stella's eyes are haunted, while Tobias seems almost angry beneath his fake smile.

Their innocent faces are enough to siphon any lingering desire from my veins and put me back on track.

I scan every pixel of the photograph, painstakingly noting the finer details. "This image is important." I raise my voice above their chatter and meet Cole's gaze. "Have you checked for the GPS details embedded in the file?"

"There's not much point," Decker replies. "The last pic didn't have any. He knows how to delete the information."

I hand Cole's phone back to him, our fingers slightly brushing. "We still need to check. And regardless of the outcome, there's a wealth of information in this picture. We might be able to pinpoint the skyline in the background. The children have been cleaned up, too. They've been given new clothes. They're even wearing T-shirts that expose their forearms, showing no signs of bruising or abuse."

"You think they're okay?" Benji asks.

"I think they're being taken care of," I correct him. "Stella's eyes aren't red, so she hasn't been crying. Yes, she's scared. But that's only natural. The kitchen is clean apart from the flour, which alludes to a healthy environment. The woman with them is showing her face, which means she doesn't see this as incriminating evidence."

"Are you saying that they might actually be keeping the kids from us because they seriously want to play happy families?" Hunter scrunches his nose in disgust. "That's insane."

"It's a possibility."

"I don't give a shit about possibilities. I just want Stella and Tobias back home." Cole taps on his phone and seconds later, a chorus of vibrations hum through the room. "I just sent you all a copy of the image. Study it. Dissect it. I don't care what it takes. We're going to work over every last detail until we find them."

The room falls silent, everyone focusing on their cells, staring blankly or tapping at the screen.

"I'm going to go back downstairs and get my laptop." Decker hobbles to his feet. "I won't take long."

We work autonomously for hours. Hunter spends his time on the balcony, speaking on his phone. Decker is constantly focused on his computer, with Benji acting like an eager assistant at his side. Cole makes calls, asking for favors from undisclosed people while demanding compliance from others.

I try to keep busy, too, but it's hard. All the resources I've come to depend on in situations like this aren't available. Normally, I could obtain warrants for phone records or credit card statements.

I could order cell traces and hopefully get a tower ping or two to narrow down a location.

Instead, I spend the entire afternoon familiarizing myself with the Costa family, delving through their company's social media to fixate on the few personal posts about Emmanuel and his children.

They seem close.

A regular hard-working family.

Their involvement in this hostage situation doesn't make sense. It's careless when they're such high-profile people.

The sun has begun to set when Hunter comes back inside. "Costa flew into the same private airport we did." He slumps onto the sofa and places his cell on the coffee table. "And it wasn't only him and his psycho wife. Two of their three sons were on the flight, along with three of their security detail."

"Reconfirming their preparation for battle," Decker mutters. "I've come close to figuring out their location from the skyline in the image." He turns the laptop screen to face Cole and I on the opposite sofa. "They're somewhere in this area." He shows a map with a highlighted circle encapsulating more than a handful of blocks. "Or they were earlier. But it doesn't mean shit when each of these city blocks would house God knows how many people."

"Can you narrow it down?" Cole massages the back of his neck. "He'd be staying somewhere expensive. Cut out all the noise and focus on penthouse suites or pricey short-stay apartments."

"To what fucking end, though?" Hunter asks. "We might narrow that list to fifty places but then what? We go searching one by one? That'll take all week, when this asshole is meant to be handing them over tomorrow anyway."

"As tough as it's going to be, I think we need to wait this out." Decker closes his laptop and places it on the sofa beside him. "The ball is in Costa's court. There's nothing we can do."

I don't voice my agreement, but it's there, burning a hole in my chest.

"We're dealing with kids now," he continues. "Even if we did know the location, we couldn't storm in there. I won't be a part of a risky operation where one stray bullet will take a child's life. I say we call it a night. Try to get some sleep. We'll reassess in the morning."

"We can't just do nothing." Benji glances between Hunter and Cole, his eyes widened with panic.

The heartbeats of silence press in like a closing vault.

Nobody has the correct answer because there isn't one.

The only choices now are to keep digging with no certainty that information will even help once we find it. Or rest and recuperate so we're ready when Emmanuel makes arrangements in the morning. *If* he makes arrangements.

Cole lets out a long huff of breath, his torment sinking under my skin. He doesn't want to say it. He doesn't want to do nothing while Stella and Tobias are suffering. But he needs sleep. They all do.

"Decker's right." I stare at Cole as his gaze raises to mine, the pain of his defeat hitting me full force. "We're better off getting some rest. You're going to need it to think clearly tomorrow."

"No." Benji pushes to his feet, shaking his head. "*No.* We can't quit."

"We're not quitting, man," Decker soothes. "I promise. We're only waiting."

"And while we're waiting, can you imagine what's happening to my daughter? She's with a man aligned with sex traffickers. They could be—" He shakes his head, wincing.

"I'll call him again." Cole stands and pulls out his cell. "I'll ask for more proof of their safety."

"Ask for a video," Hunter interjects. "Demand to speak to Stella."

"Don't demand." I approach Cole. "You need to keep a level head. Don't give him a reason to hang up on—"

"Shut the fuck up." Hunter scowls his hatred at me. "We don't need your input."

"I want to speak to her." Benji strides around the sofa, approaching. "Let me talk to my daughter." He reaches for the cell.

Cole broadens his shoulders and straightens to his full height. He transforms from tired and lethargic to territorial and lethal in the blink of an eye. "Get out of my face before I give you what you deserve. I don't care about your wants or needs. My only concern is for those kids."

His vehemence is beyond scathing. It's downright cruel.

"Cole…" His name is whispered from my lips. It's pulled from me in sympathy for a man who is clearly hurting. But I get no response.

The call is made as Cole moves to the main bedroom.

Benji follows.

"Don't step foot in that room," Hunter threatens. "You've pushed your luck too far. There's no more lenience now."

I don't understand why they're hating on Benji. They're treating him like an enemy, not a distraught father.

I glance to Decker for understanding, then Hunter. Both of them scowl at me in return, leveling me with the same contempt. "What's going on?" I ask.

"Mind your own business." Hunter shoves from the sofa and stalks to the kitchen as Cole starts talking in the bedroom.

I switch my attention to the conversation, moving to the doorway alongside Benji to watch Cole pace before the wall of windows.

"I'm being patient," he mutters. "But I need more proof that those kids are okay. I want video or—"

He quits speaking. Stops moving.

"Yes." His chin hikes. "I understand."

He turns toward us and raises a hand, one finger pointed in warning before he lowers the cell and taps the screen. He places the call on speaker, the rustle of unknown sounds rumbling from the phone.

"Uncle Cole?"

The young girl's voice devastates my composure, dragging all the air from my lungs.

"Stella?" Benji gasps.

I grab his arm, taking the curl of Cole's lip as a sign that the rule of necessary distance hasn't changed.

"Be patient," I whisper. "Let him handle this."

"It's me, princess." Cole keeps his tone level. "How are you?"

"I want to go home. Where are you? Where's my mom? Are you coming to get us?"

"We'll be there in the morning. I promise. Are you okay?"

"Yes." One word. No conviction.

It's hard to tell if she's being coerced.

"I don't know what happened." She lowers her voice. "We woke up here and we don't know these people. They say they're friends with Grandpa, but I've never seen them before. Did something happen to Mom and Dad? Is that why we're here?"

Benji jostles his arm, attempting to loosen my grip.

"Please, Benji." I cling to him. "Let Cole handle this."

"Your mom and dad are fine, Stella." Cole remains incredibly strong, not showing an ounce of panic or heartache. He knows exactly how to speak to her fear to strengthen her. "You'll see them tomorrow."

"What about Penny and Uncle Luca? Tobias is worried. Emmanuel said there was an issue last night and that's why he's looking after us, but he won't say what happened. Why haven't you come to get us?"

Benji's face crumples. He grabs my wrist, clinging to me like I'm clinging to him.

"There was an issue." Cole rakes a hand through his hair. "But it's been taken care of. Everyone is okay. There's nothing for you to worry about."

"Then why haven't you come?"

"We are coming, sweetheart. We'll be there tomorrow. Is Emmanuel looking after you? Do you feel safe?"

There's a pause. A frantic heartbeat where my fear overrides comprehension.

"Yes." She stalls again. "Mrs. Costa has been watching movies with us all afternoon. We've eaten cakes and pastries and ice cream. We had pizza for dinner."

Cole's gaze meets mine. His eyes are questioning. Hopefully pleading.

He wants to know if I believe her. If I'm hearing anything he's not. And I honestly can't tell.

I'm too invested now. Emotion has taken over my intelligence.

I shake my head and shrug, mouthing, *"I don't know."*

"Is anyone else with you?" he asks. "Other men, or—"

A rustle emanates from the speaker.

"I think that's enough for tonight," Emmanuel's voice cuts in. "The children are tired and need to get ready for bed. I will contact you in the morning to make arrangements. Good night, Mr. Torian."

"Wait." Benji runs for Cole. "I'm here, baby. You're daddy's here."

There's no answer.

No response.

No noise at all.

"He disconnected the call." Cole's jaw ticks as he pockets the cell, his attention focused over my shoulder. "What are your thoughts?"

I turn, finding Hunter and Decker standing a few feet behind me, their faces solemn.

"She didn't seem under duress." Decker limps closer. "And I don't think a kid that age would follow a script if she feared for her life."

"She's our little ball-busting princess," Hunter adds. "She would've screamed the house down at the first sound of your voice if they were hurting her."

"Unless she's already been beaten into submission," Benji snaps. "How can you give up on her so easily?"

"We're not giving up on anyone." Hunter speaks through clenched teeth. "And before you go blaming anything else on us, you might want to take the time to remember why she was taken in the first place."

"You know why she was taken?" I glance at Cole. "Why haven't I been told? That information could be—"

"We're calling it a night." He speaks over me. "I trust that Stella and Tobias are okay for now. Hire another suite. Eat and get some rest. Tomorrow is going to be another long day."

"Fuck you." Benji continues toward the hall. "Fuck you all for giving up on my daughter." He yanks the front door wide and slams it on his way out.

"Is someone going to tell me what's happening?" I glance from one man to the next, taking in their stubborn resolve to shut me out.

"Go after him." Cole jerks his chin at Hunter. "Make sure he doesn't cause any trouble."

"What about me?" Decker asks as Hunter stalks for the door. "What do you want me to do?"

"Update the women. Keep them calm. Make sure they have dinner and an early night."

"Can I opt for being shot in the leg again instead? Don't get me wrong, I can handle Keira, but Layla? And Sarah? Those two aren't going to appreciate sitting on their hands for another fourteen hours. They'll tear me to fucking pieces."

"Do you want me to speak to them?" I ask.

Decker ignores me apart from the upturn of his nose.

"No, he can deal." Cole makes his way out of the bedroom, passing me to stand near his younger sister's partner. "Tell everyone to keep their cells close by. I'll let you know if I hear anything else."

Decker gives me a scorn-filled look before he nods and hobbles toward the hall, closing the penthouse door behind him.

Then it's just the two of us.

Cole and I.

Alone.

Again.

17

ANISSA

Cole strolls across the living area to stand before the floor-to-ceiling glass, staring down at the city below.

He doesn't break the eerie quiet and neither do I. There's nothing but hollow isolation until my stomach rumbles, demanding sustenance loud enough to wake the dead.

I'm not hungry, but I need to eat. My energy reserves are low. I even struggle to drag my feet to the kitchen to mumble a random selection from the room service menu to the operator.

Cole is still at the wall of glass after I hang up. His silence is in stark contrast to the storm raging through his tight posture and I can't help wishing I could do something to gentle the turmoil.

"I hope you don't mind me ordering you dinner." I walk around the kitchen counter to lean against the armrest of a sofa. "I thought taking a wild guess at what you might eat would be better than asking you to make menial decisions."

"I appreciate it."

I hear the truth in his words. The utter fatigue.

"I should head out and get something to wear tomorrow," he murmurs. "I have no clothes. I didn't plan on staying overnight."

"Is that something the concierge could organize?"

He shrugs, not meeting my gaze.

My hunger pangs turn into cramps, my insides twisting and

squeezing in empathetic meltdown. "What are your sizes? I'll get the hotel staff to arrange something."

He relays measurements I note down in my cell, then I turn my back as I reclaim the penthouse phone. I can't look at him anymore. Not when all I want to do is comfort him.

I've witnessed male suffering before. But never like this. Not with a man who prides himself on strength of character and sterility of emotion.

I distract myself with the concierge, asking about dry-cleaning timelines and personal shopper availability. This time when I hang up, I swing around to find an empty room. There's no image of sorrowful mourning at the window. There's not even a glimpse of the crime lord who's battling against a devastating downfall.

"Cole?"

"In here."

I follow his voice toward the bedroom. "The concierge said he would send someone to arrange a selection of suits for you to wear tomorrow." I enter the doorway, finding him at the side of the bed, unbuttoning his shirt and throwing it on the mattress.

My heart quickens without my consent. My stomach twists. I force myself to look away, focusing on the closed curtains across the room. "He also mentioned you can have your current suit dry-cleaned within the hour, so I asked for him to send someone up to retrieve it."

"Thanks."

There's a clink of a belt. A grate of a zipper.

My quickening heart and twisting stomach increase, my insides somersaulting like an Olympic gymnast despite my exhaustion.

"I didn't even think about dry-cleaning," he mutters. "I can hardly think at all."

"That's why you need sleep."

"The sun has barely set."

"But it's currently setting the day *after* you last slept." I chance a glance in his direction, and there he stands, gloriously naked except for his boxer briefs, his chest a masterpiece of tanned, defined muscles as he pulls on a hotel robe.

He cinches it tight around his waist and grabs the discarded clothes from the bed. "I'll leave these at the door." He starts toward me, the approaching proximity causing arrhythmia.

"Here." I hold out my hands. "Let me do it."

He pauses before me, meeting my gaze. I'm sure there's skepticism hidden in those dark blue depths, resentment at my coddling, too. But he doesn't voice a protest. Only stares, melting me into a puddle.

"Go to bed." I reach for the clothes. "I'm going to stay awake for a while and do more research."

"You need the rest as much as I do." He keeps his folded suit tight within his strong hands and continues into the living room, his retreating footsteps carrying down the hall until the penthouse door opens and closes.

I have a few moments to breathe freely before his dominating presence returns.

"The food shouldn't take long." He strides back into the room, still a sight to behold even in a plush white bathrobe. "I'm going to take a shower."

He continues into the bathroom, not closing the door.

I remain nailed in place as the sound of rushing water seduces my ears.

I don't know if he's attempting to entice me, or if he's so entirely bone-weary he doesn't have the strength to close the barrier between us. It has to be option one. It always is.

I become entranced by the melodic flow of water, the gentle sound soothing parts of me hardened from the last twenty-four hours. I've showered with him before. I know what it feels like to be surrounded by warmth. And hunger. I remember how powerless I was to resist Cole when the world had faded from view and it was only the two of us.

My stomach hurts with the memory. With the lost affection.

I'd thought he was falling in love with me. I truly had.

The worst part was those feelings had been reciprocated.

I had loved a *criminal*.

A *murderer*.

And now those feelings are clawing their way back from the depths of my despair.

"No," I whisper to the empty room. "Not again."

I drag my feet to the living room to sit on the sofa. He's so quiet it's unnerving.

He remains in the shower long after our food is delivered and I've eaten my burger and fries. He stays in there while I fight against concern for his welfare. To the point where I'm almost ready to check on him. Then the water finally turns off.

"Your dinner is out here." I raise my voice to carry through the rooms. "Hurry, while it's still warm."

"I'm not hungry."

"You need to eat." I grab a plate filled with fries, steak and salad, along with a set of cutlery, and return to the main bedroom only to pause at the threshold.

He stands at the bed, a towel wrapped around his hips, his chiseled chest on full display as he ruffles his damp hair.

He's gorgeous. Purely divine. So incredibly tempting it pains me to keep my distance.

I wish I understood the effect he has on me.

I should be daunted by the ease with which he displays himself. He doesn't care that he's naked beneath that towel. The bigger problem is—I don't either.

It feels natural to be here like this. But it's not. I just don't get why panic isn't setting in.

"Here." I pad forward, placing the plate and cutlery on the end of the bed before backing away. "Eat."

"I've lived a long time without a mother, Nis. You don't need to baby me."

"Even someone as ruthless as you needs to be taken care of every once in a while."

He quirks a brow. "And you're the person for the job?"

"I'm the only one here."

He inclines his head. "Be careful, Nis. You might start to expose feelings for me other than lust."

I don't let the strike penetrate. It hits hard though, the efficient barb making me wince.

"Just eat," I beg. "Neither one of us has the patience to argue."

He surprises me by doing exactly as I ask, stepping forward the few feet to grab some fries. Everything about him is smooth. His chest. His composure. The way he continues to lazily eat, his gaze raking me the entire time.

"What happened between you and Benji?" I rest my shoulder against the doorjamb. "What's with the hostility?"

"It's family business. You don't need to concern yourself with the details."

"It must be something big for you to be angry at him during what has to be the most excruciating time of his life."

He grabs a piece of cucumber and throws it into his mouth, chewing with casual arrogance.

The shower must have pepped him up. He's got energy back in those eyes. Lethal efficiency.

"Is it that you don't trust me with the information?" I ask. "You don't want me to know?"

"You don't need to know."

"But I'd like to."

He gives a snake of a grin. "There's many things I'd like from you, too. Will I get those in return?"

Heat skitters along my skin, the flashover wild and intense. I picture what he wants as payment. I *feel* it. Lucky for me I have just enough strength to look away from his demanding gaze in the hopes of severing his train of thought.

He sighs in response. "Benji is a snitch. He's been ratting on me to my father for God knows how long at my sister's request."

"Layla betrayed you?" The question leaves my lips in a rapid evacuation of breath. "Why?"

"Money. Security. Intimidation. Who the fuck cares? There's no excusable reason to make their actions acceptable."

Holy Jesus.

This isn't good. Not for Cole's reputation or his stronghold in Portland.

"Don't look so worried, little fox. I'll sort it out."

"How?" I push from the doorframe. "How can you sort something like that?"

"You don't want to know." He holds my gaze, the slightest conniving smile tilting his lips. He's alluding to violence. To torture. Possibly death. But the thirst for bloodshed doesn't reach his eyes. All I see is hardship in the ocean-blue depths.

He wouldn't kill Benji, would he?

"What about my phone?" The question rushes from my lips in an attempt to change the subject. "You deliberately turned off my data before sending that video to Easton. Why?"

He resumes ruffling his hair, scattering water droplets over his bare shoulders. "Because I knew I would get the desired effect without having to risk your reputation."

There's another twist to my heart. A cautionary tweak. "And what was the desired effect?"

"Does it really matter?" He starts toward me, his relaxed stride seeming predatory. "You already judged me for my actions."

"Why, Cole?"

He stops before me, the scent of soap filtering into my lungs as he reaches out to run gentle fingers along my jaw.

My nerves tingle in response. My throat dries.

I should run. I should scream. I should do anything other than stand here basking in his touch, but I don't.

"Your initial response wasn't to blame me for manipulating you. Or to rail on me for playing games. You didn't even claim some pathetic mental excuse for your enjoyment of that kiss. Instead, you got angry because I exposed the truth."

I close my eyes, hating his accuracy.

"You threw your phone at me because you could no longer hide behind lies." His fingers grip my chin, lifting my face upward. "But I'm not entirely heartless, Nis. Not when it comes to you. If you want to keep your job I would never take it away."

I squeeze my eyes tighter, wishing the darkness could shut out my growing need. "Not heartless, yet you still threatened my shrink."

"I was concerned for your well-being. I won't apologize for that." The pad of his thumb brushes my lower lip, back and forth, stimulating every nerve in my body. "But I admit taking you to Greece wasn't one of my finest moments. I did things I regret. And I needed to make sure my actions didn't have a lasting effect on you."

They did.

They always will.

I open my eyes and immediately regret the decision when I'm

ensnared by the intensity peering back at me. His fierce scrutiny. His inviting mouth.

"You suffer because of me." He continues to rub his thumb over my lip. "I don't like it."

"Be careful, Cole. If you keep talking like this you might expose a soft side." I throw his own taunt back at him. We're all about games and ridicule. Even now. It's all I've got to shield myself.

"I'm more concerned with how hard you make me." His mouth kicks in a faint smile.

Goddamnit.

My pussy clenches at the thought of his arousal. My nipples bead.

I'm a vibrating mess of building adrenaline and humming endorphins as his fingers tease along my jaw to my cheek, gently guiding stray strands of hair behind my ear.

"I asked you to be my queen once. I wanted you to stand by my side. That hasn't changed."

I shake my head. "I'm a Fed. You're a murderer."

"Yes, I'm a murderer. But so are you. You killed my father and didn't report it. You remained silent while Luca and I disposed of bodies. You're a criminal, too, Nis."

"Don't." I pull back. "Please don't throw my mistakes in my face. I know exactly what I've done."

"It wasn't a mistake. You rid the world of a man underserving of life. You saved tortured women. You ensured no more would be targeted by him. How can you still not see that?"

"Because I didn't do it the right way."

"The *right* way?" His jaw ticks, nostrils flare. "What was wrong about it?"

I don't answer. There's no point. He'll only twist my words and use them against me.

He'll break me down with his infallible logic.

"Please don't," I beg.

He holds me captive beneath those hard eyes for long moments, my pulse pounding in my throat. "Have it your way then."

He turns and makes for the bathroom, momentarily

disappearing inside before returning without the towel as he thrusts his arms into the robe.

I get an eyeful of his perfect body. Head to toe. Nothing left unseen. Especially not the hardened length of his cock.

The display is deliberate. A calculated reminder of how easily he can make me burn.

"It's my dad." I finally answer his question, needing the necessary distraction. "You told me in Greece that he turned bad because of me."

He frowns, cinching the robe's belt around his waist. "That's not what I said."

"You told me he sought out your father to help protect me and my mother. You said he had no choice but to hire a hitman. And he lost everything because of it." I clasp my hands in front of me, tangling my fingers tight. "He made shady decisions to keep me safe. He threw away all he had. All so I could have this life. This career."

"So you plan to live the life he couldn't? You're giving up on your own freedom for him?"

Hearing my feelings spoken so simply makes them seem naive. Wrong.

"Doing the right thing isn't giving up on my freedom. I made the choice to distance myself from you because I cherish his sacrifice."

"My family *helped* yours. Yet you make it sound like we did the opposite." He huffs out a laugh. "You treat me as if I'm the scum of the Earth, but when the rest of the world failed your father, he turned to us. And we saved him. We saved *you*. And still you punish me for it."

I wince.

"The thing is, you don't know the half of it," he growls. "You've only heard the start of your father's story. He's not—"

"*No*. Please." I hold up a hand for him to stop. "Don't manipulate the memories I have of him. They're all I've got left."

He drags his gaze away, returning his attention to the food on the bed, claiming another piece of cucumber. "I wouldn't dream of it."

His cell vibrates on the bedside table beside his gun. He moves to snatch up the device, his expression remaining unchanged as he reads the screen.

"What is it?" I start toward him, stopping at his side to read the message from Luca.

We've arrived. Hunt filled me in on what's happening. We're booking another room. Call if you need anything.

"He made good time." I step back, removing myself from Cole's personal space.

"I'm surprised they made it at all." He begins typing a reply. "After what they've both been through in the last twenty-four hours, I've been waiting to hear news of a car accident."

He's been worried.

Why am I surprised?

He continues to tap, tap, tap on the screen, then returns the cell to the bedside table and runs his hands through his hair in a slow glide of tired frustration.

"You've handled this situation well." My comfort is barely audible. It's as if saying it too loud will mean I've finally switched sides, when I've already done far worse.

"Have I?" Sad eyes meet mine. Sad, defeated eyes.

My walls fall. Crumbling. Brick by brick, they succumb to his vulnerability.

What makes it worse is that I'm sure he's never shown this side of himself to anyone else before. Just me.

I'm the only one he's let in.

"You've done everything you can. There's nothing left to do but wait."

A knock sounds from the front of the suite, the interruption filling me with trepidation.

"Don't worry." Cole grabs his gun from the bedside table and some cash from his wallet. "It should be the dry-cleaning."

I follow him to the living room and watch, on alert, as he opens the door, reclaims his clothes, and tips the hotel staff.

It's then that I realize there are no more scheduled interruptions coming to save me.

He needs rest and I'm going to remain awake, stewing on all the bad decisions I've made.

Cole and I always seem to move in circles. Around and around. Never getting anywhere. Never learning from our mistakes.

It's such a demeaning routine, but the worst part is how right it feels.

The closeness. The exposed vulnerabilities. Even the passion… It seems like I've been pulled toward this by fate.

He pads back into the living room, the crinkle of plastic the only sound as he continues into the bedroom and out of sight.

"Can you come in here for a minute?" he asks moments later.

I'm loath to walk back in there.

Well, my mind is. My heart and nerve endings are the opposite as I enter the doorway.

"I'm going to sleep." He grabs the plate of food from the mattress and places it on the armchair in the corner. "Which side of the bed do you prefer?"

I huff out a half-hearted chuckle. "Nice try."

"The left side it is." He makes his way to the right and pulls back the covers. "It's time you got some rest, too."

He's right. I'm dead tired. But Goldilocks is *not* suited for this bed.

"I'll sleep in the spare room."

"No, you won't." There's no authority in his tone. No demand. Just pure, one hundred percent expectation.

"Good night, Cole." I back away, my heart thudding when he turns to me with narrowed eyes.

"I currently don't have the energy to chase you and haul you over my shoulder, but I assure you, I'll find it."

A chill skitters down my spine—a short, sharp thrill that leaves a hollow aftertaste. "You're only doing this for a distraction." I shake my head, correcting myself. "No, you consider me a challenge, don't you? That's why this time between us is never-ending. It's a cat and mouse game neither of us can win."

"You're no challenge, Nis. I had you in Greece. You threw yourself on me earlier in the hall. And you came on my fingers at the dining table. What part of that do you think was challenging for me?"

Shame heats my cheeks. Building disgust.

His face softens and it seems as though pity now stares back at me. "You stopped being a challenge and a game a long time ago."

The humiliation multiplies. Suffocates.

"What we have is far more complex than that." He drops the corner of the bedcovers and faces me. "You've become everything to me."

I haven't believed it before—his words of devotion, his continued commitment. Yet now it sinks in, warming the edges of my frigid insecurities. I'm a slave to his admission. A captive.

"We're made for each other. But you already know that." He discards the robe and slides onto the mattress, gloriously naked. "Now get in bed. I won't sleep unless I know you're safe at my side."

18

COLE

I expect her to continue protesting.

I'm more intrigued than relieved when she doesn't, instead turning on her heel after announcing she's going to get a change of clothes.

She returns moments later to enter the bathroom and close the door with a definitive click of the lock. She showers, the water's spray tempting me to break the barrier between us, but I force myself to remain in bed.

I don't even protest when she reenters the room covered neck to foot in soft-pink winter pajamas.

"Don't say a word." She turns off the light and rounds the bed to climb in the opposite side. "I'm doing this for safety's sake."

Sure she is.

If this is an attempt to throw me off my game by surrendering without a fight, it won't work. I'll take being near her any way I can.

She lays down as far away from me as humanly possible, then turns her back. The snub is an annoyance I don't have the energy to rally against.

I'm fucking dead inside. I need her warmth. But I'm done pushing. At least for now. Instead, I stare at the ceiling and watch the city lights peeking through the curtains as I brainstorm strategies for tomorrow.

I need to find leverage. Blackmail. I have to figure out a way to extort Emmanuel into giving those kids back without placing them in harm's way. Maybe his own children are the answer. But once I have Stella and Tobias safe in my care, I'll burn Costa's world to the ground.

I'll plant evidence. Pay law enforcement. Bribe city officials.

I'll do whatever the fuck it takes to rattle his cage. Then I'll level up to violence.

Revenge will be slow. Sweet.

It isn't long before I reach for my phone to message Hunt with tactical ideas. I tap out my anger against the glowing screen and hit send.

"What are you doing?" Nissa rolls toward me.

"Getting organized for the morning." I place the cell back on the bedside table and return to the previously broadcasted blank ceiling show.

"Why don't you reconsider letting me make a call or two? I could—"

"Don't waste your breath," I warn. "I'm not going to change my mind."

She sighs. "Then I really don't understand why I'm here. My hands are tied. I'm not helping."

"You're helping just fine."

"How?" She pushes onto her elbow, peering down at me. "What have I contributed apart from a few comments on the photos you received?"

I've asked myself the same question on repeat, and the answer has always remained the same. "You're here for me. For no other reason than to keep me grounded. I won't fail in front of you. You keep me in check."

She doesn't reply. She doesn't even move.

"Does that annoy you?" I direct the question toward the ceiling. "Do you hate knowing you're here for my benefit and nothing else?"

"It's more complicated than hatred," she whispers. "It always is with you. I just wish I would've realized sooner so I didn't mistakenly think I could've actually helped those kids."

"You're helping. Just not in the ways you planned."

She gives a breathy scoff. "Sorry, how silly of me to forget it's always your way or the highway."

"That's not the case."

"Yet here I am, in your bed, after you demanded I sleep here."

I clench my teeth, hating the way she cheapens her submission. "I didn't hear one fucking protest."

"Why bother when you always get what you want?"

"If I always got what I wanted, I would've fucked you four times by now. Once in my room this morning. Then when you plastered yourself against me in the bathroom. And again when you ground yourself into my fingers until you fucking orgasmed."

She sits up, her breathing increasing.

If I always got what I wanted, she never would've walked away from me after returning to Portland. Nothing would've stood between us. Not her morals. Not my family. And certainly not her fucking career.

"That was three, not four." She glowers down at me.

I release an anger-filled laugh. "Don't play coy, Nis. You know the fourth is right now. I'd fuck you within an inch of your life if I thought you'd consent."

"I wasn't being coy. I pointed it out because you didn't make sense. You never do. It's all smoke and mirrors. I don't understand you."

"That's another lie. You know me. You understand my motivations. You even agree with a lot of them—"

"No."

"*Yes*. You're fucking strong. You've never succumbed to my manipulations, as you like to call them. Or been tricked. Or unwillingly persuaded. You've *given* yourself to me, over and over again, because what I represent is familiar to the parts of yourself you try to hide. You like to think you've been fighting me this whole time. But the truth is, you've been fighting how much this feels like home. You've been battling your natural instincts. You've waged war with who you're meant to be."

"*No*." She slides from the bed and starts for the door. "Believe what you want but that's not true."

"Is that why you're running?" I drawl. "Because I'm wrong?"

She pauses at the threshold, back straight, shoulders stiff.

"Tell me, Nis, if I haven't got you pegged, why are you fleeing? Why not stay and prove me wrong?"

"Because there's no proving anything with you." She turns toward me. "You're always right."

I sit up. "If that were the case, you never would've returned from Greece to fuck another man, because I sure as shit didn't see that coming."

She winces.

"I wouldn't have ever expected you to move on with someone who's my complete opposite," I snarl. "Someone who isn't worthy of you. Someone who could never give you what you want."

"Don't talk about Easton."

"Why not?" I throw back the covers and slide from the bed. "Does the reality of your pathetic sex life upset you?"

"I never fucked him," she snaps.

My heart skips a beat. "No? You're telling me he practically lived in your apartment, but never had the balls to make a move?" I storm toward her, needing to see her lying eyes up close and personal.

"You said it yourself." She hikes her chin. "He's the exact opposite of you. He's a gentleman."

"So you *made love*? You didn't fuck?" My disappointment is stifling. I get in her face, wanting to taste her, to fucking claim her. My cock thickens with the need, painfully engorged. "I bet it was mediocre after what we shared."

She sucks in a breath, her shoulders hiking farther.

"If you would've come back to me I would've fucked you until your bones ached." I wrap an arm around her waist and haul her into me, pressing my dick into her abdomen. "If I always got my fucking way, little fox, you wouldn't have risen from your back since the night you returned."

"Because this is only about sex for you." She doesn't fight my hold. Not aggressively. Her only show of resistance is the way she leans away. "You claim I'm everything. But it's purely lust. You need to get laid more often."

My smirk increases. "Trust me, my sex life before you was envious."

I've bedded women who wanted nothing more than to earn my

favor through my dick. By gold-diggers who thought they could win a lifetime worth of paid bills and extravagances if only they fucked me good enough.

And none compare to her.

"You're toxic." She looks me in the eye. "One hundred percent pure poison."

Slowly, I raise my arm, teasing my fingers up her neck to grab her hair in a tight fist. I drag her forward, her lips almost against mine. "And you're a bitch. Which makes us a perfect match."

She shudders.

Her enjoyment is always evident whenever I touch her. Rough or gentle. Harsh or soft. She loves it all.

"Now, tell me you want me." I nip at her lips, breathing her fractured inhales. "Tell me you want to be fucked."

She shakes her head.

"Do you think I won't slide my fingers back into your panties to feel the evidence of what you're denying?" I run my other hand down the curve of her waist, then along the elastic band of her pajamas. "Come back to me."

"No." She grips my wrist. "Not like this."

"Then how?"

She continues shaking her head, her brows pinching. "I don't know."

"Yeah, you do." I creep my hand lower, forcing myself into her panties. "You know exactly what you want. All you need to do is ask."

"Stop. This isn't what I want." Her nails dig into my skin and she pushes me backward. My fingers reluctantly leave her.

Fuck.

I could've sworn she was malleable tonight. I would've bet my life she'd be a willing participant.

I huff out a laugh. I guess I don't know her like I thought.

"I don't want this." She keeps shaking her head at me. "I can't live like this."

"I've made you feel good before—"

"That's not what I'm talking about." Her expression turns pained, her bleak eyes all the more tortured in the dim light. "I can't live with lies and threats. Yes, the adrenaline is euphoric. And the sex was incredible. But everything else is..." She throws her arms up at her sides. "The fighting. The bickering. The constant cat and mouse game—"

"You enjoy that as much as I do."

"That doesn't mean it's healthy... And then there's my job."

Fuck this. I turn away, my cock's eagerness vanishing at the mention of her career.

She thinks she loves the Bureau. So why hasn't she gone back? Why has she remained on leave since we were together?

Denial, that's why.

"We can't exist, Cole. I enjoy my job too much."

I grind my teeth, clench my fists.

"That's all there is to it," she adds as if her words are a royal flush to win this argument.

"Your job is bullshit," I mutter under my breath. I seethe the words. "Your *job* is nothing but a scam. We've gone over how you're a puppet for the hierarchy which manipulates the constitution for its own gain." I swing around to face her. "You're not saving the world one criminal at a time. You're a meaningless soldier helping more powerful criminals."

"I don't expect you to understand."

"You don't expect *me* to understand?" Holy shit, she's fucking demeaning me? "If you had any idea of the corruption in your office alone you'd realize your badge is worthless. Everyone can be bought."

"Not me."

"Not you?" I snicker. "How about Greece? How about when I offered you the chance to take down a criminal, illegally, and you took it?"

Her eyes narrow. "That's different."

"How is it any different than if I'd paid you? You went against the law to obtain an illegal outcome."

She stands her ground, her ferocity building.

"And I could help you do it over and over again. If justice is your calling, *true* justice, then work with me. Work without confinement under my protection."

"No."

"Why? Give me one reason."

"They're my family."

"Like hell they are." I get in her face. "They treat you like shit. They ostracized you because of your father. Apart from Easton, whose only goal is to remain between your thighs, not one of them cares about you."

Her expression crumples.

"I'm the family you're meant to have. I'm the home you need to seek comfort in."

She stares at me for long moments, blinks those thick lashes. "Comfort? Is that what you think I get from Hunter's animosity? And what about Decker's seething hatred? Every single one of your *family* despises me."

I guide my hand around her waist and she trembles beneath my hold. "They're scared of you." I lean close, grazing my cheek over hers to whisper in her ear. "You're fucking fierce. They know you're a force to be reckoned with. What you see as animosity and hatred I know to be respect."

She shakes her head.

"It's true." I breathe her in, the scent of soap and sweet shampoo sinking deep into my lungs. "If you'd told them you were mine, they'd welcome you."

"You're a liar." She tilts her face away. But all it does is give me better access to her neck.

"You're my queen." I speak against her carotid, the pebble of goose bumps rising against my lips. "We're your family."

This is me begging. Pleading.

I don't do that for anyone.

Anyone but her.

I'll swallow all my pride for this woman. I'll get on my knees. Grovel. Slit my wrists at the shrine of her existence if it means seating her in the rightful place by my side.

I scrape my teeth along her neck. Kiss her jaw. Palm her face.

"It's not right." She keeps shaking her head. "*This* isn't right."

"Maybe not." I drag my lips along her skin. I nip and suck, drawing gasps from her throat, trembles from her body. "But then why does it feel so good?"

19

ANISSA

He's wrong. This doesn't feel good. It goes beyond that. Over and above.

When I'm with him, our bodies close, it seems the rest of the world exists only for us to be together. The perfection of his touch makes it hard to imagine being like this is anything other than heaven-sent.

But the devil was sent to tempt weak souls and I've proven to be the most feeble.

I place my hands on his shoulders and add pressure, hoping he'll back away.

He doesn't.

My lack of adamance seems to spur him to grab me tighter, stronger, his other arm snaking around my waist to hold me against his chest.

I whimper, wanting this and hating it, too. "I'm not like you," I whisper.

I wish I could live on sensation alone, not giving thought to morality. But once the pleasure fades and the panted breaths subside, I'll be left to wallow in self-loathing. It happens every time.

"I agree, to an extent." He brushes my lips with his fingers, the soft scrape of sensation grazing against aching nerves. "You're far better than I deserve. You're the light to my darkness."

"I don't want you to be dark."

He slides a fingertip into my mouth, only slightly, teasing the tip of my tongue. "Yes, you do."

I shudder. Tremble.

That finger in my mouth… his hard cock against my abdomen… the unrelenting strength of his chest against my breasts.

I close my eyes as his finger retreats, his mouth taking its place. He commands me with a punishing kiss, stealing my breath and my common sense.

Everything is his for the taking, including my body, which he leans down to scoop into his arms. He carries me back to the bed. Morality becomes the tiniest voice in my head, the words of warning no longer heard over the screaming desire.

He sits me on the mattress and grabs my ankles, swinging me around to face him towering above me. He stands entirely naked, remarkably hard, without one hint of insecurity. Not that I'd expect anything other than arrogant confidence from him. Not when he's carved from stone. Every muscle etched. Every limb strong.

He leans in to steal another kiss, his lips manipulating mine in a flawless dance of victory and possession. It's pure bliss. Torture, too.

Adamant hands grab my waistband, those fierce fingers gripping my pants and underwear to strip them from my body.

I should protest. I should open my goddamn mouth and stop this. But even the contemplation is laughable.

I'm lost to him. I always have been.

My surrender has never been more apparent than it is now as he holds my gaze despite my partial nudity.

"We're meant to be together." He spreads my legs apart, places a knee between my thighs, and forces me to lie down with the sheer intimidation of his approaching body. "I can't live without you."

Rough hands find my hips, skimming upward, dragging my top along with them. He exposes every inch to his hungry eyes, his adoration speaking silently in his tight expression.

I love the way he looks at me. I always have. As if he's starved and I'm his sole sustenance. But his attention only remains on my body momentarily before those eyes are back on mine.

He tugs my top over my chest, my neck, my head. In brief moments, I'm completely bare before him. At his mercy. My breathing hard to control.

"You don't know how many sleepless nights I've spent remembering your beauty." He hovers above me, one hand stabilizing his weight while the other relearns my curves. "You'll always be the most beautiful thing I've ever seen."

My heart weakens. Crumples.

He strokes the outer curve of my breast, then underneath, and over my stomach. He holds my gaze, his focus wild and intense.

"There will never be another woman for me," he vows. "There hasn't been since the moment we met."

I hear an unspoken admonishment in his admission. Or maybe it's just guilt that has me thinking he's silently accusing me of a lack of reciprocation because of Easton. The anguish lashes me regardless.

I didn't betray him.

Not the way he thinks.

But I'm compelled to seek his forgiveness.

I wrap my hand around his neck and drag his mouth back to mine. I give him my apology through the connection of eager lips. Beg for absolution in that kiss.

He matches my passion, resting his weight into me, the adamant length of his cock pressing hard into my pubic bone.

We act like teenagers. Making out. Engaging in heavy petting. Gasping for panted breaths.

He grinds his erection against me, his hand still roaming my skin, his fingers digging into my ass.

I moan, cupping his cheeks, forcing the kiss so much deeper. I can't get enough.

I claw at his hair. His shoulders. I wrap my legs around his waist and squeeze tight enough that the groan emanating in his chest rumbles through my ribs.

"You're mine, Nissa." He speaks into my mouth. "Always mine."

He reaches between us to grab his cock. It's all the prelude I get before he shoves inside me, the delicious severity making my back arch off the bed.

He thrusts hard. Over and over. Not once stopping his assault on my mouth.

It's too much. The pleasure. The consumption.

He touches every part of me. My heart. My soul.

This is why I couldn't forget him. This, right here, is why I can't move on.

This man, with his overwhelming power and undermining determination, treats me like a goddess. Like his next breath depends on my existence.

He's rabid for me, and the potency of his hunger is contagious.

"Please, don't stop." I kiss him over and over, luxuriating in his groans, demanding more of his severity.

I pulse my hips in time with his, squeezing my legs harder around him.

When he pulls back, claiming a nipple with his scorching mouth, I hiss through the burst of tingles. They're everywhere, the sensation awakening all my nerve endings.

He pays both breasts homage, licking, sucking, never stopping his thrusting assault on my pussy.

I'm a writhing, mindless mess by the time he grabs my waist and moves off the bed, his cock still inside me as he guides my ass to rest at the edge of the mattress.

"This time, I'm taking you fast and hard." His fingers dig into the flesh of my ass. "Next time, you'll be savored."

Next time.

The thought of a reoccurrence brings hope and fear. I can't commit to more. I can't even commit to a single sensible thought around him.

"Yes, you heard me." He reads my mind, his gaze narrowing. "*Next time,* you'll be savored. And the time after that. And the time after that, too."

He grips my knees, holding them at his sides as he slams into me.

Hard.

Vicious.

I claw at the bedding, needing something to cling to while he groans with the repeated impact, his eyes rolling.

Pleasure is everywhere. In my aching breasts. Tingling down my neck. No place pulsing harder than my pussy.

"I need more," I beg.

More words. More touch. More possession.

"And you'll get it," he promises. "You'll get everything you want."

I believe him. Right here, with my body at his mercy and my soul within his grasp, I unequivocally believe him.

He splays a hand over my abdomen, his thumb sliding to my clit. I gasp with the wave of bliss, my core clenching, my muscles tensing. I could come already. My mind was well within orgasm territory before he laid a hand on me. Now my body has caught up, the eager need for release growing into an obsession.

I rock into each of his thrusts and squeeze my core every time his cock slides home. I shake my head, overwhelmed, out of breath. "*Cole.*"

He doesn't quit devouring me with his gaze, wordlessly complimenting me with the hunger in his eyes.

He makes me feel adored. Cherished. I never have to question my worth when we're together this way because he stares at me like I'm his entire world.

His universe.

With the next retreat of his cock, he moves his thumb lower, sliding it inside me as he thrusts home. The delicious stretch of my core pulls a gasp from my throat. The friction of his palm against my clit brings mindlessness.

I pant. Whimper.

He doesn't stop fucking me. His rhythm only increases—harder, faster—as his thumb remains hooked inside me.

"Give me what I want," he demands. "Come on my dick."

I couldn't deny him even if I wanted to. I unravel, my neck and back arching, my core spasming with each thrust.

I don't cry his name, even though I want to. I keep the pleas locked inside as wave upon wave of pleasure wracks me. It's all I can do not to blurt my unwanted feelings as he releases inside me, his animalistic display far more erotic than I remember.

I wanted this.

I needed it.

But regret inevitably hits me before the pleasure truly subsides. He's thrusting with the last of his release when I reach rock bottom.

I'm pulled in different directions, my body begging to relax into satiation while my mind admonishes my stupidity.

"Eventually, you will stop second-guessing yourself." He steps back, leaving me cold, and makes for the bathroom to return with a damp cloth. "When you quit fighting this and realize it's fate, you'll be much happier."

"Is that what you've done? Do you simply ignore the fact we're enemies?"

He stares down at me, his eyes gentle despite his hardened face. "You're no enemy of mine. Even if you wanted to be."

His sincerity tears strips from me. Layer upon layer of hardened skin.

I ignore the offered cloth and scoot from the bed to escape into the bathroom. I lock myself inside and use the facilities. I wash my face. Scrub my hands. Glare at myself in the mirror.

"Quit fighting, Nis," he calls from the bedroom. "I won't let you shut me out again."

I clutch the counter, feeling compelled to comply.

I want to stop fighting. I want it more than anything.

It seems as though the last few years of my life have been one unending battle. First, I waged war against those who tarnished my father's name. Then I fought with my hatred toward Cole. And now, I combat my yearning for the same man.

I don't want to struggle anymore. But what's the alternative?

I grab a towel from a nearby rack and secure it around my breasts, as if the plush material can shield me against more foolish decisions, then leave the bathroom.

The bedroom is now in shadow, the soft glow from the living room seeping in from the partially opened door.

Cole is back in bed, the sheet covering him to the waist, one arm resting behind his head. "We'll make it work."

"How?" I remain a foot from the bathroom. "My conflicts aren't something that can be wished away. My career is—"

"I'll figure it out."

"You can't."

"Nissa, let me deal with one problem at a time." His voice is tired. "Let me get the kids back, then I'll convince you."

Guilt assails me at the reminder of why I'm here. But I can't help wanting him to convince me. More than anything, I want to stay in this bubble of passion and possession.

I've spent too long surrounded by people in a big city while remaining entirely alone. Even with Easton practically living in my apartment, I felt completely detached from the human race. But it's different when I'm with Cole. Our arguments are adrenaline-filled challenges. He wakes me up to the reality of the world. He teaches me—

"Get back in bed." He rolls away from me, toward the middle of the mattress, and pats my pillow. "And take off that goddamn towel."

I smother a half-hearted smile, vowing to never admit how much I love it when he slips into bouts of dictatorship. Especially when the directives are for my benefit.

I pad around the bed, meeting his gaze before I drop the towel to my feet.

His eyes don't stray from mine. He doesn't take the opportunity to visually ravage my nudity, and it's more than slightly disappointing.

"You don't care too much about looking at me anymore, do you?" I climb onto the mattress, fighting insecurity, and pull the sheet up to my shoulders.

"Why do you say that?" He reaches out, locking an arm around my waist to haul me closer.

Because since I put on the tiny bit of extra weight he so kindly pointed out this morning, he doesn't seem to want to do anything other than hold my gaze while I'm still entirely starved of the sight of his body. I could stare at the contours and sinew forever and never grow tired.

"It's just an observation, Cole."

He remains quiet for a while, his eyes holding mine, his fingertips lazily circling my back.

"I never stopped watching you in Greece," he murmurs. "I ate up every moment with you naked beside me. I watched you while you slept. I learned every curve. I even have the security footage from your room when we first arrived."

I tense, not appreciating the reminder of my invaded privacy. The hit to my pride is made all the worse when a subtle smirk curves his lips.

"Good night." I shuffle backward, moving away from his touch.

"You're not going to let me finish?"

"Nope." I roll over, turning my back to him. I need rest. It's not in my best interests to let him stir up my anger before I try to fall asleep.

He huffs out a breath. "The reason I hold your gaze is because I've never forgotten the beauty of your body, but what I struggle to recall are the memories of you looking at me in return."

My pulse increases, the gentle thump building into a tremendous boom.

"I crave the truth in your eyes, little fox. I need to see those feelings you work so hard to hide because they're what keep me fighting for you. They're the only things that help convince me you can't be entirely in love with that piece of shit who spends all his time in your apartment."

My heart squeezes, my lies gouging at me with sharp claws.

"I'm not in love with him," I admit.

He doesn't respond. The only shift in the room is the anticipation thickening the air.

"I haven't slept with Easton. I've kissed him once. And that was at the exact moment you knocked on my door the other night." I place my hands under the pillow at my cheek and tangle my fingers together. "There's never been anything substantial between us. Not even a proper date."

I wait for the gloating to start. But the boasting and bragging I expect doesn't happen.

Instead, there's a subtle shift in the bed before Cole's arm glides possessively around my waist.

"Don't." I scoot toward the edge of the mattress, needing space to come to terms with my admission. My feelings. I can't avoid them any longer.

There's no Stockholm to excuse how much I want to be with him. There's no manipulation or intimidation. Just misguided, unavoidable love. It feels like home here with him, and I don't know how to make it stop.

"Don't deny me." His arm turns to stone, imprisoning me as he closes in tight against my back. His mouth finds my shoulder, his warm lips brushing my neck. "Not when this is the best news I've heard in weeks."

"I don't want to talk about it anymore."

"Then we won't. But I *will* hold you. It's all I ask."

I shouldn't allow myself the affection. It's one thing to fuck in the heat of uncontrollable lust. It's quite another to succumb to tenderness. And that's exactly what it feels like when his lips continue to pepper kisses along my shoulder blade—pure loving tenderness.

His soft side slays me. Enslaves.

"Get some rest, my little fox," he murmurs against my skin. "I'm going to need your strength tomorrow."

I close my eyes, aching for a myriad of reasons. The danger upon us. The emotional exhaustion. The inevitable goodbye.

This will all come crashing down.

"Good night." I attempt to clear my mind, forcing unwanted thoughts away. I pretend this thing between us is normal. Natural. We're not complete opposites. Or enemies. We're everyday smitten schmucks who have white-picket-fence and two-point-five-kids potential.

His arm grows heavier, his breathing deepening into something resembling slumber. I will myself to do the same. To be at peace.

It takes forever to get to sleep, and when morning comes a few seconds pass before I register the lack of muscled warmth surrounding me.

Cole isn't in bed. He's not even in the room.

"Where are you?" I sit and throw back the covers, sliding from the mattress.

"Out here." His voice carries from the living area, behind the now closed bedroom door.

What also carries are other voices. Hunter's. Decker's. Layla's.

Shit.

I rush to tug on my pajamas and stumble to the door, pulling it open a crack to see everyone scattered around the living room. Keira, Benji, and Sarah are on the sofas. Luca and Layla drink from mugs in the kitchen. Decker and Hunter give me scathing scowls from Cole's side, while Penny smiles with gentle warmth as she picks up a piece of bacon from a large serving tray.

Goddamnit. How the hell did I sleep through this?

"Have you heard anything yet?" I pull the door open a fraction wider and rake a hand through my tangled hair.

"Not yet." Cole meets my gaze. "But one of my assets from the bank has some potential leads on where they could be."

"Why didn't you wake me?" I regret the question as soon as it comes out. I regret it even more when the knowing stares of everyone in the room weigh down on me. "Don't answer that. I'm going to get dressed."

Their murmured conversation rekindles as I retreat into the bedroom, closing the door behind me, and hustle into the bathroom. I take a quick shower and brush my teeth.

I'm barely dressed and frantically combing my hair when Cole opens the bathroom door.

"I'm leaving," he states simply. "I should be back with the kids soon."

He speaks as if he's picking them up from school or band practice, not from the clutches of a man who could potentially kill them all.

"You heard from Emmanuel?" My hands fall to my sides, my heart dropping along with them.

He pulls his cell from the pocket of his suit jacket and passes it over, showing a text message with an address.

"I want to come with you." I rush to place my brush on the counter and straighten my blouse. "I'll keep watch from nearby."

"No, you need to stay here." He steps closer, reclaiming his phone. "Look after my sisters."

"But it could be a setup. I should—"

"I know." He stands tall. Strong. Not an ounce of fear in sight. "But my hands are tied regardless. If we have to shoot our way out of this, we will, which is just another reason why I want you to stay here. If this turns south, I know you'll get my sisters home."

My stomach sinks, and not only from the responsibility he lays at my feet. This feels like goodbye.

"Cole—"

"We'll be fine. I thought about this all night and Emmanuel can't be stupid enough to risk a legitimate empire to start a war with me. The handover will be smooth."

He doesn't believe that. I know he doesn't.

No sane person would keep those kids like Costa has.

"Look after my sisters." He leans closer, pausing when he's a breath away from my mouth, as if waiting for me to back away.

I don't. I can't.

I bridge the space between us, placing my lips against his, and wither into the kiss. I don't want to be scared for him. I don't even want to care if he lives or dies. But I've never been more fearful for someone's death than I am right now.

I can't lose him.

"It'll be okay." He pulls away, turning to walk for the door before I can meet his gaze. "I'll see you soon."

20

———

COLE

Hunter and Benji climb into the Escalade with me, while the injured party of Decker and Luca ride in another vehicle behind us. It only takes a few short minutes to get to the apartment building where Emmanuel told us to meet.

I park in the one available space nearby and climb out, straightening the lapels of my suit as I stalk across the road toward the front doors of the towering construction.

My plan is fluid, the myriad of multiplying strategies dissected with my men this morning while Anissa remained asleep.

All that matters is getting those kids out.

"Decker and Luca are going to try to get on the rooftop across the street like you asked." Hunter keeps pace at my side. "Let's hope they can get eyes on us once we figure out what floor we're on."

Benji jogs to catch up. "Let's hope we're not in there long enough for them to bother."

I ignore the chitchat. I don't need the distraction.

"What happens if they're hurt?" Benji asks. "What if they're not there at all?"

I reach the glass doors at the front of the building and pull one open, letting them precede me. "They'll be there."

"But if he's done something to them—"

"The kids will be fine." I won't be able to control my rage if they're not. I'm at risk of putting all our lives on the line if Emmanuel has hurt them. "We're getting them back and taking them home. End of story."

I follow them inside, my focus switching to Hunt as we continue toward the sign pointing us to the elevators around a corner. "Are you ready?"

He nods. "Always. This isn't going to be a problem."

I don't know if he's faking the bravado, but I appreciate it. I need all the confident positivity I can get because the farther we walk through the lobby, the more this feels like a trap.

Nobody is around. Not a single soul.

I'm already antsy to draw my gun. I'll be a fucking hair-trigger away from a bloodbath by the time I face Emmanuel.

We turn the corner and find a hulking man standing in the middle of the elevator bay, the three gleaming doors positioned to his right.

He uncrosses his arms from his chest and stares past Hunter and Benji to look me up and down. "Are you Mr. Torian?"

"Yes. And you are?"

"I'm the one escorting you today. The others will need to remain in the lobby."

My plan takes its first hit. I'd hoped I wouldn't have to do this on my own. No backup. No fucking shield for those kids. But this isn't unexpected.

"Like hell," Hunter growls. "He's not going anywhere alone."

"Then he doesn't go at all." The guard shrugs. "Your choice."

Hunt reaches behind his back, preparing to retrieve his gun. "What's to stop us relieving you of your duties and going floor to floor until we find them?"

"Probably the infallible level of security." The guy smirks. "I'm merely the gatekeeper."

"You fucking son of a bitch." Benji rushes for him.

I lunge, grabbing my brother-in-law by the arm to haul him back to my side. The guard doesn't flinch. There's no fear or concern. Whatever he means by infallible security, it's enough to make him confident of his protection while in front of three men salivating for revenge.

"This is the father of the little girl." I pat Benji on the chest in a subtle warning to remain calm. "Surely he's allowed to accompany me for the sake of his daughter's comfort."

"She's comfortable enough. All you're doing is wasting time. Nobody else will accompany us. Take it or leave it."

Benji bristles. "What the fuck does that mean? If we refuse, what happens to my daughter?"

"Those decisions are above my pay grade." He steps toward the bank of elevators, hovering his finger above the call button. "Are we going up or not?"

Hunter mutters a string of unintelligible garble under his breath as he retreats, then says, "Cole, I need to speak to you."

I contemplate escaping into the elevator before he can outline more issues to compact my already heavily stacked deck. Panic isn't something I need right now.

"Give me five seconds." He continues backward.

I follow, keeping my attention on the guard. "Call the elevator. I'll return in a minute."

Benji remains at my side as we meet around the corner, Hunter immediately reaching into my suit jacket to retrieve my phone.

"What are you doing?" I scowl.

"Calling myself," he murmurs, holding the device up to my face to unlock the recognition software. He taps through screens until a vibration sounds in his pants. "I'm not going to bother talking you out of this. I already know you've made up your mind. But at least this way I can hear what's going on." He keeps his voice low, barely above a whisper as he pulls out his device and answers the call. "We'll start scouring floors. If there's all this security that asshole spoke about, it won't be hard to determine where you are."

I agree. But starting a search isn't an option. Not when Benji is fidgeting like a crack addict. He's not in his right mind. I never should've brought him along.

"I want you to remain down here." I reach into my pants pocket, pulling out the car fob. "Better yet, wait in the Escalade. I can't risk this being fucked up by someone acting on emotion."

"No." Benji gives a frantic shake of his head. "I won't fuck—"

"Go to the car." I shove the fob at Hunter's chest. "Keep him under control, and link Luca, Deck, and Anissa into the phone call."

"Anissa?" he snarls.

"You heard me. If this is a trap, I need her to be aware so she can get my sisters to safety."

His eyes harden with disapproval. I don't give a shit.

I'm so fucking impatient to have this over and done with. "Go." I jerk my chin toward the doors. "Be ready for when I return with those kids."

I don't wait for compliance. I turn on my heels and walk around the corner, coming face-to-face with the guard who shoves his finger against the elevator call button, the doors gliding open instantly.

I lead the way into the enclosed space and clear my head of toxic pessimism.

I'm going to get those fucking kids. It'll be a cakewalk. No dramatics. No foul play.

The guard follows, pressing the button to close the doors once he's inside. "I'm going to need you to surrender any weapons you might have." He holds out a hand. "And before you think about keeping any hidden, I'll be patting you down to make sure you comply."

I grind my teeth and retrieve my gun to slap it into his palm. "I expect to get that back."

"What else have you got?"

"Nothing." I spread my arms wide and glower as he frisks me.

"You're a smart man." He says once he's done. "Mr. Costa will appreciate that." He turns to the doors, using a security panel to tap in a pin code before pressing the button to the penthouse.

The restrictive coffin glides into movement, the smooth ascent raising the hair on the back of my neck. My only saving grace is the cell in my pocket giving me some sense of backup. But that's a mirage at best. Nobody can help me here. The success or failure of retrieving these kids is on my shoulders.

After the elevator stops, the doors open into an expansive sunlit entertaining area.

"Walk toward the kitchen," the guard instructs. "Once you reach the dining area, continue down the hall to the first door on your left. You'll find Mr. Costa in the study. I'll have your gun waiting for you on ground level."

I step out onto the marble tile. "Why am I not surprised he's in the penthouse?" I say for Hunter's benefit.

There's no reply apart from the gentle glide of closing steel as the elevator leaves, taking the guard with it.

This place is wide open space. The living room before me with its modular sofa and towering artistic paintings transitions into the dining area up ahead, with the kitchen beside it on the left. Closest to me is a staircase with a glass balustrade leading to a hall on the upper level.

But there's no fucking security.

There isn't a soul in sight as I continue forward, scanning nearby rooftops, hoping a familiar rifle scope is tracking my movements. There's no sound either. No voices of children or of men—only the slow thud of my footfalls.

I reach the kitchen, eying the darkened hall up ahead with the soft glow of artificial light coming from the open office doorway. I stop, waiting for a hint of the approaching trap to shut in around me, and hear the low murmur of muffled conversation in the distance.

I don't doubt it's Costa, but when there's no evidence those kids are even here I'm loath to move further. I'm lacking alternatives though.

I have to keep walking.

I follow my instructions to the start of the hall, the foreign conversation growing louder. I keep my head high, letting anyone watching via hidden surveillance know that I'm not fucking daunted in the slightest when I reach the office threshold and scowl as I look inside.

"Mr. Torian." Costa sits behind a grand oak desk in a cream woolen sweater, smiling enough to make deep wrinkles around his eyes.

Two men—his sons—flank him in black suits, their posture stiff, faces blank. Even if I hadn't done my research, it wouldn't be hard to recognize the resemblance in the chiseled jawlines and tightly pressed lips.

"It's good to see you again." The old man beams. "You were a child the last time I laid eyes on you."

I keep my mouth shut, unable to reciprocate the civility, and focus my attention on a younger man seated on what looks to be a dining chair at the left side of the desk, facing me.

There's no natural light in here. The curtains are drawn. But I can clearly see the fear emanating from the guy as his leg jolts a frantic rhythm. This fucker has *guilt* written all over his pockmarked face.

"Let me introduce you." Costa reclaims my attention, sliding backward in his plush office chair to pivot to the left, waving a hand at the raven-haired man behind him. "This is my oldest boy, Salvatore."

He swings in the other direction, indicating the son with lighter features, dark blond hair. "And Remy."

Both men are roughly my age, the spite in their eyes matching my own. They're battle ready. I may not be able to glimpse a weapon but I'm sure they're locked and loaded under their designer suit jackets.

"Enough with the pleasantries." I return my stare to Emmanuel. "Where are my niece and brother?"

"Your brother?" He raises a brow. "Interesting. I wasn't aware your father had another child."

"Where are they?" I add vehemence to my tone.

"There's no need to rush. We have a lot to discuss." He indicates one of the leather chairs in front of the desk. "Sit. Please. These unfortunate circumstances could work out to be an exciting opportunity for us all."

My palms heat, the building sweat the first sign of my waning restraint. "I have no time for exciting opportunities. My sister is beside herself with worry. And those kids must be—"

"Those kids have had a wonderful time. And I told you there was nothing to concern yourself with. We're all family here. Now sit."

Burning animosity claims me. Heat lashes my neck. Cheeks. Throat.

"Sit." His smile fades, his psychotic jubilation simmering.

"While I have you here, I want to discuss some business I had with your father."

"I'm not discussing anything until I see those kids." I stride forward, grabbing the top of the chair he's trying so hard to get me into, the leather squeaking beneath my harsh grip. "Not a damn fucking thing, old man."

He sighs. "As you wish." He glances over his shoulder to Remy. "Take him to see the children. Make it quick."

The son jerks his chin in acknowledgement and strides around the desk to the office door. I stalk after him, following back down the hall, past the kitchen.

"Wait here." He continues up the stairs to walk from view.

The eerie silence returns, the open and close of a door in the distance the only sound. None of this makes sense. Costa is far too calm and collected. There's no malice. And the fatherly act grates on my nerves.

The door opens again bringing numerous sets of footfalls. Heavy ones.

A hulking guard comes into view at the top landing. Another passes, descending to the bottom of the stairs. Then Remy escorts an older lady, two surprised kiddie faces peeking out from around her waist.

She must be Emmanuel's crazy-ass wife.

"Uncle Cole?" Stella's eyes widen before she rushes down the steps.

My relief is suffocating. I grin at her, dropping to a knee as she runs into my arms.

"I was so worried." Her arms squeeze around my neck, tight enough to stifle circulation.

"I know, princess." I return the hug, resting my head against hers. "But everything is all right. You're safe."

She clings tighter, refusing to let go.

"Did anyone hurt you?" I whisper in her ear. "Are you okay?"

"I have a big bruise on my stomach." She leans back, meeting my gaze. "And my head is sore."

My veins surge with the searing need for retaliation.

"That didn't happen on our watch." Remy makes his way

down the stairs, passing the guard. "They've been looked after since arriving here."

Stella nods, but the confirmation doesn't lessen my struggle. That fucker in the office hurt her. *Bruised* her. What else did he do while she was unconscious?

"I understand what you're thinking," the older woman adds from the upper level. "And I assure you there's nothing to worry about. I would stake my life on it."

How the fuck would she know? She better not have examined my niece.

"Don't worry, Uncle Cole." Stella cups my cheeks. "My stomach hurts a little, but I'm okay."

She calms me the slightest bit, only enough to stop me seeing red.

"And how about Tobias?" I guide Stella to my side and reach for my half-brother who slowly walks toward us. "Are you okay?"

"I'm good." His gaze seeks Remy's, as if in approval.

The man doesn't react.

Pressure builds inside my skull. Someone has to pay for what's been done. Someone here, within these walls. "Do you have any bruises?"

Tobias shrugs. Once. Succinct. "Mine aren't as bad as Stella's."

"And Emmanuel has taken good care of you?"

They both nod, not needing encouragement from the man's son to make their decision. Not that the lack of prodding makes their response genuine. It merely means it's possible they were trained prior to my arrival.

"It's time for us to get back to the office," Remy instructs. "We've got a lot to discuss. Tobias why don't you take Stella back upstairs to play for a while?"

Both children look at me with widening eyes. It isn't fear exactly. There's surprise. Followed by heartfelt disappointment.

"I want to go home." Stella grabs my hand, entwining her small fingers with mine. "They've been nice, but I don't want to stay any longer."

I raise my gaze to Emmanuel's son. "You heard her. It's time to go."

The guy smiles, the curve of his lips contrasting with his harsh eyes. "I insist." He slides a hand beneath his jacket, making a barely subtle move for his gun.

The guards do the same.

Fucking pricks.

At least they're not obvious enough to upset the children.

"Fine. I'll give you a few minutes." I untangle my fingers from Stella's.

"Wait." Tobias dives for me, wrapping his arms around my neck to snuggle close in an unexpected show of affection. He's not a clingy kid. He's barely touched me since I found out about his existence in Greece, so having him bury his face in my neck is a fucking shock.

"They're not good people," he murmurs in my ear. "They didn't hurt us, but they're not good people."

I stiffen and force myself to wrap my arms around his shoulders, the reciprocated affection the only acknowledgement I can give as the adults scrutinize us. "I miss you, too, kiddo."

"Come on now." Remy jerks his chin toward the stairs. "Go back to your room and play for a while."

"It's okay, children." The older woman coos from above. "We can start another game of Candyland."

Stella remains hesitant while Tobias releases me, slowly inching backward.

"Go." I nod. "Don't worry."

I battle an invisible army as they reluctantly walk side by side to the guard at the bottom of the stairs. I'm thrumming with the need to act. To fucking slaughter. The compulsion for revenge makes goose bumps break out along my arms. But I keep myself in check and push to my feet, not saying a word as they climb the steps to meet the woman at the top.

"My father isn't a patient man," Remy warns.

A plethora of my own subtle threats bite at the tip of my tongue, demanding to be heard. I swallow their bitter taste and glare before making my way back through the living room, down the hall, to the office, finding Emmanuel in the same place behind the desk. Salvatore has remained at his side, the jittery fucker still anxiously pulsing his foot against the floor.

"I told you they would be well looked after." Emmanuel's face lights with sickening enthusiasm. "They have been a delight for me and my wife to spend time with. We're yet to be blessed with grandchildren. So our hearts have been warmed by this act of fate."

I breathe through my temper. I clench my teeth against the possessive violence inside me.

Emmanuel is fucking insane if he isn't unsettled by the current situation. He has no clue what I'm capable of. Or if he does, he's too maniacal to care.

Either way, he'll soon learn.

"Is this the man responsible?" I glower at the young guy who repositions himself in the wooden chair. "Did you steal them from my home?"

He doesn't respond as I stalk forward, sidestepping the leather seats to stop before him. "Are you the one who bruised their skin?"

His mouth opens, closes, opens again. He's a pathetic gaping fish, gulping for air.

"Yes," Emmanuel answers. "This is Jordan. I assure you he's remorseful for his actions. And accepts whatever punishment necessary."

Whatever punishment? I scoff.

No, he would never accept if he knew what was going through my head. Instead, he'd run, and so he should.

"How did you do it?" I snarl, discreetly scanning my surroundings. I take in any potential weapon within reach, every glint of metal, every sharp, pointed object.

He shakes his head. "I just did what Robert told me to do. We timed your guards. We knew when we could slip in and out unnoticed. It wasn't hard."

His confession is a lethal hit to my pride.

He stole from me. Easily. Without concern.

"And their bruises? If the crime against me wasn't hard, then I assume hurting those kids was intentional."

He glances to Emmanuel.

"Look at me, asshole." I grab his chin, wrenching his attention back to mine. "*Why* were they hurt?"

"I-I dropped the girl while trying to climb over your wall." He frantically shakes his head. "It was an accident. I never meant to—"

"It wasn't an accident to abduct them. So what did Robert plan to do with them?"

He keeps shaking his head. "I don't know. I swear I have no idea."

"Were you aware he was a rapist? A human trafficker?" I get closer, right in his face as I dig my fingertips into his jaw. "Did you even spare a single thought to what could've been done to them?"

There's no response.

"You stole from me," I grit through clenched teeth. "You handed over two of the most valued people in my life to a man capable of unfathomable atrocities, and you don't even have the balls to answer me?"

The whites of his eyes increase. His shaking doubles.

"Did you kill their nanny?"

"No." He reaches for the edge of the desk, clinging tight. "I didn't kill her. I just injected her with some—"

I lunge for the metal letter opener partially hidden under the stack of papers on Emmanuel's desk, twisting it in my palm before stabbing it into the top of his hand, straight through to the wood beneath.

Jordan yells, the sound vibrating off the walls before I slam my palm over his mouth.

I press harder and harder, until his suffering is nothing more than smothered whimpers. "You killed her. She was barely an adult herself and you gave her a lethal dose."

Moisture fills his eyes as he frantically attempts to dislodge the weapon pinning him.

"You're struggling." I narrow my gaze. "Let me help."

He stops. I'm not sure why. Maybe he senses my delight at his suffering and the barely leashed hunger for more.

The best part is that Emmanuel doesn't say a word. He doesn't attempt to stop me. For all the wrongs he's done, the silence from him and his sons is a start toward atonement.

"Please," Jordan begs under my palm. "I'm sorry."

I nod, removing my grip from his mouth. "I'm sure you are.

Did you even know who you were messing with when you agreed to work with Robert?"

"No. I just thought you were some rich business guy. I thought—"

I tug the letter opener from its pinned place in the desk, releasing his blood-covered hand.

"Shh." I place a finger to my lips as he whimpers. "You wouldn't want to scare those children again. They've been through enough."

The first tear falls down his cheek while he sniffs back the dribble from his nose. "I'm sorry, man. You've gotta believe me."

"Don't worry. I do." I wipe the carnage from the letter opener onto his pants, and he tenses. "You made a mistake you'll never repeat."

He nods. "I promise I won't. I'll never do anything to you. I'll never even—"

"I know you won't." I keep holding his gaze, devouring his fear, letting it sink deep into my chest to soothe my anger. "I'm going to make sure of it."

I launch the letter opener at his temple.

His eyes widen. His mouth drops.

My pulse thunders as I pierce the metal blade through skin, then bone.

He shudders, then slackens, his entire body turning limp. Dead.

For a few heartbeats, there's nothing but deafening silence. Pure, euphoric revenge. Until the *drip, drip, drip* of his blood begins to pool on the carpet.

Still, there's no response from anyone in the room as I jiggle the weapon free and wipe my fingerprints from the shiny metal with the handkerchief in my pocket.

"I hope you don't mind me borrowing your letter opener." I meet Emmanuel's gaze as I return the weapon to its original place on the desk. I'd wanted to see fear reflected in his features. At the least, I expected trepidation. But he lacks emotion. All of them do.

"That was unfortunate," he murmurs. "I would've appreciated if his mistake wasn't punished with something as barbaric as death, but I understand the reputation you must need to uphold."

Unfortunate?

He's not intimidated by me at all. Or at the very least, he's fucking good at not showing it.

"Boys, drag Jordan into the bathroom. He's an unnecessary distraction, and I don't want the blood to settle into the carpet."

His sons round the table, undeterred as they grab the chair and carry the body from the room, smearing a trail of carnage along the way.

"That's better." Emmanuel holds my attention through the removal. "Now, we can finally talk."

"What's to talk about?" I try not to scramble even though my options are narrowing.

"Our future." He smiles, mischief lighting his eyes. "And the things we can achieve if we work together. Would you like a coffee or maybe some tea? We might be here a while."

After what I just did, I'm surprised this fucker is offering me a beverage. He knows I don't want anything other than those kids. At a close second, I want this psychopath to drop the joker grin and level with me.

"Please take a seat, Cole. This is important. I wouldn't hold you up if it wasn't."

I stroll to the front of the chair, sit, and lean back to cross my feet at the ankles, ignoring the deep red staining the carpet in my periphery. "Start talking."

He claps his hands together in delight. "Now, as I've mentioned numerous times, your father and I were once close friends."

"Drifting apart from him is common. He hasn't kept in touch with many people since moving to Greece. Myself included."

"That's what I'm told." He nods. "Among other things…"

He's alluding to insight. To secrets.

I don't bite. Not even a fucking nibble.

"When we were close," he continues, "we had many plans to align our families. Combining my legitimate empire with your…" He frowns as if attempting to find the right word.

"Lucrative one?" I drawl.

He chuckles. "*Criminal* was the description I was looking for. We discussed in detail how my reputable imports were a great way for your family to smuggle product into the country—either what you already specialize in, or something more diverse. And the strength of my distribution channels has only increased with my business's success."

"I have no problems with my distribution, Costa. And no interest in aligning with anyone I don't trust. So unless you have something else to offer, I'm going to have to politely decline and be on my way."

"You have no problems now. But who's to say things won't change?" His smile fades with his rising brows. "Especially if you're using the same strategies as your father. He always tended to be generous with sharing information when he had a few too many drinks."

Is he threatening to shut me down? To rat me out?

I bark a laugh. "What do you want?"

"A partnership." Those white veneers flash at me again, bright and fucking sickening. "I want in on your little slice of heaven and to expand the playing field beyond your wildest dreams."

No.

This guy wouldn't know the first thing about the drug trade. And expansion isn't for chumps like him. It takes a lot of balls to claim someone else's territory, and when this guy has come to me for help instead of trying to take for himself, it's clear he doesn't have a decent set.

"I want what your father promised me." His tone loses any hint of civility as he opens a desk drawer, retrieves a sheet of tattered paper, and slides it toward me. "And this is what I'll get."

I take the scuffed offering to read my father's handwriting, my jaw tightening with each new line of text.

"Luther promised you an arranged marriage with one of my sisters?" I place the informal signed contract down on the desk and eye the letter opener within reach. "And you think that's going to happen? We're not living in the eighteenth century."

"I'm afraid I'm at a point where I must insist."

His sons return to the room, hands clean, faces impassive as they reclaim their soldier positions behind a man who's soon to die.

"Marriage is the best option to ensure an unbreakable agreement." That indulgent fucking smile doesn't fade. "We are both going to make more money than we ever dreamed possible. And generations to come will praise us for it."

"Thanks for the generous offer." I push to my feet. "But I'm not interested."

Maybe if he'd come to me a year ago. Before my father's degradation was exposed. Before those fucking kids were stolen. Before Anissa became everything.

"Well, you should be." His tone deepens, losing the edge of delirious kindness. "You seem to be in over your head, Cole."

He stands, leaning forward to rest his knuckles on the desk. "There are rumors your father is dead. Killed by his own son, no less. I'm sure it would be harmful if that information were to begin circulating. Especially with the loyalty Luther demanded. It wouldn't just be those children you'd need to worry about. It would be your sisters. Your men. Your entire empire."

I clench my teeth, the pain radiating into my skull. "Is that a threat? Because I take just as kindly to those as I do to theft."

"Of course not." He skirts the desk to walk toward me and rests his ass against the closest edge. "I'm merely pointing out that you may have taken a path you need help to retreat from. I'm that help, son."

I have no response. Not unless it involves snatching that fucking letter opener and slamming it into his throat. But I wouldn't get close before his sons filled me with bullets.

"Layla is already married." I force a placating smile. "And Keira is committed to one of my men. So, unfortunately, your sons will have to find their own unwilling brides."

"How about you?" Salvatore speaks for the first time, his voice graveled. "From what we're told you're still unattached."

I sneer at him. "You want to marry me, asshole?"

Remy grins, the curve of lips quickly disappearing into a tight line.

"He's referring to a match with my daughter," Emmanuel clarifies. "Abri would be well suited to a man like you."

My fingers itch to claim a gun I don't have. To pull a trigger that's nowhere in reach. "Again, that's a generous offer. But an arranged marriage isn't something I'm interested in. And I'm sure your daughter would feel the same. Now, if you'll bring the children back downstairs, we'll be leaving."

Silence reigns as the three men stare at me. The sons with eagle eyes. Their father with demented optimism.

"I understand where you're coming from." He remains perched on the desk, crossing his feet at the ankles. "However, I think your father would be disappointed in me if I didn't push for this opportunity. So I'm going to insist you take a night or two to think it over. Speak to your family. Contemplate the success. I'll continue to look after the children until you've had a chance to consider this more thoroughly."

21

______

ANISSA

Penny covers her mouth with a shaking hand as she stares at my cell sitting on the coffee table, the muffled conversation from the four-way phone call filtering through the speaker.

Keira is pale beside her.

Layla quit reacting a long time ago. She's now catatonic. Apart from the relieved cry she released at the sound of her daughter's voice, she's sat in shock, the only sign of life coming from her blinking eyes and trembling fingers.

At first, I hadn't known why Hunter called me. There was no greeting. Only silence. Then Cole's voice filtered through, announcing something about a 'penthouse'.

For long minutes, we've sat listening to his exchange with Emmanuel. We heard Stella's excitement. Vaguely made out a murmur from Tobias. Through it all, I've battled not to excuse myself to the bedroom to secretly call for backup. Well, I *had*, until Cole's conversation with Jordan.

Now it's too late.

The person who drove the kids to Sacramento is dead and the man I slept with last night is responsible. There's no requesting FBI support for that. There's no longer a claim to innocence in this situation.

"He's trying to force an arranged marriage?" Keira asks. "How is this even a thing?"

Layla closes her eyes. "How can you be surprised with everything else our father has done?"

She's right. This isn't as shocking as it should be.

It's sickening, though, the sinking sensation leaving me cold.

Only yesterday I'd convinced myself there might be a way to further indulge in my feelings for Cole. To somehow make it work between us. This is a slap in the face to those ignorant wishes. A shaking of my reality to show just how different our lives are. This archaic, arranged marriage only cements the extremes.

"What are we going to do?" Sarah stares at me, waiting for an answer.

"Let me listen."

The call has gone quiet, the conversation seeming to vanish mid-threat.

"Why aren't they talking?" Keira reaches for the phone. "What happened?"

I claim the cell and raise it to my ear.

There's nothing. No sound. No hint of static.

I unlock the screen and my heart drops. "The call ended. Either Cole disconnected or Hunter kicked us from the conversation."

"Why would that happen?" Penny stumbles to her feet. "What could possibly be worse than what we already heard?"

"He would've accepted the arranged marriage," Layla whispers. "He would've given his word to get my daughter out but wouldn't have wanted anyone to overhear him bowing under pressure."

Bile screams up my throat.

This wasn't meant to happen.

"Everything will be all right." Sarah reaches for Penny, dragging her back down to the sofa. "Cole needed to say whatever necessary to bring those kids home. But we'll fix it afterward."

Keira shakes her head. "If he commits, then he won't back out. He doesn't give his word without meaning it. Not even to his enemies. He either plans to marry this woman or has every intention of killing her to nullify the agreement."

"No," I blurt. "He could've lied."

They all look at me. The sisters with pity. Penny and Sarah with confusion.

"He plays games and manipulates the truth. He won't go through with it. Once he has Stella and Tobias, he'll pretend none of this happened."

"Maybe he's done that to you." Keira cringes. "And I apologize on his behalf, but this is business. In your world, there are contracts and legal documents to outline agreements. Here, Cole's word is his bond. He won't go back on it. Otherwise he'll never be trusted again."

My heart twists.

He'd given *me* his word. He'd promised to make us work. To figure out how we could indulge in this crazy compulsion between us.

I guess I should count myself lucky the universe is acting as my handbrake when I can't keep my grip on the wheel.

"Try not to panic." Sarah gives me a pointed look. "The kids are what matter right now."

Keira wrings her hands in front of her as she stares at the carpet. "Aligning ourselves with this family after what they've done is a horrible idea. Betraying them could be even worse."

My stomach churns. "I have to use the bathroom." I escape into the main bedroom, closing the door behind me to focus on not losing my shit.

I need space. Air. Clarity would help, too.

This is what I should've wanted all along. Having a valid reason to distance myself from the temptation of Cole has been a huge issue for me. *No*, not a *valid* reason. I had a million of those all along. But this would act as an immovable stop sign between us.

A definitive brick wall.

So why does it feel like Armageddon is approaching? Why does this growing ache inside my chest resemble heartbreak? For *him*. For what he's going through.

I breathe through the searing burn in my lungs and shake off the instability. I need to forge ahead. Focus on Stella and Tobias. It's not the time to wallow.

"They're on their way back," Sarah calls out moments later. "They should be here in five."

I scramble for the doorknob and launch out of the bedroom. "All of them? Are they okay?"

Sarah raises her cell, showing me the tiny text on screen. "That's all I know—*We're on our way back. Should be there in five.*"

Layla remains catatonic on the sofa, slowly rocking back and forth.

Keira continues to wring her hands, squeezing her fingers.

Penny bites hard into her lower lip, staring into space.

I'm not helping here. Why am I not helping?

"The kids are coming home, ladies. This is good news." I force positivity into my voice and walk to the closest sofa. "We need to get our things and prepare to leave as soon as possible. We're going home."

Nobody moves. Not even Sarah.

I crouch before Layla, placing my palms on her knees. "Stella's on her way."

She stares at me. Stares right through me.

"The weapons and tactical equipment are the only things that need to be packed," Sarah murmurs from the sofa behind me. "And I'm not putting my fingerprints on those. It's best if we wait here."

"I don't want to go anywhere either." Keira stands, hugging her arms around her waist. "Let's just wait."

I rub Layla's knees, waiting for a response that doesn't come.

She's deathly quiet, yet those eyes scream with foreboding.

"It's okay. They'll be here soon." I don't know what else to say to break the building silence. There's no encouraging chatter. Not even nervous tears. The room is still and unsettling as I sit on the carpet, one palm remaining on Layla's leg.

I sink into the uncomfortable void, consumed with selfish thoughts of Cole when Sarah pushes to her feet.

"They're here." She starts for the hall. "Hunt texted that they're just about to get in the elevator from the underground parking lot."

My heart races, the arduous pace disrupting my stomach to the point of nausea as she walks from view, the swish of the penthouse door opening moments later.

I can already picture the reunion. The gasps of relief. The happy tears. The hugs and kisses… Then Cole.

I imagine meeting his eyes again and how I'll react. How *he'll* react. Will he care about my response to an upcoming marriage? Will he arrogantly expect me to be his mistress? Will my obsession for him have me stooping that low?

It takes an eternity for the elevator to *ding* in the distance. A lifetime of suffering before we all stand. Layla pushes to her feet before me to rush to the start of the hall. Keira follows close behind. Penny only takes a few steps and I remain in place, unmoving.

I don't hear the patter of kiddie steps over the thud of heavier feet. The *thump, thump, thump* is dooming as Cole strides into the open area, his expression stony. Hunter and Benji follow in single file.

"Where are they?" Layla shoves between them to clear her view down the hall. "Where's Stella?"

Nobody replies.

My throat constricts.

Their faces say it all, especially Benji's, with his nostrils flaring and eyes watering.

"Where are they?" she repeats. Louder. Frantic.

"They're still with Costa." I barely recognize Cole's voice. It doesn't hold a hint of his usual confidence.

"You left them there?" Keira rushes forward.

"You left Stella with those monsters?" Layla shrieks. "How could you?" She lunges for her brother, striking out, pummeling his chest with closed fists. *"How could you?"* she screams. "You heartless piece of shit."

Nobody attempts to stop her. Not even Cole. He stares straight ahead as she assaults him, his shoulders stiff, his chin high.

"I fucking hate you." Her voice wavers with the punches. "I'll never forgive you."

"That's enough." Hunter moves between them, grabbing Layla's wrists. "He had no choice."

"He had every choice in the world. How could he leave them?"

I don't take my eyes off Cole. I keep watching his masked pain, breathing in his resilient suffering, feeling helpless to do anything but stare.

"Layla, you need to calm down." Keira walks up behind her

sister, placing gentle hands on the thrashing woman's shoulders. "We have to figure out what comes next."

"I know what comes next," she wails. "Somebody has to go in and get my daughter. Someone who isn't willing to turn their back on my innocent baby girl."

She jerks free and lashes another strike at Cole, the meaty slap clapping across his face. Benji steps forward, trapping her arms to her sides with a bear hug before walking her backward.

"We'll figure this out." He keeps moving, forcing her to retreat as she cries in protest. "We're going to get her back."

She crumples, her knees buckling. Benji lets her drop to the floor, her sobs building for unending minutes while the rest of us remain silent. It takes forever for the tears to fade into hiccups, the sniffles transforming to ragged breaths as she curls into a ball to bury her face into her knees.

Nobody says a word.

There's no clarification. No strategy talk. No plan. Everyone appears transfixed with grief.

"What happened?" I break the awkward quiet, willing Cole to look at me.

He doesn't answer. He barely bats an eye as he walks for the bedroom, ignoring me to close the door.

I start after him.

"Don't," Hunter warns. "Give him space."

I want to argue. To fight to be with Cole. But that's selfish. My response is all about me, not him.

"Where are the others?" I ask. "Where's Decker and Luca?"

"Watching Costa's apartment from a nearby rooftop." Hunter glares at me, maintaining his hatred. "We're going to need these rooms for a while longer. Sarah, can you—"

"I'll call reception." She nods and strides for the kitchen to snatch up the penthouse phone, asking to extend our reservation.

After she hangs up, the thickening tension builds around us. The unsettling awkwardness is stifling. I want to go after Cole. To comfort him. To ask questions. But I won't add to his burden.

"Do you know what happened?" I ask Benji. "What was agreed upon?"

"Nothing was agreed upon," Hunter replies. "Torian isn't committing to anything. Not yet."

"They want in on the drug trade—that much is clear," Benji adds. "Torian's buying himself time to figure out why they're taking this strategy."

"Buying himself time? My daughter is still in there. In the same place a man was just murdered by her uncle." Layla pushes to her feet. "She's gone through hell and Cole left her there. Left his only niece." She wipes the tears from her face with her forearm and sniffs. "I think we all know the reason he paused." Her gaze turns to me, accusing and spiteful. "He didn't agree to marriage because of you. You're what's stopping me from getting my daughter back."

I frown. "No."

Cole wouldn't do that. Not for me. Not at the cost of Tobias and Stella's suffering.

"Calm down," Hunter warns. "There was no choice but to leave them. He's not going to give his word on a threatening agreement that could kill us all in the long run."

"He's right." Keira's forehead wrinkles. "But I think Layla is, too. Cole has never walked away before. Not from something like this. He would've stayed and negotiated."

I keep shaking my head. "This has nothing to do with me."

I'm ignored.

"I swear it doesn't," I add steel to my tone. "There's no way Cole would walk out on those kids for me."

They have to believe it's the truth.

I have to believe.

Because otherwise I'll fracture.

Nobody has ever risked anything for me. Nobody but my parents, and now they're gone. I've made a life on my own. I'm independent. Isolated.

For Cole to even contemplate our relationship through any of this would be... I don't know. Overwhelming... Confusing... Crazy.

A cell rings and Penny is the only one to break the statuesque stance to drag her phone from her pocket.

There are murmured affirmations. Nods of agreement. Then a

soft farewell before she disconnects. "Luca and Decker are asking for food supplies." She starts for the hall. "I'll be back later. Please keep me informed."

"Wait, I'll come with you." Keira hustles to catch up with her, both of them leaving without another word.

It returns to the bitter quiet of grief, the occasional sniffle or hiccupped breath from Layla the only thing to temporarily disrupt the hollowness. And there's so damn much of it. A wealth of unanswered questions to leave me empty. A heart full of speculation I need to fill.

"Did Cole say anything else?" I look to the men for answers. "What did you discuss in the car?"

"Look, there's nothing that can be done," Hunter sneers. "Nothing by *you* anyway. Stay out of it."

Benji moves behind his wife, clasping her shoulders. "Let's go back to our room. You should take a Valium to help settle—"

"Go to hell." She wrenches away from him. "I'm not taking another goddamn Valium just so you can shut me up. You might not care that it's our daughter who's been left in there, but I do."

Benji's face falls. "I care."

"Then show it," she demands. "Get her back."

His pain morphs to shame, then animosity. He clenches his fists, his cheeks turning red. "I'm going to our room."

"Of course you are. Leave, just when your daughter needs you the most."

"*Layla,*" Sarah snaps. "Stop it. There's nothing he can do."

Benji stalks for the hall. The penthouse door slams seconds later.

"I won't stop fighting for Stella." Layla climbs to her feet. "You can all stand here and pretend to care, but it's not your child who was abandoned by her own uncle." She storms after her husband, but it's the far bedroom door that smacks shut, the force rattling the windows.

"I don't know what to do," Sarah admits. "I feel helpless."

"It's up to Torian." Hunter slumps onto the sofa, his heavy frame dwarfing the furniture. "It's his choice whether to negotiate with these fuckers, bringing them into our lives long-term. Or to risk the safety of those kids by attempting to retrieve them with force."

"What about the man Cole killed?" I ask. "Is he just going to leave him in their hands?"

Hunter kicks his boots onto the coffee table, crossing his feet at the ankles. "Who the fuck knows?"

The master bedroom door opens and Cole steps out in a new suit, his hair damp, his arms full of clothes. He strides for Hunter, handing over the bundle of material. "I need these incinerated. Make sure nothing is left behind."

His expression is devoid of emotion. Not one hint into his psyche.

Hunter inclines his head. "I'll get it done."

The exchange is sterile. Entirely bleak. It tears me apart.

"Are you okay?" I ask.

Cole doesn't look at me. Doesn't even acknowledge my existence. "I'm taking a walk."

I start after him. "I'll come with you."

"No," he grates over his shoulder. "Stay here."

I don't know what hurts more—the dismissal or the distance he's placed between us.

I'm tempted to defy him. To follow. To insert myself into his bubble of animosity until he lets down his guard. But that's all for my benefit. To make *me* feel better. To ease *my* suffering.

I can't make this harder on him.

Instead, I let him go, my heart breaking as he walks away.

22

COLE

I CIRCLE THE BLOCK BUT THE FRIGID AIR DOES NOTHING TO DISLODGE the guilt choking my clarity.

Layla's right. I chose to walk out on those kids. I left them behind.

I could've given my word and figured out a way to break it later.

I should've agreed to marriage. To a lifelong commitment. Anything and everything to get Stella and Tobias back.

Instead, I got caught up obsessing about my reputation if I gave in to Costa. I fought against pride, disgust, and fucking rage. I struggled to come to terms with not only a conversation that was out of my control, but the potential future where my family would be the weakest link.

And I thought about *her*. Anissa. The woman I wouldn't disrespect by claiming as my mistress if I became entangled in a mess that could drag me to hell.

I contemplated her too fucking much when I should've said whatever was necessary to secure those kids.

That option is gone now.

I abandoned them and have to live with the guilt. I also have to figure out what the fuck to do next when every possible option isn't an option at all.

There's no easy way out. No cheat sheet.

I stop in the middle of the sidewalk and rake my hands through my hair, pulling at the strands. My limbs thrum with the need to retaliate. To fucking kill.

If given the chance, I'd wipe that faux smile from Emmanuel's face with a slap of his son's dismembered hand. But while those children are in his possession, I'm powerless.

I call Decker for an update, and find out Stella and Tobias are clearly visible in the living room watching television with Emmanuel's wife.

They're safe. Calm.

"He's still taking care of them," Decker assures me. "I know it felt like shit to walk away, but it was the right decision."

I disconnect the call, not wanting his goddamn approval.

I didn't make the right decision, because there wasn't one. There still isn't.

"Fuck this shit." I keep walking, circling the block—once, twice—until I find myself back in front of the hotel doors, the window to the bar a temptation I can't ignore.

I stalk my ass inside and seat myself at the back of the room, the lone staff member behind the bar eying me with unease.

She wipes her hands on her apron and makes her way toward me, her steps cautious before she stops a few feet away. "Excuse me, sir. The bar doesn't open until noon."

"Make an exception." I grab my wallet and retrieve a wad of cash, sliding it toward her. "I need a drink. Scotch. Heavy handed."

I keep my attention on the cash, not wanting her to see the devil in my eyes.

"I, umm…" She clears her throat. "I really shouldn't. I'd have to check with the manager."

"Not even for a penthouse guest?" I rest into my seat, leaving the offer on the table. "I'm sure staff of this fine establishment are told to give their highest-paying customers the best service."

She straightens. "Umm. Yes, sir, of course. I'll be right back with your drink."

"Bring the bottle. Top shelf."

She turns on her heel and hustles away, returning with my prize and a glass with ice. I stare past her to the world outside as she pours a finger, wishing I had something stronger to ease the rage. To fucking eviscerate it. But there's no escaping this.

"Can I get you anything else, sir?"

"Privacy," I grate. "I don't want to be disturbed."

She nods, retreating. "I'll be setting up the bar if you need me. The doors will open in less than an hour."

I clasp the glass, tilting it in acknowledgement before throwing back the contents. I don't question the stupidity of lowering my IQ. The liquor is a necessity. If I don't dull the sharp edges of my self-loathing none of us will make it through the day.

We're all fucked if I can't get my shit together.

My cell vibrates in my pocket before I can pour another. *Anissa.* I know it's her before I pull out the phone and read the screen.

The device flashes as it pulses in my palm, over and over, the disturbance ratcheting up my discontent. I barely blink as I will the call to end, too fucking pathetic to reject it. I can't sever anything with this woman. Never could.

The buzzing stops, bringing a surge of isolation with it.

I drop the device onto the table and drink some more, searching for clarity or maybe oblivion.

She's helped to create such a fucked up mess. All it took was one glance. A superior smirk at my uncle's funeral. A few taunting words.

Since then I've savored angering her, disgusting her. I've even lavished the struggle to turn her hatred into affection.

It was meant to be fun.

A challenge.

It never was. There's always been more—the compulsion driven by a chemical attraction I can't deny.

No female has ever distracted me the way she does. No man, woman, or child has choked me of common sense like my little fox.

My cell vibrates again, her name mocking me.

I grasp the device, itching to throw it. Like always, I succumb to the addiction and swipe the screen, listening in silence.

"Cole? Where are you?"

I close my eyes. Clench my teeth.

"Cole?" she pleads. "You're worrying the hell out of me. Tell me where you are."

I know her fears. I always have. She may be concerned for my safety, but I'd bet my life she's more worried about her freedom. Her future.

This has gone far beyond abduction.

It's blackmail now.

Extortion.

Murder.

I never should've dragged her into this.

"Listen to me," she demands. "I'm calling Easton. I can't keep quiet any longer. You need help—"

"Like hell you will." I slap my hand on the table at the whiplash of that asshole's face in my mind. "You call him and I'll make sure he's dead before he can organize any so-called help."

"Then tell me where you are."

I stiffen. Straighten.

She deliberately triggered me.

Fucking Nissa.

I scoff out a sickening laugh and pour another finger of scotch.

"Cole, please. Let me come to you so we can talk."

I clench the glass in my fist. I do the same with the cell as I attempt to withstand her allure. Effortlessly, she does a number on my pathetic weakness, calling to my obsession with her endearing voice.

"Hotel bar. Come alone." I disconnect the call and slide the cell back onto the table.

I should send her home.

Everyone else needs to be here—my sisters, Luca, Penny, Decker. They all have an emotional tie to this situation. Everyone except Anissa. She's an unnecessary risk. And becoming an even bigger crutch.

The weight of her impediment only becomes more evident when she strides into the bar, her eyes frantically seeking mine, her beauty flawless as she wordlessly strips me of strength.

Worry settles into her features as she stops at the seat across from me, eying the scotch glass. The bottle. My face.

"Tell me what happened." She pulls out the chair and sits before me.

I don't respond. Not in words. I merely stare at her, sipping my scotch, willing her to walk away.

"Cole?" She raises a brow. "Talk."

"Why? So you have more information to give your boyfriend?" I tilt my glass at her in sarcastic praise. "Nice move with threatening to call him. I should've guessed he'd be the first person you thought of when I failed."

"You didn't fail." She cringes. "And it wasn't a threat. I don't know what to do. Easton is the only person I could possibly turn to. I have no family. No friends. I'm alone here. I want to help and I have nobody else to rely on. But I didn't call him. I blocked his number yesterday because I felt guilty whenever he messaged me."

"Let me be clear." I place the glass on the table and lean close, glaring. "Involving him will never help me. Not even if I'm on death's doorstep. Do you understand?"

"I understand your stubbornness," she counters. "I understand your wounded pride."

I flash my teeth in a snarl. "Go back to the room, Anissa. I can't focus with you here."

"I'm not going anywhere. Not until you tell me what happened."

"You heard," I grate. "You were on the damn call."

"No, I heard *parts*. Snippets at best. One minute, Emmanuel was discussing an arranged marriage. The next, there was nothing. I don't know what happened after that. I don't know why you left or what agreement you made."

I swirl the remaining liquid in my glass. "Does it matter?"

Her eyes soften into a look of sympathy. Pathetic pity. "Of course it does. I'm worried about those kids." Her tongue snakes out to moisten her taut lower lip. "And I'm worried about you. Are you considering marrying this woman?"

"I have little choice." I hold her gaze, attempting to decipher her thoughts over the prospect of my pending nuptials. "Right now, Costa has all the power. I can't wait around while he's got Stella and Tobias."

She swallows, her nose crinkling.

She's hurting.

I'm hurting her.

"It would be temporary." I want to reach out. To touch the pain away. "If I take that option, I'd marry her until I was in a position to get rid of her without leaving my hands dirty."

She winces, shaking her head. "Wouldn't Costa assume as much? Why would he risk his daughter?"

"My guess is that he either thinks I'm not capable of killing a woman, or that he can convince me of the benefits of the marriage before she's dead."

She keeps shaking her head. Keeps denying what has to happen if I take that route. "Would you at least meet her first? To see who she is? What she's like?"

"This is a business decision. Not a love match. Looks and personality don't matter."

Her wince deepens, her unease multiplying.

"You don't agree with what has to be done?" I ask. "Do you have a better idea?"

"It's not that I don't agree. I just don't understand. If this was the only choice, why didn't you commit straight away and bring those kids home?"

She's fishing for answers I don't want to give. Admitting my exposure is loathsome. Fucking deplorable. But maybe that's what needs to be brought to light to help cement my way forward.

"Only one thing stopped me from giving in to Costa on the spot," I admit.

She sucks in a breath as if sensing the severity of my approaching truth. "What was it?"

I throw back the remainder of scotch, needing the burn to lessen the instinct to keep my mouth shut. "You, little fox. You're the only thing."

It wasn't the freedom of those children I thought about when the arranged marriage was put on the table. It wasn't my sister's pain or Benji's struggle.

My mind had focused on Anissa. The fucking Fed. The woman who has brought me to my knees without even knowing it.

I've convinced myself the kids were relatively safe under the watchful eye of the old woman. I've told myself that buying time to strategize was the only option.

But there was little strategy in my delay.

It all came down to selfishness.

I hesitated because I didn't want to give Nissa up.

If it wasn't for my narcissism, those kids could already be free.

Stella would be in Layla's arms. Tobias would be snuggled close with Penny. The jet would be in the air, taking us home, and I'd be making wedding plans with a woman I'd soon dispose of.

But at least the children would be safe.

"Say something," I demand.

For numerous pained heartbeats Anissa stares right through me, blinking her wild eyes. "What do you want me to say?"

I scoff. "I dunno. Maybe something to address the fact I risked everything for you. For *us*." I slam my glass down on the table. "I should've agreed to marriage as soon as it was mentioned and worried about figuring out a way to gain the upper hand over Emmanuel later. But what I couldn't do is spit in the face of what we have without speaking to you first."

"You shouldn't have." She shudders. Cringes. Shakes her head some more. "Why would you do that? I don't understand why I was a part of your process at all. It's too much."

"Is it? Have I got us so completely wrong that I'm imagining shit that doesn't even exist between us?"

"It existed." She looks at me with despair. "But it shouldn't have. This is getting too complicated."

"So that's your decision? You're telling me to marry her?"

"No." She balks. "I'm not telling you to do anything. It's not my choice to make."

"That's exactly what this is," I add spite to my tone. "I'm letting you know right now, my decision to marry this woman rests firmly on your shoulders."

"No." She glares and pushes to her feet.

I do the same, grabbing her wrist to drag her back down and hold her across the table. "You're meant to be at my side," I snarl. "It's where you belong."

"I don't know where I belong." Her voice cracks. "But I'm certain it's meant to be in a far simpler life than this."

There's a plea in her words. An unspoken cry for help.

It fucking kills me.

"I'm drowning, Cole. I don't know how to help you."

"Then go." I release her. "I'll book you a flight and arrange a car. I'll have the concierge send your belongings back tomorrow. You don't even need to go upstairs to pack."

She continues to glare, yet there's no venom in her focus. The viciousness is smothered under a far heavier emotion. She wants to admit her desire to stay. She needs to, if only she wasn't more stubborn than I am.

"Leave, Anissa." I jerk my head toward the lobby. "Go and don't look back. I won't stop you. I won't seek you out again either. If you want this to be done, it's done."

The admission burns holes in my throat. But it's the truth. If she walks, I'll give my promise to be married, and retrieve those kids. I'll figure out how to break ties with Costa later, while siphoning revenge along the way.

She pushes to her feet, this time slower, her weary caution staring down at me. "You need to do whatever it takes to get Stella and Tobias back. You never should've hesitated for me."

"Wouldn't you have done the same?"

She flinches, her chin hitching slightly before she glances away, denying the truth.

She doesn't need to admit it out loud. I already know. Her initial reaction would've revolved around me, just like mine did for her. It's the settled dust that causes the problems. The callousness of the decision.

"We're meant to be together," I growl. "I've been committed to you since the day we met. But now it's your turn to decide. You can't sit on the fence anymore. Do you pick me or your unhappy life?"

"That's unfair." She crosses her arms over her chest, building a barrier between us. "You can't make me decide your future."

"You were my only future until today. So quit thinking of life as unfair and just. Good and bad. Moral and corrupt. Say you'll be my wife and I'll do anything to make that happen. I'll tell Costa his daughter isn't an option because I've vowed myself to you."

She sucks in a breath, the shock fading under a quickly descending frown. "Stop it."

"Why? Because you're scared?"

"Of course I'm scared. My chest physically hurts due to my fear for you and those kids, but I also don't want to spend a lifetime in prison."

"Instead you'd prefer to spend the rest of your life in misery? Wasting every day wondering what it would've been like to be happy with me? Prison is a minimal risk, Nissa. I'd always protect you. You'd have the world at your feet if you were with me. I could give you the opportunity to set up foundations. Charities. I'd give you all the money you'd need—"

"I don't want your money," she snaps.

"Then what do you want?" I shove the scotch bottle and glass to the side, leaving nothing between us. "Why are you still here? Why haven't you thrown my marriage proposal back in my face and stormed out?"

"That was a proposal?" Her mouth gapes. "You're serious?"

"Marry me." I say it louder, strengthening the words. "Commit to me and be my wife. Show my family I haven't made the wrong choice in hesitating with those kids, because you make me stronger. You make me fucking unstoppable."

She winces, those beautiful hazel eyes pinching as she swipes her tongue frantically over her lower lip. When she glances over her shoulder to the lobby, I'm in trouble.

Her doubts are winning the fight.

"You've never felt at home in the FBI, Nis. They're not your family."

Her fingers twitch at her side, her gaze once again returning to the lobby.

She's going to run.

"I'm sorry," she murmurs. "I can—"

"I know more about your father," I cut her off, using the low blow as a leash to keep her with me. "I know so much more than you'd want to believe."

Her face pales, the color draining to reveal the starkness of the heartache I'm causing.

"You wanted him to be moralistic and pure. To be an agent who everyone looked up to, but—"

"*Don't.*" This time her plea is pained, torn from the depths of her soul. "Don't start the games again. Don't say something you can't take back."

"He's exactly who you're meant to be. He makes his own rules. Follows his own path. He's on my side now."

The color continues to fade from her features. "I don't believe you. You're only saying this because you know things are—"

"You're right. I'm telling you because I know you're going to run." I push to my feet. "Because like I said, I can't follow this time. And even if this shitstorm could work out, I have pride, little fox. I won't chase you again."

She squares her shoulders. "Where is he?"

"Chicago. Working for an associate of mine. Slowly paying off the debt he owes my family."

Her lips press tight, her stubborn disbelief creeping in as she says, "He wouldn't have stayed away."

"Are you sure? Do you really think he could've faced returning to you?" I make my way around the table. "He threw away the career you idolize. He turned to criminals for help. And he left you alone while you grieved your mother's death."

She retreats a step. "You're doing this to hurt me."

"Maybe." I take caution in my approach. "Maybe I'm doing it in retaliation for you wanting to walk away from me again. Or maybe I'm trying to make you fucking realize this is where you're meant to be."

"You're lying. He wouldn't have abandoned me."

"Who says he did? Haven't you ever wondered why you have such remarkable rent control? Not one damn change in your payments in how many years?"

She straightens, her face betraying her shattering emotions. She glances toward the bar, her arms finding their way around her chest again, her sniffle an agonizing grate against my ears as she blinks through rapidly building tears.

"Why didn't you tell me?" she whispers. "Were you waiting for a time to use this as ammunition?"

"It wasn't my plan to keep the information from you. But laying his secrets bare in Greece was too soon. You wouldn't have believed me. And after we returned, you made it your mission to build distance between us."

I hate her suffering.

When we're fighting and spiteful, it's different. I usually thrive on her venom. Not when she's like this, though. Not when her pain is palpable and her devastation is threatening to break free.

Her lips part, then close again. She struggles to remain composed as she keeps eying the escape.

I grab her arm, ignoring how she stiffens as I drag her into me. "I was going to tell you. You need to believe that."

"I don't know what to believe. My entire reality is changing. Nothing is what it's supposed to be. Not my memories of my father. Not my feelings toward you. I can't make sense of any of it."

I hold her through the arduous heartbeats, her palms resting gently against my chest. I've always loved her strength. Her tenacity. But this—the lost, vulnerable side of her—is what breaks down my walls to leave me a chained slave at the altar of her existence.

She owns me.

She always will.

"Be my wife," I whisper. "Give me a reason to take a different path with Costa."

She doesn't move, doesn't even say a word as I struggle through her silence.

"My life will be yours." I rake a hand through her hair, placing my lips to her forehead. "You'll be happy with me."

She sucks in a shuddering breath and holds it tight. She doesn't return my hug. Doesn't reciprocate the affection at all, except for the subtle lowering of her head to my shoulder.

I could hold her like this forever. My possession. My treasure.

Before I can get enough, she steps back, sniffing away her emotions to stand tall. "I appreciate you telling me about my father. Although, I'm sure you could've found a way to do it sooner."

She looks anywhere but my eyes—at the bar, the lobby, my fucking suit.

She's about to leave.

"I, umm." She frowns, the words seeming to be agonizing. "I

need to go. Like you said—I'm a distraction. And that's not helping get those kids back."

"So you're telling me to marry her?"

Her nose crinkles as she nods. "If that's what you think needs to be done… If that's how your world works…" She shrugs. "I don't know. I'm out of my league here. This is all beyond my comprehension."

"It's not my usual wheelhouse either, little fox."

Her lips curve in a pained smile. It's only brief. The slightest glimpse of heartfelt beauty before it slips beneath her suffering. "I really need to go." She jerks her head toward the lobby, killing me slowly. "I'm not going to waste any more of your time."

"Nissa." Her name is a warning. A brutal fucking plea.

She can't walk out on me again.

She has to know I won't chase her a second time.

"Leaving is the right thing to do." Her face crumples. "But I want you to know I wouldn't go back and change anything. Not even what happened in Greece. Luther needed to be taken down and I'm glad I was there to do it. Everything worked out the way it was meant to."

Even us?

Even the sweat and seduction? The addiction and compulsion?

I want to ask, but my pride won't allow it.

I'm done. Fucking shattered.

"Go get those kids." She retreats. "Do whatever needs to be done."

I want this conversation to stop. I fucking need it to, if only severing her words didn't mean cutting short the last moments we have left.

"Goodbye, Cole." She scrunches her nose and swallows hard. "Stay safe."

23

―――――

COLE

She leaves me standing there, her head hung as she walks through the lobby to the city street, disappearing into foot traffic.

I don't follow.

Some sick, sorry part of me thinks she'll come back. That she can't possibly leave me again. But deep down, I know that's not my Nissa.

When times get tough my woman clings to stability, and obviously, I don't make the cut.

"Can I get you anything else, sir?" the bartender asks from behind me.

"No." I pull out my wallet and throw more cash on the table. I have to get away from here.

I reach the penthouse, finding the kitchen and living room empty. Everyone's gone. Even my sisters. There's no note on the counter. No sign of life… apart from a faint rustle coming from the main bedroom.

"Hunt?" I palm my gun and aim it at the open door.

"Yeah. In here."

I stash my weapon and stalk to the threshold, finding him standing near the bed. "What are you doing?"

He shrugs. "I just got back from grabbing something to eat."

I scrutinize the room. The bed is still unmade. The bathroom door is wide. Everything seems normal except for Nissa's suitcase that was neatly packed on the floor the last time I checked and is now a pile of tangled clothes.

My pulse quickens, the heavier beat inspired by a protective nature I need to ditch.

"I came in here looking for you," he adds.

"Did you think you were going to find me in Nissa's suitcase?" I can't keep the aggression from my tone. "Why were you touching her things?"

He grins. "It's my job to make sure you're safe. I bet you wouldn't have checked to make sure she didn't stash anything suspicious."

He's right. I didn't.

I trust her. Even despite the threats to involve Easton.

"Leave her shit alone. She's not your concern." I check the safety on my gun, then lob it toward him. "Give this a once-over to make sure the guard didn't tamper with it. When you're done, relieve Luca from his watching post. I need him back here digging up information."

"Benji's already on his way to them now."

"Jesus Christ. Why the fuck would you think that's a good idea?"

He waves me away as he releases the magazine and drops it to the bed. "He wanted to see his daughter. And from what you've told me, it won't be a major issue if the sight of her gets the better of him. If he jumps off the roof and plummets to his death, it saves you from doing it, right?"

He keeps dismantling my gun, feigning disinterest even though I know that fucker is starving for a nibble of insight.

"Benji's a problem I don't want to think about right now." I discard my jacket and walk forward to throw it against the bed coverings. I can't get Nissa out of my head. Even with her gone and the ties severed, she's still the air I breathe. "Instead, we should start planning my buck's party."

"Yeah?" He starts inspecting each piece of my gun, not showing any shock. "You're going to cave to Costa? You don't want to go in there guns blazing?"

"I'm not placing those kids in the line of fire. It was bad enough leaving them behind."

"You had to stall. The old man is testing you. He's trying to figure out what you're made of."

I scoff. "I thought so, too. I anticipated him backing off once I killed the fucker who drove Stella and Tobias from Portland. But then he doubled down."

"He's a prick, that's for sure." Hunt starts clasping my gun back together. "There aren't many men who would witness murder, then immediately offer their daughter's hand in marriage. This girl of his must be nasty."

I don't give a fuck what she is. All that matters is that she's not Nissa. And I'll make sure she knows it, too.

"It might not work out too bad, though," he continues. "If you marry this bitch, then slowly knock them off one by one, starting with the father, you could end up owning a fashion label. Wouldn't that be ironic?"

"Ironic?" I grate. "How?"

"Because you're the least fucking fashionable guy I know." He shoves the magazine back into the gun and grins. "You've got one look and it's been done to death, my friend."

He's attempting humor. He might even be aiming to raise my sour mood. But he only has the opposite effect. Trying to make light of this situation when Nissa is already on her way home is eating me alive.

He sighs and lobs the weapon my way. "Where's the Fed? Who's keeping an eye on her?"

"She's gone." I return the gun to the back of my waistband.

"Gone where? To get her hair done? To paint her nails?"

I glare, despising the constant ridicule of a woman undeserving of his spite. "She's on her way home. She won't be back."

His grin increases. "Good riddance."

I clench my fingers, biting back the need to lash out. He's testing me. He wants to know where my head's at, and I don't want anyone aware of my lacking mental state.

"Go relieve Benji of his position. I don't want him watching those kids. I can't trust him to keep his head."

He watches me release the buttons on my sleeve cuffs. I need more room to breathe. These clothes are fucking choking me.

"Yeah, I can do that. But what do you have planned? What's

your next move?"

"I'll let you know when I figure it out." I sit on the mattress and kick off my shoes. I need a shower. A cold one. To wash Anissa from my life.

"She messed with you, didn't she?"

I don't react to Hunt's question as I unclasp my belt and slide it from my pants.

"How the fuck did she get under your skin?"

I push to my feet. "I've asked you to do something."

"Damn. When you said she was gone, I assumed you kicked her to the curb, but you didn't, did you? She walked." He huffs out a laugh. "What the fuck have you become?"

"Leave," I warn. "*Now.*"

"What are you going to do?" He straightens his shoulders. "You've gone soft, Torian. The man I originally came to work with would've thrived on Costa's proposal. You would've taken it as the perfect opportunity to infiltrate his business and pull it apart from the inside out. Especially after he dared to involve children in the games of men. But I'm beginning to think you're doing it as an easy out. You won't attack because you've become a pussy, and you're caving to him for the same fucking reason."

I glare, my anger fighting to break free.

"Holy shit." He laughs. "I'm right."

"No, you're not fucking right," I lie. "Kids are involved. I won't risk—"

"Fuck the kids. Don't let them be a weakness. Tobias has gone through heavier shit than this. The boy is Satan's fucking prodigy, for Christ's sake. And Stella isn't your responsibility. None of this is. Layla knew what world she was bringing her daughter into. She fucking knew. Yet she was the one who went behind your back. She risked that little girl when she started talking to Robert. This is on her head, not yours."

"You're a heartless son of a bitch, Hunt."

He inclines his head. "And you used to be, too. It's how we've survived this long. But the future is fucking grim if you're negotiating with assholes for the wrong reasons. If you cave because you think they're in control, then I'm out. I'm done. I won't work for someone with no backbone."

I gnash my teeth. I fucking thrum with volatility.

"You know it all started to go downhill when you set your sights on that bitch," he continues. "You got drawn in by a Fed and you couldn't even see that she was taking you down."

I grin. It's all I can do to stop myself from killing him. "You don't know the first damn thing about her."

"You might be right, but I know the exact effect she has on you." He looks me up and down, his nose scrunched in disdain. "She made you sloppy. You're not focused."

"Without her, I never would've taken down my father. She's far more valuable than you give her credit for."

"I'm aware of her value," he grates. "I always have been. Having a Fed in your pocket is far better than having one on the loose, but she wasn't in your pocket. She was riding your damn cock while she held the fucking reins."

My pulse pounds in my ears. My eyes burn with hatred. "Relieve Benji before you get yourself in trouble."

"I don't give a shit about trouble. I'm not leaving until you shake her off. The Fed's gone. Get over it."

I suck in a slow breath, willing the rage to subside without success. "You've always had a problem saying her name. Why is that?" I cock a brow. "Could it be because you're threatened by her? Maybe even a little jealous?"

"Jesus. You're losing your fucking mind."

"No, I don't think so. Not on this. You know she belongs here. You could see it just as well as I could, and that worried you."

"Of course it fucking worried me," he snaps. "She's the enemy and you gave her the keys to the kingdom."

She deserved them. Those keys were hers.

"Torian, listen to me." He moves closer, grabbing my shoulders with force, digging his fingers into muscle. "I wasn't threatened by *her*. I was threatened by what she could do to *you*. To our whole fucking set up. And I was right. You missed things you never would've missed before. You didn't even notice the betrayal from your sister and Benji because you were too head-fucked."

I launch a fist, striking a warning punch to his gut.

He takes the hit with a puff of air.

"You're wrong." I shove him backward. "My failings are mine

and mine alone. She hasn't fucking weakened me. *Life* has done that." I shove him again. "Finding out the degree of my family's filth has caused this. Burying my fucking uncle. Discovering what was done to Keira. Not to mention Decker's betrayal, and yours, for that matter. Then there was Greece. Now this." I stalk forward and shove him again. "That fucking *Fed* is the only reason I'm still standing. She's the strength that got me to this point. She's the only goddamn thing that kept me going."

"She was a distraction."

"No," I snarl. "She was my peace. My fucking redemption. And you owed her respect, not animosity."

His chin hikes, his hands fisted at his sides.

"I would've made her mine." I hold his gaze, letting him know the brutal truth. "She would've helped right this fucking shitshow. She would've had authority over you. Over everything. And I would've trusted her with it."

His jaw ticks. "Then you're a fool."

Maybe. But I would've done it without regret.

Nissa was a risk I couldn't back away from. Even now, I regret vowing not to chase her. I need her here. I crave the adrenaline-filled clarity she provides.

"Look..." Hunt huffs out a breath. "I get the infatuation. Seriously, I understand how messed up that shit is after meeting Sarah. But her leaving is the best thing—"

A knock at the door cuts him short.

He raises a brow, silently asking if I'm expecting visitors.

It could be anyone—my heartbroken sisters, any of my men, or goddamn housekeeping for all I know.

The knock sounds again, this time louder.

"I guess I'm answering that." Hunt stalks from the room, retrieving his gun from the back of his pants.

I follow into the living area as the knock comes again, and again.

"I'm coming," Hunt yells. He reaches the door, places his barrel against the wood and checks the peephole. "Jesus *fucking* Christ."

The hair on my nape prickles as I start toward him, my hand on my weapon. "Who is it?"

He snarls, "Trouble."

24

ANISSA

I sit my ass in the gutter between two parked cars, hiding from people passing by the front of the hotel.

Marriage.

Cole proposed marriage. Not just from left field, but from outer fucking space.

There's no way it would work. Not in a million years.

So why does it feel like I've made a mistake? Why is it so hard to now be separated from him?

My insides churn with abandonment, as if he's the guilty party who left me, instead of the other way around. This is exactly what it felt like when I turned my back on him after Greece. Only this time, it's stronger. The invisible hands wrapped around my throat are tighter.

I pull out my phone, needing to find grounding in the one person I can rely on, and ignore the guilt as I unblock Easton's number.

He'll know how to right this train wreck. He'll give me a dose of that Cole-is-a-maniacal-psychopath speech and I'll be pulled back from the brink of disaster. It's my trembling heart that makes it hard, even now, to defy Cole.

Message after message downloads to my cell, all the vibrating notifications coming from Easton. There are phone calls. Texts. Emails.

The guilt thickens over blocking him in the first place, followed by more shame over the barrage of unanswered communication. But I'd wanted the barrier. It felt right to be with Cole without distraction. At least until now.

I dial Easton's number and don't have a chance to back out before the line connects.

"Where the hell are you?" he demands in greeting. "I've been worried sick."

Despite his anger, it's good to hear his voice. "I needed to get away." I bend my knees, dragging them to my chest. "But I'm fine. There's nothing to worry about."

"Why do I find that hard to believe?"

"No, truly. I'm okay." I nod, attempting to convince myself of the lie. "Things just got a little hectic with my shrink, and us, and…"

"And Torian," he finishes for me.

I don't verbalize my agreement. We both know I don't have to.

"Take all the time you need, Fox—just quit ignoring me. I was about to file a missing person's report."

"I'm glad you didn't." I rub the heel of my palm over my sternum, attempting to dislodge the ache beneath it. I want to tell him everything. About Cole. And Emmanuel. Even the increase in my psychosis. But I can't get those words out yet. I need to fill the void with something else.

"I'm sorry." My voice cracks. "I shouldn't have kissed you the other night."

There's a beat of silence. The slightest pause that pummels me with remorse.

"Don't worry about it," he murmurs. "It was nice."

He nailed it. Out of every possible description, he picked the perfect one to explain our brief press of lips.

It was agreeable. Friendly. And in complete contrast to the sheer force of nature that happens when my mouth is on Cole's.

"Look, I know things are complicated with us working together," he continues. "But sometimes it's okay to do the wrong thing when it feels right. We're not always meant to follow the rules. We're born with instincts for a reason. That, by far, should be the ultimate measure of what's right and wrong."

I squeeze my eyes closed, hating that he's putting voice to what I've been trying to deny with Cole. The instinct to be with a man I'd usually despise goes far beyond anything I've ever experienced. I'm drawn to him. Even now, I want to run back to his side.

"I've hidden feelings for you for a long time, Anissa. We'll figure this out. There's no rush."

I shield my face with a hand, so fucking ashamed to have led Easton to this point when I'm in a completely different mental space to him.

The last twenty-four hours have solidified that there can never be a future between us. Maybe even between me and any other man. I'm lost to the hunger of Cole. Trapped in this thrilling desperation. I may have left him, but there's no returning to normal life after what we shared.

"I'm sorry but you misunderstood." I swallow over my agonizingly parched throat. "I don't feel the same way."

His silence is deafening. A car horn blares in the distance. The brakes of a bus hiss nearby.

"I wish I did," I murmur. "I wanted to feel the same. I pushed and pushed in an attempt to create those emotions because you're everything that's right in this world. But..." I shake my head, unable to explain. Or maybe I'm just scared to admit that even though something good was wrapped in a bow and placed before me like a prize, I decided to throw it away.

"It's him, isn't it?" He sighs. "What I feel for you, you somehow feel for him."

I'd love to be able to agree, but his statement holds no accuracy. There's nothing nice between Cole and I. There's fire and passion and flame. There's battle and so much bloody war, and beneath it all, there's a devastatingly sweet rebirth that captures my breath and infuses me with unbelievable strength.

"Are you with him now?" he asks.

"No." It's not a lie. I'm not with Cole. Not anymore. Even though my heart still is.

"But you want to be." He announces my weakness with bitter simplicity. "Is that why you're calling? Because you want me to make you feel better about throwing your life away?"

That hadn't been my intent at all. But maybe I'd been kidding myself.

I bury my head in my hand. "What sort of person does it make me if I say yes?"

"I guess it makes you more brutally honest than I anticipated."

I crinkle my nose to fight the burn. "My father works for him," I admit. "Or for someone aligned with the family. All this time, I thought he was one of the good guys. I pictured him as this unflinching voice of integrity and honor. Now I've found out he's…"

"He's what?"

"I don't know." I shrug to myself. "Like Cole. Like the person I feel drawn to become."

"You're not a bad person, Anissa. I don't know what happened to make you think you've got anything in common with those people, but it's not true. You're one of the good guys. You're one of the fucking best."

His words don't hit their mark. I'm not persuaded by his beliefs this time. And I'm unsure if I still want to be.

Being *good* doesn't hold the warm fuzzies it once did. There's no comfort.

"You're wrong." My conviction builds. "I've done things that go against everything I signed up for with the Bureau. I've committed crimes and—"

"Fox, this isn't a conversation to have over the phone. Why don't you come to my place? We can talk this out face-to-face."

No, I don't think I can.

Conviction is gaining the better of me. It's intensifying. Strengthening. The pull toward what I want is outweighing what I'd once thought was right.

"I'm like him, Easton. I'm exactly like Cole. And all the illegal things I've done lately don't come with remorse. If anything, I'm proud." I want to tell him about Luther. That a monstrous sex trafficker is now unable to hurt more women because of my actions. I've done bad things for good reasons and I'm okay with that. I'm emboldened. "I did something you would never forgive me for. It wasn't by the book and I don't regret—"

"Anissa, I'm hanging up. This line isn't secure."

"No, wait. I just need..." God, I don't know what I need. Approval, maybe. Acceptance? Closure?

Cole is an adamant vision in my mind. His hold on my heart is strengthening the more I fight it.

He's everything. And I don't think I can live through more weeks fighting where I'm drawn to. I can't let him go again.

"You've decided to be with him." The words seem to fall easily from his lips when I'm still trying to deny them.

I've relied on Easton to remind me of Cole's abhorrence. I've used him as a shield against my cravings when I never truly believed the negativity he spoon-fed me. I even had to self-diagnose a mental illness in an effort to protect myself. Yet, it's now clear Cole is a calling.

He's my path.

"Yes," I admit. "I have."

Easton's ragged exhale carries down the line, his pained emotion coming with it. "Do you realize you're going to lose everything? Your job. Your friends. Your life."

"Yes." And still I can't walk away. From Cole. From this compulsion that's worked its way into the marrow of my bones.

"That means me, too," he adds. "I can't stick by you through this. I won't watch you ruin your life."

My self-loathing builds. I hate even more that the decision to go after Cole still feels right. It's all there is. Conviction and growing determination.

"I'm sorry." I squeeze the cell tighter. "I wish I could explain—"

"Don't. I'd never understand anyway." There's no bite to his words. Only resignation. "But if you ever need a way out, I'll still be here. You'll always know where to find me, even if you can't find yourself."

I want to tell him I'm found. That after so long running, I'm right where I need to be. No longer a special agent of the FBI. Not the isolated woman who couldn't find her place in the world.

I'm Anissa Fox. Current lover to an underworld mastermind. Future queen to a lawless empire. And devoted slave to a man I never imagined I could admire.

As long as I'm not too late to claim what's mine.

25

——

COLE

"She's gone, is she?" Hunt shoots me a glare and yanks the door wider. "Doesn't look gone to me."

I stand tall as Anissa walks into the penthouse, keeping her distance from Hunt to continue along the hall toward me.

"Come back for your things?" I keep my tone level, not buying into the optimistic throb in my gut. "I told you I'd have them sent to you."

She stops at the entry to the open living area and glances over her shoulder, eying Hunt before shaking her head. "No."

"I swear to God," he growls. "You two are the stupidest fucks I know."

I scowl at him. "Go get Benji."

"Do you want me to tell the others what's happening?" He pastes on a malicious smile. "I'm happy to break the news of your agreement to the arranged marriage."

Anissa stands straighter, her chin inching higher.

I flex my fingers. "I suggest you keep your mouth shut."

"Well, I'd suggest you keep your dick in your pants, but we both know that ain't gonna happen."

He storms out, slamming the door behind him, the vibrations momentarily ringing through the penthouse until the noise fades into uncomfortable quiet.

The distant sound of city traffic is the only reminder of the outside world. But I don't break the silence. Not for a long time. I lean against the wall, pretending I'm okay with the suspense, as she rounds the sofa to stop at the glass doors and stares across the Sacramento skyline.

She doesn't talk. She merely stands there with her back to me, chin high, shoulders straight, posture perfect.

"What are you doing here, Nis?"

Her head bows momentarily before returning to the confident angle. "I came back."

"I can see that. What I want to know is why?" I should kick the superior undertone from my voice. I really fucking should. But superiority is all I have until she retrieves the knife she embedded between my ribs.

"I thought you'd already be halfway to the airport by now." I push from the wall. "Do you need me to arrange a car?"

"No."

She's fucking killing me with this subdued bullshit. I want to shake the answers from her. And maybe I will. I can't handle this twenty-question routine.

"Nis, I don't have time for whatever the hell this is. What do you want from me?"

She turns my way with stark eyes, her fragility clearly visible in those hazel-green depths. "I called Easton."

Motherfucker.

The rage is instantaneous. The heat suffusing my face becomes a fucking furnace.

"Don't look at me like that." Her expression hardens. "I didn't do it to upset you."

"Give me your phone." I stalk toward her, thrusting out a hand. She's played this card before. I need to make sure she's not bluffing again. "*Now.*"

She raises her brows as she pulls the device from her pants pocket with a faint sniff. "Are you going to break it?"

Not as much as I'm going to break him. "Unlock it."

She does that too, her stare turning haughty as I scroll through her recent calls, finding the truth about her deception.

"Fucking hell." I lob the device at the sofa. "What did you tell him?"

She holds my gaze, her jaw tight.

"What the fuck did you tell him, Anissa?" I close in on her, almost nose to nose, making it impossible for her to escape my fury.

She crosses her arms over her chest and raises her chin, attempting to stare me down. "I said goodbye."

Shock hits me. Confusion, too.

The silence returns, but this time it's loud. The absence of sound deafens me. The beat of my pulse thunders.

"He doesn't know where I am," she murmurs. "But he knows I'm choosing you—your life, your world."

This is a trick. A game.

She's telling me exactly what I want to hear, and I'm not sure why.

"Now it's your turn to say something." Her teeth dig into her lower lip. "What are you thinking?"

"I want to know what you're playing at."

She winces. "I'm not playing. I told him how I feel about you."

"And how is that?" I growl, biting back the tension growing in my gut.

She breaks eye contact to stare at the sofa. "You already know."

"I certainly thought I did back in Greece. Then again after last night. But you've walked away from me twice now. I'd be a fool to give you the opportunity to do it a third time."

"No, you'd be a fool for not realizing I wasn't walking from you, but instead attempting to hide from what I didn't want to accept." Her gaze raises to mine. "Fear drove me away. Nothing else. I understand that now."

I want to gorge on her words. To dive into them with unwavering faith. If only it were that easy. "What changed?"

"The thought of losing you outweighs the fear." Her arms fall to her sides as her chin regains the slightest hitch of determination. "I can't see you with someone else."

That's good to know. But still, I won't sink my teeth into the prize standing before me. Not when I'm sure it's a mirage.

She sighs. "You're not going to make this easy on me, are you?"

"It wasn't easy watching you walk away."

"I'm sorry, okay? You say things that scare the hell out of me. Marriage, for starters. Then the constant talk of ownership."

"That's this life, Nis. It's how I live. If I don't own every single aspect of my existence, I'm as good as dead. I need to own every move I make, every thought, every action, and every damn woman I stake a claim to, otherwise my enemies target the weakness, just like they did with those kids."

She hikes her chin. "I won't be owned, Cole."

"Why not? You've owned every damn inch of me for too fucking long. Is it really that demeaning to return the favor?"

Her eyes flare before she quickly hides the shock. "I don't own you."

"Yes, you do."

"Well, I don't want to. I need something less sterile." Her throat works over a heavy swallow. "I want to know there's more than just heated games between us. Ownership means nothing to me when it's your heart I want." Her cheeks darken as if she's embarrassed by her admission. Such pink, beautiful cheeks that emphasize the intensity in her gaze.

I prowl closer, her request a lead weight in my throat. "You want love."

She shifts her focus over my shoulder, denying me eye contact.

"You can't admit it?" My palms sweat, demanding touch. "Why is that?"

"Is that emotion even possible for you?" Her attention snaps back to mine in accusation. "Do you even know what love is?"

I take her savage blows without retaliation. "Yes, I know." I reach out, brushing my hand over her neck.

She flinches, attempting to back away only to be captured in my grip, my fingers tight around her throat.

I get in her face, demanding her attention, her heated breath brushing my lips. "I fell in love with you that night under the tree in Greece. With your makeshift shiv and your desperation to stab me. And I've loved you in every moment since."

Her pulse quickens beneath my touch, her inhales increasing.

"There's nobody else, little fox. There never will be."

Her throat convulses under my palm, her gaze growing with determination.

"You *will* marry me." My murmured demand snaps her rigid. "Maybe not this week or the next. But you will be my wife." I lean closer, unable to resist the need to taste her as I press my mouth to her jaw. "And you will be happy. I vow this to you."

She shudders, closing her eyes. "I think I fell in love with you before Greece. Back in that café, when you manipulated me with so much ease and confidence before Luther's escape from custody that it was impossible not to appreciate your brilliance."

I grin, falling victim to her admission. Her truth warms me in a way I've never experienced. It brings weakness yet so much fucking fortitude.

There's no going back from this.

No walking away.

No goodbyes.

"Tell me you're mine." I kiss her chin, her cheek, the corner of her mouth. "I need to hear you say it."

She whimpers. "I don't know—"

I slam my lips against hers, still holding her neck tight. I punish her with my tongue, dragging her body into mine with the tight wrap of my arm. When I ease back, she gasps for air, clinging to my shirt.

"Cole, I—"

"Tell me," I demand. "Convince me you're done walking away."

She shakes her head. "What about the children? And this woman you're meant to marry? What about Hunter and your sisters?"

"Leave that shit to me." I'll figure a way to right this train wreck. What I need is to know she'll be waiting for me at the end.

"I don't want to lie to you." She inches back. "I'm in love, Cole. I'm just not sure how this can work."

"*Trust* me," I growl. "Forget Costa. Forget Hunter and anything else outside this room. And tell me, right now, that I'm what you want. That *this*—" I point between us. "—is how you want to live your life."

She licks her lips, her brows pinched.

I'm waiting for her to attempt to look at the door, and holy fuck, I'll hold her head in place if I have to. She wants this. I need her to have the conviction to own it.

She swallows, holding my gaze, her eyes glassy with vulnerability. "This is what I want."

Relief is an overwhelming bitch.

I plaster my mouth to hers, sinking my fingers into the flesh of her hip. I devour her, stealing her breath and losing my own.

She mewls against my lips, her hands clutching tight against my shirt. She's fucking everything. My guidance. My meaning. She's going to pull me out of the shitshow that has become my life and help right the downfall, but more than that—she's going to be there. Beside me. Always.

Forever mine.

"God, I want you." She grabs my waistband, unclasps my belt. "I need you."

I'm rock hard before she's yanking at my zipper. I'm fumbling to catch my gun, my dick fucking throbbing by the time she grabs at my boxer briefs.

"Wait." I snatch her wrist in warning. "This time you're meant to be savored."

She shakes her head, her eyes wild with lust. "Call me impatient."

I snicker as I release her arm to place my gun on the sofa. "You need to be taught some restraint."

"To hell with restraint." She kicks off her shoes and steps closer, placing her hands around my neck. "We have the rest of our lives to savor. I want what comes naturally."

A growl of appreciation vibrates in my chest. "Natural means rough." I grasp her hips, yanking her into me. "Natural means we get our fill, fast and intense."

She tilts her pelvis, grinding against my dick, making us both moan.

"That's what I want." She reaches between us, unbuttons my shirt, exposes my chest. "I can't do slow right now."

I swoop forward and pick her up, one arm cradling her back, the other behind her knees, and carry her to the bedroom. I sit her on the mattress as she scrambles to pull out her gun, shoving it toward the top of the bed.

She reefs off her suit jacket. Discards her holster. Undoes her pants.

"Stop." I kick off my shoes. "You're unwrapping my present without permission."

"This isn't your birthday. We don't have time to mess around with packaging."

I grin, unwilling to further my protest as she fumbles to release her blouse buttons, then leans forward to shove down my open pants and boxer briefs, exposing my dick.

She grasps my length in her hands, squeezing the hardness. Tempting fate.

"Wait," I growl.

Her eagerness is killing me, especially when I'm being denied the full sight of her.

I grab her panties, forcing her to let go of me as I yank them off. Her socks, too. "Spread those gorgeous legs."

She rests back on her elbows, splayed before me like an artist's inspiration. I want to remember this until the day I die—the burn in my chest, the hunger in my veins.

Her knees part slightly as a faint grin teases her lips.

"I said, spread 'em." I grasp her knees, forcing them wide, making her gasp.

This sight is even better, her pussy lips parted, her arousal glistening.

I should do as I promised and savor her. I should dive between those legs and eat my fill. I could do a million things to ensure she's aware of my unwavering commitment, but my vow to go slow means nothing when pitted against what she wants from me.

"There's no going back." I place my palms on her thighs, sliding them upward. "This is your life now."

She blinks those dark lashes my way, a lock of hair hanging low to seductively cover one eye. "I know."

She's utter brilliance.

My complete downfall.

"Forever, Nis. Not just until the next hurdle or you grow tired of me." I swoop over her, climbing onto the bed from between her thighs. My chest brushes her stomach along the way, my mouth latching on to one nipple to suck and tease as I reclaim her throat in my grip.

"I won't grow tired."

I pay those breasts homage, kissing one, then the other, until my dick can't take it any longer. I move higher, trekking my lips over her sternum. Shoulder. Jaw.

"No other man will experience this again," I whisper in her ear, settling my hips into hers. "No other man will even dare to touch you."

"That works both ways." She grasps my shoulders, digging her nails into my skin. "Now stop attempting to scare me off and fuck me."

"My pleasure." I grasp my dick, take a second to reposition myself, then give her what she wants, thrusting hard inside her, all the way to the hilt.

Her tight pussy fits me like a glove. The ultimate vice.

Her mewl of rapture only affirms the perfection.

I fuck her rough. Savage thrusts. Slamming home. Over and over, the brutal repetition burning my muscles with fatigue.

I keep my hand tight around her throat, the high tilt of her neck making it obvious she wants more as my other hand digs into the soft flesh of her hip.

I squeeze. Claiming her. Owning her.

Her breaths become fractured—broken and manic. So fucking delectable.

She digs her claws into my wrist, her gaze holding mine as she whispers, "I own you."

I grin. "Yes, you own me."

I fuck her harder, wanting to temper her sass and increase it all at the same time. But she feels so fucking good, those legs around my hips holding tight.

"Oh, fuck." She tilts her head back, closing her eyes, and shudders.

She's fucking coming.

Already. Without me.

I grind harder, thrust deeper.

I pound into her until she screams, the sound echoing off the walls and into my chest.

Her orgasm is the greatest show I've had the pleasure of witnessing. Her euphoria. Her peace. Those nails dig deeper into my wrist.

Her core pulses around me, the agonizing shudders making it almost impossible not to follow along with her. But this isn't over. Not yet. Not even when her body becomes soft beneath mine, her bliss turning into relaxation.

"You done?" I drawl.

She smiles, her eyes still closed. "Like you wouldn't believe."

I can definitely believe it. I'll never forget it either—the moment when she truly succumbed to me will forever be a treasured memory.

I lean closer, my stubble grazing her cheek as I growl in her ear. "Don't for one second think this is anywhere near over, little fox."

She chuckles. "I wouldn't dream of it."

I release her neck, trailing kisses where my fingers have heated her skin until her breathing levels. I want her to start all over again. From beginning to end.

I grind slowly, coaxing her into a moan, but instead of enjoying my gentle lethargy, she places her hands on my chest and pushes me backward.

"Off," she demands. "Get off the bed."

I frown. "We're not done."

"I know." She pushes again, and this time I oblige despite the vacuum of bliss that's sucked from my senses when my cock leaves her pussy.

I raise to my knees between her thighs, then climb off the mattress. I stand before her, tall, proud, with my fucking cock bobbing like a buoy in troubled waters.

But she won't leave me unsatisfied. I know she won't. It's not her style.

My fear is that she'll give more than what I deserve. Too much pleasure. A dose of something beyond lust to make me fall deeper into this mind-fuck of slavery.

"Step back." She slowly rises, creeping from the bed, as I do her bidding.

She holds my gaze as she stands before me, chin high, eyes

glazed, cheeks flushed. Then she descends, falling to her knees to deliver my wildest fantasies.

"I want to taste you," is all she says before her unfathomably brilliant mouth engulfs my cock, her lips sliding halfway down my shaft with exquisite suction.

I groan, clenching every fucking muscle imaginable as she tongues my length.

It's beyond words—the lust, the waning restraint.

I could come with one stroke, but I force myself to prolong this, to take her offering as the gift it is and treasure it.

I slide my fingers through her hair, unable to stop myself from squeezing tight as she sucks harder.

"*Fuck.*" My pulse becomes a pounding beat in my ears. There's so much pressure. Beneath my ribs. In my temples. No place more adamant than my fucking balls.

Her tongue works overtime along the underside of my shaft. I can't help directing her, my hands almost balled into fists in her hair as I force her back and forth, back and forth.

She groans with my force, the vibration adding a new layer to my torment.

"You're going to make me come," I speak through clenched teeth.

She nods, taking me all the way to the back of her throat, her eyes rolling as she retreats and starts all over again. Her hands slide to my ass, her nails digging deep.

I groan, my orgasm building beyond my control.

"Keep sucking like that and this will be over real soon."

Those pretty eyes meet mine, her mouth stretched over my dick, the glistening juices of her arousal and saliva coating her lips.

She bobs faster, keeping the attention at the sensitive head of my cock, knowing exactly what I need. Those nails dig deeper. Those lips suck harder. She moans again, and I'm almost done for.

"Don't stop," I growl. "Keep sucking until I come down the back of your throat. Then swallow everything I give you."

I pull at her hair, thrusting my hips into her mouth, inspiring more of her moans.

But it's her nod that sends me over the edge. The sweet

acquiescence that draws the orgasm out of me and makes me buck uncontrollably.

She doesn't stop. There's not even a pause as my cum releases down the back of her throat, those eyes forever holding mine.

"Jesus," I groan. "*Fuck*."

The euphoria continues, the drawn-out bliss on a whole new level until the last of my seed escapes.

She may not be convinced about marrying me, but that right there was a commitment pledged by both of us.

There's nobody else now.

Just the two of us. All I have to do is keep her safe in my fucked up world.

She releases my length with a loud pop, then swallows in a show of erotic simplicity, her tongue confidently swiping her glistening lips.

"That was perfect." I grip her chin to drag her to her feet, placing my mouth on hers. "*You're* fucking perfect."

"That's because I now own every part of you." She pulls back with a smirk and walks for the bathroom. "And those were some of my favorite inches."

"Feel free to pay homage whenever you like, little fox. Those inches are yours to command."

She chuckles and closes the door behind her.

It takes a split second for the high to fade. As soon as she's out of sight, the darkness of reality creeps in to steal the warmth.

I can't mess around anymore. I can't lose myself in distraction or put off the upcoming war with Emmanuel. I have to get us all home. I've finally got what I've craved for too long—and I won't let anyone fuck with it.

I've pulled my clothes back on and I'm buttoning my shirt by the time she returns to the bedroom, still gloriously naked with a subtle afterglow.

The space around us isn't the same though.

I see her differently, too.

She'll have a bigger target on her back now. One unlike anything I'm accustomed to. Law enforcement will see her as a traitor. Those I work with may never fully accept her despite my threats for them to comply.

The road forward won't be easy for either of us.

"Are you okay?" She moves in behind me as I fix the last button on my shirt, and wraps her arms around my waist.

"Yeah. You?" I turn to face her subtle wince.

"The after-sex vibe with us is never kind." She keeps her arms locked around me, her fingers working intricate patterns on the low of my back.

"We haven't had the best start. But things will change once we return to Portland."

"What's going to happen in between now and then?"

"I don't know. I still have no clue what Costa's capable of." I press my lips to her forehead, picturing that asshole's smirking face. "I anticipate having to negotiate with him for a long time. But we'll eventually come to some sort of agreement."

"What if you don't?"

"Every man can be bought. One way or another. I just have to find the right price."

Her arms fall to her sides as she leans back to meet my gaze. "Do you truly believe that?"

"In ten years, I haven't been proven wrong. But the right price might not necessarily be money. Getting out of this could mean getting my hands on what he values most." I glide my fingers through the silken strands of her hair. "That could mean his sons. Or his wife."

"What would you do to them?"

"Whatever necessary."

I brace for her flinch of disgust. It never comes.

Instead, she holds my gaze with steadfast assurance. "Do whatever it takes. This has gone on long enough."

The hardened pressure of pride strips me of my defenses. I'm so fucking besotted, and even though I know it's a deficiency, I can't help wanting more of her.

"I will." I drag her back to me with a gentle grip around her neck. "And no matter what carnage I create, you'll be waiting for me once it's all over."

She nods. "No matter what."

This thing between us doesn't make sense. There's no rhyme or reason. It's mindless obsession and uncontrollable fascination. But it's here to stay.

Nobody will take her from me.

"Get dressed—" My cell vibrates in my pants, the buzz bringing unwelcome dread as I pull the device from my pocket to stare at the screen.

"Who is it?" Nissa grabs her clothes from the floor to pile them on the bed.

"Layla."

The endorphin binge is well and truly over. I swipe to connect the call and raise the cell to my ear. "Where are you?"

"Our hotel suite." Her voice is brittle, the tone doing a number on my guilt. "Please, tell me you've figured out how to get my little girl back."

26

ANISSA

Cole tells his sister to meet us in the penthouse in half an hour then disconnects the call.

"She's coming up here?" I keep my gaze on him.

"They all are." His posture tightens as he taps at his cell screen and walks for the door. "Get dressed and meet me in the living room."

I make quick work of my underwear, blouse, and jacket, then shimmy into my pants. I'm striding from the bedroom, finger-combing my hair when I find him in the kitchen, his back to me as he stands in front of the coffee machine watching dark liquid gurgle and spit into two mugs.

"How was Layla?" I cock my hip against the counter, giving him space.

"Predictably upset." He grabs the filled mugs and approaches, placing one in front of me. "There's no escaping her suffering until I can get Stella back."

He's different now. Hardened. Focused.

"I know she's hurting, but it's unfair for her to blame you for this."

"Blame keeps her occupied." He sips his coffee, not holding my gaze. "It's a better alternative to letting her mind run wild with thoughts of what her daughter could be going through."

"But it upsets you, right?" I cock my head, forcing myself into his line of sight. "You seem different after the phone call. Are you worried about facing her again?"

He huffs out a breathy laugh. "No."

"Then what is it?"

He eyes me over the rim of his mug and leisurely takes another sip, as if waiting for me to figure out the answer.

"Cole?" I raise a brow.

He places the mug on the counter, giving me his attention. "I'm worried about you."

"Me? Why?"

"Nobody will appreciate this new turn of events between us." A subtle grin tilts his lips. "Vowing my life to a Fed isn't a typical day at the office."

"Wait." I bristle at the declaration, my mug clattering to the counter, coffee sloshing over the rim. "You're going to tell them?"

"Layla may have stopped screaming at me but she's going to expect answers. They all need to know."

My heart grows claws, the sharp tips digging into tender tissue.

"This isn't the right time." I'm still treading water with my own feelings. I need to get used to this reality first.

"No, it's not. But it's necessary. They already know you slept in my bed last night." Those deep blue eyes hold mine as if trying to give me strength. "They're fully aware something has been going on between us. It's time they learned to trust you."

I shake my head. They can't trust me. Not yet.

God, I don't even trust myself right now.

"They're going to attempt to tear you limb from limb," he continues. "If not physically, then mentally."

"Jesus Christ." I release the air in my lungs with a heavy heave. "You didn't want to break that to me a little more gently?"

"There's no time for gentle. They'll be here soon."

My throat threatens to close.

They're going to kill me.

"You'll be fine." He takes another sip, those eyes still intently coaxing me to be stronger.

"Fine?" No, not fine. Anything but fine. "Hunt wanted me dead *before* we started sleeping together. Finding out we've committed to some sort of permanence will... I don't know. It's just not the right time. Can't you let me get used to us first?"

"For starters, there's not *some sort* of permanence. This is infinite, little fox." He places his mug on the counter and bridges the space between us. "I also know you're going to take your sweet-ass time getting used to this, and I have no plan to coddle you with postponements."

"Well, I hope your impatience is worth my death."

His grin returns. "Hunter is protective. He knows you're a threat and not because of your badge. He was well aware of your hold on me before I was. Same goes for Luca, although, unlike Hunt, he's slightly conflicted about hurting women."

"Slightly?" I roll my eyes. "Your gushing words of comfort fill me with confidence."

He chuckles, soft and breathy. "You can handle it."

"You're joking, right? We haven't even touched base on Decker, who I dragged to hell and back to get information on you and your family. Which is why Keira will never trust me." I swallow to ease the ache in my throat. "It's too soon, Cole."

"It's no longer up for discussion." He wraps a hand around my wrist and pulls me in for a hug. His lips find my temple, his gentle warmth enveloping me. "You can be quite endearing when you're vulnerable. It's not my favorite facet of you, but it's growing on me."

"This isn't funny." I lean back to meet his gaze. "What are you going to say exactly?"

"I don't have a script, little fox." He glides strong fingers through my hair, teasing my scalp. "But they'll be told you're here to stay. And that they now have to answer to you."

My heart lurches. "Again. That's not funny."

"As far as I'm concerned, you're an extension of me. They will answer to both of us."

He's sincere. Batshit, loco serious.

"You'd be throwing me to the dogs." I step back, demanding space.

"I'm placing you on your throne."

Hell no.

Luca doesn't approve of me. Decker despises me. Hunter wants to slay me alive. And I have no clue what the women in Cole's life are capable of.

"Nobody is ready for this." The weak defense is murmured from my lips.

He reaches out, his hands sliding up my forearms, over my shoulders to my neck. His fingers work their magic at the base of my skull. Teasing. Coaxing. "Holding off will only delay the confrontation."

"I'm good with a delay."

He grins, half-hearted and incredibly sly at the same time. "You can handle this. The faster we put this behind us, the sooner we can focus on the bigger picture."

The bigger picture.

I slump my shoulders, my perspective finally settling on what matters most—Stella and Tobias. The only thing that matters is those kids.

"Okay?" He leans in, placing his forehead to mine.

My stomach lurches. I'm not merely drowning in the deep end. The water here is one unending rip filled with bloodthirsty sharks and pummeling waves.

"Okay." I suck in a breath. "But I came to Sacramento in an attempt to make things easier, and it seems I've done the opposite."

He huffs out a laugh. "You never make things easier, yet I keep coming back—"

A knock raps at the door, flooding me with panic. "I thought you said we had half an hour."

He gives me a quick kiss and starts for the hall. "It sounds like the attack dogs came early."

He's such a masochist, deriving pleasure from my suffering. Yet in the same heartbeat, I know he's taunting me out of a desire to create strength.

I'm about to be attacked. My choices. My loyalty. My life. He needs me to be resilient.

I square my shoulders at the sound of the door opening, bracing for the upcoming onslaught.

But it's not his sisters' voices I hear. It's men, their grumbled undertones unfamiliar.

No, not entirely foreign—just initially indistinguishable. The longer they mumble, the more I remember.

I dash for the hall, finding Cole at the door, his profile a tight line of hostility.

"Our father wants to see you," the unseen man says. "Now."

I don't stop running, not until Cole raises a hand at me in warning, his gaze snapping to mine.

"Stay there." There's no fear in his eyes, only angered determination before he returns his attention back to the men. "Where are we going?"

"You'll see."

The response sickens me. If Emmanuel's sons had to dispose of one body today, there's nothing to stop them from getting rid of two.

"Don't go." I creep forward, my throat drying when the men come into sight.

They're both tall, broad, lethal, their hard stares and tight lips exuding malice.

"You know the drill," the blond with the beard says. "No weapons."

Cole reaches behind his waist, flipping the back of his suit jacket to retrieve his gun.

"No." I grab for his arm, but he counters by snatching my wrist to guide the weapon into my palm.

"It's okay." His features don't soften as he meets my gaze. "I'll call you when I can."

"No, you won't," the taller man mutters. "Leave your cell behind, too. We don't want any distractions."

My panic increases, hollowing my stomach. They want Cole entirely vulnerable, with no ability to escape.

"Look after this." He retrieves his cell from his jacket pocket, holding it out to me.

I'm too numb to take it. Too busy scrambling for a way to stall while his gun remains a heavy weight in my hand.

"Please listen to me." Cole's team is meant to be here soon. Any minute now there could be a wall of backup to stop this from happening. All I need to do is buy time. "You're meant to be meeting your sisters. Don't leave until they show up."

Cole slides his cell into my pocket and leans close, kissing my cheek, using his proximity to murmur in my ear, "The password is your birthday. Call Hunter."

I shake my head and whisper, "If you go with them, you might not come back."

"And if I don't, then the same can be said for those kids."

Every organ in my body twists, demanding action.

I can't let him go. He can't stay either.

I have to find a middle ground and I don't know how. I just need a little more time to figure this out.

"Let me go with you." I step away from Cole, pushing in front of him to block the doorway as I face Emmanuel's sons. "He's not leaving on his own."

"Nissa," Cole warns.

"Stop wasting our time." The blond stares over my shoulder. "We're not taking anyone except you."

Strong hands fall on my hips, the pressure building to move me out of the way.

"No." I raise the gun in both hands, mindless of what else to do. "He's not going anywhere. Not like this."

The men don't move. Don't even flinch.

They remain standing there as if I don't exist, their attention focused on Cole.

"We retrieved those children for you," the guy with the dark stubble says. "We cleaned up the mess you left behind in the penthouse. And our father has even offered you an opportunity most people would sell their soul for. Yet this is how we're repaid?"

A hard body settles in behind me. "Lower the gun, little fox," The growled demand brushes the back of my neck, making me shiver. "Trust that I'll sort this out."

I ignore him, switching my aim from one brother to the next. I can't trust anyone when there's no humanity to be seen in the men before me. "You're going to bring those kids here and end this."

"Get your bitch under control," the blond snaps.

"Anissa, lower my gun," Cole sneers this time, his arm wrapping around my stomach. "Because if he calls you a bitch again, I'm going to have to kill him."

I need more time. Just a few more minutes. I don't know how to win in their world. I haven't learned the ropes. The only thing I'm familiar with is intimidation and threats. Whoever calls chicken is the loser, right?

"Now, Nissa." Cole's hold tightens. "Before they lose patience."

The darker-haired man reaches into his suit jacket, completely undaunted by my threat. Is he going for a gun?

Shit. He probably knows I won't shoot, and I have no doubt he will.

"Okay." *Fuck.* I raise my hands in surrender and stumble as Cole pulls me back into the penthouse.

"Behave." His hand sweeps over my wrist, giving a gentle squeeze. "Get in contact with the others. Make sure nobody meddles. *Including you.* I'll return with those kids soon. Be ready to leave."

I'm scraped hollow as he turns his attention to the threat and walks directly toward it. Fearless.

My insides scream at me to do something. Anything. But I'm clueless when my only experience involves avenues Cole would despise me for taking.

I can't alert the authorities.

I can't make threats revolving around the law.

The three of them walk to the elevator, the two men flanking Cole as he presses the call button and waits for the doors to open.

I'm a trembling mess of internal suffering by the time they step inside the small space and swing around to face me with matching expressions of cold calculation.

I hold my breath, holstering the gun in my waistband while the doors close. As soon as they're gone I run after them, diving deep into my pocket to snatch Cole's phone. I press the button to call for another elevator, then unlock the cell by entering my birthday.

My pulse is erratic as I scroll through the contact list to find Hunter's name and connect the call, the *ding* of the elevator's arrival filling me with temporary relief.

I dash inside, slamming my hand against the lobby button as the line connects.

"Yeah?" Hunt says in greeting.

"It's Anissa." The elevator jolts into movement, slowly descending. "Emmanuel's sons showed up and took Cole."

"Wh—you—Torian." His gruff words are cut short, the garble undecipherable.

Shit. "I can't hear you. I'm in the elevator. They made him leave his gun and phone behind."

"Get—there—wait."

Goddamnit.

I hang up and stare at the descending numbers on the indicator screen, silently begging them to move faster. Once I stop at ground level, I reef the doors open and run barefoot to the front of the building, rushing to the city street, spinning in a full circle in the middle of the sidewalk.

Cole's nowhere in sight. Not in the passing cars. Not walking nearby.

They can't have disappeared. I wasn't far behind them.

The cell vibrates in my hand, Hunter's name appearing on the screen.

"Cole's gone," I answer in a rush. "They took him."

"Yeah, I got that part. You don't know where they're going?"

"No." I rake a hand through my hair, my toes throbbing from the frozen cement. "They didn't say."

"Well, I've got eyes on the kids. They haven't moved. My guess is they're bringing him here. So you can tap out." His voice fills with annoyance. Disdain. "Mind your own business, and leave Cole to me."

27

COLE

I'M TAKEN TO THE HOTEL'S UNDERGROUND PARKING LOT WHERE A black sedan idles a few feet outside the elevator, the windows tinted.

"Do you plan on telling me where we're going?" I stop a few feet from the vehicle, not overly enthusiastic about being at their mercy.

"It's a surprise." Salvatore opens the back door. "Get in."

His audacity is becoming more than a thorn in my side.

He's nobody.

Nothing.

Yet he dares to throw his weight around, and his brother is stupid enough to call my woman a bitch.

I'd slit their throats right here if they didn't have me by the balls. Instead, I calmly step forward, biding my time until I can gain the upper hand as I take a look inside.

Emmanuel sits on the far back seat, his wrinkled face smiling up at me. "Let's go for a drive."

I fucking hate this guy. I'm unsure if I've hated anyone else more. But strangely enough, I have an unwanted appreciation for his unprecedented level of cockiness.

"Are you going to be more hospitable about where we're going?" I place a hand on the roof, another on the open door and check the interior. There's no sign of Stella or Tobias. No blatant show of weaponry either.

"I have something you need to see. Call it an incentive." He pauses, holding up a finger as if to warn me from taking his words as a taunt. "A gift," he clarifies. "All I want to do is show it to you."

He can call it a gift, a bribe, or a fucking curse for all I care. In the end, it will only ever be a delay in getting those kids.

I slide in, sticking to my side of the car as the door is slammed behind me.

"Your seat belt, please." Emmanuel watches me patiently. "It's going to be quite a drive."

I keep my mouth shut and fasten the belt as Salvatore climbs in behind the steering wheel while Remy takes shotgun.

"Good." Emmanuel nods in appreciation. "Let's go."

We exit the underground parking lot to stop out the front of the hotel and wait for passing traffic. That's when I see her. Barefoot. Her face pale with panic.

Nissa stares at the car, her focus on Salvatore, her hand sliding beneath her jacket.

"Is she going to be a problem?" Emmanuel asks.

I try to ignore my anger at him recognizing her even though he wasn't upstairs, but my aggression is unescapable. It consumes me, increasing my need to protect her.

"She pulled a fucking gun on us," Remy grates as we accelerate onto the road. "She's lucky to still be breathing."

The hair rises on the back of my neck, the distinct prickle crawling its way down my spine. Nissa runs after us, her hand still inside her jacket, her hair flipping around her face.

"She isn't a problem." I feign disinterest, unwilling to reveal her true value just yet. "What's this *gift* you have for me?" I turn to meet Emmanuel's kind, lying eyes as Nissa haunts my periphery. "Has your wife grown tired of the kids already?"

"On the contrary. She's become quite attached."

I stiffen.

"There's no need to fear, Mr. Torian. I assure you, they're in good hands and will be returned to you as soon as our business dealings are taken care of."

"Where are they?"

We turn a corner, and I fight to ignore relief when Anissa disappears from view.

"Where you left them. But it's come to my attention that we're running out of time. I heard news of a scene between you and that woman at the hotel bar, and I must admit I was a little disappointed when rumors of your FBI fling proved true."

"Disappointed?" I scoff. "I thought a man of your underhanded capabilities would understand the benefit of having an agent in their pocket."

He raises a brow. "Is she in your pocket, though, or in your bed? I heard whispers of a marriage proposal and wanted to make sure you were still considering my generous offer."

"Have you been spying on me, Costa?" This asshole is more thorough than I anticipated. "All this strategy and foresight is leading me to believe you were in on Robert's abduction plan from the beginning."

"I give my word that I wasn't. Like I told you, my involvement started once I heard Jordan had the children in his possession. I've helped you ever since."

I scoff a laugh.

Maybe he believes he helped. Maybe he's so fucked up that he's convinced his actions are benign instead of an act of hostility.

"What about the proposal?" he asks. "Is what I heard true?"

We drive onto the I-5 heading away from the hustle of the compacted city streets.

"It's true." I meet his gaze. "I'm sorry to inform you I won't be aligning our families through marriage. But I'm sure we can come to some other kind of arrangement."

Disappointment enters his features. Calculated, fraudulent disappointment.

He nods and tangles his fingers in his lap. "That's okay. I'm not giving up."

Of course he isn't. He doesn't plan to stop until he has me nailed to a wall.

"I've made up my mind, Costa. Whatever you plan to threaten me with won't work."

He clucks his tongue. "I've never threatened you. And I don't plan to start. What I offer is enlightenment. I want to show you the alternate options to marrying a Fed who will only threaten your empire."

"Why don't you just tell me what—"

He holds up a hand. "Please. Give me this last opportunity to prove myself. I've lived long enough to make many mistakes. All I'm doing is trying to stop you from making one yourself."

"I can handle my own problems."

He inclines his head. "I admire your confidence, son. But marriage isn't just a personal commitment. Not for men like us. You're balancing the success of your entire empire on this woman. And I assure you the lust won't last. You might be having fun now, but soon it will wear off."

Bullshit.

I know things with Anissa will be challenging. But my want for her goes beyond lust. It always has.

"How many long-term relationships have you had?" he asks without curiosity, because I swear he's already aware. This asshole has dug deep enough into my past to understand my previous lack of interest in commitment. "Have you shared your house before? Your belongings? Your trust? What will you do if she betrays you? What will happen if after you commit to her in the eyes of the Lord, things don't work? Will she walk away with a lifetime's worth of your secrets? Or will you be able to silence her?"

Silence? No, he means kill, and for once, the imagery of that act leaves me cold.

"Weren't you the one trying to tempt me into marrying your daughter?" I scowl. "You're not doing a good job selling commitment."

"That's the thing, son. My daughter is malleable. You can shape Abri however you like. If you want a doting wife, she can be that for you. If you prefer a business partner, she's smart enough to hold her own. And if you desire no strings, she can stand by your side in name alone, turning a blind eye to a long line of mistresses." He sighs and relaxes back into his seat. "What I'm trying to say is that a marriage to someone in law enforcement will forever be a noose around your neck, waiting for you to slip. Yet the alternate option of my Abri will bring nothing but ease and prosperity."

"And if things don't work out with her?" I drawl. "Does she walk away with a lifetime of my secrets, or do I get to *silence* her?"

"You will never need to worry about that. As I will be as heavily invested in a successful marriage as you, I'll make it my duty to ensure my daughter is everything you need her to be."

This fucker is proving to be more like my father with every word. Maybe more misogynistic and cruel.

"Trust me, Cole. You don't want to align yourself with a woman for anything other than financial gain."

I hadn't planned to marry at all. Until Anissa.

There'd been no concept of commitment. No desire to slice myself open and share my secrets with anyone until my little fox came along.

Now, life is different.

"I appreciate your concern. Unfortunately, it won't change my mind." I stare out the side window as we drive farther away from the city. "How long until we reach our destination?"

"A while." Salvatore grunts. "We're heading out of Sacramento."

I'm getting farther and farther away from those kids. From civilization and witnesses.

"I understand you're not convinced." Emmanuel leans closer and lowers his voice. "I was young and hopeful once. But tell me, how can this woman possibly improve your future? What will she bring to your family other than risk?"

I don't owe him answers. I shouldn't even acknowledge his question. Yet his scrutiny eats at me, coarsely grating away layers of protective coating to expose flaws in my future.

"Perspective," I say on instinct. "Insight. Strength. New blood."

Anissa isn't a prop or a fling. She's the outsider who will fortify my empire.

"And you've weighed this perspective and insight above the threat she will pose when everyone who has ever worked with your family begins to question your sanity? What do your men think of her? What about your suppliers? Your informants?"

His biting inquisition isn't new. I've been through all this on my own. I've weighed the options. And every time I convince myself Anissa is worth the risk.

Emmanuel heaves an exhale, as if hating to be the bearer of bad news. "The cartel won't be pleased—"

"Enough," I growl. "I'm done talking about her."

He sucks in a long breath and slowly nods. "I understand."

The ride becomes silent as we coast for miles. The further we go, the less traffic follows. Away from the city, past the outer suburbs, until there are few cars on the road and even fewer houses in sight.

They want desolation, and we're close to getting it.

This ride could be my last.

This old fuck, with his disturbing smirk and lack of self-preservation, might be making a move to wipe me out now rumors of my father's death have started to circulate.

And why wouldn't he? I have no successor. My sisters are neither capable nor inclined. Decker lacks the ingrained brutality. Luca hasn't been around long enough. Benji is a fucking traitor. And although Hunter knows every aspect of my business and could handle taking over, he wouldn't want the responsibility or the leadership.

Tobias is the only replacement who can rule my family, and he's not even within a few years of being able to grasp the helm.

Salvatore takes an exit off the I-5, taking us over a bridge to cross a river. My prospects are even worse out here. Houses are separated by numerous acres. We pass a vineyard as the sun lowers toward the horizon and I'm sure the approaching darkness is all a part of their plan.

"It's not much farther." Emmanuel stares down the middle of the car, focusing out the front windshield.

We follow alongside a wire fence for mile after mile of farmland before the road curves wide, taking us in a new direction.

"Here." Emmanuel points up ahead. "We've arrived."

We approach a dense barrier of trees on the left, bordered by a white ranch fence, the billowing scrub blocking the view of what I presume is a house yard. I remain quiet as we pull into the property, passing open metal gates and the thick tree line into an expansive manicured garden.

This place is its own oasis shielded from the rest of civilization.

The trees block out the world, enclosing us amongst the dense lawn, sculpted rose bushes, and, from what I can see, an impressive farmhouse up ahead.

"Is this place one of yours?" I ask.

"No. Just a rental in a perfect location. I want you to have privacy while you reconsider your future with Ms. Fox."

I stiffen at her name.

His insight into Anissa is no longer a revelation—it only makes the dust settle on the level of exposure I've placed upon her. The risks will increase once the world learns of her value to me. But I've known that all along. It's the distance currently between us that makes the reminder fucking brutal.

"My gift." Costa juts his chin at the lavish house as the car pulls up a few yards from the wraparound porch. "Have an open mind."

I drag my gaze along the pristinely painted exterior, the orange glow of the late afternoon sun gleaming off the windows. For a second I think he's offering to buy me the property, until I see the woman leaning against the porch railing near the front doors.

Slim, blonde, and cover-model pretty, she's a vision of perfectly choreographed temptation that fills me with adrenaline. "Your daughter, I presume?"

"She's beautiful, isn't she?" He releases his seat belt and opens his door. "Come meet her."

"This is a waste of time, old man."

He slides out to peer down at me. "Maybe. But humor me. Spend some time with her before you make a rash decision." He closes the door on the conversation, leaving Salvatore to glare at me through the rearview mirror.

"We'll be watching," he warns. "Don't do anything stupid."

I laugh. Can he sense my sudden thrill?

This woman is exactly what I've been looking for—their fucking soft underbelly.

I get out, the smirk still haunting my mouth as I leisurely stroll after Emmanuel and climb the three stairs to the front porch.

The woman eyes my approach, her appraisal sly as she seductively bites her lower lip.

"Cole, I'd like you to meet Abri." Costa greets his daughter with a kiss on the temple, then retreats. "Abri, this is the man I've been telling you all about."

I don't take my gaze off her, scrutinizing every detail from the deep blue eyes that sparkle with mischief to the way her fingers loosely tangle in front of her, showing no hint of apprehension.

She's beyond visually appealing, with high cheekbones and enough subtle makeup to accentuate her beauty. And even though she's covered from shoulder to foot in her designer sheer blouse, peach blazer, and tight white pants, it's clear she's sporting an astronomical body.

She's a viper.

I may have been born to rule and lead, but this woman was a strategically raised Trojan horse who only has one aim in mind —temptation.

"Cole." She says my name like a lover's call, the syllable whispering past my ears as she saunters forward in ankle boots to offer her hand. "I've been told a lot about you."

"I promise it was all lies." I play the game, sweeping my palm over hers for a quick shake, the connection increasing my thrill.

"I assure you, every word was kind." She chuckles.

"Like I said, all lies."

Her laughter continues, bubbling like a gentle brook. "Let's take a walk."

My pulse quickens as I remain in place, anticipating discouragement from Costa that never comes. He doesn't voice disapproval of me being alone with his daughter. He doesn't even drop the faux friendly expression.

"That's a great idea. Just don't go too far." He claps me on the shoulder and strides away, his polished shoes thudding along the porch. "Take this seriously, son. I assure you my Abri is a far better option for your future."

Leaving me alone with this woman, even though unarmed, is senseless. He's banking her safety on my reputation for not involving women in the games of men. But that moral high ground is no longer on the table.

"You seem worried." Abri inches closer as her brothers leave the car, their stares fixed on us. "Don't you want to be alone with me?"

I meet her gaze, searching for sincerity, and grin when I don't see any. "I'm not the one who should be worried."

She rolls her pretty eyes and passes me to descend the stairs. "I'm far too prepared to be worried."

Meaning?

Maybe she has a weapon. Or more eyes are watching from the overbearing tree line, even though the sedan is the only car out here.

Neither would matter, though, if I wanted her dead.

Problem is, she only holds value as a hostage. Breath needs to remain in her lungs.

"Where are we going?" I stroll after her, catching up on the pebbled drive to head in the opposite direction to the men in her family.

"Anywhere." She shrugs. "I don't care, as long as we can talk."

So she plans to lure me into marriage through conversation and the gentle sway of her lush hips? This bitch gets ten points for optimism.

"What do you want to talk about, snowflake?" I hold the aggression from my tone.

Fuck this beating-around-the-bush bullshit. I need to get back to Anissa. She's exposed without me. And the thought of Stella and Tobias approaching another night without their family is gnawing at my impatience.

Abri shoots me a grin. "We need to talk about us, of course. *You* mainly. Tell me about yourself."

"You want menial chitchat?" I shoot a glance over my shoulder. Her brothers still eyeball me.

"It's not menial anything. We'd be creating a foundation that will hopefully start a very beneficial future for all of us. You're a highly successful businessman, Cole. But your wealth can't be anywhere near the level of my father's. Aren't you excited at the prospect of unimaginable success?"

"I'm satisfied with where I'm at."

"Liar." She snickers. "Men like you are never satisfied. I bet you thrive on new opportunities. You're just daunted by how different my father's offer is from what you're used to."

"And you appreciate the prospect of marrying someone you don't know?"

She pauses, her smile remaining in place as she focuses aimlessly across the yard. "Let's just say you're a far better prospect than I anticipated."

"That doesn't answer my question. If you want to talk, then tell me how a pretty girl like you would ever agree to an arranged marriage."

She stops and turns to face me, her expression remaining bright as she raises a brow in condescension. "For starters, I'm no girl, tough guy. And agreeing to marry you didn't take much convincing. I do what needs to be done for the success of my family."

I'm not buying it. Not unless she's clueless.

"Do you know who I am, Abri?" I stare into those sky-blue eyes. "Do you have any idea what being with me would entail? It would be a loveless marriage completely devoid of emotional connection. Surely you want more than that."

Her sly smile widens, exposing a dimple in her left cheek. "I'd never set my sights on something so pathetically whimsical as love. I know it doesn't exist. Neither does God, for that matter. Both were created to appease the masses." She pivots on her heel and continues forward. "What I *do* know is that you're a piece of the puzzle that will help bring diversity to my family's wealth. And I can do the same for you."

"You didn't answer my question." I grab the crook of her arm, making her stop. "Do you have any idea who I am?"

She snaps rigid.

In the distance, a throat clears in subtle warning.

I grind my teeth, struggling not to tighten my fingers as her haughty gaze lowers to my grip.

"Sorry. I thought you were being rhetorical." Her menial expression remains in place as she yanks her arm away. "But my answer is yes. I know who you are. Somewhat." She shrugs again. "I don't have specifics. I don't need them. I'm well aware your business dealings are more aligned with my mother's side of the family, and that doesn't faze me."

Her mother's side of the family? Who the fuck is her mother?

"See?" She beams at me. "This is why we need to talk. Clearly you're at a disadvantage with information. Let me enlighten you." She keeps walking, reaching the end of the house to lead the way around the side.

She doesn't give a shit that she's now out of sight from her protectors. She gives no fucks at all because she knows I'm currently a sucker waiting to be ass fucked by her father. But that won't last forever.

"Cole?" She pauses a few yards around the corner. "Come on. This is good news."

Like fuck it is.

I've been blindsided again, and the worst part is knowing that seemingly kind old woman looking after Stella and Tobias may have blood like mine running through her veins. She might not have a loving heart or gentle intentions. She could be just another fucking Trojan horse.

I glance over my shoulder again, glaring at Salvatore and Remy who stand at the front porch steps before I stalk after Abri, my palms itching to squeeze the life from Costa's only daughter.

I scrutinize the tree line to our left as I catch up to her. Someone has to be hiding in the scrub. Someone with a rifle scope to stop me from giving this family what they deserve.

"My mother has a large extended family." She holds my focus as she speaks. "She's a Cappelletti."

The name hits like a physical blow.

Italian fucking mafia.

I let out a long, slow breath, refusing to let shock grip me by the balls, and focus straight ahead. The tall trees stop at the edge of the side boundary to give sight to the leveled paddock of dry grass and dirt behind the house yard. "This obviously isn't public knowledge."

Decker and Luca would've found the information otherwise.

"My father went to great lengths to cover up the connection before they were married. He previously wanted nothing to do with their reputation. Our legitimate businesses would've suffered—"

"Previously? What about now?"

She's quiet for a moment, nothing but the building chorus of cicadas calling to the approaching night.

"Abri?" There's a warning in my tone. "You wanted to talk, so fucking talk."

She sweeps her arm out to snap a rose from a nearby bush. "Yes, previously. Don't ask me why he's had the sudden change of heart. I'm not privy to his reasons. All I know is that he's now eager to diversify, and sees you as the golden goose."

Not a force to be reckoned with. Not a threat to his future or an upcoming menace to his existence. A fucking golden goose.

"You have no idea what you're getting yourself into," I seethe. "If I were you, I'd reassess your willingness to help your family with anything that involves mine."

She leads me to the back fence, placing her booted foot on the bottom rung of the white horizontal railing as she picks petals from the rose and throws them one by one to the ground.

"Why?" she asks simply. "I don't understand your refusal to contemplate the possibilities. You don't even know what my father has planned."

I grasp the fence tight enough to make my fingers ache, my anger volatile beneath the surface as she rambles on about our future and unfathomable potential for too fucking long.

She has no clue of my desire to choke her.

To make her fucking scream.

I want her entire family's blood spilled at my feet, their pleas for mercy tattooing my memory.

"Cole?" Her attention bores into the side of my face. "Are you listening?"

"No. I'm not fucking listening. What I'm doing is waiting for you to drop this act." I push from the fence. "Up until now I've kindly ignored your father's attempts to start a war, but that window is closing." I turn toward the house, still trying to see the audience I know hovers nearby.

"Look, I know you're reluctant to be here." She throws the flower stem to the grass. "But you also need to understand that my father went to a lot of trouble renting this house and flying me here to meet you. He's gone to great lengths to welcome you into—"

"He's gone to great lengths to test my patience."

She sighs. "Please, Cole, you need to loosen up. Neither one of us will be allowed to leave until we've given this partnership ample consideration. So relax, and stop thinking you can rush this." She raises her brows, waiting for a response I'm not restrained enough to give. "Why don't we go inside and have a drink? It might help take the edge off."

I don't want a fucking drink. Or to waste ample time, considering this bogus bullshit.

What I need is a new plan to get those kids, the intricacies seeming all the harder to finesse now that they're being held by a woman with mafia ties.

"Come on." She sidles up to me, running her fingers along the sleeve of my jacket as she continues toward the back of the house. "One drink. That's all I ask."

"Then what?" I growl.

"Well, if you hear me out and finally realize this opportunity is too good to pass up, my father will call in the helicopter. We could be married in Vegas by the end of the night. And those kids would be right by your side."

Laughter festers in my throat, the slightest hint of mania edging its way into my psyche. "And when I don't?"

She keeps walking for the house. "That isn't for me to decide."

I don't follow. Instead, I clench my hands, struggling to hide my instability.

The Cappellettis aren't people who mess around. They're big fish in a pond I don't want my family dragged into. It doesn't matter that they're based on the other side of the country. This shit is too close to home.

"Come on, Cole." This time Abri's voice holds sympathy. The slightest edge of compassion. "Let alcohol take the edge off your concerns. You'll see sense afterward."

She doesn't wait for a response as she weaves around the rose bushes and steps onto the porch, heading toward French doors with the glass windows illuminated by the warm light inside. She pulls both handles wide, disappearing into the house, leaving me with the cicadas and whoever lurks close by.

Maybe it's just her brothers.

Maybe the whole East Coast mafia are watching.

Either way, I'm running low on options for a resolution. At least ones that don't involve high risk. Or marriage.

"*Fuck.*" I run a hand through my hair, digging my nails into my scalp.

Hunt was right.

Before Nissa, I would've handled this situation differently.

I would've jumped at the marriage opportunity, either eager to be aligned with another like-minded family, diving in headfirst, palms itching for action, or salivating at the prospect of taking them down from the inside out for daring to intimidate me.

This inaction is a deficiency I can no longer allow.

I need to make a decision and stick with it.

No path is without risk or suffering. No choice is devoid of pain. But I have to make one, and fast.

I follow after her, my determination reaffirmed, my focus steady. I step onto the porch, my pulse thundering as I stop at the open doors to an expansive living room, the ceilings high, the thick draped curtains open, the furnishings expensive.

"I've heard scotch is your drink of choice." She stands before a freestanding alcohol gurney beside one of the brown leather sofas, her long hair draped over her shoulder as she holds up a bottle of Macallan single malt. "Would you like me to pour you a glass?"

"No."

She shrugs. "Have it your way."

She ditches the scotch and claims a bottle of champagne from an ice bucket, taking a few seconds to struggle with the cork before pouring herself a glass. "This was meant to be reserved for good news, but I'm confident I'm only jumping the gun a little."

I ignore her and scope the room, searching for make-shift weapons. There are no knick-knacks that could be used to bludgeon. No vases or sculptures able to be smashed. There's nothing but books and furniture... unless I take into account the champagne bottle in her hand and the Macallan within her reach.

"Looking for something in particular?" Her faux curiosity

pisses me off. "My brothers swept the house clean earlier. They took out anything sharp and pointy."

I lean against the doorjamb, crossing my arms over my chest. "And you're not daunted by the need for that preparation?"

She shoves the champagne bottle back into the ice, the crunch and swish momentarily drowning out the internal whispers of vengeance before she saunters to the sofa to take a seat. "You don't seem like an animal."

Her assessment is inaccurate. I'm nothing if not entirely feral right now.

"Come sit with me." She crosses her legs and pats the space beside her. "I've already told you we won't be able to leave until my father is satisfied."

Yes, I heard her the first time, but now I home in on her words.

We won't be allowed to leave.

Not just me. Both of us.

"Suit yourself." She gives a wicked grin. "I don't mind admiring you from afar."

"Admiring? Is that how you're going to play this?"

"What other way is there? You're a handsome man, Cole, and although I know no marriage of convenience can start perfectly, you'll come to learn I'm quite a catch." She tweaks that grin up a notch, her dimple resurfacing. "I have many talents I'm sure you'll enjoy."

"You're quite the generous offer."

Her expression doesn't falter. "But you're hung up on someone else."

"I am." I cross my arms over my chest as she sips the champagne, her tongue sneaking out to swipe her glossy lips.

"If the woman is your reason for denying me, I can assure you she's the wrong choice." She places the flute on the coffee table and slowly glides to her feet. She's lithe as she saunters toward me with a complete lack of self-preservation. "A man like you can't be naive to the risks involved in pairing with a Fed. How do you know she won't double-cross you?"

"She's aware of what happens to those who mess with me." There's a harshness to my tone I can't suppress.

"Careful, big guy." Her brows rise as she sidles closer, sliding her palms over my biceps. "A lady might consider that a threat."

"Maybe a lady should." I remain still while she dares to skirt those hands higher, up to my shoulders, around my neck. "You wouldn't last a week under my roof."

"I don't know about that." She laughs, the husky sound brushing my ears like a lover's touch. "Your devilishness only makes me eager for more."

She's definitely beautiful. Flawless, even. Given normal circumstances I'd fuck the spark from those dazzling eyes. But right now, all I want to do is suffocate it.

"Your delicious dominance doesn't frighten me." She lowers her voice to a teasing whisper. "I don't scare easily." Her fingernails tease my nape, sending a rush of sensation down my spine.

"You're making a mistake with the Fed." She leans closer. "Women love a bad boy. But only temporarily. The timeline is even shorter for someone with a strict moral compass, and I'm assuming that's what this woman has." Her eyes fill with lust, whether it's fake or not, I'm unsure. "You're a phase, Cole. Her interest in you won't last. Eventually, she'll humiliate you."

She nips at my triggers. Her teeth dig deep into insecurities I never wanted exposed.

"I know women like her," Abri continues, her voice soft. "Strong, forthright women. Even if she did stick around, your lifestyle would change her."

The clarity of her insight slices deep.

That's what I've been worried about. That Anissa, with her unshakable determination and infallible fortitude, would weaken in my world.

I don't want that for her.

"She'll become someone else," Abri whispers. "Someone you're not infatuated with. You know she will."

"So marrying you is the best option?"

"Marrying me is the only option. I'm the perfect replacement— easy on the eye, yet strong, smart, and determined. I'm everything you need, with the bonus of financial security instead of ruin. And strings that never need to be attached."

She's a choice of convenience and prosperity in comparison to the path with Anissa, which is riddled with landmines.

"Let me show you one of the benefits of having my company." She slides a hand down my arm and grabs my wrist to lead me to the sofa. "And as soon as you realize being together is the best option, we can tell my father and have the kids brought out here to celebrate."

28

ANISSA

It's been hours without word from Cole and no movement from the children as I sit in the Escalade parked across the road from Emmanuel's building.

Normally, I'd keep myself busy through a case by chasing leads. I'd run Costa's license plates and track them through traffic surveillance. I'd have the option to call local law enforcement for assistance. I'd even go through the process of watching credit card transactions in the hopes of pinpointing Emmanuel's location.

But I chose to be here as part of Cole's team—his partner—and legitimate, legal means are only used if they're discreet and without trace, which is something I can't provide.

I've done my best to ensure all our bases are covered though.

Penny is in the hotel lobby if Cole returns.

Keira and Layla remain in the penthouse suite in case his arrival bypasses the front doors.

Luca and Decker are situated on different rooftops, giving us numerous angles of sight on the children, while Sarah and Benji are in another car at the back of Emmanuel's building, watching the exit to the parking lot.

If anything happens, we'll know.

But nothing has happened. Not since Cole was taken.

It's been radio silence, and the quiet is killing me.

"Would you quit jolting your fucking leg," Hunter snarls from the driver's seat. "You're pissing me off."

I plant my foot and glare straight ahead.

Why I got paired with this asshole is beyond me. He's made it damn clear he would love to see me disemboweled and rotting in a shallow grave.

"You should go wait with Sarah and Benji," I snap. "I'm sure you'd prefer their company."

"No shit. I'm only here to keep an eye on you." He white-knuckles the steering wheel. "I'm playing goddamn babysitter because I don't trust you."

He's itching for a fight, and I'm beyond tempted to give it to him. But the distraction won't help Cole. At this point, I'm not sure if anything will.

"You'd make my job a lot fucking easier if you'd just leave." Hunt looks at me, his angry stare haunting my peripheral vision. "I bet you've been tempted to call in the license plates on the black sedan. Or to cave to your impatience by contacting the cops."

"It's not impatience. It's concern. I'm worried about him."

"And you think that makes you special? We're all fucking worried, but the rest of us know to trust his ability to handle the situation if he specifically said not to meddle." He lowers his window, letting the chilled air sweep in. "No matter how bad Torian wants to believe you can be one of us, you never will be. You're too much of a high and mighty bitch to change your ways."

I drag in a long breath to keep myself composed. "There's no going back. I've made my choice. So get used to me being here."

"I've got no plans to get used to anything where you're concerned. You'll be gone soon enough."

"Not if I get rid of you first."

He laughs. "You think that's possible?"

"I don't know." I look him in the eye. "But I'd sure enjoy trying."

He stares daggers at me. "I suggest you mind your manners."

"And I suggest you focus on why we're here and quit being distracted. It's unprofessional."

His nostrils flare. "Fucking bitch," he mutters under his breath, then turns his attention out the windshield.

More time passes as Cole's phone remains silent in my hand. I grow nauseous. Anxious. Angry. Anything would be better than sitting here doing nothing, because the sound of Hunter's barely audible breathing is enough to make me homicidal.

"We've got movement." Luca's voice carries through the car speakers. "Get ready."

Hunter reaches for his cell propped against the vehicle's display screen and turns the call off mute. "What's happening?"

"The woman and the two guards are escorting the kids into the elevator," Decker announces through the four-way conversation. "It looks like everyone is leaving."

I sit forward, scrutinizing the street. There are no lingering cars at the front of Emmanuel's building. "They're either leaving on foot or not coming out this way."

Nobody acknowledges me. Not even with a scoff of dismissal.

"I'm coming down," Luca says. "There's no point keeping two of us in the sky if they're on the move."

Cole's phone vibrates in my hand, ratcheting my pulse. I rush to unlock the screen and open the awaiting text from Costa.

"What is it?" Hunt asks.

I click the notification, find a video recording, and immediately press play.

The first sight of Cole makes my eyes burn with overwhelming relief.

He's alive. Uninjured.

It's the passing seconds of what appears to be a surveillance feed that suck the gratitude from my system.

I watch as a beautiful woman straddles his lap on a sofa, her blouse loose, maybe even gaping at the front. I can't tell from the angle of the camera. His hands are on her thighs though, his gaze intent on her face.

"I said, what the fuck are you looking at?" Hunter leans forward, muting his cell again before snatching Cole's phone from my grip. His expression doesn't change as he replays the video while I struggle not to vomit. "This must be Costa's daughter." He pivots the screen in my direction and raises a taunting brow. "They look cozy, don't they?"

Bile climbs my throat as I glare.

"Your man didn't stay loyal for long." He lobs the device back at me and I fumble to catch it in my lap. "Are you ready to walk yet? If I were you, I'd take off and never look back."

I clench the cell in my fist. "You'd love that, wouldn't you?" My voice cracks with bitterness. "I bet all your dreams would come true if I scrambled out of here with my tail between my legs."

"If the collar fits, why not run with it?"

My hatred of this man knows no bounds. I want to shove my gun down his throat. To claw at his eyes and slap that superiority from his arrogant face.

"I'm not going any-fucking-where." I pivot in my seat, turning my whole body to him. "Not now. Not because of this. That video means nothing. I know Cole. I trust him."

"You don't know shit. You've got no fucking clue what he's like."

He pokes at my insecurities.

No, he punches them, beating me into a submissive state where I question my choices all over again.

"We've got eyes on them." Sarah's voice breaks through my turmoil. "It looks like those guards are driving a black Lincoln from the parking lot. They're pulling onto the side street."

Hunter remains focused on me, cocking his head in question. "This is your last chance to bail."

I should. For self-preservation's sake. For sanity and safety, too. But I won't give up on Cole. Not this easily.

I pull on my seat belt and find the black Lincoln waiting at the traffic lights up ahead.

"I see it." I jerk my head toward the intersection. "Hurry up and follow."

He doesn't comply. He keeps sitting there, staring at me. "Stop fighting this and fucking go. You know this bullshit between the two of you won't last."

"*Drive*," I snap, unleashing my anger and animosity, even my fear.

Again, the car doesn't move.

My pulse quickens with the closing window of opportunity to tail the Lincoln. We can't lose them. We can't miss the only chance to find Cole.

"I said fucking drive, you arrogant prick." I snatch the gun from inside my jacket and slam the barrel against his forehead. *"Now."*

There's a beat of volcanic animosity where I question who the hell I've become, my pulse ratcheting higher, my heart thundering. Threatening him like this goes against everything I used to stand for. It's careless and impulsive. And feels so fucking right I can't quit.

"Where are you guys?" Sarah asks. "Does anyone else have eyes on them?"

Hunter smirks, the curve of lips more of a sneer.

"So help me God, motherfucker, if you don't hurry up and follow I'll pull the trigger and dump your ass in the street. There's no way I'm losing that car."

He keeps the grin in place as he rolls his eyes, then without a word, he starts the ignition, my gun still digging into his head as he cuts into traffic.

"Hunt, where are you?" Sarah's' frantic voice adds to my building adrenaline. "What's going on?"

He bats away my arm and unmutes the call. "I'm following. We'll be a few cars behind the Lincoln."

"What was with the radio silence?" Benji interrupts.

"We've had contact from Costa." Hunt indicates into the middle lane, remaining a few vehicles behind our target. "He sent a video of Torian."

"What video?" Decker demands. "Is he still breathing?"

"He's breathing just fine." Hunter shoots me a grin. "Isn't he, Miss Piggy?"

I clench my teeth and shove my gun back into its holster before I'm more tempted to squeeze the trigger.

"The footage showed Torian with a woman. I assume it's Costa's hot-as-fuck daughter. And the two seem to be getting along well, if her position over his dick is anything to go by."

"A sex tape?" Sarah scoffs. "Are you serious?"

"Not a sex tape." Hunt takes a left, following the Lincoln down a busy street compacted with traffic. "Just the prelude."

"Fuck you," I mutter under my breath. He's only saying this to destroy me. To cut and slice at what I have with Cole. "I'm not leaving, no matter how hard you push."

"We'll see."

"We can figure out motives later." Luca talks over our mutterings. "For now, keep an eye on those kids and give me directions. I've only just made it to my rental."

Sarah relays the information from her position somewhere behind us, while I force myself to remain focused on things that don't whip up volatile emotion.

"We're moving onto the I-5." Hunter pulls onto the exit, remaining out of sight behind other vehicles as daylight fades to black.

The cover of darkness will work in our favor, as long as we don't lose the Lincoln.

And if we do... My throat squeezes, the dryness of apprehension taking over my mouth.

I can't handle the unknown. My fear over what happens next is blinding. Suffocating. It doesn't help that riding alongside Hunter is a task drowning in complete sterility.

We don't communicate through the passing miles. Not apart from the telepathic messages of hatred I send his way.

He's entirely cold to my existence. An invisible barrier has been built between us.

As the minutes drag by, I unlock Cole's phone and replay the video. I watch it over and over, reading expressions and body language. I scrutinize Cole's fingers on the woman's thigh and his intent focus on her face so close to his.

Their physical contact turns my veins to ash, my thoughts to suffering. I press play so many times I memorize the footage from start to finish, the valves in my heart seeming to rip apart from one another to create a chasm of carnage.

"Quit looking at it." Hunt reaches out to mute his cell. "You're eating out of their fucking hands. Buying into their stupid game."

I can't stop. All I want is one hint to ease my suffering. Just one little clue to tell me Cole hasn't succumbed to Emmanuel's plan. I keep watching. One more time. Then two.

"Fucking stop," he grates. "They sent it to make you jealous, and it's working."

"How do you know?"

"Why else would they send it? Do you think Torian asked for a souvenir?" He rests one arm against the car door, chilled as fuck in the middle of a wildfire. "My guess is he declined the arranged marriage. And they're attempting the soft-cock option of getting rid of you."

I replay the footage again. The hands. The proximity.

"If it were me—" Hunt indicates into the second lane, passing another vehicle. "—I would've taken pleasure in putting a bullet through your brain. But women usually cut and run when they see their man fucking around with someone else. So I guess whatever works…"

I wince, even though the slightest sense of hope warms me. "You think this is staged?"

"Not staged. But not a true indication of what's going down." He doesn't look at me. There's no emotion to his words either. He's still calm. Cool. Arctic. Yet his insight could almost be considered an act of kindness. *Almost.* If I wasn't fully aware of his raging asshole status.

"Why are you telling me this?" I attempt to read his caged expression through the soft glow of the dashboard lights and come up with nothing.

"The shooting you part or…?"

"No," I grate. "Why did you say he must've declined the arranged marriage? Why be nice enough to tell me the one thing I want to hear when you've made it clear how you feel about me?"

His jaw ticks, his fingers tightening on the steering wheel.

"Hunter? Why say anything at all?"

"It's my job," he snarls. "I do what's in his best interests."

"But you didn't when the video first arrived."

"Yes, I did."

I don't understand. "How?"

"Jesus *fucking* Christ," he mutters under his breath. "I didn't think you would stick around. I thought you'd walk."

"So you taunted me about the recording to speed up the process?"

He keeps staring straight ahead. "I should've tried harder."

"And now you suddenly think it's in his best interest to have me here?"

"Hell no. I still want you to fuck off. The only difference now is that I don't think you will."

He's right.

I won't.

At least not unless I'm forced out by an arranged marriage.

I want to explore what life could be like in the grey, where things aren't clear-cut and right or wrong. I want to hold on to the strength and confidence he's stoked inside me. I want to delve deeper beneath his vicious love.

"That video means nothing," Hunter mutters. "There's nobody more loyal than Torian, not only to his men, but also his women. He'd never stoop low enough to cheat on you. He's more likely to kill you than ever go behind your back to fuck someone else."

I huff out a breath, strangely comforted.

"What I'm saying," he continues, "is that there's a story behind that video and it's got nothing to do with him wanting her to ride his dick and everything to do with strategy."

"And you're telling me because I stuck around," I repeat, needing validation.

"I'm telling you because you're his now, which means you're also mine to inform and protect, no matter how much I fucking hate the prospect."

I want to scoff. To laugh in the face of his admission. But there's something in his words that brings me more comfort than I care to admit. In his own fucked up way, Hunter has made me feel at home in this foreign world.

"*Shit.*" He slaps a meaty finger against his cell. "We're heading off the I-5. Nobody follow. We don't want to make this obvious."

I lock Cole's phone and shove it into the glove compartment, sitting forward in my seat as Hunter waits for the Lincoln to take the exit and drive from view before he cuts his headlights and continues with the pursuit.

We're out in the middle of nowhere, surrounded by darkness. There's no glow from nearby houses. No sign of life.

"This doesn't look good." I take off my jacket and drape it over the illuminated dash screen, blanketing us in shadow. "Why would Costa want the kids out here?"

"Your guess is as good as mine." He eases off the accelerator as the road straightens, the red tail lights of the Lincoln now tiny dots in the distance.

We struggle to keep up through the limited vision, crossing a bridge we almost miss, only to have our target disappear.

"We lost them." My chest squeezes with impatience. "Where did they go?"

"We didn't lose shit. The road curves up ahead. So pipe down and let me do what I do."

We drive with nothing but the full moon to cast the slightest glimmer over the asphalt.

I fidget, my leg returning to the constant jostle. "Whatever you do, don't touch the brakes. They'll see our lights."

"Are you fucking serious right now?" He shoots me a glare. "You're really going to give me pointers?"

I ignore his ego and the constant churn of nausea in my belly. We can't have much farther to go. This has to end soon.

"Sarah, kill your headlights and follow." Hunt raises his voice and jerks his head at me. "Send her our GPS location."

I do his bidding, using his cell to text the information.

"I'm on my way," she responds. "Luca is riding with us now. We'll catch up soon."

When I raise my vision from his phone, the Lincoln seems so far away. The tail lights are barely a blip in the distance. "We're losing them. You need to catch up."

"I know what I'm doing." He waits until the red glow disappears, then presses his foot down. For long minutes, we drive like this. Slow, then fast. Following lights, then seeing nothing but darkness, until we reach a sweeping curve that sends us in a different direction.

"Where the fuck are they going?" Hunter grates. "This could be a goddamn trap."

We round the bend and he leans forward at the sight of an illuminated entrance to a property roughly half a mile away.

There's no Lincoln in sight. No sign of another car at all. Only a wall of trees stretching along the property's border, the towering barrier stretching into the night.

"Look." I point to a speck of red through the dense foliage. "A tail light."

He jerks his chin in acknowledgement. "And house lights."

I see them, the slithers of orange slipping through the thick trunks.

"Sarah, we're stopping." Hunter quietens his voice. "I'm going to hang up and send through our final location but make sure you lay low. There's nothing out here. Any noise will draw attention." He pulls off the road, inching the vehicle slowly through long grass before cutting the engine. "I'll have earpieces and extra ammo waiting for you. Let me know when you arrive."

"We will."

He grabs the phone, disconnects, and taps his screen a few times before shoving it into his pocket. "This is it, boss bitch." He reaches into the back seat to retrieve a duffle. "Are you going to do me a solid and stay in the car?"

My adrenaline and apprehension surge, flooding me, the energy buzzing through my veins. "You know the answer to that."

Hunter reefs open the duffle and pulls out a hard plastic case to reveal earpieces hidden inside. Six different sets. All encased in foam padding. "I know what I want your answer to be." He settles back in his seat to look at me. "Whatever is happening in there isn't going to be pretty. And it sure as shit won't be legal."

"I've made my decision." My chest tightens. Restricts. I made the choice back in Greece. My future was always going to revolve around Cole. "I'm all in. He means too much to me."

Hunter sighs and lobs an earpiece in my direction. "Then keep your fucking head in the game and make sure your heart stays out of it."

29

COLE

"I THINK IT'S TIME FOR THAT DRINK." I SPREAD MY ARMS ALONG THE back of the sofa, allowing my gaze free rein to stalk Abri's body as she straddles my hips like a stripper itching for a generous tip.

"Okay." She slides off me, clearly doing her best to provide as much friction as possible before she walks to the alcohol cart. "See? I'm not too proud to do your bidding."

"I can definitely see that."

I've given her what she wanted.

Time. Attention. Indulgence.

I've listened to her husky promises of a bright future. I held my disinterest at bay as she removed her blazer and undid the top button of her blouse, attempting to seduce me with the barest hint of cleavage.

I even ate up my rage and frustration, humoring her enthusiasm while I gained insight.

Now, I'm done playing with my food.

"Tell me, Abri, why did you say earlier that we wouldn't be able to leave unless your father was satisfied with the time we spent here?"

She frowns and grabs the bottle of Macallan. "Because he wants to make sure you think this through properly."

"You said *'we,'* though. Not just me. But both of us." I scrutinize her, noting the slightest twang of tension entering her shoulders.

"We're both involved." She pours my liquor, then dumps the bottle back onto the cart. "I thought that would be obvious."

I incline my head. "It's the way you said it. It made me think you're not such a willing participant in this after all."

She chuckles, the jovial show unconvincing. "I'm willing." She pastes on a smile and saunters back to me, handing over the scotch before reclaiming her seat on my dick, her hands finding my shoulders.

"Well, unfortunately, my feelings haven't changed. I won't be humoring you or your father any longer."

She reaches for me, raking her fingers through the hair at my nape. "He'll be disappointed. Why don't we sleep on it?"

"I'll pass." It's my turn to laugh, the low snicker encouraging her genuine smile to return. "You also said you know who I am. What information did your father give you? How deep did Daddy dig into my life?"

"I was smart enough to do my own research."

I latch on to more clues, eating up her crumbs as she continues her seduction.

"Your own? Interesting." I swirl the liquor in the glass, my arms remaining outstretched over the back of the sofa. "Doesn't your father keep you well informed?"

"On the things that matter, yes. Of course he does."

"Good." I nod, doing my best to resist the numbing bliss of the alcohol. I've used the sedative trick too many times to fall for it myself. "That means you'll be able to alleviate my concerns about what happened with the body this morning. What did your brothers do with the guy executed in the penthouse?"

Her expression pauses. Confusion sets in.

"Where did they dump him? And the blood…" I lower my free hand, placing it on her hip. "Did they get it out of the office carpet? I've got a man who knows a trick or two about cleaning up a scene."

She breaks eye contact to reach for her champagne flute on the corner table. "I'm sure everything was handled properly." She raises the glass to her lips, gently sipping, pretending she's okay with the information she clearly hadn't been privy to.

"Yeah." I swirl a lone fingertip in a slow pattern along her leg. "I'm sure you're right."

Her sickeningly sweet smile is no longer fixed on me when she places the flute back onto the table. She's let down her mask enough to show I rattled her.

"How do your brothers usually handle clean-up?" I tilt my head, attempting to regain eye contact. "Are they the type to dump a body in a river? Or do they prefer the 'dismember and dissolve' trick?"

She doesn't look at me as she huffs in humorous disbelief. "I'm not sure."

"So you're not informed on those type of things?" I keep trailing a swirling pattern with my fingertip, lazily taunting. "What about information about the people your father does business with? Are you aware that my family isn't new to yours?"

"Yes." She raises her chin slightly, emboldened by her insight. "Your father and uncle attended some of our house parties when I was little. They were both ladies' men, if I recall. Always surrounded by a swarm of beautiful women."

"Slaves," I correct. "Beautiful women, yes. But slaves who had no choice in the company they kept."

Those lashes continue to bat. Her chin remains high.

For brief seconds, she stares at me in silence before she says, "I know what you're trying to do and it won't work."

"What am I trying to do, snowflake?" I swirl my scotch and slide my other hand higher, over her hip, her waist, all the way up to her shoulder. "Other than continue the discussion you've forced upon me."

"You're attempting to frighten me. Even after I've made it clear I don't scare easily."

I guide my palm to her neck, a move once reserved for Anissa, but this has nothing to do with pleasure and everything to do with destruction.

"I'm beginning to see that. It's admirable." I tighten my hold, firm and fucking direct. "Especially if you're undeterred by the knowledge of your family's association with sex trafficking. Or that the hand gripping your vulnerable throat is the same one that stabbed a letter opener through a man's temple mere hours ago."

She purses her lips. "You're lying."

"If you think so, why not ask your father?" I keep adding pressure against her neck, tighter and tighter until she begins lifting her chin from the restriction.

"Careful," she warns. "They're watching."

I keep my hand in place, undaunted.

"Cameras." She hikes her brows with confidence. "Two of them. On opposite sides of the room."

"You think cameras will save you?" A slow grin spreads across my lips. "You have my brother and niece." I keep my voice low as I dig my fingertips into her delicate skin. "You're holding children hostage from a man who's spent his life perfecting the art of revenge. Do you really think I'll spare voyeurs a second thought if I decide I want you dead?"

Her throat works over a heavy swallow, her pulse increasing beneath my fingers.

"What's wrong?" I lean closer, grazing the stubble of my cheek against hers as I murmur in her ear. "You seem unsettled."

She doesn't answer. Not in words. Her continued rigidity is enough of a response.

"You don't want to marry me, Abri. You don't want to live with a man who is currently eager to see you suffer."

Her breathing deepens—long, measured inhales followed by heaving exhales.

"So tell me how I get out of this." I nuzzle her jaw. "Tell me how to wake your father up to the slaughter he's approaching."

She swallows again, remaining quiet.

"I'm convinced you're a smart woman. But you'll be a dead one if you continue to play his games." I claw my fingers, digging nails into flesh.

"I don't know."

"Sure you do." I lean back. "Are there any other men on the property? Any guards? Or security?"

She doesn't respond.

I squeeze tighter. "Abri?"

"No." She chokes in a strangled breath. "Nobody else is here."

"No fucking snipers? Don't you have another brother somewhere?"

"He's not here." She licks her lips in a frantic rush. "Nobody else is, either. It's just us."

I can't figure out if she's telling the truth. She seems panicked enough not to lie, but that could be an act, too. "What does your father have planned if I deny him?"

"I don't know."

"I'm losing patience," I growl. "That doesn't work in your favor."

She lowers her attention to stare at my chest. "I swear—"

"Look me in the fucking eye when you talk to me." I release her neck and grasp her chin, demanding compliance. "Give me the respect I deserve."

Her attention gradually raises to mine, the sparkling blue gleaming back at me with vehemence.

"Dear ol' dad hasn't come to save you yet. Why is that?"

Her nostrils flare, her jaw ticking.

I've hit a nerve.

This is what I've been digging for. The anger. The bitter truth in her emotions.

"Tell me, Abri, if he's watching, why hasn't he run to your rescue?"

She struggles over her answer, her lips tight before she admits, "He can't hear what you're saying. He can only watch. He probably thinks your attention is a good sign."

"You don't think your discomfort is obvious?"

She glares her hatred, but it doesn't seem aimed at me. My guess is that her animosity is toward the man leaving her in danger.

"He doesn't give a shit about me," she grates through clenched teeth. "He never has. I'm an asset to him and nothing else."

Perfect. So fucking perfect. "Then why maintain this charade?"

She plasters her mouth shut, holding her answer hostage.

"Come on now. Why are you shy all of a sudden?" I dig my fingers harder into her chin, making her grimace. "Tell me why you're playing along."

"You're a way out." She unsuccessfully attempts to tug her head away.

"Of what?"

"This hell." Strength enters her tone. "He controls everything I do. Who I speak to. When I work. My goddamn money. He acts as if he's doing me a favor by choreographing my life, but all I am is a commodity in some sick game."

She's convincing, yet she's also a manipulative actress.

"And your brothers?"

"They're biding their time until they can take over the family estate."

I release her, allowing her to inch back a little. "Then tell me what he's attempting to achieve with this marriage and I'll help you."

She blinks as if startled by my offer. "I have no idea."

"Yeah, you do. Maybe not directly, but you would've heard something. You'd have a fucking clue."

"I'd only be guessing."

"Then fucking guess."

Her mouth opens, her lips working over silent contemplation. "It has to have something to do with my uncles. My dad could be trying to prove a point."

I tense at the Cappelletti reminder. I don't want those fuckers anywhere near this. "What point?"

"I don't know. They always ridicule our side of the family—our business. They think my father is weak. Maybe this has something to do with him showing them he's more than a fashion label."

I'm not buying it. There has to be another reason. "What would your father do if you were under threat?"

Her eyes flare, the whites blazing as she pulls away from my grip on her chin. "I have no idea."

"Yes, you do. Tell me what he'd do if I held you hostage."

"You don't have a weapon."

"Anything can be a weapon when you have a thirst for blood." I grab her around the back of the neck and pull her toward me. "What would he do, Abri? Would he care enough about your safety to negotiate the release of those kids? Or would he cut and run from his so-called asset?"

There's a faint crunch of noise outside. The cacophony of cicadas is replaced by the disturbance of pebbles. A car approaches.

"Someone else has arrived." I narrow my gaze. "Who?"

"It has to be my mother with the kids. As far as I know, she's the only other person here in Sacramento."

Apart from those fucking guards.

"Why would she come out here?" I flick my gaze to the open doors leading to the porch before returning my glare to Abri. "What's going on?"

"My father must think I've either convinced you or he's given up waiting." She shakes her head. "He said I'd have a few hours. After that…"

"After that, what?" I grab her throat again, my impatience about to detonate.

"I don't know." Her expression transforms to a plea. "I swear."

"Then tell me what he'd do if you were under threat." I jolt her with a quick shove of my hand. "*Now*, Abri."

She whimpers, clutching her hands onto mine to fight against my grip. "If I'm right about my mother being here, he'd do everything he could to protect me. He wouldn't be careless with my life in front of her."

Good. That gives me options. Not many, but enough.

I smash my scotch glass against the side table, sending liquid and shards scattering, the sound loud in the silent house.

"Oh, God." She screams and attempts to scramble off my lap. "Stop. *Please.*"

I hold tight, demanding her compliance. "Calm down."

She claws at my wrist, scratching and shoving. "What are you doing?"

"I'm finishing this. I just have to spill a little blood first."

30

────

COLE

Claret oozes between my fingers clamped against Abri's neck as I stand, dragging us both to our feet.

She releases another bone-chilling scream, her heart and soul belting out with the piercing decibels.

"Be quiet, snowflake." I drag her backward into me, holding her against my chest. I feel her terror in her trembling limbs. Despite her tough act, she's petrified. "Don't struggle or this will all be for nothing."

Footsteps thunder toward us from the porch. A door squeaks somewhere inside the house. Her brothers clamber through the French door entry, guns drawn moments before her father fills the archway from the hall.

All three of them stop in rage-induced panic.

"How valuable is she to you?" I jab a shard of glass toward the exposed side of her throat. "Lower your weapons or I slice the other side, too."

Emmanuel takes a cautious step forward, raising his hands.

"Stop." I use his daughter as a shield and dig the shard into her skin, making her whimper. "My hand around her throat is the only thing keeping her from bleeding out." I relax my grip, proving my point by allowing the carnage to freely flow down her neck, soaking her blouse.

This time she sobs, her fingers clinging to my wrist. "Please don't let me die."

"Everyone relax." Emmanuel takes another step. "I think we can all agree this has gone too far."

"Too far?" I ask. "You've held me to a disadvantage from the beginning. I've merely leveled the playing field."

"I'll fucking kill you." Salvatore keeps his gun trained on me. "If anything happens to her, I'll make you suffer."

"I don't doubt it for a second. But can you achieve greatness before your sister dies of blood loss? Because if it were me, I'd be setting my sights on getting her out of here as soon as possible."

"Salvo, please." Abri's breathing becomes labored. "Do what he says. Call in the helicopter. I need a hospital."

"It's done," Emmanuel growls at me. "I'd already organized our departure. There was no need for this."

"There was always a need." I smirk, giving him a healthy dose of flipped history. "You step on my toes and I cut off your feet. You threaten my family and I destroy yours."

"Enough." He stands taller. "You're making a big mistake."

"I don't think so. Tell your boys to drop the weapons."

His jaw ticks as the faint *whoop, whoop* of a chopper approaches in the distance. He wasn't lying. At least, not about his departure. I'm well aware he didn't say shit about whether or not he planned to take the children with him.

"I'm lowering my gun." Remy leans over, placing the Glock on the floor. His brother reluctantly copies. "Just stay calm."

"Where's my niece and brother?" I glance between them, waiting for someone to offer an answer they all seem reluctant to give. "You brought them here, right? You were going to take this excursion to the next level by flying them out of Sacramento."

"No. This was over." Emmanuel shakes his head, showing minimal sympathy for his daughter. He doesn't look at her, not her neck or the threatening glass. He's more fixated on leveling me with spite. "I never threatened you, son."

I ignore him and jerk my chin at Remy. "Kick the guns my way. One of you is going to want to get a first-aid kit. The other can retrieve the kids and bring them to me."

"No," Emmanuel repeats.

"Please, Dad." Abri shudders against me. "Do what he says."

"Let her go first,' he demands. "Let her come to me."

I dig the pointy tip of the broken glass into her throat, making her squeal. "I'm afraid your time to manipulate and make demands is finished." I turn my attention to Salvatore. "Do as I asked before I lose my temper."

The noise from the chopper increases as everyone remains in place.

They don't listen.

Don't move.

I drag the glass down Abri's neck, lightly, but enough to draw blood.

"You fucking prick." Remy starts for the porch, doing my bidding.

But Salvatore still doesn't move. "There's no fucking first-aid kit here, you piece of shit. We removed anything with scissors or sharp blades before you arrived."

"That's too bad." I shrug. "You might want to take off that shirt then so she's got something to stem the blood."

His lip curls in a sneer as he shucks his suit jacket to the floor, then starts on the buttons of his white shirt. "If she so much as loses consciousness, I swear to God—"

"You'll do what?" I rage. "Endanger my family? You'll take our children hostage? This is the result of your actions. However this ends is your doing, not mine."

He yanks off the shirt, his muscles tense, waiting for a chance to strike. He juggles the material in his hands, finding a sleeve, then proceeds to rip it off. "Help her secure this around her neck. Make sure it's tight." He throws the makeshift bandage to his sister, his eyes leveled on her in concern. "Are you okay?"

"Please just do what he says," Abri pleads. "Bring the kids in here."

"He will *not* bring those kids." Emmanuel storms for the French doors now rattling from the whip of outside air. "One of the guards will hand them over at the back of the house yard once my family is already safely in the helicopter."

"No, *Remy* will hand them over," I clarify. "Your two for my two, old man."

His shoulders straighten in response but he doesn't say a word before escaping onto the porch. He doesn't even give a heartfelt farewell to his petrified daughter as he steps into the thrashing air to walk out of view.

Abri wasn't lying about him after all.

"Let me help you bandage her throat." Salvatore steps forward.

"Get out of here." I yank her farther into me. "Make sure your father doesn't try any shady shit. I'll be holding you responsible if he does."

He stares at his sister. At the blood dripping from my fingers.

"Hurry." Abri clings to the hand at her throat as if struggling to remain upright. "I don't want to die here."

His nostrils flare. His father might not care about her, but he does.

"She'll be fine," I drawl. "As long as none of you try anything stupid."

"Give your word that you won't do anything else to hurt her." His glare cuts to me. "That once the helicopter leaves the ground, this all ends. No repercussions. No more acts of vengeance."

No. I won't.

"Fucking give your word, Torian." He clenches his fists. "My father will kill those kids—"

"No." Abri struggles. "He wouldn't."

"He's lost his fucking mind." He raises his hands to his head, shoving them through his hair. "You know he doesn't give a shit about you. He's only complying because our mother is here. He won't risk her life. Nobody else matters to him." His arms drop to his sides, his surrender on display as he meets my gaze again, this time without hostility. "Give your word and I'll make sure to keep him under control."

I don't have to give him a damn thing. Not promises. Not protection. Nothing other than pain and suffering.

But those kids are out there somewhere. In the dark. Scared and vulnerable. They don't deserve to be tortured by another second of delay.

"You have my word."

His shoulders straighten in response.

"I said, you have my fucking word. Now *go*." I jerk my chin at the French doors. "Before your sister runs out of time."

A second of contemplation passes before he nods. "I'll get everyone in the helicopter."

"We'll be right behind you." I increase the wattage of my smirk. "Won't we, snowflake?"

She shudders out a breath and trembles in my hold.

She's the perfect victim. Her vulnerability is flawless.

"I'm holding you accountable, Torian." Salvatore trudges to the door. "Don't fuck this up." He disappears outside, his footsteps thundering back down the porch, the sound quickly fading under the mass of swirling air.

I wait one second. Two. Then release her throat and turn her toward me. "Give me the shirtsleeve."

"Are you crazy?" She grabs my wrist, flipping over my hand to inspect the deep gash along my palm. "You're the one who needs a bandage."

"Stop fucking around." I ignore the biting sting of the open wound and focus on her neck. "I need to cut you so they don't think you were in on this."

"No." She retreats, running her fingers over the slight scratch on the other side of her throat. "You've already done enough of that. I'll make up a story later."

"Get over here. Have you forgotten the cameras? And what motherfucking story are you going to make up?" I start after her, the shard of glass ready in my hand. "I won't cut deep. Only enough for them to think you believed you were dying."

"Seriously. *No.* Just help me with this." She raises Salvatore's shirtsleeve and begins wrapping it around her neck. "I'll keep the bandage on until I get to a hospital. If I have to cut myself then I will. There's no way my dad is out there watching the security feed right now. He's furious. He probably can't even see straight."

"You better be right, otherwise you're on your own after this."

We made a deal.

She'd play along with my slice-and-dice act if I vowed to get her away from her family when she decided it was time. But that agreement only holds up if this goes off without a hitch.

"Don't worry; he bought it." She inches back toward me and

raises her head to allow me access to secure the material around her throat.

"Maybe he did. But we need to finish this before any of them start to question why you're still conscious." I place my sliced palm against the spot where her cut carotid is meant to be, letting the blood oozing from my wound seep into the material. "Don't fuck this up."

I spin her, reversing her into my chest to drag her toward the porch. I pick up the guns along the way, shoving one into the back of my waistband, out of her reach. The other takes the place of the jagged glass to point against her cheek.

"Do everything I say." I grasp her throat with my bloodied hand. "One wrong move and you'll regret it."

She nods as I lead her outside, the air whipping around us.

Immediately, I feel eyes on me. I don't see them through the darkness. But they're there. Watching. Waiting.

"Where are they?" I scan the shadows, unwilling to expose my back until I can see my enemy. The chopper whoops close by, the floodlights from beneath the metal bird illuminating part of the open field up ahead.

"There's my mother." Abri tilts her chin a smidge. "At the back of the house yard."

I squint, scanning the night to find the silhouette of the woman being escorted through the wooden slats of the fence with what looks to be the two guards from the penthouse.

"I told you my father is taking you seriously." Abri's voice is barely loud enough for me to hear. "This is working."

Not good enough though. I want eyes on everyone before I step away from the house. One bullet to the back of the head is all that's needed to take me out.

"Find your father," I grate in her ear. "We don't move until we see him."

Her head pivots, scoping the yard, while I do the same.

There's not enough light. Too much noise.

"Over there." Abri shrugs her right shoulder.

I follow her line of sight, finding Emmanuel on the pebbled path, Salvatore at his side, both hustling toward the helicopter. "I don't see the kids."

Where is my fucking niece and brother?

"We're running out of time, snowflake. And if this doesn't work, nobody is going to like what I do next."

She stands taller, her posture rigid despite our agreement. "Give Remy a few more seconds. He won't hurt them, I promise. He'd never harm a child. And he'd never risk my life either."

My adrenaline kicks up a notch. My paranoia, too.

I need to come up with another plan.

Fast.

"Look," she blurts. "There they are."

Remy walks out from beside the house, the kids in front of him, his grip on their shoulders one of casual intimidation.

"You better hope you're right about him." I snarl, despising his audacity to touch them, and take the first step away from the house. "Otherwise my hand won't be the only thing that's left bleeding."

31

—————

ANISSA

DIRT SCRATCHES MY EYES AS HUNTER AND I LAY ON THE MOIST GRASS, the chopper's blades whipping dust and mulch around our faces.

We've stuck to the shadows, slowly creeping past the tree line and farther into the house yard as Cole stands on the porch with the woman, one bloodied hand around her throat, the other holding a gun to her head.

"They're leading Stella and Tobias toward the helicopter." Benji's voice carries through my earpiece, his tone frantic. "I won't let them take her again."

"Stay out of sight," Hunter warns. "We don't know what's going on yet."

That's not true.

We know Cole has taken a woman hostage. He's hurt her, the carnage from her neck soaking into her white blouse, the liquid staining his hand.

I should feel sympathy. Even compassion.

I don't.

I can't muster anything with this gnawing hunger to get the kids and Cole to safety eating away at my soul.

"We're not going to let anyone take them away from here." I have no basis for my assurance. Not when the Costa's bearded son is marching the children toward the fence leading to the open field. All I know is that I'll risk my life before I let Emmanuel succeed.

"You can't expect me to wait, Hunt," Benji growls. "Make a move before I do it myself."

"I swear to God, if you don't fucking stick to the shadows I'm going to have an even bigger issue with you than I already do." Hunter crawls farther along the grass, keeping in line with Cole.

I glance behind me, toward the house and into the darkness, trying to find the rest of our team among the trees.

Hunter and I took the far side of the property. Sarah, Luca, and Benji took the opposite. They're meant to be mimicking our position, staying in line with Cole, waiting for any sign that he's lost control of the situation.

"We need to wait." I keep my voice low. "We don't want to scare anyone into making a rash decision. Cole included."

I keep slithering along the grass as our target walks the woman through the garden and around some bushes, approaching the wooden fence. The kids climb through a few feet ahead, the man guiding them closer and closer to the helicopter.

"Still feel loyal to him with what he's doing to that woman?" Hunter asks beside me.

"Yes." I don't hesitate.

She's one of them—the enemy.

If anything, Cole is teaching her a valuable lesson about straddling the laps of men who are spoken for.

"Maybe we're wearing off on you after all." He raises into a crouch, retrieves his gun, and starts moving forward again.

"Wait." I hustle to keep up. "What are you doing?"

"We need to—"

"Benji, pull back." Sarah's concern cuts into my ear. "They're going to see you."

I swivel, panicked, and scan the other side of the yard.

"You better fucking listen to her." Hunter's voice is lethal. "You're walking a knife's edge as it is."

"That's my daughter," Benji pleads. "What the fuck would you do in my position?"

"Listen," Luca cuts in. "I'd fucking listen. Now get your ass back here."

The bearded blond leads the kids away from the fence, as Cole and the woman climb through the railings. They're too close to the helicopter. I can already picture Costa's son hauling their little bodies under his arms to run them toward his family.

"*Stop.*" Cole's shout is heard over the constant whip of air. "Stay there."

The blond shakes his head, relaying something indecipherable in return. He indicates for his sister to move forward with a wave of his hand.

They're doing an exchange.

"This isn't going to work." Benji's voice is brutal. "As soon as he lets her go, he's dead."

Tobias and Stella's faces are pale against the floodlights, their eyes wide with panic.

"He's got a plan. He knows what he's doing. Just look at him." I keep crawling as I focus on Cole. He stands tall, confident, unshakable. He isn't cowering. The gun in his hand doesn't tremble. He believes he has this under control, and we need to trust him.

"Fucking hell." Hunter points across the yard, his finger leading to Benji who steps from the shadows in his tailored suit to stand in plain sight, his gun raised.

My stomach nosedives. "If they see him…"

I can't finish the sentence; the fear is too much.

"Get back," I snarl the demand, my vehemence explosive. "Before I take you down myself."

Cole keeps the woman tight against his chest, the guards, the sons, and Costa all watching him as Benji continues to inch forward.

It's only a matter of time before he's seen.

I huddle next to Hunter. "We need to get closer." I raise into a crouch and pull out my gun. "Once they notice—"

"Benji *no*," Sarah's shout rings through my earpiece.

"Fuck." Hunter takes off in a run.

I do the same, not understanding what's happening or where I'm going until I see Benji sprinting through the garden, his gun bobbing in front of him, his focus on his daughter.

I witness the moment the guards notice. I see them aim their weapons as the older son shoves his father into the helicopter.

"*Benji,*" Luca yells. "*Stop.*"

Shots are fired. Stella screams. Men shout.

Hysteria descends as Hunter drops to his knees in front of me, raining bullets at the helicopter.

"Take cover." He grabs for me as I pass.

I don't listen. I don't stop.

I slap away his hand and push my legs as fast as they'll carry me, diving between the fence railings while the bearded man sprints for his family.

"*Get down*," Cole roars at the children, still standing tall, his gun blasting at the enemy as he pushes the woman free.

There's so much noise. Destruction bombards my ears, filling me with terror.

A guttural shout breaks through the commotion. A guard falls to his knees, clutching his thigh.

I anticipate the pain of that shot. I imagine the impact of a life-threatening bullet as my legs burn from exertion. Still, I don't stop. I'm the closest protection the children have and I won't let them down. Not even when Stella and Tobias turn to me in fear, Cole's niece taking a backward step at my approach.

I barrel into them, arms outstretched, slamming us all to the ground.

"Don't move." I stay on top of them as Stella gasps for air and tries to scream. I use my body as a shield in the dry grass, cradling their heads with my hands. "Stay down."

So many shouts break through the night. Demands. Threats.

The whip of the chopper increases, the swish of blades kicking up dirt and twigs. I squeeze my eyes shut as I drag the kids farther into me, covering them the best I can as more gunfire rains down around us.

A tornado of movement swirls above my head, the brightness from the floodlights dimming behind my eyelids.

"You're okay." I talk to the children, rambling nonsense. "This will all be over soon."

Footsteps thunder toward us. A heavy weight slams into my back.

"I've got you."

It's him. *Cole.*

He helps to shield the children as the noise above us lessens, the whoosh of air fading with each heartbeat until the storm of sound is almost gone.

I could cry with relief, the burn of threatening tears taking over my closed eyes… until the pungent smell of blood fills my lungs, the scent stealing my hope to leave me cold.

32

COLE

"*Daddy.*" Stella scrambles out from beneath us and runs for her father.

"Toby?" Luca yells. "Where are you?"

"He's here." Nissa shifts, giving the boy freedom to rush to his feet.

I don't move. I barely budge an inch from my resting place against her back while the commotion of a heartfelt reunion sounds behind us.

I need a moment. Just one. To breathe her in and remember she's mine.

"Is everyone accounted for?" Hunt shouts. "Torian, where the fuck are you?"

"I'm here."

Anissa wiggles, attempting to free herself.

"Don't move." I speak against her neck, drawing the scent of her deep into my lungs. I'm owed one fucking second of calm before I have to concentrate on getting everyone out of here. "Tell me you're okay."

She stills, relaxing. "I'm fine."

"Good." I shift to the side and help her turn to face me, those emotional eyes staring back at me through the night. "That didn't go down how I'd expected."

"I know." She cringes. "I'm sorry. Benji wouldn't listen."

I ignore the anger over my brother-in-law's actions, not wanting anything other than my little fox claiming my attention through the adrenaline detox.

"I smell blood." Her tongue anxiously slides out to swipe her lower lip. "Are you hurt?"

"My palm is going to need a few stitches."

"Why?" She grabs for my wrist, turning over my hand to inspect the injury. "Jesus Christ, what happened?"

"I told Costa I'd sliced his daughter's neck. It had to look real."

"So you stabbed yourself?" she asks. "Next time draw the enemy's blood, not your own."

"I'll make sure to do that." I grin and lean in, pressing my forehead to hers. "How'd you find me?"

"We followed the scent of your dumbass decisions. Didn't you ever learn not to get into a car with strangers?"

I snicker, plastering my mouth to hers. I part her lips with my tongue, delving deep, drowning in her. All it takes is a taste and I'm grounded.

"Let's get out of here." Sarah claps her hands nearby. "If a helicopter and gunfire don't draw the cops, I don't know what will."

I'm not ready. Not even close.

I keep my lips smashed to Nissa's, needing her, craving her.

"Come on, Torian." Hunt approaches, his boots crunching in the grass. "We've gotta move."

"He's right." Anissa breaks the kiss, placing her hands on my chest to push me back. "I can't be here if police arrive." She climbs to her feet and waits for me to follow. "We've got two cars parked at the front of the property."

"We're going to need to clean up inside first. My blood is on the floor."

"Where?" Hunt walks backward toward the house, reaching into his pants pocket.

"Through the French doors. Maybe on the porch."

"Leave it with me. You guys get out of here." He lobs a car fob through the darkness at Nissa. "Take the kids and Benji. We'll follow a few minutes behind."

"Are you sure?" she asks.

He turns his back, striding hard. "Get the fuck out of here."

"Come on." I grab her hand and lead her toward Benji and Luca who are huddled with the kids on the pebbled path. "Let's go." I raise my voice, drawing their attention. "Benji, you and the kids are coming with us. Everyone else can get a ride in the second car."

"Sure thing." Luca grabs Toby's shoulders. "It's all over now, little man. Penny's waiting for you back in the city. We won't be far behind you."

I slow my steps at the sight of my half-brother. The poor kid is going to have a lot of unpacking to do once we get home. His mental suitcases were already stuffed with trauma before he arrived in Portland; now he's got this shit to deal with, too.

"Hey." I stop before him, looking down at the resilient jut of his chin. "How are you holding up?"

He nods. There's no reassuring expression or search for comfort —just wide eyes and thin lips.

"Are you ready to get back to Penny?"

Another nod. No emotion. No warmth.

"Come on." Anissa places a hand on his shoulder, leading him along the path.

I lag a step behind, giving him space. In the coming days, I'll need to make decisions about his future—who he'll live with, what school he'll go to, what role he'll play within the family.

If he doesn't already despise me, I'm sure he will by then. But right now, I have enough of that toxicity focused toward Benji to drown out the static of what's to come.

We pass the house, then the front porch, with Stella and her father dragging their feet behind us. Every scrape of his shoes against the stones grates on my nerves, building my resentment.

I'd had the situation with Costa under control. I'd been fucking heartbeats from getting Stella and Tobias free without a goddamn bullet exchange, until he fucked it up.

Now he has even more to answer for.

Nissa leads the way out the front gates and along the road, the distance growing between us and the huddled father and daughter duo trailing behind. When she reaches the Escalade, she helps

Tobias into the back seat, closing the door behind him before meeting up with me at the front of the car.

"I can already tell you're pissed at Benji. But go easy on him. He was worried for his daughter."

"Don't soften for him, little fox." I glide stray strands of hair behind her ear, smudging blood near her temple. "He caused this. Not only tonight, but the entire situation. If it wasn't for—"

"I know." She steps into me. Foot to foot. Hands to my chest. "I really do. Just let it go for now. Let him be with Stella without having to worry about what lies ahead. If not for him, do it for her. She needs her father's comfort after everything that's happened."

She's right. But it doesn't lessen my animosity.

Benji needs to be dealt with. There's no escaping punishment. Whatever that is, I still haven't determined.

"Please, Cole." She twists her fingers in my shirt. "Let them have a few days."

"Yeah. Okay." I hold out my good hand. "Give me the keys."

"I'm driving." She turns for the car, striding away like a confident warrior. "You have to bandage yourself up."

"When did you turn into an overlord?"

She laughs. "When you left me alone with your thugs."

"I guess I need to do that more often in the future." I head toward the passenger side, ignoring the humorous glare she gives me.

"Don't even joke about it. Hunter and I almost killed each other."

"But you didn't, which is better than ninety percent of the people he works with." I open my door and slide in, Nissa doing the same on the driver's side.

She starts the engine once Stella and Benji round the hood, the headlights illuminating Sarah, Hunt, and Luca casually jogging toward us in the distance.

It's all done. Over. Yet there's no sense of relief when the damage has already been inflicted.

"That was quick." She waits for the father-daughter duo to climb inside, then puts the car into gear.

"Hunt knows what he's doing." I turn, meeting my niece's gaze as she crawls into the middle seat and clasps her belt. "Ready to go, little one?"

She nuzzles into Benji's side and nods.

"How about you, Toby?" I switch my focus to the boy who stares out the window, not meeting my gaze.

"Yeah," he mutters.

The poor kid deserves a lot better than what I've given him.

"Time to go home." Nissa pulls onto the road, doing a U-turn to drive back toward the city.

We sit in silence, rounding the wide corners as we skirt the darkened farmland.

I glance at my niece and Benji every now and then, needing the sight of their bond to soften my thoughts for his future.

They're arm in arm, huddled close. Stella blinks back at me each time, but Benji is lost in the moment, his eyes closed, his face hard with emotion as he clings to his little girl.

He may not be a loyal soldier, but I'll admit he's a good father. A doting dad.

That's the only thing working in his favor.

"Where's Mom?" Stella murmurs.

"She's waiting for you." Benji's voice is roughened. Emotional. And so it should be.

We wouldn't have a building vendetta against Costa if it wasn't for him. There'd be no mental scars for Stella. No death of her babysitter. No bullshit to cover up with Robert.

I turn back toward the road, my thoughts of punishment building.

I'd worked out a plan with Abri—one where I'd promised no retaliation toward her father. One where I could be left in peace to enjoy Anissa. Now all the future holds is vengeance for the motherfuckers who dared to fire their weapons in the presence of children.

"Why didn't she come to get me?" Stella asks.

"We weren't sure…" Benji grunts, the sound born from pain.

Nissa shoots me a glance, frowning in question as the hair on the back of my nape rises.

"She's waiting in the hotel." Benji's words are forced. Labored. "You'll see her soon."

I peer at him over my shoulder, his eyes opening to meet mine. Even in the dim light, the grip of agony lancing his features is clear. "What happened to you?"

"It's a scratch." He winces. "I'll be fine."

"Are you hurt?" Stella raises her frantic gaze to her father, sitting up straight. "Daddy, you're wet." She pulls her arm away from his waist to inspect her sleeve. "Uncle Cole…" The terror in her voice cuts through me. "He's bleeding."

"What's going on?" Nissa glances from me to the road and back again.

"Slow down." I reach for the roof, flicking on the interior light, then hold in a curse.

A sheen of liquid is cast over the lower left side of his suit jacket, the shirt beneath drenched in blood, his face now a sickening shade of grey.

"Pull over." I release my belt as the car brakes. I'm shoving open my door and jumping out before we come to a stop. I skirt the hood, anger and dread thrumming through me.

Anissa is right behind me, cutting the engine to climb out, the beam of Hunt's approaching headlights blinding me as I pull open Benji's door.

"I'm okay," he rasps. "You need to get Stella back to her mother."

My niece sobs, her hands covered in dark crimson as she clutches her father's fingers. "What's happening?" she pleads. "Is he dying?"

"He'll be fine." I flick back Benji's jacket and raise the sodden material of his shirt, exposing something far more sinister than a scratch.

He's got two fucking bullet wounds to the abdomen, the holes purging blood.

Nissa draws in a breath behind me. "He needs a hospital."

It's too late for that.

We're in the middle of nowhere. We'd never make it in time, and the condemned look in Benji's eyes says he knows it.

"Cole." Nissa grabs my arm. "You need to get back in the car."

"No." Benji winces and leans down to kiss Stella's forehead.

"This is payment for my mistakes. Please just let me be with my daughter."

Jesus. *Fuck.* Bile stirs in my gut as my pulse thunders. The trauma only increases when Hunt's car pulls up beside us, the windows lowered.

Benji was always meant to pay for his mistakes with his life. But not like this. Not in front of his daughter. Not in a way that would devastate my niece beyond repair.

Hell, I might've even weakened and let him run, as long as he ghosted for the rest of his snake-ish existence. He could've started a new life far away from here. Now that option has been taken away from us all.

"What's going on?" Luca asks from the back seat.

I meet his gaze, relaying the seriousness of the situation without saying a word.

He frowns, scrambling to unclasp his belt, then flings open his door. Hunt and Sarah follow.

"Uncle Cole, do something," Stella pleads. "Help him."

Her agony pierces me deep, destroying the hardened parts of me as Luca bumps Anissa out of the way to reach my side.

"There's nothing to be done." Benji cups Stella's face in shaky hands, her wide eyes filled with despair as her father strokes her cheeks with his thumbs. "You're going to be okay. I promise. I'm not going anywhere. I'll always be with you."

"No," she sobs. "You're hurt. You need help."

"I love you, baby girl."

"No, Daddy. Please." Her voice trembles. "Tell Uncle Cole to take you to the hospital."

Luca freezes beside me, staring down at his brother, taking a split second of contemplation before he shucks his jacket in a rush and lunges into the car. "We need to stem the bleeding." He grabs Stella's hands. "Hold this, sweetheart. Push as hard as you can."

She wails, the tears beginning to fall as Luca glances over his shoulder at me. "Get back in the car. We need to leave. *Now.*"

I don't move. Don't answer.

Nothing I say will help the information sink in until he's ready to understand it.

"Did you hear me?" He straightens and swings around to face me. "Get in the fucking car, Torian."

I remain in place, hating his suffering, but unwilling to humor his attempts to save an unsalvageable life.

Hunt comes up behind him, placing strong hands on his shoulders. "You know he's not going to make it back to the city, bro."

"Don't fucking give up on him." Luca glares at me in accusation. "Get in the fucking car."

I step back, lowering my voice so Stella can't hear. "You have a decision to make—fight the inevitable and tarnish his final moments, or leave him in peace to be with his daughter."

"No." His face crumples as he violently swings his shoulders, dislodging Hunt's hold. "Get the fuck off me."

"Luca, please." Sarah inches toward him, her hands held up in surrender, her eyes glistening with building tears. "I know you're hurting. But Stella needs you to be strong. They both do."

"No." He makes toward the car again and Hunt grabs him, hauling him backward, battling the thrashing and jerking. "*No.*"

"Stop fighting it." Benji croaks from inside the Escalade. "I need you to be strong."

Luca slumps. Surrenders. Stumbles, almost falling to his knees.

I clench my jaw as he suffers before me, the grief already stealing his breath.

"I'll get Tobias out of the car," Anissa whispers. "He shouldn't be left in there."

She hustles to the other side of the vehicle to help my brother out, then guides him across the road, leading him into the solitude of darkness, murmuring words of comfort.

I love her more than I ever have in this moment.

Her level head. Her compassion.

"I can't just stand here." Luca shoves his fingers into his hair, choking on breath. "What the fuck do I do?"

"Give them space." Hunt walks him toward Anissa and Tobias. "It's out of our hands now."

"I'll stay with Stella." Sarah creeps closer to the open door, inching herself inside to offer comfort.

I don't feel my feet as I follow Luca's reluctant steps. I don't feel anything.

I'm numb to the world. Hollowed by this vicious poetic justice. But the crunch of my shoes against the asphalt isn't enough to drown out Benji's voice.

"Tell your momma I love her, okay?"

"No," Stella pleads. "Daddy, no."

Giving her these moments alone with him might be a mistake. The trauma could be too deep to surface from. But I can't strip her of these last memories.

I would've killed to be by my mother's side when she died. To make the promise that her legacy would live on. To hold her one last time.

"*Daddy?*" My niece's cry cuts through the night, her pain scarring me as Luca forges back toward the car.

"Nothing can be done." Hunt grabs him. "Let him go."

"No." Luca reignites his fight, striking a punch to Hunt's ribs, scrambling to break free. "*No.*" His demands turn into guttural pleas. "Don't you fucking die on me, brother."

"I love you, baby girl." There's no strength left in Benji's quiet voice. No life. "Never forget how special you are."

Anissa comes to my side, Tobias peering up at me with anguish.

The silence that follows is deafening.

The five of us stand at the edge of the road, the grim reaper at our backs, the ghosts of our sins fast approaching.

Sarah's cries drift softly from the car. Luca's breathing becomes harder. I reach for Nissa, dragging her against me, Tobias following along with her to stand at my feet, his head resting into my stomach.

I squeeze his arm, not giving a shit about the pain in my palm or my blood staining his clothes. "I've got you."

My promise is all I have to give.

I can't fix this mess. I can't stop the misery.

All I can do is vow retribution and make sure the punishment goes above and beyond the crime.

"*No,*" Stella's wail carries through the night. "No, Daddy, please don't go."

33

———

ANISSA

The funeral was low-key. Close family. No outsiders.

Stella cried rivers, the wetness on her cheeks dripping down to leave damp patches at the top of her floral dress while Layla remained quiet at her side, her face an emotionless mask.

Luca took a different approach. His anger shrouded the room, his glare baring down on the coffin as it lowered into the ground. With every breath, he silently promised vengeance and all of us agree that time will come. Maybe not in the coming days. But eventually. Once we've pulled ourselves together.

None of us have been the same since Sacramento.

Not Hunt and Decker, who were left in charge of driving Benji's body home and paying off medical officials to hide his cause of death. Not Layla, who blames herself for what happened to her husband. Not Stella, who is plagued by ongoing nightmares. Or Cole, who acts as if he's immune to their suffering even when I know it's killing him to remain emotionless.

Not even me, because I can't ditch the rage that's made its home under my skin. It keeps me up at night, the anger making me toss and turn until Cole wraps his arms around me, his proximity the only thing capable of lulling me to sleep.

"How's he holding up?" Hunter comes to stand beside me in the kitchen, mimicking my position leaned against the counter, his focus straight ahead on Cole and the others in the living room. "Does he need anything?"

"He's doing okay." I shrug. "I think everyone is dealing the best they can."

"Yeah." He pauses a moment before turning to me. "I'm going to have to deal some more bad news, though."

I stiffen and tilt my head to look at him. "What is it?"

"I'm getting Sarah out of here for a while." He meets my gaze with indifference. There's still no love lost between us, but since returning to Portland, the animosity has taken a back seat. "We're eloping. With all the shit that's gone down, she needs something good in her life. It's time to make her mine."

"That's far from bad news."

"Maybe." He shrugs. "I know Torian needs me here. But she needs me more."

"I don't think you have to worry. Cole would appreciate what you're doing. You should tell him."

His brows pull tight. "Nah. I'll leave that to you. You'll know when the timing is right better than I will."

My brow quirks before I can stop it. He wants *me* to do something for *him*... because I'd be a *better* option?

"Don't look at me like that. We won't be gone long. A week. Or two. If that's suitable."

"You're asking me?" I fight not to give him a side-eye of disbelief. Who the hell is this man and what did he do with the dumpster fire of a thug I previously knew?

"Yeah." His frown deepens. "Is that a problem?"

"No. I think you should take all the time you need." I swallow over the awkward lump in my throat. "I'll let him know. When do you plan on leaving?"

"Now. I'm not going to say goodbye. But I want you to make sure you don't make a move on Costa until I get back."

"I can't promise that. Cole deserves closure, and I won't stand in his way."

He scoffs, a saccharine grin quirking the corner of his lips. "Look at you being a heartless bitch all in the name of revenge."

"And look at you, giving up the opportunity for vengeance because you're pussy whipped."

He snickers, sly and half-hearted. "Touché." He walks from the kitchen, giving a subtle jerk of his head to Sarah who strides forward to take his hand.

They disappear down the hall, nobody else noticing their departure as the murmured conversations continue around the room. Cole chats with Decker and Keira. Luca and Penny snuggle on the opposite sofa. Tobias and Stella play a subdued board game on the dining table, while Layla stands at the glass doors, alone, blankly staring into the backyard.

I want to go to her, offering my millionth condolence. Instead, I stack dirty plates in the dishwasher and busy myself wiping the counter.

I'm not a part of the inner circle yet and I get it. No matter how many promises Cole makes or the devoted level of his attention, the others aren't used to having me here.

It's going to take time to build on the smidge of trust I've earned.

"Anissa?" Penny walks into the kitchen, her hands clasped in front of her.

"Hey." I smile. "How are you?"

"Good." She sucks in a fortifying breath and lowers her voice. "I realize this is a day of mourning and I'm truly hurting for Luca's loss, but I didn't know Benji so the devastation is kept at a distance, if that makes sense."

"I understand."

Her eyes drift to her partner still on the sofa, the adoration in her expression clear. "My life is incredibly different now. I'm starting to finally find my feet. He's such a good man. Even with everything he's going through, he always puts me first."

"I'm glad to hear it."

She nods. "I knew you would be. That's why I wanted to thank you for all you've done. Both in Greece and back here in Portland. You changed my life, and I'll be forever grateful."

My heart pangs at her sincerity. "You don't need to thank me."

"Yes, I do." She unclasps her hands to place a palm over her heart. "I'm so unbelievably grateful for every morning that I wake up with Luca. He's..." She releases a heavy breath. "He's my happiness. He's everything. And I never would've met him if all our paths didn't converge."

My eyes tingle. "You need to stop before you make me cry."

She laughs. "I wouldn't want that. Not in a room full of these guys. I know you need to stay tough, and I've definitely got your back."

I keep the humor in my voice despite the reminder of the potential snake pit I now live in. "You make it sound like I shouldn't walk around without a bodyguard."

"No, not at all. I don't think anyone would be stupid enough to even risk offending you with the level of devotion Cole has shown toward his queen." She snickers. "But in all honesty, Sarah and I think incredibly highly of you. Apparently, Hunter does, too."

"Hunter?" I scoff.

"No, seriously, he does. Sarah said he spent most of the drive home from Sacramento berating my brother on how he now needs to treat you with respect. He instigated some sort of no tolerance policy on giving you a hard time."

Hunter wouldn't have instigated it. Those directives would've come from Cole. But I appreciate knowing the big, bad wolf is willing to throw his weight around for me.

"I bet Decker didn't take the news kindly." I act blasé, pretending I'm not impatiently waiting for a response. "I did some pretty shitty things to him when we first met."

"Don't worry. I heard that, too. But you did them because you were trying to take down Luther, which, in my book, gave you grounds to do absolutely anything in the name of success." She shrugs. "Sebastian will come around soon enough. I'm sure, deep down, he appreciates what you did."

"Deep, deep, *deep* down." Maybe buried under layer upon hardened layer of macho aggression and thick hostility.

She smiles again. "You're meant to be here. Just like I am. Despite how different this is from the future we envisaged for ourselves."

I don't voice my agreement. I keep my thoughts to myself in the hopes of preventing the tightening in my throat from exposing how emotional I am about being here.

It feels right to spend time under Cole's roof. In his bed. Held in his arms.

Even with their world hitting rock bottom and the depth of misery suffocating us, this place has become my new home.

Each day I learn more and more about the way Cole lives. His agenda. His thought process. And for every one of those days, my understanding of him grows.

I've been exposed to the corruption that I've always been blind to. I'm discovering the false reality I once existed in, which makes the way these people live not only justifiable but logical.

"You soften his ragged edges." Penny inches forward, grasping my wrist for a light squeeze. "He's a harsh man, but so uniquely honest and clear-cut that it's hard not to appreciate him. I'm glad the two of you found each other."

My eyes burn hotter, the heat filtering to my cheeks. "Thank you."

"*Hey.*" Cole's shout steals my attention, his pointed frown fixing on me. "What are you two talking about that's made you upset?"

"Oh, boy," Penny mutters under her breath. "Please don't let him kill me."

I chuckle and sniff back the emotion tingling in my nose. "We're just chatting."

"Well, come chat over here. No woman of mine is going to look unsettled unless I'm the one unsettling her." He pats his lap with a wink.

I roll my eyes, my heart fluttering as I walk toward him. Then I tingle with warmth as he grabs my arm and drags me to sit on his thighs.

"You okay?" he murmurs against my neck, his delicate lips in contrast to the possessive hand on my hip. "Need me to destroy someone for bothering you?"

I glide my fingers over his, entwining our hands. "You're not funny."

"Sure I am." He kisses my nape, increasing the flutters and tingles. "Decker just admitted I'm hilarious."

"What's that?" Decker interrupts. "Are you talking about me?"

"Yes." His hold tightens on my hip. "I was just about to tell Nis how we were discussing leaving the past in the past."

Decker's eyes harden. The tight set of his jaw does, too.

It's now obvious what past they're referring to—my history with Decker. Specifically the sex and manipulation to make him my informant.

Tension settles around us. Quiet falls.

I shift uncomfortably. "Maybe this is a discussion for another—"

"No." Cole's hold strengthens, the hand on my hip becoming possessive, his fingers tangling tighter. "From this moment on, no grudges will be held between those in this room. The time for spite and animosity is over. Are we all clear?"

"I think that's a good idea." Keira meets my gaze. "You're welcome here and you always will be, especially when you keep my brother in line."

I smile at her, but it's forced. I can't hold the kind expression when Decker continues to scowl.

"I agree." Luca's eyes hold a sense of pleading sincerity as he looks at me. "I'd be thankful if the messed up shit I contributed to in Greece was left behind us."

"It's already forgotten." There's a slight falsity to my admission. I don't think I'm capable of fully forgetting the role he played during my abduction. However, the way he selflessly saved Penny, and the way he's conducted himself toward her ever since, is enough evidence to prove to me that he's an incredible man.

"What about you, Decker?" Cole prods. "Do you have something to say?"

The guy flares his nostrils and takes a few moments to mask his intolerance. "I'm more than happy to forget everything to do with this woman. I—"

"Watch your tone." Cole's fingers grip tighter around mine.

"More importantly," Penny adds, "watch your goddamn disrespect toward someone who helped rescue me. You, of all people, should be thankful—"

"It's complicated," he grates.

"It's only as complicated as you want to make it." Keira nestles into him. "You slept together. She played you. Move on. Lots of other people have been forgiven for a whole lot worse."

"She's not wrong." Luca leans back into the sofa, crossing his legs at the ankles. "And all this drama has me well and truly cooked. I'm over it. Can't we have some peace for once?"

Decker sucks in a long breath and lets it out on a huff. "Fine. I accept that she was a contributing factor toward getting Penny back. And yes, she risked her life for those kids in Sacramento, too. She's an asset. Not to mention some sort of balm against you being such an asshole." He jerks his chin at Cole. "I'll try my best to treat her with respect from now on, if she can do the same."

"I respect you." I admire him, too. He's yet another great man who risked everything for someone he loved. "And I know me being here doesn't feel right. It's going to take a while for this to be normal."

"It'll take no time at all. It's a cakewalk in comparison to the shit we usually do." Luca pushes from the sofa to walk toward Penny. "We're going to head home."

"Us, too." Keira stands, dragging Decker with her as she looks at her brother. "Are you going to be okay with Layla and the kids?"

"They're fine." Cole drags me back into his chest. "I'm going to take them out for ice cream later. They all need some fresh air."

They leave after subdued farewells to the children and Layla, the house descending into quiet calm.

"Hunt and Sarah didn't say goodbye." Cole's breath brushes my neck. "Did my two favorite people get into another fight?"

"No. We're fine." I drag my feet onto the sofa and turn into him, meeting his gaze. "Hunter actually asked me to tell you something."

He frowns. "I'm listening."

"He's heading out of town for a while. Eloping."

His brows rise in casual surprise.

"You're not angry I didn't stop him, are you?"

He glides a stray strand of hair behind my ear. "No. If anything, I'm envious."

"That he told me?"

"No, that he gets to marry his woman. Somehow I don't think you're ready to walk down the aisle."

"Not ready in the slightest. And yet again, you're not funny, Cole."

"This time I agree." He holds my gaze. "Because I wasn't joking. I'm prepared to make this official whenever you are."

"You're incorrigible."

"I'm determined." He kisses below my ear. My jaw. "And impatient. There's no changing my mind on this. When you know, you know."

I push back against his chest, getting a better look at him as he stares at me without an ounce of sarcasm.

"You're seriously ready to marry me?" I shake my head. "How…?"

"There's nobody else for me, Nis. There never will be."

Emotion drowns me in a wave, squeezing my chest, clogging my throat.

"Does your silence count as a yes?" He drags me back against him, one hand gently wrapping around my neck. "If so, I could have us on a jet to Vegas in less than thirty."

"It wasn't an affirmation." I melt into him, smiling.

"But it wasn't a no."

"Cole," I warn. "This isn't the time to talk about this." It's not even close to the time to think about making a time to talk about this.

"Agree to marry me then." He kisses my jaw. My ear. "Be my fiancé."

I fight not to moan against the pleasure of his lips, my heart searing and sizzling like a firework waiting to explode. "Your family is in mourning."

"Exactly. They need some happiness in their lives. You'd be cruel to deny them."

I chuckle, the sound morphing into a groan when his teeth dig into my neck.

"Commit to marrying me," he growls. "Agree to be my wife. My queen."

"I can't."

He continues torturing my neck, kissing and nipping and teasing. "Then say yes to saying yes in the future."

"I don't even know what that means."

He releases my throat and leans to the side to retrieve something from his pocket.

No, not something. *Everything.* A small velvet jewelry box that sits on the palm of his hand right in front of me. He opens it, shocking me with a dazzling diamond ring.

I'm momentarily lost for words. For breath. Then the questions start to pummel my mind, scratching and clawing for answers. "How long have you had this?"

"Since we got back from Greece." He rests his stubbled cheek against mine, both of us staring at his offering. "There's never been any doubt."

"Cole…" It's too much, too soon.

I'm crazy for this man, and he knows it. I ended my lease to move in with him. I quit my job. But this…

"Say yes to saying yes," he repeats. "Agree to accept my proposal when I ask."

My head says no. Nope. No way.

But my heart. Oh, *God,* my heart flutters and thunders *yes, yes, yes.*

"Nissa?" His fingers glide over my chin, tilting my face to meet his. "Say yes."

"Okay." My voice cracks with the onslaught of adrenaline. "I say yes to saying yes when you ask."

"Promise?" He brushes his lips against mine, teasing me with a kiss.

"Yes," I whisper. Melting. "I promise."

"Good." He gives me another chaste kiss then grabs my hips, shifting me off his lap.

I'm underwhelmed with the whiplash of his departure. That is, until he drops to one knee in front of me, still holding the ring box open. "Marry me, little fox."

I frantically shake my head, my gaze finding Layla at the glass doors as she watches us with a sad yet encouraging smile. "You said when you ask in the *future.*"

"This is the future. The conversation we just had is already in the past."

I glare at him even though I want to tackle him to the floor and smother him in kisses. "You tricked me."

"I did." He smirks. "And after everything we've been through, you still fell for it. So make good on your promise and commit to being my wife because you're all I'll ever want."

Read Layla's story in Seeking Vengeance.

Please consider leaving a review on your book retailer
website or Goodreads

Titles in the Hunting Her World

Hunter

Decker

Torian

Savior

Luca

Cole

Seeking Vengeance

Ruthless Redemption

Bishop

**Information on Eden's other books can be found at
www.edensummers.com**

ABOUT THE AUTHOR

Eden Summers is a bestselling author of contemporary romance with a side of sizzle and sarcasm.

She lives in Australia with a young family who are well aware she's circling the drain of insanity.
Eden can't resist alpha dominance, dark features and sarcasm in her fictional heroes and loves a strong heroine who knows when to bite her tongue but also serves retribution with a feminine smile on her face.

If you'd like access to exclusive information and giveaways, join Eden Summers' newsletter via the link on her website.

For more information:
www.edensummers.com
eden@edensummers.com

www.ingramcontent.com/pod-product-compliance
Lightning Source LLC
Chambersburg PA
CBHW050749190726
48285CB00005B/1594